THE PURPLE LAND

THE PURPLE LAND

BY
W. H. HUDSON

INTRODUCTION BY
WILLIAM McFEE

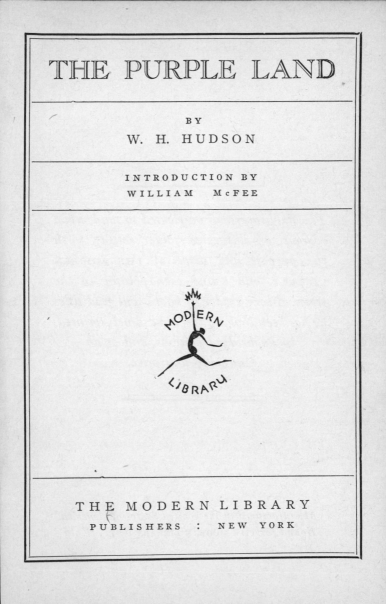

THE MODERN LIBRARY
PUBLISHERS : NEW YORK

Manufactured in the United States of America
Bound for THE MODERN LIBRARY *by* H. Wolff

PREFACE TO THE NEW EDITION

THIS work was first issued in 1885, by Messrs. Sampson Low, in two slim volumes, with the longer and, to most persons, enigmatical title of *The Purple Land that England Lost*. A purple land may be found in almost any region of the globe, and 'tis of our gains, not our losses, we keep count. A few notices of the book appeared in the papers, one or two of the more serious literary journals reviewing it (not favourably) under the heading of "Travels and Geography"; but the reading public cared not to buy, and it very shortly fell into oblivion. There it might have remained for a further period of nineteen years, or for ever, since the sleep of a book is apt to be of the unawakening kind, had not certain men of letters, who found it on a forgotten heap and liked it in spite of its faults, or because of them, concerned themselves to revive it.

We are often told that an author never wholly loses his affection for a first book, and the feeling has been likened (more than once) to that of a parent towards a first-born. *I* have not said it, but in consenting to this reprint I considered that a writer's early or unregarded work is apt to be raked up when he is not standing by to make remarks. He may be absent on a journey from which he is not expected to return. It accordingly seemed better that I should myself supervise a new edition, since this would enable me to remove a few of the numerous spots and pimples which decorate the ingenuous countenance of the work before handing it on to posterity.

Besides many small verbal corrections and changes, the deletion of some paragraphs and the insertion of a few new ones, I have omitted one entire chapter containing the Story of a Piebald Horse, recently reprinted in another book entitled *El Ombu*. I have also dropped the tedious introduction to the former edition, only preserving, as an appendix, the historical part, for the sake of such of my readers as may like to have a few facts about the land that England lost.

W. H. H.

September, 1904.

CONTENTS

INTRODUCTION TO "THE PURPLE LAND"

The vicissitudes of authorship are admirably revealed in the history of Hudson's novel of the *Banda Oriental* since its publication, forty-two years ago, under the title *The Purple Land that England Lost*. It had apparently died, and was buried deep among other forgotten books of the eighties. Nineteen years later it experienced a resurrection. It came out again, with the title shortened to its present form, and since that day its vogue has gradually spread among the lovers of books. In 1916 it was published in America, and in the course of the next ten years eight printings were required to cope with the growing interest in this remarkable series of *Reisebilder*. Now no apology is expected for its inclusion in the Modern Library. It is known to all men by name, it is a peculiar favorite among those members of the reading public who enjoy a narrative which is not constructed upon the fashionable contemporary model.

In an introduction to a book, which has grown like seed buried in a tomb, by reason of its own vitality, out of oblivion into a secure position in

modern literature, it would be impertinent and
cheap to indulge in the excited phraseology which
has been pilfered from our flamboyant essayists
by the writers of "jacket blurbs." *The Purple
Land* needs no purple language. It is described
from time to time as "a novel." If there is any
meaning at all left in that word, Hudson's book
is not a novel. It has been called "a romance,"
and here again one addicted to romances might
easily feel cheated after reading it. It is as much
of a novel, as much of a romance, as Mr. Belloc's
classic *The Path to Rome,* as De Quincy's *Opium
Eater* or Mr. O'Brien's *White Shadows in the
South Seas.* That is to say, it is a misnomer to include it among those novels and romances which
are accepted as such by the general public. Hon-
esty is imperative in dealing with the works of a
man like Hudson, and very little imagination is
needed to evoke the distaste he himself would
have manifested if he had heard anybody trying
to pass off one of his books for something it did
not happen to be.

The Purple Land indeed, appears to me a very
successful example of the kind of book which
eventually succeeds for the very reason that it is
not a novel or even "a romance." Hudson's
equipment did not include a mastery of what we
call novel-technique. He was, I maintain against
all comers, primarily a naturalist with bohemian
habits, a queer, lovable fellow. Such a man
cherishes a philosophy which makes it difficult for

him to move easily within the somewhat artificial
limitations of conventional fiction. To expect
Hudson to conform to the usages of a modern
story magazine, for example, would be like fitting
an Argentine *vaquero* with a suit of hunting pink
from a Bond Street tailor. It might be a consum-
mate fit, but the moment he began to exercise his
body according to his custom on the pampas the
coat would split down the back. So with Hudson
as a novelist. The conventional form never fitted
his mind. To tell the truth briefly, there was a
quality of simplicity in Hudson's mind which made
the sophisticated novel-form seem grotesque and
unreal to him. And it is that same simplicity of
spirit which attracts men and women to a book
like *The Purple Land*. It is responsible, moreover, for the deceptive simplicity of his style, because unless you have a spirit like his, a spirit
happier among birds in the forest than among men
in the city, you will never achieve a style like his.
Joseph Conrad said, in an oft-quoted passage,
"You can't tell how this fellow gets his effects.
He writes as the grass grows; the good God makes
it there, and that is all there is to it." The above
suggestion may help us to a guess, that it was because he was not overly occupied with "getting
an effect," that Hudson's prose steals upon us like
a change in the evening sky, or on the surface of
the sea at sunrise. This marvelously "natural"
ease of execution delights both professional novel-
ists like Conrad, Galsworthy and Ford Madox

Ford, all of whom knew and loved Hudson as a personal friend, and the average reader. The latter, a much-maligned person given to surprising his traducers, reveals at times a decided preference for a rambling narrative not overburdened with an artificial plot. He enjoys a traveler's tale, and the remoteness of Hudson's *Purple Land* is no obstacle to his interest when it is seen through that serene crystalline style, which like the clear air of tropical regions makes distant objects seem miraculously close at hand.

It is unexpectedly embarrassing to discuss this book as a piece of fiction, which of course it is, after denying it a place among formal novels and romances. But a certain amount of criticism is allowed even to writers of introductions, and no ultimate advantage accrues to Hudson by claiming for *The Purple Land* the thrilling appeal of the modern cowboy book. For myself, the fable of the book was never indispensable. The young Englishman whose amorous adventures precipitated his flight from Buenos Aires to Montevideo across those "unlovely red billows" of the La Plata River, is not entirely successful in disentangling his personality from Hudson's own, and it is for this reason the story falls into the class of travel-narratives, or if you prefer it, travel-pictures, like Heine's, or Sterne's *Sentimental Journey*. And this is the more true because, as Mr. Galsworthy points out, Hudson depicts not only what he saw but the emotion behind the observation—"the spirit of his vision." He never ceases to be a fine type of the adventurous young Englishman; and let the reader who is interested in character-drawing note how sharply the young man's racial traits stand out at the very moment when he is among men of his own race. The colony of drunken and shiftless scions of "old families" exiled for the good of their country to the *Banda Oriental*, is remarkably well done in *The Purple Land*. It is a peculiar commentary upon history that great leaders have usually emerged out of such groups of nonentities to influence the destinies of unborn millions. The whole point of Hudson's original title, *The Purple Land that England Lost*, is that no such leader appeared on this occasion. It is strange to read Hudson's very emotional regrets—he who was the least jingoistic of men, who had such scant sympathy for the inevitable changes which afflict a region when his countrymen embark upon their schemes of imperial development. It might be said with truth that here Hudson was inconsistent because in general his opinion of birds and savages was higher than his opinion of civilized humanity. He seems to have had something of the elusiveness of a gentle wild creature in himself. And whatever justice there may be in the dislike of the English people for Mr. Epstein's strange sculpture of the Hudson Memorial in a London park, that sculpture, if it means anything at all, is a bold attempt to express in stone the strangeness of

Hudson's lovable personality. In Ford Madox
Ford's book on Conrad there is an unforgetable
allusion to a visit Hudson paid to Conrad's Kentish
home. At first it was believed to be the bailiff,
then a man come to discuss the sale of a horse,
when "an extremely tall man, with a dispropor-
tionately small head," went "stalking past the
window." It was Hudson, come to visit the
Polish seaman who had written "Almayer's
Folly." In some ways those two men were far
apart. Yet significant traits they had in common.
They were both original literary artists. Both
were so little rewarded by the public that Civil
List pensions stood between them and penury.
To both the spectacle of civilized man, against the
background of tropical vegetation and the stupendous grandeur of the untamed earth and sea,
evoked ironic sentiments. And both, in large
measure, stand out from their own generation on
account of their success in giving us authentic in-
terpretations of alien psychologies. The author
of *The Purple Land* would know how to estimate
the author of *Nostromo*. They were both romantic realists, creating out of their own experiences a world of bright glamor, shot through
with a lofty skepticism of man's ultimate destiny.
Neither of them ever successfully achieved the
modern rapid fire method of telling a story. They
speak to us from an age which is nowadays being
subjected to much cynical analysis. But it is one
of the most astonishing characteristics of the Vic-

torian Era that the great men of that era are so often great men still, especially those of them who did not make much money.

The present age of literature will be known, no doubt, for its satirical curiosity. We are going about equipped with text-books of psycho-analysis, discovering, to our own satisfaction, that the men and women of all ages, who achieved anything in the way of fame, suffered from various mental lesions to which we give learned names. It must be confessed, by one who remembers the vogue of Max Nordau's *Degeneration*, in which most of the great Victorians were catalogued as psycho-pathic specimens, that the popular fashion in biography is no more than the child of modern fiction, sired by modern publishing and born in a hospital. It is a literary expression of the age of jazz. It will pass, if it be not already passing. But behind the tumult of those who surge to and fro in the market place, seeking some new thing, worshipping unknown gods, dwells another pub-lic, less sophisticated and less certain that we are at the apex of human culture.

This public *The Purple Land* has pleased and will continue to please. To most of us today this romantic narrative of life fifty years ago in the *Banda Oriental* seems as fanciful as Gulliver's Travels or Marco Polo's account of the Great Khan. The *Banda Oriental* itself has vanished and has become the model republic of Uruguay, the virtuous child of the South America family.

Roads and railways cut through the vast savannahs over which Hudson's youthful hero rode in company with heroes, ne'er do weels, rogues, vagabonds and patriots. The incredibly innocent and romantic young ladies whom he met have borne daughters, who visit Paris and New York and take back with them shingled heads, golf-sticks and police-dogs. Uruguayans may still proclaim themselves Reds or Whites, Colorados or Blancos, just as we are labelled Republicans or Democrats. But the golden age of which Hudson wrote is gone like the Creole days of Cable's *Grandissimes* or the maritime era of New England. It is gone, yet it is preserved forever in the crystal clarity of these pages, the legacy of one of the great spirits of his age.

WILLIAM McFEE

WESTPORT, CONN.,
December, 1926

THE PURPLE LAND

CHAPTER I

RAMBLES IN MODERN TROY

THREE chapters in the story of my life—three
periods, distinct and well defined, yet consecutive
—beginning when I had not completed twenty-
five years and finishing before thirty, will probably prove the most eventful of all. To the very
end they will come back oftenest to memory and
seem more vivid than all the other years of existence—the four-and-twenty I had already lived,
and the, say, forty or forty-five—I hope it may be
fifty or even sixty—which are to follow. For
what soul in this wonderful various world would
wish to depart before ninety! The dark as well as
the light, its sweet and its bitter, make me love it.
Of the first of these three a word only need be
written. This was the period of courtship and
matrimony; and though the experience seemed to
me then something altogether new and strange in
the world, it must nevertheless have resembled
that of other men, since all men marry. And
the last period, which was the longest of the three,
occupying fully three years, could not be told. It
was all black disaster. Three years of enforced

1

separation and the extremest suffering which the
cruel law of the land allowed an enraged father
to inflict on his child and the man who had ventured to wed her against his will. Even the wise
may be driven mad by oppression, and I that was
never wise, but lived in and was led by the passions and illusions and the unbounded self-con-
fidence of youth, what it must have been for me
when we were cruelly torn asunder; when I was
cast into prison to lie for long months in the company of felons, ever thinking of her who was also
desolate and breaking her heart! But it is ended
—the abhorred restraint, the anxiety, the brood-
ing over a thousand possible and impossible
schemes of revenge. If it is any consolation to
know that in breaking her heart he, at the same
time, broke his own and made haste to join her
in that silent place, I have it. Ah no! it is no
comfort to me, since I cannot but reflect that before he shattered my life I had shattered his by
taking her from him, who was his idol. We are
quits then, and I can even say, "Peace to his
ashes!" But I could not say it then in my frenzy
and grief, nor could it be said in that fatal country
which I had inhabited from boyhood and had
learned to love like my own, and had hoped never
to leave. It was grown hateful to me, and, flying
from it, I found myself once more in that Purple
Land where we had formerly taken refuge together, and which now seemed to my distracted
mind a place of pleasant and peaceful memories.

During the months of quietude after the storm, mostly spent in lonely rambles by the shore, these memories were more and more with me. Sometimes sitting on the summit of that great solitary hill, which gives the town its name, I would gaze by the hour on the wide prospect towards the interior, as if I could see and never weary of seeing all that lay beyond—plains and rivers and woods and hills and cabins where I had rested, and many a kindly human face. Even the faces of those who had ill-treated or regarded me with evil eyes now appeared to have a friendly look. Most of all did I think of that dear river, the unforgettable Yí, the shaded white house at the end of the little town, and the sad and beautiful image of one whom I, alas! had made unhappy.

So much was I occupied towards the end of that vacant period with these recollections that I remembered how, before quitting these shores, the thought had come to me that during some quiet interval in my life I would go over it all again, and write the history of my rambles for others to read in the future. But I did not attempt it then, nor until long years afterwards. For I had no sooner begun to play with the idea than something came to rouse me from the state I was in, during which I had been like one that has outlived his activities, and is no longer capable of a new emotion, but feeds wholly on the past. And this something new, affecting me so that I was all at once myself again, eager to be up and doing, was nothing more than a casual word from a distance, the cry of a lonely heart, which came by chance to my ear; and hearing it I was like one who opening his eyes from a troubled doze unexpectedly sees the morning star in its unearthly lustre above the wide, dark plain where night overtook him—the star of day and everlasting hope, and of passion and strife and toil and rest and happiness.

I need not linger on the events which took us to the Banda—our nocturnal flight from Paquíta's summer home on the pampas; the hiding and clandestine marriage in the capital and subsequent escape northwards into the province of Santa Fé; the seven to eight months of somewhat troubled happiness we had there; and finally, the secret return to Buenos Ayres in search of a ship to take us out of the country. Troubled happiness! Ah yes, and my greatest trouble was when I looked on her, my partner for life, when she seemed loveliest, so small, so exquisite in her dark blue eyes that were like violets, and silky black hair and tender pink and olive complexion—so frail in appearance! And I had taken her—stolen her—from her natural protectors, from the home where she had been worshipped—I of an alien race and another religion, without means, and, because I had stolen her, an offender against the law. But of this no more. I begin my itinerary where, safe on our little ship, with the towers of Buenos Ayres fast fading away in the west, we began to feel free from apprehension and to give ourselves up to the contemplation of the delights before us. Winds and waves presently interfered with our raptures, Paquíta proving a very indifferent sailor, so that for some hours we had a very trying time of it. Next day a favourable north-west breeze sprang up to send us flying like a bird over those unlovely red billows, and in the evening we disembarked in Montevideo, the city of refuge. We proceeded to an hotel, where for several days we lived very happily, enchanted with each other's society; and when we strolled along the beach to watch the setting sun, kindling with mystic fire heaven, water, and the great hill that gives the city its name, and remembered that we were looking towards the shores of Buenos Ayres, it was pleasant to reflect that the widest river in the world rolled between us and those who probably felt offended at what we had done.

This charming state of things came to an end at length in a somewhat curious manner. One night, before we had been a month in the hotel, I was lying wide awake in bed. It was late; I had already heard the mournful, long-drawn voice of the watchman under my window calling out, "Half-past one and cloudy."

Gil Blas relates in his biography that one night while lying awake he fell into practising a little introspection, an unusual thing for him to do, and the conclusion he came to was that he was not a very good young man. I was having a somewhat similar experience that night when, in the midst

of my unflattering thoughts about myself, a profound sigh from Paquíta made me aware that she
too was lying wide awake and also, in all prob-
ability, chewing the cud of reflection. When I
questioned her concerning that sigh, she endeavoured in vain to conceal from me that she was
beginning to feel unhappy. What a rude shock
the discovery gave me! And we so lately married! It is only just to Paquíta, however, to say
that had I not married her she would have been
still more unhappy. Only the poor child could
not help thinking of father and mother; she
yearned for reconciliation, and her present
sorrow rose from her belief that they would
never, never, never forgive her. I endeavoured,
with all the eloquence I was capable of, to dispel
these gloomy ideas, but she was firm in her conviction that precisely because they had loved her
so much they would never pardon this first great
offence. My poor darling might have been reading "Christabel," I thought, when she said that
it is toward those who have been most deeply
loved the wounded heart cherishes the greatest bitterness. Then, by way of illustration, she told me
of a quarrel between her mother and a till then
dearly loved sister. It had happened many years
ago, when she, Paquíta, was a mere child; yet the
sisters had never forgiven each other.

"And where," I asked, "is this aunt of yours,
of whom I have never heard you speak until this
minute?"

"Oh," answered Paquíta, with the greatest simplicity imaginable, "she left this country long,
long ago, and you never heard of her because we
were not even allowed to mention her name in
the house. She went to live in Montevideo, and
I believe she is there still, for several years ago
I heard some person say that she had bought herself a house in that city."

"Soul of my life," said I, "you have never left
Buenos Ayres in heart, even to keep your poor
husband company! Yet I know, Paquíta, that
corporeally you are here in Montevideo conversing
with me at this very moment."

"True," said Paquíta; "I had somehow forgotten that we were in Montevideo. My thoughts
were wandering—perhaps it is sleepiness."

"I swear to you, Paquíta," I replied, "that you
shall see this aunt of yours to-morrow before set
of sun; and I am positive, sweetest, that she will
be delighted to receive so near and lovely a relation. How glad she will be of an opportunity of
relating that ancient quarrel with her sister and
ventilating her mouldy grievances! I know these
old dames—they are all alike."

Paquíta did not like the idea at first, but when
I assured her that we were getting to the end of
our money, and that her aunt might be able to put
me in the way of obtaining employment, she consented, like the dutiful little wife she was.

Next day I discovered her relation without very
much trouble, Montevideo not being a large city.

We found Doña Isidora—for that was the lady's name—living in a somewhat mean-looking house at the eastern extremity of the town, furthest away from the water. There was an air of poverty about the place, for the good dame, though well provided with means to live comfortably, made a pet of her gold. Nevertheless, she received us very kindly when we introduced ourselves and related our mournful and romantic story; a room was prepared for our immediate reception, and she even made me some vague promises of assistance. On a more intimate acquaintance with our hostess we found that I had not been very far out in guessing her character. For several days she could talk of nothing except her immemorial quarrel with her sister and her sister's husband, and we were bound to listen attentively and to sympathise with her, for that was the only return we could make for her hospitality. Paquíta had more than her share of it, but was made no wiser as to the cause of this feud of long standing; for though Doña Isidora had evidently been nursing her wrath all those years to keep it warm, she could not, for the life of her, remember how the quarrel originated.

After breakfast each morning I would kiss her and hand her over to the tender mercies of her Isidora, then go forth on my fruitless perambulations about the town. At first I only acted the intelligent foreigner, going about staring at the public buildings, and collecting curios—strangely marked pebbles, and a few military brass buttons, long shed by the garments they once made brave; rusty misshapen bullets, mementoes of the immortal nine or ten years' siege which had won for Montevideo the mournful appellation of modern Troy. When I had fully examined from the outside the scene of my future triumphs—for I had now resolved to settle down and make my fortune in Montevideo—I began seriously to look out for employment. I visited in turn every large mercantile establishment in the place, and, in fact, every house where I thought there might be a chance of lighting on something to do. It was necessary to make a beginning, and I would not have turned up my nose at anything, however small, I was so heartily sick of being poor, idle, and dependent. Nothing could I find. In one house I was told that the city had not yet recovered from the effects of the late revolution, and that business was, in consequence, in a complete state of paralysis; in another that the city was on the eve of a revolution, and that business was, in consequence, in a complete state of paralysis. And everywhere it was the same story—the political state of the country made it impossible for me to win an honest dollar.

Feeling very much dispirited, and with the soles nearly worn off my boots, I sat down on a bench beside the sea, or river—for some call it one thing, some the other, and the muddied hue and freshness of the water, and the uncertain words of geographers, leave one in doubt as to whether Montevideo is situated on the shores of the Atlantic, or only near the Atlantic and on the shores of a river one hundred and fifty miles wide at its mouth. I did not trouble my head about it; I had other things that concerned me more nearly to think of. I had a quarrel with this Oriental nation, and that was more to me than the greenness or the saltness of the vast estuary that washes the dirty feet of its queen—for this modern Troy, this city of battle, murder, and sudden death, also calls itself Queen of the Plata. That it was a very just quarrel on my part I felt well assured. Now, to be even with every human being who despitefully uses me has ever been a principle of action with me. Nor let it be said that it is an unchristian principle; for when I have been smitten on the right or left cheek (the pain is just the same in either case), before I am prepared to deliver the return blow so long a time has often elapsed that all wrathful or revengeful thoughts are over. I strike in such a case more for the public good than for my own satisfaction, and am therefore right in calling my motive a principle of action, not an impulse. It is a very valuable one too, infinitely more effective than the fantastical code of the duellist, which favours the person who inflicts the injury, affording him facilities for murdering or maiming the person injured. It is a weapon invented for us by Nature before Colonel Colt ever lived, and it has this advantage, that one is permitted to wear it in the most law-abiding communities as well as amongst miners and backwoodsmen. If inoffensive people were ever to cast it aside, then wicked men would have everything their own way and make life intolerable. Fortunately the evil-doers always have the fear of this intangible six-shooter before them; a wholesome feeling, which restrains them more than reasonableness or the law courts, and to which we owe it that the meek are permitted to inherit the earth. But now this quarrel was with a whole nation, though certainly not with a very great one, since the population of the Banda Orientál numbers only about a quarter of a million. Yet in this sparsely settled country, with its bountiful soil and genial climate, there was apparently no place for me, a muscular and fairly intelligent young man, who only asked to be allowed to work to live! But how was I to make them smart for this injustice? I could not take the scorpion they gave me when I asked them for an egg, and make it sting every individual composing the nation. I was powerless, utterly powerless, to punish them, and therefore the only thing that remained for me to do was to curse them.

Looking around me, my eyes rested on the famous hill across the bay, and I all at once resolved to go up to its summit, and, looking down on the Banda Orientál, pronounce my imprecation in the most solemn and impressive manner.

The expedition to the *cerro,* as it is called,

proved agreeable enough. Notwithstanding the
excessive heats we were just then having, many
wild flowers were blooming on its slopes, which
made it a perfect garden. When I reached the
old ruined fort which crowns the summit, I got
upon a wall and rested for half an hour, fanned
by a fresh breeze from the river and greatly enjoying the prospect before me. I had not left
out of sight the serious object of my visit to that
commanding spot, and only wished that the male-
diction I was about to utter could be rolled down
in the shape of a stupendous rock, loosed from its
hold, which would go bounding down the mountain, and, leaping clear over the bay, crash through
the iniquitous city beyond, filling it with ruin and
amazement.

"Whichever way I turn," I said, "I see before
me one of the fairest habitations God has made
for man: great plains smiling with everlasting
spring; ancient woods; swift beautiful rivers;
ranges of blue hills stretching away to the dim
horizon. And beyond those fair slopes, how many
leagues of pleasant wilderness are sleeping in the
sunshine, where the wild flowers waste their sweet-
ness and no plough turns the fruitful soil, where
deer and ostrich roam fearless of the hunter, while
over all bends a blue sky without a cloud to stain
its exquisite beauty? And the people dwelling in
yon city—the key to a continent—they are the
possessors of it all. It is theirs, since the world,
out of which the old spirit is fast dying, has

suffered them to keep it. What have they done
with this their heritage? What are they doing
even now? They are sitting dejected in their
houses, or standing in their doorways with folded
arms and anxious, expectant faces. For a change
is coming: they are on the eve of a tempest. Not
an atmospheric change; no blighting simoom will
sweep over their fields, nor will any volcanic eruption darken their crystal heavens. The earth-
quakes that shake the Andean cities to their foun-
dations they have never known and can never
know. The expected change and tempest is a political one. The plot is ripe, the daggers sharp-
ened, the contingent of assassins hired, the throne
of human skulls, styled in their ghastly facetious-
ness a Presidential Chair, is about to be assaulted.
It is long, weeks or even months, perhaps, since
the last wave, crested with bloody froth, rolled its
desolating flood over the country; it is high time,
therefore, for all men to prepare themselves for
the shock of the succeeding wave. And we consider it right to root up thorns and thistles, to drain
malarious marshes, to extirpate rats and vipers;
but it would be immoral, I suppose, to stamp out
these people because their vicious natures are disguised in human shape; this people that in crimes
have surpassed all others, ancient or modern, until
because of them the name of a whole continent has
grown to be a byword of scorn and reproach
throughout the earth, and to stink in the nostrils
of all men!

"I swear that I, too, will become a conspirator if I remain long on this soil. Oh, for a thousand young men of Devon and Somerset here with me, every one of them with a brain on fire with thoughts like mine! What a glorious deed would be done for humanity! What a mighty cheer we would raise for the glory of the old England that is passing away! Blood would flow in yon streets as it never flowed before, or, I should say, as it only flowed in them once, and that was when they were swept clean by British bayonets. And afterwards there would be peace, and the grass would be greener and the flowers brighter for that crimson shower.

"Is it not then bitter as wormwood and gall to think that over these domes and towers beneath my feet, no longer than half a century ago, fluttered the holy cross of St. George! For never was there a holier crusade undertaken, never a nobler conquest planned, than that which had for its object the wresting this fair country from unworthy hands, to make it for all time part of the mighty English kingdom. What would it have been now—this bright, winterless land, and this city commanding the entrance to the greatest river in the world? And to think that it was won for England, not treacherously, or bought with gold, but in the old Saxon fashion with hard blows, and climbing over heaps of slain defenders; and after it was thus won, to think that it was lost—will it be believed?—not fighting, but yielded up without a stroke by craven wretches unworthy of the name of Britons! Here, sitting alone on this mountain, my face burns like fire when I think of it—this glorious opportunity lost for ever! 'We offer you your laws, your religion, and property under the protection of the British Government,' loftily proclaimed the invaders—Generals Beresford, Achmuty, Whitelocke, and their companions; and presently, after suffering one reverse, they (or one of them) lost heart and exchanged the country they had drenched in blood, and had conquered, for a couple of thousand British soldiers made prisoners in Buenos Ayres across the water; then, getting into their ships once more, they sailed away from the Plata for ever! This transaction, which must have made the bones of our Viking ancestors rattle with indignation in their graves, was forgotten later on when we seized the rich Falklands. A splendid conquest and a glorious compensation for our loss! When yon queen city was in our grasp, and the regeneration, possibly even the ultimate possession, of this green world before us, our hearts failed us and the prize dropped from our trembling hands. We left the sunny mainland to capture the desolate haunt of seals and penguins; and now let all those who in this quarter of the globe aspire to live under that 'British Protection' of which Achmuty preached so loudly at the gates of yon capital, transport themselves to those lonely antarctic islands to listen to the thunder of the waves on the grey shores and shiver in the bleak winds that blow from the frozen south!"

After delivering this comminatory address I felt greatly relieved, and went home in a cheerful frame of mind to supper, which consisted that evening of mutton scrag, boiled with pumpkins, sweet potatoes, and milky maize—not at all a bad dish for a hungry man.

CHAPTER II

SEVERAL days passed, and my second pair of boots had been twice resoled before Doña Isidora's schemes for advancing my fortunes began to take form. Perhaps she was beginning to think us a burden on her somewhat niggardly establishment; anyway, hearing that my preference was for a country life, she gave me a letter containing half a dozen lines of commendation addressed to the Mayordomo of a distant cattle-breeding establishment, asking him to serve the writer by giving her *nephew*—as she called me—employment of some kind on the estancia. Probably she knew that this letter would really lead to nothing, and gave it merely to get me away into the interior of the country, so as to keep Paquíta for an indefinite time to herself, for she had become extremely attached to her beautiful niece. The estancia was on the borders of the Paysandù department, and not less than two hundred miles from Montevideo. It was a long journey, and I was advised not to attempt it without a *tropilla*, or troop of horses. But when a native tells you that you cannot travel two hundred miles without a dozen horses, he only means that you cannot do the distance in two days;

for it is hard for him to believe that one may be satisfied with less than one hundred miles a day. *I* travelled on one horse, and it therefore took me several days to accomplish the journey. Before I reached my destination, called *Estancia de la Virgen de los Desamparados*, I met with some adventures worth relating, and began to feel as much at home with the *Orientales* as I had long been with the *Argentinos*.

Fortunately, after I left the town, a west wind continued blowing all day, bringing with it many light flying clouds to mitigate the sun, so that I was able to cover a good number of leagues before the evening. I took the road northwards through Camelones department, and was well on into the Florida department when I put up for the night at the solitary mud rancho of an old herdsman, who lived with his wife and children in a very primitive fashion. When I rode up to the house, several huge dogs rushed out to attack me: one seized my horse by the tail, dragging the poor beast about this way and that, so that he staggered and could scarcely keep his legs; another caught the bridle-reins in his mouth; while a third fixed his fangs in the heel of my boot. After eyeing me for some moments, the grizzled old herdsman, who wore a knife a yard long at his waist, advanced to the rescue. He shouted at the dogs, and finding that they would not obey, sprang forward and with a few dexterous blows, dealt with his heavy whip-handle, sent them away howling with rage and pain. Then he welcomed me with great courtesy, and very soon, when my horse had been unsaddled and turned loose to feed, we were sitting together enjoying the cool evening air and imbibing the bitter and refreshing maté his wife served to us. While we conversed I noticed numberless fireflies flitting about; I had never seen them so numerous before, and they made a very lovely show. Presently one of the children, a bright little fellow of seven or eight, came running to us with one of the sparkling insects in his hand, and cried—

"Look, tatita, I have caught a *linterna*. See how bright it is!"

"The Saints forgive you, my child," said the father. "Go, little son, and put it back on the grass, for if you should hurt it, the spirits would be angry with you, for they go about by night and love the *linterna* that keeps them company."

What a pretty superstition, I thought; and what a mild, merciful heart this old Oriental herdsman must possess to show so much tenderness towards one of God's tiny creatures. I congratulated myself on my good fortune in having fallen in with such a person in this lonely place.

The dogs, after their rude behaviour to me and the sharp punishment they had suffered in consequence, had returned, and were now gathered around us lying on the ground. Here I noticed, not for the first time, that the dogs belonging to these lonely places are not nearly so fond of being noticed and caressed as are those of more populous and civilised districts. On attempting to stroke one of these surly brutes on the head, he displayed his teeth and growled savagely at me. Yet this animal, though so truculent in temper, and asking for no kindness from his master, is just as faithful to man as his better-mannered brother in the more settled country. I spoke on that subject to my gentle herdsman.

"What you say is true," he replied. "I remember once during the siege of Montevideo, when I was with a small detachment sent to watch the movements of General Rivera's army, we one day overtook a man on a tired horse. Our officer, suspecting him to be a spy, ordered him to be killed, and after cutting his throat we left his body lying on the open ground at a distance of about two hundred and fifty yards from a small stream of water. A dog was with him, and when we rode off we called it to follow us, but it would not stir from its dead master's side.

"Three days later we returned to the same spot, to find the corpse lying just where we had left it. The foxes and birds had not touched it, for the dog was still there to defend it. Many vultures were near, waiting for a chance to begin their feast. We alighted to refresh ourselves at the stream, then stood there for half an hour watching the dog. He seemed to be half-famished with thirst, and came towards the stream to drink; but before he got half-way to it the vultures, by twos and threes, began to advance, when back he flew and chased them away barking. After resting for a few minutes beside the corpse, he came again towards the stream, till, seeing the hungry birds advance once more, he again flew back at them, barking furiously and foaming at the mouth. This we saw repeated many times, and at last, when we left, we tried once more to entice the dog to follow us, but he would not. Two days after that we had occasion to pass by that spot again, and there we saw the dog lying dead beside his master."

"Good God," I exclaimed, "how horrible must have been the feelings you and your companions experienced at such a sight!"

"No, señor, not at all," replied the old man. "Why, señor, I myself put the knife into that man's throat. For if a man did not grow accustomed to shed blood in this world, his life would be a burden to him."

What an inhuman old murderer! I thought. Then I asked him whether he had ever in his life felt remorse for shedding blood.

"Yes," he answered; "when I was a very young man, and had never before dipped weapon in human blood; that was when the siege began. I was sent with half a dozen men in pursuit of a clever spy, who had passed the lines with letters from the besieged. We came to a house where, our officer had been informed, he had been lying concealed. The master of the house was a young

man about twenty-two years old. He would confess nothing. Finding him so stubborn, our officer
became enraged, and bade him step out, and then
ordered us to lance him. We galloped forty yards
off, then wheeled back. He stood silent, his arms
folded on his breast, a smile on his lips. Without
a cry, without a groan, with that smile still on his
lips, he fell pierced through with our lances. For
days afterwards his face was ever present to me.
I could not eat, for my food choked me. When
I raised a jug of water to my lips I could, señor,
distinctly see his eyes looking at me from the
water. When I lay down to sleep, his face was
again before me, always with that smile that
seemed to mock me on the lips. I could not understand it. They told me it was remorse, and
that it would soon leave me, for there is no ill that
time will not cure. They spoke truth, and when
that feeling left me I was able to do all things."

The old man's story so sickened me that I had
little appetite for supper, and passed a bad night
thinking, waking or sleeping, of that young man
in this obscure corner of the world who folded his
arms and smiled on his slayers when they were
slaying him. Very early next morning I bade my
host good-bye, thanking him for his hospitality,
and devoutly hoping that I should never look
upon his abhorred face again.

I made little progress that day, the weather
proving hot, and my horse lazier than ever. After
riding about five leagues, I rested for a couple of

hours, then proceeded again at a gentle trot till about the middle of the afternoon, when I dismounted at a wayside *pulperia*, or store and public-house all in one, where several natives were sipping rum and conversing. Standing before them was a brisk-looking old man—old, I say, because he had a dark dry skin, though his hair and moustache were black as jet—who paused in the discourse he appeared to be delivering, to salute me; then, after bestowing a searching glance on me out of his dark hawk-like eyes, he resumed his talk. After calling for rum and water, to be in the fashion, I sat down on a bench, and, lighting a cigarette, prepared to listen. He was dressed in shabby gaucho habiliments—cotton shirt, short jacket, wide cotton drawers and *chiripà*, a shawl-like garment fastened at the waist with a sash, and reaching down half-way between the knees and ankles. In place of a hat he wore a cotton handkerchief tied carelessly about his head; his left foot was bare, while the right one was cased in a colt's-skin stocking, called *bota-de-potro*, and on this distinguished foot was buckled a huge iron spur, with spikes two inches long. One spur of the kind would be quite sufficient, I should imagine, to get out of a horse all the energy of which he was capable. When I entered he was holding forth on the pretty well-worn theme of fate *versus* free will; his arguments were not, however, the usual dry philosophical ones, but took the form of illustration, chiefly personal reminiscences and strange incidents in the lives of people he had known, while so vivid and minute were his descriptions—sparkling with passion, satire, humour, pathos, and so dramatic his action, while wonderful story followed story—that I was fairly astonished, and pronounced this old *pulperia* orator a born genius.

His argument over, he fixed his keen eyes on me and said—

"My friend, I perceive you are a traveller from Montevideo: may I ask what news there is from that city?"

"What news do you expect to hear?" said I; then it came into my thought that it was scarcely proper to confine myself to mere commonplace phrases in replying to this curious old Oriental bird, with such ragged plumage, but whose native woodnotes wild had such a charm in them. "It is only the old story over again!" I continued. "They say there will be a revolution some day. Some of the people have already retired into their houses, after chalking in very big letters on their front doors, 'Please come into this house and cut the owner's throat for him, so that he may rest at peace, and have no fear of what may happen.' Others have climbed on to their roofs and occupy themselves there looking at the moon through spyglasses, thinking that the conspirators are concealed in that luminary, and only waiting for a cloud to obscure it, in order to descend upon the city unobserved."

"Hear!" cried the old man, rapping delighted applause on the counter with his empty glass.

"What do you drink, friend?" I asked, thinking his keen appreciation of my grotesque speech deserved a treat, and wishing to draw him out a little more.

"Rum, friend, thank you. They say it warms you in winter, and cools you in summer—what can you have better?"

"Tell me," said I, when his glass had been refilled by the storekeeper, "what I shall say when I return to Montevideo, and am asked what news there is in the country?"

The old fellow's eyes twinkled, while the other men ceased talking, and looked at him as if anticipating something good in reply to my question.

"Say to them," he answered, "that you met an old man—a horse-tamer named Lucero—and that he told you this fable for you to repeat to the townspeople: Once there was a great tree named Montevideo growing in this country, and in its branches lived a colony of monkeys. One day one of the monkeys came down from the tree and ran full of excitement across the plain, now scrambling along like a man on all fours, then erect like a dog running on its hind legs, while its tail with nothing to catch hold of wriggled about like a snake when its head is under foot. He came to a place where a number of oxen were grazing, and some horses, ostriches, deer, goats, and pigs.

'Friends all,' cried the monkey, grinning like a skull, and with staring eyes round as dollars, 'great news! great news! I come to tell you that there will shortly be a revolution.' 'Where?' said an ox. 'In the tree—where else?' said the monkey. 'That does not concern us,' said the ox. 'Oh, yes it does!' cried the monkey, 'for it will presently spread about the country and you will all have your throats cut.' Then the ox replied, 'Go back, monkey, and do not molest us with your news, lest we get angry and go to besiege you in your tree, as we have often had to do since the creation of the world; and then, if you and the other monkeys come down to us, we will toss you on our horns.' "

This apologue sounded very well, so admirably did the old man picture to us with voice and gesture the chattering excitement of the monkeys and the majestic *àplomb* of the ox.

"Señor," he continued, after the laugh had subsided, "I do not wish any of my friends and neighbours here present to fly to the conclusion that I have spoken anything offensive. Had I seen in you a Montevidean I should not have spoken of monkeys. But, señor, though you speak as we do, there is yet in the pepper and salt on your tongue a certain foreign flavour."

"You are right," I said; "I am a foreigner."

"A foreigner in some things, friend, for you were doubtless born under other skies; but in that chief quality, which we think was given by the

Creator to us and not to the people of other lands
—the ability to be one in heart with the men you
meet, whether they are clothed in velvet or in
sheep skins—in that you are one of us, a pure
Oriental."

I smiled at his subtle flattery; possibly it was
only meant in payment of the rum I had treated
him to, but it pleased me none the less, and to his
other mental traits I was now inclined to add a
marvellous skill in reading character.

After a while he invited me to spend the night
under his roof. "Your horse is fat and lazy," he
said with truth, "and unless you are a relation of
the owl family, you cannot go much further before to-morrow. My house is a humble one, but
the mutton is juicy, the fire warm, and the water
cool there, the same as in another place."

I readily accepted his invitation, wishing to see
as much as I could of so original a character, and
before starting I purchased a bottle of rum, which
made his eyes sparkle so that I thought his name
—Lucero—rather an appropriate one. His rancho
was about two miles from the store, and our ride
thither was about as strange a gallop as I ever
took. Lucero was a *domador*, or horse-tamer, and
the beast he rode was quite unbroken and vicious
as it could be. Between horse and man a fierce
struggle for mastery raged the whole time, the
horse rearing, plunging, buck-jumping, and putting into practice every conceivable trick to rid
itself of its burden; while Lucero plied whip and

spur with tremendous energy and poured out torrents of strange adjectives. At one moment he
would come into violent collision with my cold
sober beast, at another there would be fifty yards
of ground between us; still Lucero would not stop
talking, for he had begun a very interesting story
at starting and he stuck to his narrative through
everything, resuming the thread after each tempest of execration vented on his horse, and raising
his voice almost to a shout when we were far apart.
The old fellow's staying powers were really extraordinary, and when we arrived at the house he
jumped airily to the ground and seemed fresh and
calm as possible.

In the kitchen were several people sipping maté,
Lucero's children and grandchildren, also his wife,
a grey old dame with dim-looking eyes. But then
my host was old in years himself, only, like
Ulysses, he still possessed the unquenched fire and
energy of youth in his soul, while time bestowed
infirmities together with wrinkles and white hairs
on his helpmate.

He introduced me to her in a manner that
brought the modest flame to my cheek. Standing
before her, he said that he had met me at the
pulpería and had put to me the question which a
simple old countryman must ask of every traveller
from Montevideo—What the news was? Then,
assuming a dry satirical tone, which years of practice would not enable me to imitate, he proceeded

to give my fantastical answer, garnished with much original matter of his own.

"Señora," I said when he had finished, "you must not give me credit for all you have heard from your husband. I only gave him brute wool, and he has woven it for your delight into beautiful cloth."

"Hear him! Did I not tell you what to expect, Juana?" cried the old man, which made me blush still more.

We then settled down to maté and quiet conversation. Sitting in the kitchen on the skull of a horse—a common article of furniture in an Oriental rancho—was a boy about twelve years old, one of Lucero's grandchildren, with a very beautiful face. His feet were bare and his clothes very poor, but his soft dark eyes and olive face had that tender half-melancholy expression often seen in children of Spanish origin, which is always so strangely captivating.

"Where's your guitar, Cipriano?" said his grandfather, addressing him, whereupon the boy rose and fetched a guitar which he first politely offered to me.

When I had declined it, he seated himself once more on his polished horse skull and began to play and sing. He had a sweet boy's voice, and one of his ballads took my fancy so much that I made him repeat the words to me while I wrote them down in my notebook, which greatly gratified Lucero, who seemed proud of the boy's accom-

plishment.   Here are the words translated almost
literally, therefore without rhymes, and I only
regret that I cannot furnish my musical readers
with the quaint, plaintive air they were sung to:—

O let me go—O let me go,
Where high are born amidst the hills
The streams that gladden all the south,
And o'er the grassy desert wide,
Where slakes his thirst the antlered deer,
Hurry towards the great green ocean.

The stony hills—the stony hills,
With azure air-flowers on their crags,
Where cattle stray unowned by man;
The monarch of the herd there seems
No bigger than my hand in size,
Roaming along the tall, steep summit.

I know them well—I know them well,
Those hills of God, and they know me;
When I go there they are serene,
But when the stranger visits them
Dark rain-clouds gather round their tops—
Over the earth goes forth the tempest.

Then tell me not—then tell me not
'Tis sorrowful to dwell alone:
My heart within the city pent
Pines for the desert's liberty;
The streets are red with blood, and fear
Makes pale the mournful women's faces.

O bear me far—O bear me far,
On swift, sure feet, my trusty steed:
I do not love the burial-ground,
But I shall sleep upon the plain,
Where long green grass shall round me wave—
Over me graze wild herds of cattle.

CHAPTER III

MATERIALS FOR A PASTORAL

LEAVING the eloquent old horse-tamer's rancho early next morning, I continued my ride, jogging quietly along all day and, leaving the Florida department behind me, entered upon that of the Durazno. Here I broke my journey at an estancia where I had an excellent opportunity of studying the manners and customs of the Orientals, and where I also underwent experiences of a mixed character and greatly increased my knowledge of the insect world. This house, at which I arrived an hour before sunset to ask for shelter ("permission to unsaddle" is the expression the traveller uses), was a long, low structure, thatched with rushes, but the low, enormously thick walls were built of stone from the neighbouring sierras, in pieces of all shapes and sizes, and presenting, outwardly, the rough appearance of a stone fence. How these rudely piled-up stones, without cement to hold them together, had not fallen down was a mystery to me; and it was more difficult still to imagine why the rough interior, with its innumerable dusty holes and interstices, had never been plastered.

I was kindly received by a very numerous family, consisting of the owner, his hoary-headed old mother-in-law, his wife, three sons, and five daughters, all grown up. There were also several small children, belonging, I believe, to the daughters, notwithstanding the fact that they were un-married. I was greatly amazed at hearing the name of one of these youngsters. Such Christian names as Trinity, Heart of Jesus, Nativity, John of God, Conception, Ascension, Incarnation, are common enough, but these had scarcely prepared me to meet with a fellow-creature named—well, Circumcision! Besides the people, there were dogs, cats, turkeys, ducks, geese, and fowls with-out number. Not content with all these domestic birds and beasts, they also kept a horrid, shriek-ing paroquet, which the old woman was inces-santly talking to, explaining to the others all the time, in little asides, what the bird said or wished to say, or, rather, what she imagined it wished to say. There were also several tame young ostriches, always hanging about the big kitchen or living-room on the look-out for a brass thimble, or iron spoon, or other little metallic *bonne bouche* to be gobbled up when no one was looking. A pet ar-madillo kept trotting in and out, in and out, the whole evening, and a lame gull was always stand-ing on the threshold in everybody's way, perpetu-ally wailing for something to eat—the most persistent beggar I ever met in my life.

The people were very jovial and rather indus-trious for so indolent a country. The land was their own, the men tended the cattle, of which they appeared to have a large number, while the women made cheeses, rising before daylight to milk the cows.

During the evening two or three young men—neighbours, I imagine, who were paying their addresses to the young ladies of the establishment—dropped in; and after a plentiful supper we had singing and dancing to the music of a guitar, on which every member of the family—excepting the babies—could strum a little.

About eleven o'clock I retired to rest, and stretching myself on my rude bed of rugs, in a room adjoining the kitchen, I blessed these simple-minded hospitable people. Good heavens, thought I to myself, what a glorious field is waiting here for some new Theocritus! How unutterably worn out, stilted, and artificial seems all the so-called pastoral poetry ever written when one sits down to supper and joins in the graceful *Cielo* or *Pericon* in one of these remote semi-barbarous South American estancias! I swear I will turn poet myself, and go back some day to astonish old *blasé* Europe with something so—so—— What the deuce was that? My sleepy soliloquy was suddenly brought to a most lame and impotent conclusion, for I had heard a sound of terror—the unmistakable *zz-zzing* of an insect's wings. It was the hateful vinchuca. Here was an enemy against which British pluck and six-shooters are of no avail, and in whose presence one begins to experience sensations which are not usually supposed to enter into the brave man's breast. Naturalists tell us that it is the *Connorhinus infestans*, but as that information leaves something to be desired, I will proceed in a few words to describe the beast. It inhabits the entire Chilian, Argentine, and Oriental countries, and to all the dwellers in this vast territory it is known as the vinchuca; for, like a few volcanoes, deadly vipers, cataracts, and other sublime natural objects, it has been permitted to keep the ancient name bestowed on it by the aborigines. It is all over of a blackish-brown colour, as broad as a man's thumb-nail, and flat as the blade of a table-knife—when fasting. By day it hides, bug-like, in holes and chinks, but no sooner are the candles put out, than forth it comes to seek whom it may devour; for, like the pestilence, it walks in darkness. It can fly, and in a dark room knows where you are and can find you. Having selected a nice tender part, it pierces the skin with its proboscis or rostrum, and sucks vigorously for two or three minutes, and, strange to say, you do not feel the operation, even when lying wide awake. By that time the creature, so attenuated before, has assumed the figure, size, and general appearance of a ripe gooseberry, so much blood has it drawn from your veins. Immediately after it has left you the part begins to swell up and burn as if stung by nettles. That the pain should come after and not during the operation is an arrangement very advantageous to the vinchuca, and I greatly doubt whether any other blood-sucking parasite has been equally favoured by nature in this respect.

Imagine then my sensations when I heard the sound of not one, but two or three pairs of wings! I tried to forget the sound and go to sleep. I tried to forget about those rough old walls full of interstices—a hundred years old they were, my host had informed me. Most interesting old house, thought I; and then very suddenly a fiery itching took possession of my great toe. There it is! said I; heated blood, late supper, dancing, and all that. I can almost imagine that something has actually bitten me, when of course nothing of that kind has happened. Then, while I was furiously rubbing and scratching it, feeling a badger-like disposition to gnaw it off, my left arm was pierced with red-hot needles. My attentions were quickly transferred to that part; but soon my busy hands were called elsewhere, like a couple of hard-worked doctors in a town afflicted with an epidemic; and so all night long, with only occasional snatches of miserable sleep, the contest went on.

I rose early, and going to a wide stream, a quarter of a mile from the house, took a plunge which greatly refreshed me and gave me strength to go in quest of my horse. Poor brute! I had intended giving him a day's rest, so pleasant and hospitable had the people shown themselves; but now I shuddered at the thought of spending another night in such a purgatory. I found him so lame that he could scarcely walk, and so returned to the house on foot and very much cast down. My host consoled me by assuring me that I would sleep the siesta all the better for having been molested by those "little things that go about," for in this very mild language he described the affliction. After breakfast, at noon, acting on his hint, I took a rug to the shade of a tree and, lying down, quickly fell into a profound sleep which lasted till late in the afternoon.

That evening visitors came again and we had a repetition of the singing, dancing, and other pastoral amusements, till near midnight; then, thinking to cheat my bedfellows of the night before, I made my simple bed in the kitchen. But here also the vile vinchucas found me, and there were, moreover, dozens of fleas that waged a sort of guerilla warfare all night, and in this way exhausted my strength and distracted my attention, while the more formidable adversary took up his position. My sufferings were so great that before daybreak I picked up my rugs and went out a distance from the house to lie down on the open plain, but I carried with me a smarting body and got but little rest. When morning came I found that my horse had not yet recovered from his lameness.

"Do not be in a hurry to leave us," said my host, when I spoke of it; "I perceive that the lit-

tle animals have again fought with and defeated
you. Do not mind it; in time you will grow accustomed to them."

How *they* contrived to endure it, or even to
exist, was a puzzle to me; but possibly the vinchucas respected them, and only dined when, like
the giant in the nursery rhyme, they "smelt the
blood of an Englishman."

I again enjoyed a long siesta, and when night
came resolved to place myself beyond the reach
of the vampires, and so, after supper, went out to
sleep on the plain. About midnight, however, a
sudden storm of wind and rain drove me back to
the shelter of the house, and the next morning
I rose in such a deplorable state that I deliberately caught and saddled my horse, though the
poor beast could scarcely put one foot on the
ground. My friends laughed good-humouredly
when they saw me making these resolute preparations for departure. After partaking of bitter
maté, I rose and thanked them for their hospitality.

"You surely do not intend leaving us on that
animal!" said my host. "He is unfit to carry
you."

"I have no other," I replied, "and am anxious
to reach my destination."

"Had I known this I should have offered you
a horse before," he returned, and then he sent
one of his sons to drive the horses of the estancia
into the corral.

Selecting a good-looking animal from the herd, he presented it to me, and as I did not have money enough to buy a fresh horse whenever I wanted one, I accepted the gift very gladly. The saddle was quickly transferred to my new acquisition, and once more thanking these good people and bidding adieu, I resumed my journey.

When I gave my hand before leaving to the youngest, and also, to my mind, the prettiest of the five daughters of the house, instead of smiling pleasantly and wishing me a prosperous journey, like the others, she was silent, and darted a look at me, which seemed to say, "Go, sir; you have treated me badly, and you insult me by offering your hand; if I take it, it is not because I feel disposed to forgive you, but only to save appearances."

At the same moment, when she bestowed that glance on me which said so much, a look of intelligence passed over the faces of the other people in the room. All this revealed to me that I had just missed a very pretty little idyllic flirtation, conducted in very novel circumstances. Love cometh up as a flower, and men and charming women naturally flirt when brought together. Yet it was hard to imagine how I could have started a flirtation and carried it on to its culminatory point in that great public room, with all those eyes on me; dogs, babes, and cats tumbling about my feet; ostriches staring covetously at my buttons with great vacant eyes; and that intolerable paroquet perpetually reciting "How the waters came down at Lodore," in its own shrieky, beaky, birdy, hurdy-gurdy, parrot language. Tender glances, soft whispered words, hand-touchings, and a thousand little personal attentions, showing which way the emotions tend, would scarcely have been practicable in such a place and in such conditions, and new signs and symbols would have to be invented to express the feelings of the heart. And doubtless these Orientals, living all together in one great room, with their children and pets, like our very ancient ancestors, the pastoral Aryans, do possess such a language. And this pretty language I should have learnt from the most willing of teachers, if those venomous vinchucas had not dulled my brain with their persecutions and made me blind to a matter which had not escaped the observation of even unconcerned lookers-on. Riding away from the estancia, the feeling I experienced at having finally escaped from these execrable "little things that go about" was not one of unmixed satisfaction.

CHAPTER IV

VAGABONDS' REST

CONTINUING my journey through the Durazno district, I forded the pretty River Yí and entered the Tacuarembó department, which is immensely long, extending right away to the Brazilian frontier. I rode over its narrowest part, however, where it is only about twenty-five miles wide; then crossing two very curiously named rivers, Rios Salsipuedes Chico and Salsipuedes Grande, which mean Get-out-if-you-can Rivers, Little and Big, I at length reached the termination of my journey in the province or department of Paysandù. The *Estancia de la Virgen de los Desamparados*, or, to put it very shortly, Vagabonds' Rest, was a good-sized square brick house built on very high ground, which overlooked an immense stretch of grassy undulating country. There was no plantation about the house, not even a shade tree or cultivated plant of any description, but only some large *corrales*, or enclosures, for the cattle, of which there were six or seven thousand head on the land. The absence of shade and greenery gave the place a desolate, uninviting aspect, but if I was ever to have any authority here this would soon be changed. The Mayordomo, or manager, Don Policarpo Santierra de

Peñalosa, which, roughly done into English, means Polycarp of the Holy Land abounding in Slippery Rocks, proved to be a very pleasant, affable person. He welcomed me with that quiet Oriental politeness which is never cold and never effusive, and then perused the letter from Doña Isidora. Finally he said, "I am willing, my friend, to supply you with all the conveniences procurable at this elevation; and, for the rest, you know, doubtless, what I can say to you. A ready understanding requires few words. Nevertheless, there is here no lack of good beef, and, to be short, you will do me a great favour by making this house with everything it contains your own, while you honour us by remaining in it."

After delivering himself of these kindly sentiments which left me rather in a mist as to my prospects, he mounted his horse and rode off, probably on some very important affair, for I saw no more of him for several days.

I at once proceeded to establish myself in the kitchen. No person in the house appeared ever to pay even a casual visit to any other room. This kitchen was vast and barn-like, forty feet long at least, and proportionately wide; the roof was of reeds, and the hearth, placed in the centre of the floor, was a clay platform, fenced round with cows' shank-bones, half buried and standing upright. Some trivets and iron kettles were scattered about, and from the centre beam, supporting the roof, a chain and hook were suspended to which a vast iron pot was fastened. One more article, a spit about six feet long for roasting meat, completed the list of cooking utensils. There were no chairs, tables, knives, or forks; everyone carried his own knife, and at meal-time the boiled meat was emptied into a great tin dish, whilst the roast was eaten from the spit, each one laying hold with his fingers and cutting his slice. The seats were logs of wood and horse-skulls. The household was composed of one woman, an ancient, hideously ugly, grey-headed negress, about seventy years old, and eighteen or nineteen men of all ages and sizes, and of all colours from parchment-white to very old oak. There was a *capatas*, or overseer, and seven or eight paid *peones*, the others being all *agregados*—that is, supernumeraries without pay, or, to put it plainly, vagabonds who attach themselves like vagrant dogs to establishments of this kind, lured by the abundance of flesh, and who occasionally assist the regular *peones* at their work, and also do a little gambling and stealing to keep themselves in small change. At break of day everyone was up sitting by the hearth sipping bitter maté and smoking cigarettes; before sunrise all were mounted and away over the surrounding country to gather up the herds; at midday they were back again to breakfast. The consumption and waste of meat was something frightful. Frequently, after breakfast, as much as twenty or thirty pounds of boiled and roast meat would be thrown into a wheelbarrow and carried out to the dust-heap, where it served to feed scores of hawks, gulls, and vultures, besides the dogs.

Of course, I was only an *agregado*, having no salary or regular occupation yet. Thinking, however, that this would only be for a time, I was quite willing to make the best of things, and very soon became fast friends with my fellow *agregados*, joining heartily in all their amusements and voluntary labours.

In a few days I got very tired of living exclusively on flesh, for not even a biscuit was "procurable at this elevation"; and as for a potato, one might as well have asked for a plum-pudding. It occurred to my mind at last that, with so many cows, it might be possible to procure some milk and introduce a little change into our diet. In the evening I broached the subject, proposing that on the following day we should capture a cow and tame her. Some of the men approved of the suggestion, remarking that they had never thought of it themselves; but the old negress, who, being the only representative of the fair sex present, was always listened to with all the deference due to her position, threw herself with immense zeal into the opposition. She affirmed that no cow had been milked at that establishment since its owner had paid it a visit with his young wife twelve years before. A milch-cow was then kept, and on the señora partaking of a large quantity of milk "before breaking her fast," it produced such an indigestion in her that they were obliged to give her powdered ostrich stomach, and finally to convey her, with great trouble, in an ox-cart to Paysandù and thence by water to Montevideo. The owner ordered the cow to be released, and never, to her certain knowledge, had cow been milked since at La Virgen de los Desamparados.

These ominous croakings produced no effect on me, and the next day I returned to the subject. I did not possess a lasso, and so could not undertake to capture a half-wild cow without assistance. One of my fellow *agregados* at length volunteered to help me, observing that he had not tasted milk for several years, and was inclined to renew his acquaintance with that singular beverage. This newfound friend in need merits being formally introduced to the reader. His name was Epifanio Claro. He was tall and thin, and had an idiotic expression on his long, sallow face. His cheeks were innocent of whiskers, and his lank, black hair, parted in the middle, fell to his shoulders, enclosing his narrow face between a pair of raven's wings. He had very large, light-coloured, sheepish-looking eyes, and his eyebrows bent up like a couple of Gothic arches, leaving a narrow strip above them that formed the merest apology for a forehead. This facial peculiarity had won for him the nickname of Cejas (Eyebrows), by which he was known to his intimates. He spent most of his time strumming on a wretched old cracked guitar, and singing amorous ballads in a lugubrious whining falsetto, which reminded me not a little of that hungry, complaining gull I had met at the estancia in Durazno. For though poor Epifanio had an absorbing passion for music, Nature had unkindly withheld from him the power to express it in a manner pleasing to others. I must, however, in justice to him, allow that he gave a preference to ballads or compositions of a thoughtful, not to say metaphysical character. I took the trouble of translating the words of one literally, and here they are:—

> Yesterday my senses opened,
> At a rap-a-tap from Reason,
> Inspiring in me an intention
> Which I never had before,
> Seeing that through all my days
> My life has been just what it is.
> Therefore when I rose I said,
> To-day shall be as yesterday,
> Since Reason tells me I have been
> From day to day the self-same thing.

This is very little to judge from, being only a fourth part of the song; but it is a fair specimen, and the rest is no clearer. Of course it is not to be supposed that Epifanio Claro, an illiterate person, took in the whole philosophy of these lines; still it is probable that a subtle ray or two of their deep meaning touched his intellect, to make him a wiser and a sadder man.

Accompanied by this strange individual, and with the grave permission of the *capatas*, who declined, however, in words of many syllables all *responsabilidad* in the matter, we went out to the grazing grounds in quest of a promising-looking cow. Very soon we found one to our liking. She was followed by a small calf, not more than a week old, and her distended udder promised a generous supply of milk; but unfortunately she was fierce-tempered, and had horns as sharp as needles.

"We will cut them by-and-by," shouted Eyebrows.

He then lassoed the cow, and I captured the calf, and lifting it into the saddle before me, started homewards. The cow followed me at a furious pace, and behind came Claro at a swinging gallop. Possibly he was a little too confident, and carelessly let his captive pull the line that held her; anyhow, she turned suddenly on him, charged with amazing fury, and sent one of her horrid horns deep into the belly of his horse. He was, however, equal to the occasion, first dealing her a smart blow on the nose, which made her recoil for a moment; he then severed the lasso with his knife, and shouting to me to drop the calf, made his escape. We pulled up as soon as we had reached a safe distance, Claro drily remarking that the lasso had been borrowed, and that the horse belonged to the estancia, so that we had lost nothing. He alighted, and stitched up the great gash in the poor brute's belly, using for a thread a few hairs plucked from its tail. It was a difficult task, or would have been so to me, as he had to bore holes in the animal's hide with his knife-point, but it seemed quite easy to him. Taking the remaining portion of the severed lasso, he drew it round the hind and one of the fore feet of his horse, and threw him to the ground with a dexterous jerk; then, binding him there, performed the operation of sewing up the wound in about two minutes.

"Will he live?" I asked.

"How can I tell," he answered indifferently. "I only know that now he will be able to carry me home; if he dies afterwards what will it matter?"

We then mounted and rode quietly home. Of course we were chaffed without mercy, especially by the old negress, who had foreseen all along, she told us, just how it would be. One would have imagined, to hear this old black creature talk, that she looked on milk-drinking as one of the greatest moral offences man could be guilty of, and that in this case Providence had miraculously interposed to prevent us from gratifying our depraved appetites.

Eyebrows took it all very coolly.

"Do not notice them," he said to me. "The lasso was not ours, the horse was not ours, what does it matter what they say?"

The owner of the lasso, who had good-naturedly lent it to us, roused himself on hearing this. He was a very big, rough-looking man, his face covered with an immense shaggy black beard. I had taken him for a good-humoured specimen of the giant kind before, but I now changed my opinion of him when his angry passions began to rise. Blas, or Barbudo, as we called the giant, was seated on a log sipping maté.

"Perhaps you take me for a sheep, sirs, because you see me wrapped in skins," he observed; "but let me tell you this, the lasso I lent you must be returned to me."

"These words are not for us," remarked Eyebrows, addressing me, "but for the cow that carried away his lasso on her horns—curse them for being so sharp!"

"No, sir," returned Barbudo, "do not deceive yourself; they are not for the cow, but for the fool that lassoed the cow. And I promise you, Epifanio, that if it is not restored to me, this thatch over our heads will not be broad enough to shelter us both."

"I am pleased to hear it," said the other, "for we are short of seats; and when you leave us, the one you now encumber with your carcass will be occupied by some more meritorious person."

"You can say what you like, for no one has yet put a padlock on your lips," said Barbudo, raising his voice to a shout; "but you are not going to plunder me; and if my lasso is not restored to me, then I swear I will make myself a new one out of a human hide."

"Then," said Eyebrows, "the sooner you provide yourself with a hide for the purpose, the better, for I will never return the lasso to you;

for who am I to fight against Providence, that took it out of my hands?"

To this Barbudo replied furiously—

"Then I will have it from this miserable starved foreigner, who comes here to learn to eat meat and put himself on an equality with men. Evidently he was weaned too soon; but if the starveling hungers for infant's food, let him in future milk the cats that warm themselves beside the fire, and can be caught without a lasso, even by a Frenchman!"

I could not endure the brute's insults, and sprang up from my seat. I happened to have a large knife in my hand, for we were just preparing to make an assault on the roasted ribs of a cow, and my first impulse was to throw down the knife and give him a blow with my fist. Had I attempted it I should most probably have paid dearly for my rashness. The instant I rose Barbudo was on me, knife in hand. He aimed a furious blow, which luckily missed me, and at the same moment I struck him, and he reeled back with a dreadful gash on his face. It was all done in a second of time, and before the others could interpose; in another moment they disarmed us, and set about bathing the barbarian's wound. During the operation, which I daresay was very painful, for the old negress insisted on having the wound bathed with rum instead of water, the brute blasphemed outrageously, vowing that he would cut out my heart and eat it stewed with onions and seasoned with cummin seed and various other condiments.

I have often since thought of that sublime culinary conception of Blas the barbarian. There must have been a spark of wild Oriental genius in his bovine brains.

When the exhaustion caused by rage, pain, and loss of blood had at length reduced him to silence, the old negress turned on him, exclaiming that he had been rightly punished, for had he not, in spite of her timely warnings, lent his lasso to enable these two heretics (for that is what she called us) to capture a cow? Well, his lasso was lost; then his friends, with the gratitude only to be expected from milk-drinkers, had turned round and well-nigh killed him.

After supper the *capatas* got me alone, and with excessive friendliness of manner, and an abundance of circumlocutory phrases, advised me to leave the estancia, as it would not be safe for me to remain. I replied that I was not to blame, having struck the man in self-defence; also, that I had been sent to the estancia by a friend of the Mayordomo, and was determined to see him and give him my version of the affair.

The *capatas* shrugged his shoulders and lit a cigarette.

At length Don Policarpo returned, and when I told him my story he laughed slightly, but said nothing. In the evening I reminded him of the subject of the letter I had brought from Montevideo, asking him whether it was his intention to give me some employment on the estancia.

"You see, my friend," he replied, "to employ you now would be useless, however valuable your services might be, for by this time the authorities will have information of your fight with Blas. In the course of a few days you may expect them here to make inquiries into that affair, and it is probable that you and Blas will both be taken into custody."

"What then would you advise me to do?" I asked.

His answer was, that when the ostrich asked the deer what he would advise him to do when the hunters appeared, the deer's reply was, "Run away."

I laughed at his pretty apologue, and answered that I did not think the authorities would trouble themselves about me—also that I was not fond of running away.

Eyebrows, who had hitherto been rather inclined to patronise me and take me under his protection, now became very warm in his friendship, which was, however, dashed with an air of deference when we were alone together, but in company he was fond of parading his familiarity with me. I did not quite understand this change of manner at first, but by-and-by he took me mysteriously aside and became extremely confidential.

"Do not distress yourself about Barbudo," he

said. "He will never again presume to lift his hand against you; and if you will only condescend to speak kindly to him, he will be your humble slave, and proud to have you wipe your greasy fingers on his beard. Take no notice of what the Mayordomo says, he also is afraid of you. If the authorities take you, it will only be to see what you can give them: they will not keep you long, for you are a foreigner, and cannot be made to serve in the army. But when you are again at liberty it will be necessary for you to kill some-one."

Very much amazed, I asked him why.

"You see," he replied, "your reputation as a fighter is now established in this department, and there is nothing men envy more. It is the same as in our old game of *Pato*, where the man that carries the duck away is pursued by all the others, and before they give up chasing him he must prove that he can keep what he has taken. There are several fighters you do not know, who have re-solved to pick quarrels with you in order to try your strength. In your next fight you must not wound but kill, or you will have no peace."

I was greatly disturbed at this result of my accidental victory over Blas the Bearded, and did not at all appreciate the kind of greatness my of-ficious friend Claro seemed so determined to thrust upon me. It was certainly flattering to hear that I had already established my reputation as a good fighter in so warlike a department as

Paysandù, but then the consequences entailed were disagreeable, to say the least of it; and so, while thanking Eyebrows for his friendly hint, I resolved to quit the estancia at once. I would not run away from the authorities, since I was not an evil-doer, but from the necessity of killing people for the sake of peace and quietness I certainly would depart. And early next morning, to my friend's intense disgust, and without telling my plans to anyone, I mounted my horse and quitted Vagabonds' Rest to pursue my adventures elsewhere.

CHAPTER V

A COLONY OF ENGLISH GENTLEMEN

FAITH in the estancia as a field for my activities had been weak from the first; the Mayordomo's words on his return had extinguished it altogether; and after hearing that ostrich parable I had only remained from motives of pride. I now determined to go back towards Montevideo, not, however, over the route I had come by, but making a wide circuit into the interior of the country, where I would explore a new field and perhaps meet with some occupation at one of the estancias on the way. Riding in a south-westerly direction towards the Rio Malo in the Tacuarembó department, I soon left the plains of Paysandù behind me, and being anxious to get well away from a neighbourhood where I was expected to kill someone, I did not rest till I had ridden about twenty-five miles. At noon I stopped to get some refreshment at a little roadside *pulpería*. It was a wretched-looking place, and behind the iron bars protecting the interior, giving it the appearance of a wild beast's cage, lounged the storekeeper smoking a cigar. Outside the bar were two men with English-looking faces. One was a handsome young fellow with a somewhat worn and dissipated look on his bronzed face; he was leaning against the counter, cigar in mouth, looking slightly tipsy, I thought, and wore a large revolver slung ostentatiously at his waist. His companion was a big, heavy man, with immense whiskers sprinkled with grey, who was evidently very drunk, for he was lying full-length on a bench, his face purple and swollen, snoring loudly. I asked for bread, sardines, and wine, and careful to observe the custom of the country I was in, duly invited the tipsy young man to join in the repast. An omission of this courtesy might, amongst proud and sensitive Orientals, involve one in a sanguinary quarrel, and of quarrelling I had just then had enough.

He declined with thanks, and entered into conversation with me; then the discovery, quickly made, that we were compatriots gave us both great pleasure. He at once offered to take me to his house with him, and gave a glowing account of the free, jovial life he led in company with several other Englishmen—sons of gentlemen, every one of them, he assured me—who had bought a piece of land and settled down to sheep-farming in this lonely district. I gladly accepted the invitation, and when we had finished our glasses he proceded to wake the sleeper.

"Hullo, I say, Cap, wake up, old boy," shouted my new friend. "Quite time to go home, don't you know. That's right—up you come. Now let me introduce you to Mr. Lamb. I'm sure he's an acquisition. What, off again! Damn it, old

Cloud, that's unreasonable, to say the least of it."

At length, after a great deal of shouting and shaking, he succeeded in rousing his drunken companion, who staggered up and stared at me in an imbecile manner.

"Now let me introduce you," said the other. "Mr. Lamb. My friend, Captain Cloudesley Wriothesley. Bravo! Steady, old cock—now shake hands."

The Captain said nothing, but took my hand, swaying forwards as if about to embrace me. We then with considerable difficulty got him on to his saddle and rode off together, keeping him between us to prevent him from falling off. Half an hour's ride brought us to my host Mr. Vincent Winchcombe's house. I had pictured to myself a charming little homestead, buried in cool greenery and flowers, and filled with pleasant memories of dear old England; I was, therefore, grievously disappointed to find that his "home" was only a mean-looking rancho, with a ditch round it, protecting some ploughed or dug-up ground, on which not one green thing appeared. Mr. Winchcombe explained, however, that he had not yet had time to cultivate much. "Only vegetables and such things, don't you know," he said.

"I don't see them," I returned.

"Well, no; we had a lot of caterpillars and blister beetles and things, and they ate everything up, don't you know," said he.

The room into which he conducted me con-

tained no furniture except a large deal table and
some chairs; also a cupboard, a long mantelpiece,
and some shelves against the walls. On every
available place were pipes, pouches, revolvers,
cartridge boxes, and empty bottles. On the table
were tumblers, cups, a sugar-basin, a monstrous
tin teapot, and a demijohn, which I soon ascer-
tained was half-full of Brazilian rum, or caña.
Round the table five men were seated smoking,
drinking tea and rum and talking excitedly, all of
them more or less intoxicated. They gave me a
hearty welcome, making me join them at the table,
pouring out tea and rum for me, and generously
pushing pipes and pouches towards me.

"You see," said Mr. Winchcombe, in explanation of this convivial scene, "there are, altogether,
ten of us settlers here going in for sheep-farming
and that sort of thing. Four of us have already
built houses and bought sheep and horses. The
other six fellows live with us from house to house,
don't you know. Well, we've made a jolly arrangement—old Cloud—Captain Cloud, don't
you know, first suggested it—and it is that every
day one of the four—the Glorious Four we are
called—keeps open house; and it's considered the
right thing for the other nine fellows to drop in
on him some time during the day, just to cheer
him up a bit. Well, we soon made the discovery
—old Cloud, I fancy, made it—that tea and rum
were about the best things to have on these occasions. To-day it was my day and to-morrow it

will be some other fellow's, don't you know. And, by Jove, how lucky I was to meet you at the *pulpería!* It will be ever so much jollier now."

I had certainly not stumbled upon a charming little English paradise in this Oriental wilderness, and as it always makes me uncomfortable to see young men drifting into intemperate habits and making asses of themselves generally, I was not rapturously delighted with "old Cloud's" system. Still I was glad to find myself with Englishmen in this distant country, and in the end I succeeded in making myself tolerably happy. The discovery that I had a voice pleased them greatly, and when, somewhat excited from the effects of strong cavendish, rum, and black tea, I roared out—

> And may his soul in heaven dwell,
> Who first found out the leather botél,

they all got up and drank my health in big tumblers, and declared they would never let me leave the colony.

Before evening the guests departed, all except the Captain. He had sat with us at the table, but was too far gone in his cups to take part in the boisterous fun and conversation. Once in about every five minutes he had implored someone in a husky voice to give him a light for his pipe, then, after two or three ineffectual puffs, he would let it go out again. He had also attempted two or three times to join in the chorus of a song, but soon relapsed again into his imbecile condition.

Next day, however, when he sat down refreshed by a night's sleep to breakfast, I found him a very agreeable fellow. He had no house of his own yet, not having received his money from home, he confidentially informed me, but lived about, breakfasting in one house, dining in a second, and sleeping in a third. "Never mind," he would say, "by-and-by it will be my turn; then I will receive you all every day for six weeks to make it all square."

None of the colonists did any work, but all spent their time lounging about and visiting each other, trying to make their dull existence endurable by perpetual smoking and tea and rum drinking. They had tried, they told me, ostrich-hunting, visiting their native neighbours, partridge-shooting, horse-racing, etc.; but the partridges were too tame for them, they could never catch the ostriches, the natives didn't understand them, and they had finally given up all these so-called amusements. In each house a peon was kept to take care of the flock and to cook, and as the sheep appeared to take care of themselves, and the cooking merely meant roasting a piece of meat on a spit, there was very little for the hired men to do.

"Why don't you do these things for yourselves?" I innocently asked.

"I fancy it wouldn't quite be the right thing, don't you know," said Mr. Winchcombe.

"No," said the Captain gravely, "we haven't quite come down to that yet."

I was greatly surprised to hear them. I had seen Englishmen sensibly roughing it in other places, but the lofty pride of these ten rum-drinking gentlemen was quite a new experience to me.

Having spent a somewhat listless morning, I was invited to accompany them to the house of Mr. Bingley, one of the Glorious Four. Mr. Bingley was really a very nice young fellow, living in a house far more worthy of the name than the slovenly rancho tenanted by his neighbour Winchcombe. He was the favourite of the colonists, having more money than the others, and keeping two servants. Always on his reception-day he provided his guests with hot bread and fresh butter, as well as with the indispensable rum-bottle and teapot. It therefore happened that, when his turn came round to keep open house, not one of the other nine colonists was absent from his table.

Soon after our arrival at Bingley's, the others began to appear, each one on entering taking a seat at the hospitable board, and adding another cloud to the dense volume of tobacco smoke obscuring the room. There was a great deal of hilarious conversation; songs were sung, and a vast amount of tea, rum, bread and butter, and tobacco consumed; but it was a wearisome entertainment, and by the time it was over, I felt heartily sick of this kind of life.

Before separating, after "John Peel" had been sung with great enthusiasm, someone proposed that we should get up a fox-hunt in real English style. Everyone agreed, glad of anything, I suppose, to break the monotony of such an existence, and next day we rode out, followed by about twenty dogs, of various breeds and sizes, brought together from all the houses. After some searching about in the most likely places, we at length started a fox from a bed of dark-leafed Mio-mio bushes. He made straight away for a range of hills about three miles distant, and over a beautifully smooth plain, so that we had a very good prospect of running him down. Two of the hunters had provided themselves with horns, which they blew incessantly, while the others all shouted at the top of their lungs, so that our chase was a very noisy one. The fox appeared to understand his danger and to know that his only chance of escape lay in keeping up his strength till the refuge of the hills was reached. Suddenly, however, he changed his course, this giving us a great advantage, for by making a short cut we were all soon close at his heels, with only the wide level plain before us. But reynard had his reasons for what he did; he had spied a herd of cattle, and in a very few moments had overtaken and mixed with them. The herd, struck with terror at our shouts and horn-blowing, instantly scattered and flew in all directions, so that we were able still to keep our quarry in sight. Far in advance of us the panic in the cattle ran on from herd to herd, swift as light, and we could see them miles away fleeing from us, while their hoarse bellowings and thundering tread came borne by the wind faintly to our ears. Our fat lazy dogs ran no faster than our horses, but still they laboured on, cheered by incessant shouts, and at last ran into the first fox ever properly hunted in the Banda Orientál.

The chase, which had led us far from home, ended close to a large estancia house, and while we stood watching the dogs worrying their victim to death, the *capatas* of the establishment, accompanied by three men, rode out to inquire who we were, and what we were doing. He was a small, dark native, wearing a very picturesque costume, and addressed us with extreme politeness.

"Will you tell me, señores, what strange animal you have captured?" he asked.

"A fox!" shouted Mr. Bingley, triumphantly waving the brush, which he had just cut off, over his head. "In our country—in England—we hunt the fox with dogs, and we have been hunting after the manner of our country."

The *capatas* smiled, and replied that if we were disposed to join him, it would afford him great pleasure to show us a hunt after the manner of the Banda Orientál.

We consented gladly, and mounting our horses, set off at a swinging gallop after the *capatas* and his men. We soon came to a small herd of cattle; the *capatas* dashed after them, and unloosening the coils of his lasso, flung the noose dexterously over the horns of a fat heifer he had singled out, then started homewards at a tremendous pace. The cow, urged forward by the men, who rode close behind and pricked it with their knives, rushed on, bellowing with rage and pain, trying to overtake the *capatas*, who kept just out of reach of its horns; and in this way we quickly reached the house. One of the men now flung his lasso and caught the beast's hind leg; pulled in two opposite directions, it quickly came to a standstill; the other men now dismounting, first hamstrung, then ran a long knife into its throat. Without removing the hide, the carcass was immediately cut up, and the choice pieces flung on to a great fire of wood, which one of the men had been making. In an hour's time we all sat down to a feast of *carne con cuero*, or meat roasted in the hide, juicy, tender, and exquisitely flavoured. I must tell the English reader who is accustomed to eat meat and game which has been kept till it is tender, that before the tender stage is reached, it has been permitted to get tough. Meat, game included, is never so tender or deliciously flavoured as when cooked and eaten immediately after it is killed. Compared with meat at any subsequent stage, it is like a new-laid egg or a salmon with the cream on, compared with an egg or a salmon after a week's keeping.

We enjoyed the repast immensely, though Captain Cloud bitterly lamented that we had neither rum nor tea to wash it down. When we had thanked our entertainer and were about to turn our horses' heads homewards, the polite *capatas* once more stepped out and addressed us.

"Gentlemen," he said, "whenever you feel disposed to hunt, come to me and we will lasso and roast a heifer in the hide. It is the best dish the republic has to offer the stranger, and it will give me great pleasure to entertain you; but I beg you will hunt no more foxes over the ground belonging to this estancia, for you have caused so great a commotion amongst the cattle I am placed here in charge of, that it will take my men two or three days to find them all and bring them back again."

We gave the desired promise, plainly perceiving that fox-hunting in the English fashion is not a sport adapted to the Oriental country. Then we rode back, and spent the remaining hours at the house of Mr. Girling, of the Glorious Four, drinking rum and tea, smoking unlimited pipes of cavendish, and talking over our hunting experience.

CHAPTER VI

THE COLONY UNDER A CLOUD

I spent several days at the colony; and I suppose the life I led there had a demoralising effect on me, for unpleasant as it was, every day I felt less inclined to break loose from it, and sometimes I even thought seriously of settling down there myself. This crazy idea, however, would usually come to me late in the day, after a great deal of indulgence in rum and tea, a mixture that would very soon drive any man mad.

One afternoon, at one of our convivial meetings, it was resolved to pay a visit to the little town of Tolosa, about eighteen miles to the east of the colony. Next day we set out, every man wearing a revolver slung at his waist and provided with a heavy poncho for covering; for it was the custom of the colonists to spend the night at Tolosa when they visited it. We put up at a large public-house in the centre of the miserable little town, where there was accommodation for man and beast, the last always faring rather better than the first. I very soon discovered that the chief object of our visit was to vary the entertainment of drinking rum and smoking at the "Colony," by drinking rum and smoking at Tolosa. The bibulous battle raged till bedtime, when the only sober member of our party was myself; for I had spent the greater part of the afternoon walking about talking to the townspeople, in the hope of picking up some information useful to me in my search for occupation. But the women and old men I met gave me little encouragement. They seemed to be a rather listless set in Tolosa, and when I asked them what they were doing to make a livelihood, they said they were *waiting*. My fellow-countrymen and their visit to the town was the principal topic of conversation. They regarded their English neighbours as strange and dangerous creatures, who took no solid food, but subsisted on a mixture of rum and gunpowder (which was the truth), and who were armed with deadly engines called revolvers, invented specially for them by their father the devil. The day's experience convinced me that the English colony had some excuse for its existence, since its periodical visits gave the good people of Tolosa a little wholesome excitement during the stagnant intervals between the revolutions.

At night we all turned into a large room with a clay floor, in which there was not a single article of furniture. Our saddles, rugs, and ponchos had all been thrown together in a corner, and anyone wishing to sleep had to make himself a bed with his own horse-gear and toggery as best he could. The experience was nothing new to me, so I soon made myself a comfortable nest on the floor, and, pulling off my boots, coiled myself up like an

opossum that knows nothing better and is friendly
with fleas. My friends, however, were evidently
bent on making a night of it, and had taken care
to provide themselves with three or four bottles
of rum. After conversation, with an occasional
song, had been going on for some time, one of
them—a Mr. Chillingworth—rose to his feet and
demanded silence.

"Gentlemen," he said, advancing into the middle of the room, where, by occasionally throwing
out his arms to balance himself, he managed to
maintain a tolerably erect position, "I am going
to make a what-d'ye-call-it."

Furious cheers greeted this announcement,
while one of the hearers, carried away with enthusiasm at the prospect of listening to his friend's
eloquence, discharged his revolver at the roof,
scattering confusion amongst a legion of long-
legged spiders that occupied the dusty cobwebs
above our heads.

I was afraid the whole town would be up in
arms at our carryings on, but they assured me that
they all fired off their revolvers in that room and
that nobody came near them, as they were so well
known in the town.

"Gentlemen," continued Mr. Chillingworth,
when order had been at length restored, "I've been
thinking, that's what I've been doing. Now let's
review the situation. Here we stand, a colony of
English gentlemen: here we are, don't you know,
far from our homes and country and all that sort

of thing. What says the poet? I daresay some of you fellows remember the passage. But what for, I ask! What, gentlemen, is the object of our being here? That's just what I'm going to tell you, don't you know. We are here, gentlemen, to infuse a little of our Anglo-Saxon energy, and all that sort of thing, into this dilapidated old tin-pot of a nation."

Here the orator was encouraged by a burst of applause.

"Now, gentlemen," he continued, "isn't it hard —devilish hard, don't you know, that so little is made of us? I feel it—I feel it, gentlemen; our lives are being frittered away. I don't know whether you fellows feel it. You see we ain't a melancholy lot. We're a glorious combination against the blue devils, that's what we are. Only sometimes I feel, don't you know, that all the rum in the place can't quite kill them. I can't help thinking of jolly days on the other side of the water. Now don't you fellows look at me as if you thought I was going to blubber. I'm not going to make such a confounded ass of myself, don't you know. But what I want you fellows to tell me is this: Are we to go on all our lives making beasts of ourselves, guzzling rum—I—I beg your pardon, gentlemen. I didn't mean to say that, really. Rum is about the only decent thing in this place. Rum keeps us alive. If any man says a word against rum, I'll call him an infernal ass. I meant to say the country, gentlemen—this rotten old country, don't you know. No cricket, no society, no Bass, no anything. Supposing we had gone to Canada with our—our capital and energies, wouldn't they have received us with open arms? And what's the reception we get here? Now, gentlemen, what I propose is this: let's protest. Let's get up a what-d'you-call-it to the thing they call a government. We'll state our case to the thing, gentlemen; and we'll insist on it and be very firm; that's what we'll do, don't you know. Are we to live amongst these miserable monkeys and give them the benefit of our—our—yes, gentlemen, our capital and energies, and get nothing in return? No, no; we must let them know that we are not satisfied, that we will be very angry with them. That's about all I have to say, gentlemen."

Loud applause followed, during which the orator sat down rather suddenly on the floor. Then followed "Rule Britannia," everyone assisting with all the breath in his lungs to make night hideous.

When the song was finished the loud snoring of Captain Wriothesley became audible. He had begun to spread some rugs to lie on, but becoming hopelessly entangled in his bridle-reins, surcingle, and stirrup-straps, had fallen to sleep with his feet on his saddle and his head on the floor.

"Hallo, we can't have this!" shouted one of the fellows. "Let's wake old Cloud by firing at the wall over him and knocking some plaster on to his head. It'll be awful fun, you know."

Everybody was delighted with the proposal, except poor Chillingworth, who after delivering his speech had crept away on all fours into a corner, where he was sitting alone and looking very pale and miserable.

The firing now began, most of the bullets hitting the wall only a few inches above the recumbent Captain's head, scattering dust and bits of plaster over his purple face. I jumped up in alarm and rushed amongst them, telling them in my haste that they were too drunk to hold their revolvers properly, and would kill their friend. My interference raised a loud, angry remonstrance, in the midst of which the Captain, who was lying in a most uncomfortable position, woke, and, struggling into a sitting posture, stared vacantly at us, his reins and straps wound like serpents about his neck and arms.

"What's all the row 'bout?" he demanded huskily. "Getting up rev'lution, I s'pose. A'right; only thing to do in this country. Only don't ask me to be pres'dent. Nor good enough. Goo' night, boys; don't cur my throat by mistake. Gor bless you all."

"No, no, don't go to sleep, Cloud," they shouted. "Lamb's the cause of all this. He says we're drunk—that's the way Lamb repays our hospitality. We were firing to wake you up, old Cap, to have a drink——"

"A drink—yes," assented the Captain hoarsely.

"And Lamb was afraid we would injure you. Tell him, old Cloud, whether you're afraid of your friends. Tell Lamb what you think of his conduct."

"Yes, I'll tell him," returned the Captain in his thick tones. "Lamb shan't interfere, gentlemen. But you know you took him in, didn't you now? And what was my opinion of him? It wasn't right of you fellows, was it, now? He couldn't be one of us, you know, could he now? I'll leave it to you, gentlemen; didn't I say the fellow was a cad? Why the devil doesn't he leave me alone then? I'll tell you what I'll do with Lamb, I'll punch his damned nose, don't you know."

And here the gallant gentleman attempted to rise, but his legs refused to assist him, and, tumbling back against the wall, he was only able to glare at me out of his watery eyes.

I went up to him intending, I suppose, to punch *his* nose, but suddenly changing my mind I merely picked up my saddle and things, then left the room with a hearty curse on Captain Cloudesley Wriothesley, the evil genius, drunk or sober, of the colony of English gentlemen. I was no sooner outside the door than the joy they felt at being rid of me was expressed in loud shouts, clapping of hands, and a general discharge of firearms into the roof.

I spread my rugs out of doors and soliloquised myself to sleep. "And so ends," said I, fixing my somewhat drowsy eyes on the constellation of Orion, "adventure the second, or twenty-second —little does it matter about the exact number of them, since they all alike end in smoke—revolver smoke—or a flourish of knives and the shaking of dust from off my feet. And, perhaps, at this very moment Paquíta, roused from light slumbers by the droning cry of the night-watchman under her window, puts out her arms to feel me, and sighs to find my place still vacant. What must I say to her? That I must change my name to Ernandes or Fernandes, or Blas or Chas, or Sandariaga, Gorostiaga, Madariaga, or any other *aga*, and conspire to overthrow the existing order of things. There is nothing else for me to do, since this Oriental world is indeed an oyster only a sharp sword will serve to open. As for arms and armies and military training, all that is quite unnecessary. One has only got to bring together a few ragged, dissatisfied men, and, taking horse, charge pellmell into poor Mr. Chillingworth's dilapidated old tin-pot. I almost feel like that unhappy gentleman to-night, ready to blubber. But, after all, my position is not quite so hopeless as his; I have no brutalised, purple-nosed Briton sitting like a nightmare on my chest, pressing the life out of me."

The shouts and choruses of the revellers grew

fainter and fewer, and had almost ceased when I sank to sleep, lulled by a solitary tipsy voice droning out in a lugubrious key:—

We won't go—gome till morring.

CHAPTER VII

LOVE OF THE BEAUTIFUL

EARLY next morning I left Tolosa and travelled the whole day in a south-westerly direction. I did not hurry, but frequently dismounted to give my horse a sip of clear water and a taste of green herbage. I also called during the day at three or four estancia houses, but failed to hear anything that could be adavntageous to me. In this way I covered about thirty-five miles of road, going always towards the eastern part of the Florida district in the heart of the country. About an hour before sunset I resolved to go no further that day; and I could not have hoped to find a nicer resting-place than the one now before me—a neat rancho with a wide corridor supported by wooden pillars, standing amidst a bower of fine old weeping willows. It was a calm, sunshiny afternoon, peace and quiet resting on everything, even bird and insect, for they were silent, or uttered only soft, subdued notes; and that modest lodge, with its rough stone walls and thatched roof, seemed to be in harmony with it all. It looked like the home of simple-minded pastoral people that had for their only world the grassy wilderness, watered by many clear streams, bounded ever by that far-off unbroken ring of the horizon, and arched over with blue heaven, starry by night and filled by day with sweet sunshine.

On approaching the house I was agreeably disappointed at having no pack of loud-mouthed, ferocious dogs rushing forth to rend the presumptuous stranger to pieces, a thing one always expects. The only signs of life visible were a white-haired old man seated within the corridor smoking, and a few yards from it a young girl standing under a willow tree. But that girl was a picture for one to gaze long upon and carry about in his memory for a lifetime. Never had I beheld anything so exquisitely beautiful. It was not that kind of beauty so common in these countries, which bursts upon you like the sudden south-west wind called *pampero*, almost knocking the breath out of your body, then passing as suddenly away, leaving you with hair ruffled up and mouth full of dust. Its influence was more like that of the spring wind, which blows softly, scarcely fanning your cheek, yet infusing through all your system a delicious magical sensation like—like nothing else in earth or heaven. She was, I fancy, about fourteen years old, slender and graceful in figure, and with a marvellously clear white skin, on which this bright Oriental sun had not painted one freckle. Her features were, I think, the most perfect I have ever seen in any human being, and her golden brown hair hung in two heavy braids behind, almost to her knees. As I approached, she looked up to me out of sweet, grey-blue eyes; there was a bashful smile on her lips, but she did not move or speak. On the willow branch over her head were two young doves; they were, it appeared, her pets, unable yet to fly, and she had placed them there. The little things had crept up just beyond her reach, and she was trying to get them by pulling the branch down towards her.

Leaving my horse I came to her side.

"I am tall, señorita," I said, "and can perhaps reach them."

She watched me with anxious interest while I gently pulled her birds from their perch and transferred them to her hands. Then she kissed them, well pleased, and with a gentle hesitation in her manner asked me in.

Under the corridor I made the acquaintance of her grandfather, the white-haired old man, and found him a person it was very easy to get on with, for he agreed readily with everything I said. Indeed, even before I could get a remark out he began eagerly assenting to it. There, too, I met the girl's mother, who was not at all like her beautiful daughter, but had black hair and eyes, and a brown skin, as most Spanish-American women have. Evidently the father is the white-skinned, golden-haired one, I thought. When the girl's brother came in, by-and-by, he unsaddled my horse and led him away to pasture; this boy was also dark, darker even than his mother.

The simple spontaneous kindness with which these people treated me had a flavour about it, the like of which I have seldom experienced elsewhere. It was not the common hospitality usually shown to a stranger, but a natural, unstrained kindness, such as they might be expected to show to a beloved brother or son who had gone out from them in the morning and was now returned.

By-and-by the girl's father came in, and I was extremely surprised to find him a small, wrinkled, dark specimen, with jet-black, bead-like eyes and podgy nose, showing plainly enough that he had more than a dash of aboriginal Charrua blood in his veins. This upset my theory about the girl's fair skin and blue eyes; the little dark man was, however, quite as sweet-tempered as the others, for he came in, sat down and joined in the conversation, just as if I had been one of the family whom he had expected to find there. While I talked to these good people on simple pastoral matters, all the wickedness of Orientals—the throat-cutting war of Whites and Reds, and the unspeakable cruelties of the ten years' siege—were quite forgotten; I wished that I had been born amongst them and was one of them, not a weary, wandering Englishman, overburdened with the arms and armour of civilisation, and staggering along, like Atlas, with the weight of a kingdom on which the sun never sets on his shoulders.

By-and-by this good man, whose real name I never discovered, for his wife simply called him

Batata (sweet potato), looking critically at his pretty girl, remarked: "Why have you decked yourself out like this, my daughter—it is not a Saint's day?"

His daughter indeed! I mentally ejaculated; she is more like the daughter of the evening star than of such a man. But his words were unreasonable, to say the least of it; for the sweet child, whose name was Margarita, though wearing shoes, had no stockings on, while her dress—very clean, certainly—was a cotton print so faded that the pattern was quite undistinguishable. The only pretence of finery of any description was a narrow bit of blue ribbon tied about her lily-white neck. And yet had she been wearing richest silks and costliest gems she could not have blushed and smiled with a prettier confusion.

"We are expecting Uncle Anselmo this evening, papita," she replied.

"Leave the child, Batata," said the mother. "You know what a craze she has for Anselmo; when he comes she is always prepared to receive him like a queen."

This was really almost too much for me, and I was powerfully tempted to jump up and embrace the whole family on the spot. How sweet was this primitive simplicity of mind! Here, doubtless, was the one spot on the wide earth where the golden age still lingered, appearing like the last beams of the setting sun touching some prominent spot, when elsewhere all things are in shadow.

Ah, why had fate led me into this sweet Arcadia, since I must presently leave it to go back to the dull world of toil and strife,

> That vain low strife
> Which makes men mad, the tug for wealth and power,
> The passions and the cares that wither life
> And waste its little hour?

Had it not been for the thought of Paquíta waiting for me over there in Montevideo I could have said, "O good friend Sweet Potato, and good friends all, let me remain for ever with you under this roof, sharing your simple pleasures, and, wishing for nothing better, forget that great crowded world where all men are striving to conquer nature and death and to win fortune; until, having wasted their miserable lives in their vain endeavours, they drop down and the earth is shovelled over them!"

Shortly after sunset the expected Anselmo arrived to spend the night with his relations, and scarcely had he got down from his horse before Margarita was at his side to ask the avuncular blessing, at the same time raising his hand to her delicate lips. He gave his blessing, touching her golden hair; then she lifted her face bright with new happiness.

Anselmo was a fine spécimen of the Oriental gaucho, dark and with good features, his hair and moustache intensely black. He wore costly clothes, while his whiphandle, the sheath of his

long knife, and other things about him were of
massive silver. Of silver also were his heavy
spurs, the pommel of his saddle, his stirrups and
the headstall of his bridle. He was a great talker;
never, in fact, in the whole course of my varied
experience have I encountered anyone who could
pour out such an incessant stream of talk about
small matters as this man. We all sat together in
the social kitchen, sipping maté; I taking little
part in the conversation, which was all about
horses, scarcely even listening to what the others
were saying. Reclining against the wall, I occupied myself agreeably, watching the sweet face of
Margarita, which in her happy excitement had become suffused with a delicate rosy colour. I have
always had a great love for the beautiful: sun-
sets, wild flowers, especially verbenas, so prettily
called margaritas in this country; and beyond
everything the rainbow spanning the vast gloomy
heavens with its green and violet arch when the
storm-cloud passes eastward over the wet sun-
flushed earth. All these things have a singular
fascination for my soul. But beauty when it pre-
sents itself in the human form is even more than
these things. There is in it a magnetic power
drawing my heart; a something that is not love,
for how can a married man have a feeling like that
towards anyone except his wife? No, it is not
love, but a sacred ethereal kind of affection, resembling love only as the fragrance of violets resembles the taste of honey and the honey-comb.

At length, some time after supper, Margarita to my sorrow rose to retire, though not without first once more asking her uncle's blessing. After her departure from the kitchen, finding that the inexhaustible talking-machine Anselmo was still holding forth fresh as ever, I lit a cigar and prepared to listen.

CHAPTER VIII

MANUEL, ALSO CALLED THE FOX

WHEN I began to listen, it was a surprise to find that the subject of conversation was no longer the favourite one of horse-flesh, which had held undisputed sway the whole evening. Uncle Anselmo was just now expatiating on the merits of gin, a beverage for which he confessed to a special liking.

"Gin is, without doubt," said he, "the flower of all strong drinks. I have always maintained that it is incomparable. And for this reason I always keep a little of it in the house in a stone bottle; for, when I have taken my maté in the morning, and, after it, one or two or three or four sips of gin, I saddle my horse and go out with a tranquil stomach, feeling at peace with the whole world.

"Well, sirs, it happened that on the morning in question, I noticed that there was very little gin left in the bottle; for, though I could not see how much it contained, owing to its being of stone and not of glass, I judged from the manner in which I had to tip it upwards when pouring it out. In order to remember that I had to bring home some with me that day I tied a knot in my handkerchief; then, mounting my horse, I rode out towards the side on which the sun sets, little expecting that anything unusual was going to happen to me that day. But thus it often is; for no man, however learned he may be and able to read the almanac, can tell what a day will bring forth."

Anselmo was so outrageously prosy, I felt strongly inclined to go to bed to dream of beautiful Margarita; but politeness forbade, and I was also somewhat curious to hear what extraordinary thing had happened to him on that very eventful day.

"It fortunately happened," continued Anselmo, "that I had that morning saddled the best of my cream-noses; for on that horse I could say without fear of contradiction, I am on horseback and not on foot. I called him Chingolo, a name which Manuel, also called the Fox, gave him, because he was a young horse of promise, able to fly with his rider. Manuel had nine horses—cream-noses every one—and how from being Manuel's they came to be mine I will tell you. He, poor man, had just lost all his money at cards—perhaps the money he lost was not much, but how he came to have any was a mystery to many. To me, however, it was no mystery, and when my cattle were slaughtered and had their hides stripped off by night, perhaps I could have gone to Justice—feeling like a blind man for something in the wrong place—and led her in the direction of the offender's house; but when one has it in his power to speak, knowing at the same time that his words will fall like a thunderbolt out of a blue sky upon a neighbour's dwelling, consuming it to ashes and killing all within it, why, sirs, in such a case the good Christian prefers to hold his peace. For what has one man more than another that he should put himself in the place of Providence? We are all of flesh. True, some of us are only dog's flesh, fit for nothing; but to all of us the lash is painful, and where it rains blood will sprout. This, I say; but, remember, I say not that Manuel the Fox robbed me—for I would sully no man's reputation, even a robber's, or have anyone suffer on my account.

"Well, sirs, to go back to what I was saying, Manuel lost everything; then his wife fell ill with fever; and what was there left for him but to turn his horses into money? In this way it came about that I bought the cream-noses and paid him fifty dollars for them. True, the horses were young and sound, nevertheless it was a great price, and I paid it not without first weighing the matter well in my own mind. For in things of this nature if a person makes not his reckoning beforehand, where, let me ask, sirs, will he find himself at the year's end? The devil will take him with all the cattle he inherited from his fathers, or got together by his own proper abilities and industry.

"For you see the thing is this. I have a poor head for figures; all other kinds of knowledge come easy to me, but how to calculate readily has never yet found an entrance into my head. At the same time, whenever I find it impossible to make out my accounts, or settle what to do, I have only to take the matter to bed with me and lie awake thinking it over. For when I do that, I rise next morning feeling free and refreshed, like a man that has just eaten a water-melon; for what I have to do and how it is to be done is all as plain to my sight as this maté-cup I hold in my hand.

"In this difficulty I therefore resolved to take the subject of the horses to bed with me, and to say, 'Here I have you and you shall not escape from me.' But about supper-time Manuel came in to molest me, and sat in the kitchen with a sad face, like a prisoner under sentence of death.

"'If Providence is angry against the entire human race,' said he, 'and is anxious to make an example, I know not for what reason so harmless and obscure a person as I am should have been selected.'

"'What would you have, Manuel?' I replied. 'Wise men tell us that Providence sends us misfortunes for our good.'

"'True, I agree with you,' he said. 'It is not for me to doubt it, for what can be said of that soldier who finds fault with the measures of his commander? But you know, Anselmo, the man I am, and it is bitter that these troubles should fall on one who has never offended except in being always poor.'

"'The vulture,' said I, 'ever preys on the weak and ailing.'

" 'First I lose everything,' he continued, 'then this woman must fall ill of a calenture; and now I am forced to believe that even my credit is gone, since I cannot borrow the money I require. Those who knew me best have suddenly become strangers.'"

" 'When a man is down,' said I, 'the very dogs will scratch up the dust against him.'"

" 'True,' said Manuel; 'and since these calamities fell on me, what has become of the friendships that were so many? For nothing has a worse smell, or stinks more, than poverty, so that all men when they behold it cover up their faces or fly from such a pestilence.'"

" 'You speak the truth, Manuel,' I returned; 'but say not all men, for who knows—there being so many souls in the world—whether you may not be doing injustice to someone.'"

" 'I say it not of you,' he replied. 'On the contrary, if any person has had compassion on me it is you; and this I say, not in your presence only, but publicly proclaim it to all men.'"

"Words only were these. 'And now,' he continued, 'my cards oblige me to part with my horses for money; therefore I come this evening to learn your decision.'"

" 'Manuel,' said I, 'I am a man of few words, as you know, and straightforward, therefore you need not have used compliments, and before saying this to have said so many things; for in this you do not treat me as a friend.'"

" 'You say well,' he replied; 'but I love not to dismount before checking my horse and taking my toes from the stirrups.'

" 'That is only as it should be,' I said; 'nevertheless, when you come to a friend's house, you need not alight at such a distance from the gate.'

" 'For what you say, I thank you,' he answered. 'My faults are more numerous than the spots on the wild cat, but not amongst them is precipitancy.'

" 'That is what I like,' said I; 'for I do not love to go about like a drunk man embracing strangers. But our acquaintance is not of yesterday, for we have looked into and know each other, even to the bowels and to the marrow in the bones. Why, then, should we meet as strangers, since we have never had a difference, or any occasion to speak ill of each other?'

" 'And how should we speak ill,' replied Manuel, 'since it has never entered into either of us, even in a dream, to do the other an injury? Some there are, who, loving me badly, would blow up your head like a bladder with lies if they could, laying I know not what things to my charge, when—heaven knows—they themselves are perhaps the authors of all they so readily blame me for.'

" 'If you speak,' said I, 'of the cattle I have lost, trouble not yourself about such trifles; for if those who speak evil of you, only because they themselves are evil, were listening, they might say, This man begins to defend himself when no one has so much as thought of drawing against him.'

" 'True, there is nothing they will not say of me,' said Manuel; 'therefore I am dumb, for nothing is to be gained by speaking. They have already judged me, and no man wishes to be made a liar.'

" 'As for me,' I said, 'I never doubted you, knowing you to be a man, honest, sober, and diligent. If in anything you have given offence I should have told you of it, so great is my frankness towards all men.'

" 'All that you tell me I firmly believe,' said he, 'for I know that you are not one that wears a mask like others. Therefore, relying on your great openness in all things, I come to you about these horses; for I love not dealing with those who shake you out a whole bushel of chaff for every grain of corn.'

" 'But, Manuel,' said I, 'you know that I am not made of gold, and that the mines of Peru were not left to me for an inheritance. You ask a high price for your horses.'

" 'I do not deny it,' he replied. 'But you are not one to stop your ears against reason and poverty when they speak. My horses are my only wealth and happiness, and I have no glory but them.'

" 'Frankly then,' I answered, 'to-morrow I will tell you yes or no.'

" 'Let it be as you say; but, friend, if you will close with me to-night I will abate something from the price.'

" 'If you wish to abate anything,' said I, 'let it be to-morrow, for I have accounts to make up to-night and a thousand things to think of.'

"After that Manuel got on to his horse and rode away. It was black and rainy, but he had never needed moon or lantern to find what he sought by night, whether his own house, or a fat cow—also his own, perhaps.

"Then I went to bed. The first question I asked myself, when I had blown out the candle, was, Are there fat wethers enough in my flock to pay for the cream-noses? Then I asked, How many fat wethers will it take at the price Don Sebastian—a miserly cheat be it said in passing—offers me a head for them to make up the amount I require?

"That was the question; but you see, friends, I could not answer it. At length, about midnight, I resolved to light the candle and get an ear of maize; for by putting the grains into small heaps, each heap the price of a wether, then counting the whole, I could get to know what I wanted.

"The idea was good. I was feeling under my pillow for the matches to strike a light when I suddenly remembered that all the grain had been given to the poultry. No matter, said I to myself, I have been spared the trouble of getting out of bed for nothing. Why, it was only yesterday, said I, still thinking about the maize, that Pascuala, the cook, said to me when she put my dinner before me, 'Master, when are you going to buy some grain for the fowls? How can you expect the soup to be good when there is not even an egg to put in it? Then there is the black cock with the twisted toe—one of the second brood the spotted hen raised last summer, though the foxes carried off no less than three hens from the very bushes where she was sitting—he has been going round with drooping wings all day, so that I verily believe he is going to have the pip. And if any epidemic comes amongst the fowls, as there was in neighbour Gumesinda's the year before last, you may be sure it will only be for want of corn. And the strangest thing is, and it is quite true, though you may doubt it, for neighbour Gumesinda told me only yesterday when she came to ask me for some parsley, because, as you know very well, her own was all rooted up when the pigs broke into her garden last October; well, sir, she says the epidemic which swept off twenty-seven of her best fowls in one week began by a black cock with a broken toe, just like ours, beginning to droop its wings as if it had the pip.'

" 'May all the demons take this woman!' I cried, throwing down the spoon I had been using, 'with her chatter about eggs and pip and neighbour Gumesinda, and I know not what besides! Do you think I have nothing to do but to gallop about the country looking for maize, when it is not to be had for its weight in gold at this season, and all because a sickly spotted hen is likely to have the pip?'

" 'I have said no such thing,' retorted Pascuala, raising her voice as women do. 'Either you are not paying proper attention to what I am telling you, or you pretend not to understand me. For I never said the spotted hen was likely to have the pip; and if she is the fattest fowl in all this neighbourhood you may thank me, after the Virgin, for it, as neighbour Gumesinda often says, for I never fail to give her chopped meat three times a day; and that is why she is never out of the kitchen, so that even the cats are afraid to come into the house, for she flies like a fury into their faces. But you are always laying hold of my words by the heels; and if I said anything at all about pip, it was not the spotted hen, but the black cock with the twisted toe, I said was likely to have it.'

" 'To the devil with your cock and your hen!' I shouted, rising in haste from my chair, for my patience was all gone and the woman was driving me crazy with her story of a twisted toe and what neighbour Gumesinda said. 'And may all the curses fall on that same woman, who is always full as a gazette of her neighbours' affairs! I know well what the parsley is she comes to gather in my garden. It is not enough that she goes about the country giving importance to the couplets I sang to Montenegro's daughter, when

I danced with her at Cousin Teodoro's dance after the cattle-marking, when, heaven knows, I never cared the blue end of a finger-nail for that girl. But things have now come to a pretty pass when even a chicken with a broken toe cannot be indisposed in my house without neighbour Gumesinda thrusting her beak into the matter!'

"Such anger did I feel at Pascuala when I remembered these things and other things besides, for there is no end to that woman's tongue, that I could have thrown the dish of meat at her head.

"Just then, while occupied with these thoughts, I fell asleep. Next morning I got up, and without heating my head any more I bought the horses and paid Manuel his price. For there is in me this excellent gift, when I am puzzled in mind and in doubt about anything, night makes everything plain to me and I rise refreshed and with my determination formed."

Here ended Anselmo's story, without one word about those marvellous matters he had set out to tell. They had all been clean forgotten. He began to make a cigarette, and, fearing that he was about to launch forth on some fresh subject, I hastily bade good night and retreated to my bed.

CHAPTER IX

THE BOTANIST AND THE SIMPLE NATIVE

EARLY next morning Anselmo took his departure, but I was up in time to say good-bye to the worthy spinner of interminable yarns leading to nothing. I was, in fact, engaged in performing my morning ablutions in a large wooden bucket under the willows when he placed himself in the saddle; then, after carefully arranging the drapery of his picturesque garments, he trotted gently away, the picture of a man with a tranquil stomach and at peace with the whole world, even neighbour Gumesinda included.

I had spent a somewhat restless night, strange to say, for my hospitable hostess had provided me with a deliciously soft bed, a very unusual luxury in the Banda Orientál, and when I plunged into it there were no hungry bedfellows waiting my advent within its mysterious folds. I thought about the pastoral simplicity of the lives and character of the good people slumbering near me; that inconsequent story of Anselmo's about Manuel and Pascuala caused me to laugh several times. Finally my thoughts, which had been roaming around in a wild, uncertain manner, like rocks "blown about the windy skies," settled quietly down to the consideration of that beautiful anomaly, that mystery of mysteries, the white-faced Margarita. For how, in the name of heredity, had she got there? Whence that pearly skin and lithesome form; the proud sweet mouth, the nose that Phidias might have taken for a model; the clear, spiritual, sapphire eyes, and the wealth of silky hair, that if unbound would cover her as with a garment of surpassing beauty? With such a problem vexing my curious brain, what sleep could a philosopher get?

When Batata saw me making preparations for departure, he warmly pressed me to stay to breakfast. I consented at once, for, after all, the more leisurely one does a thing the sooner will it be accomplished—especially in the Banda Oriental. One breakfasts here at noon, so that I had plenty of time to see, and renew my pleasure in seeing, pretty Margarita.

In the course of the morning we had a visitor; a traveller who arrived on a tired horse, and who slightly knew my host Batata, having, I was told, called at the house on former occasions. Marcos Marcó was his name; a tall sallow-faced individual about fifty years old, slightly grey, very dirty, and wearing threadbare gaucho garments. He had a slouching gait and manner, and a patient, waiting hungry animal expression of face. Very, very keen were his eyes, and I detected him several times watching me narrowly.

Leaving this Oriental tramp in conversation

with Batata, who with misplaced kindness had offered to provide him with a fresh horse, I went
out for a walk before breakfast. During my walk,
which was along a tiny stream at the foot of the
hill on which the house stood, I found a very
lovely bell-shaped flower of a delicate rose-colour.
I plucked it carefully and took it back with me,
thinking it just possible that I might give it to
Margarita should she happen to be in the way.
On my return to the house I found the traveller
sitting by himself under the corridor, engaged in
mending some portion of his dilapidated horse-
gear, and sat down to have a chat with him. A
clever bee will always be able to extract honey
enough to reward him from any flower, and so I
did not hesitate tackling this outwardly very un-
promising subject.

"And so you are an Englishman," he remarked,
after we had some conversation; and I, of course,
replied in the affirmative.

"What a strange thing!" he said. "And you
are fond of gathering pretty flowers?" he continued, with a glance at my treasure.

"All flowers are pretty," I replied.

"But surely, señor, some are prettier than
others. Perhaps you have observed a particularly
pretty one growing in these parts—the white margarita?"

Margarita is the Oriental vernacular for ver-
bena; the fragrant white variety is quite common
in the country; so that I was justified in ignoring

the fellow's rather impudent meaning. Assuming as wooden an expression as I could, I replied, "Yes, I have often observed the flower you speak of; it is fragrant, and to my mind surpasses in beauty the scarlet and purple varieties. But you must know, my friend, that I am a botanist, that is, a student of plants, and they are all equally interesting to me."

This astonished him; and pleased with the interest he appeared to take in the subject, I explained, in simple language, the principles on which classification of plants is founded, telling him about that *lingua franca* by means of which all the botanists in the world of all nations are able to converse together about plants. From this somewhat dry subject I launched into the more fascinating one of the physiology of plants. "Now look at this," I continued, and with my penknife I carefully dissected the flower in my hand, for it was evident that I could not now give it to Margarita without exposing myself to remarks. I then proceeded to explain to him the beautiful complex structure by means of which this campanula fertilises itself.

He listened in wonder, exhausting all the Spanish and Oriental equivalents of such expressions as "Dear me!" "How extraordinary!" "Lawks a mussy!" "You don't say so!" I finished my lecture, satisfied that my superior intellect had baffled the rude creature; then, tossing away the fragments of the flower I had sacrificed, I restored the penknife to my pocket.

"These are matters we do not often hear about in the Banda Orientál," he said. "But the English know everything—even the secrets of a flower. They are also able to do most things. Did you ever, sir botanist, take part in acting a comedy?"

After all, I had wasted my flower and scientific knowledge on the animal for nothing! "Yes, I have!" I replied rather angrily; then, suddenly remembering Eyebrow's teaching, I added, "and in tragedy also."

"Is that so?" he exclaimed. "How amused the spectators must have been! Well, we can all have our fill of fighting presently, for I see the *White Flower* coming this way to tell us that breakfast is ready. Batata's roast beef will give something for our knives to do; I only wish we had one of his own floury namesakes to eat with it."

I swallowed my resentment, and when Margarita came to us looked up into her matchless face with a smile, then rose to follow her into the kitchen.

CHAPTER X

MATTERS RELATING TO THE REPUBLIC

AFTER breakfast I bade a reluctant good-bye to my kind entertainers, took a last longing lingering look at lovely Margarita, and mounted my horse. Scarcely was I in the saddle before Marcos Marcó, who was also about to resume his journey on the fresh horse he had borrowed, remarked—

"You are travelling to Montevideo, good friend; I am also going in that direction, and will take you the shortest way."

"The road will show me the way," I rejoined curtly.

"The road," he said, "is like a lawsuit; roundabout, full of puddles and pitfalls, and long to travel. It is only meant to be used by old half-blind men and drivers of bullock carts."

I hesitated about accepting the guidance of this strange fellow, who appeared to have a ready wit under his heavy slouching exterior. The mixed contempt and humility in his speech every time he addressed me gave me an uncomfortable sensation; then his poverty-stricken appearance and his furtive glances filled me with suspicion. I looked at my host, who was standing near, thinking to take my cue from the expression of his face; but it was only a stolid Oriental face that revealed nothing. An ancient rule in whist is to play trumps when in doubt; now my rule of action is, when two courses are open to me and I am in doubt, to take the bolder one. Acting on this principle, I determined to go with Marcos, and accordingly we rode forth together.

My guide soon struck away across country, leading me wide of the public road, through such lonely places that I at length began to suspect him of some sinister design against my person, since I had no property worth taking. Presently he surprised me by saying—"You were right, my young friend, in casting away idle fears when you accepted my company. Why do you let them return to trouble your peace? Men of your blood have never inflicted injuries on me that cry out for vengeance. Can I make myself young again by shedding your life, or would there be any profit in changing these rags I now wear for your garments, which are also dusty and frayed? No, no, sir Englishman, this dress of patience and suffering and exile, my covering by day and my bed by night, must soon be changed for brighter garments than you are wearing."

This speech relieved me sensibly, and I smiled at the poor devil's ambitious dream of wearing a soldier's greasy red jacket; for I supposed that that was what his words meant. Still, his "shortest way" to Montevideo continued to puzzle me considerably. For two or three hours we had been riding nearly parallel to a range of hills, or cuchilla, extending away on our left hand towards the south-east. But we were gradually drawing nearer to it, and apparently going purposely out of our way only to traverse a most lonely and difficult country. The few estancia-houses we passed, perched on the highest points of the great sweep of moor-like country on our right, appeared to be very far away. Where we rode there were no habitations, not even a shepherd's hovel; the dry, stony soil was thinly covered with a forest of dwarf thorn trees and a scanty pasturage burnt to a rust-brown colour by the summer heats; and out of this arid region rose the hills, their brown, woodless sides looking strangely gaunt and desolate in the fierce noonday sun.

Pointing to the open country on our right, where the blue gleam of a river was visible, I said—"My friend, I assure you, I fear nothing, but I cannot understand why you keep near these hills when the valley over there would have been pleasanter for ourselves, and easier for our horses."

"I do nothing without a reason," he said, with a strange smile. "The water you see over there is the Rio de las Canas (River of grey hairs), and those who go down into its valley grow old before their time."

Occasionally talking, but oftener silent, we jogged on till about three o'clock in the afternoon, when suddenly as we were skirting a patch of scraggy woodland, a troop of six armed men emerged from it, and wheeling about came directly towards us. A glance was enough to tell us that they were soldiers or mounted policemen, scouring the country in search of recruits, or, in other words, of deserters, skulking criminals, and vagabonds of all descriptions. I had nothing to fear from them, but an exclamation of rage escaped my companion's lips, and turning to him I perceived that his face was of the whiteness of ashes. I laughed, for revenge is sweet, and I still smarted a little at his contemptuous treatment of me earlier in the day.

"Is your fear so great?" I said.

"You do not know what you say, boy!" he returned fiercely. "When you have passed through as much hell-fire as I have and have rested as sweetly with a corpse for a pillow, you will learn to curb your impertinent tongue when you address a man."

An angry retort was on my lips, but a glance at his face prevented me from uttering it—it was, in its expression, the face of a wild animal worried by dogs.

In another moment the men had cantered up to us, and one, their commander, addressing me, asked to see my passport.

"I carry no passport," I replied. "My nationality is a sufficient protection, for I am an Englishman as you can see."

"We have only your word for that," said the

man. "There is an English consul in the capital, who provides English subjects with passports for their protection, in this country. If you have not got one you must suffer for it, and no one but yourself is to blame. I see in you only a young man complete in all his members, and of such the republic is in need. Your speech is also like that of one who came into the world under this sky. You must go with us."

"I shall do nothing of the sort," I returned.

"Do not say such a thing, master," said Marcos, astonishing me very much with the change in his tone and manner. "You know I warned you a month ago that it was imprudent to leave Montevideo without our passports. This officer is only obeying the orders he has received; still he might see that we are only what we represent ourselves to be."

"Oh!" exclaimed the officer, turning to Marcos, "you are also an Englishman unprovided with a passport, I suppose? You might at least have supplied yourself with a couple of blue crockery eyes and a yellow beard for your greater safety."

"I am only a poor son of the soil," said Marcos meekly. "This young Englishman is looking for an estancia to buy, and I came as his attendant from the capital. We were very careless not to get our passports before starting."

"Then, of course, this young man has plenty of money in his pocket?" said the officer.

I did not relish the lies Marcos had taken upon

himself to tell about me, but did not quite know what the consequences of contradicting them might be. I therefore replied that I was not so foolish as to travel in a country like the Banda Oriental with money on my person. "To pay for bread and cheese till I reach my destination is about as much as I have," I added.

"The government of this country is a generous one," said the officer sarcastically, "and will pay for all the bread and cheese you will require. It will also provide you with beef. You must now come with me to the Juzgado de las Cuevas, both of you."

Seeing no help for it, we accompanied our captors at a swinging gallop over a rough, undulating country, and in about an hour and a half reached Las Cuevas, a dirty, miserable-looking village, composed of a few ranchos built round a large plaza overgrown with weeds. On one side stood the church, on the other a square stone building with a flagstaff before it. This was the official building of the Juez de Paz, or rural magistrate; just now, however, it was closed, and with no sign of life about it except an old dead-and-alive-looking man sitting against the closed door, with his bare, mahogany-coloured legs stretched out in the hot sunshine.

"This is a very fine thing!" exclaimed the officer with a curse. "I feel very much inclined to let the men go."

"You will lose nothing by doing so, except, perhaps, a headache," said Marcos.

"Hold your tongue till your advice is asked!" retorted the officer, thoroughly out of temper.

"Lock them up in the calaboso till the Juez comes to-morrow, Lieutenant," suggested the old man by the door, speaking through a bushy white beard and a cloud of tobacco smoke.

"Do you not know that the door is broken, old fool?" said the officer. "Lock them up! Here I am neglecting my own affairs to serve the state, and this is how I am treated. We must now take them to the Juez at his own house and let him look after them. Come on, boys."

We were then conducted out of Las Cuevas to a distance of about two miles, where the Señor Juez resided in the bosom of his family. His private residence was a very dirty, neglected-looking estancia-house, with a great many dogs, fowls, and children about. We dismounted and were immediately taken into a large room, where the magistrate sat at a table on which lay a great number of papers—goodness knows what they were about. The Juez was a little hatchet-faced man, with bristly grey whiskers, standing out like a cat's moustache, and angry eyes—or, rather, with one angry eye, for over the other a cotton handkerchief was tied. No sooner had we all entered than a hen, leading a brood of a dozen half-grown chickens, rushed into the room after us, the chickens instantly distributing themselves about the floor in quest of crumbs, while the mother, more ambitious, flew on the table, scattering the papers right and left with the wind she created.

"A thousand demons take the fowls!" cried the Juez, starting up in a fury. "Man, go and bring your mistress here this instant. I command her to come."

This order was obeyed by the person who had ushered us in, a greasy-looking, swarthy-faced individual, in threadbare military clothes; and in two or three minutes he returned, followed by a very fat, slatternly woman, looking very good-tempered, however, who immediately subsided, quite exhausted, into a chair.

"What is it, Fernando?" she panted.

"What is it? How can you have the courage to ask such a question, Toribia? Look at the confusion your pestilent fowls are creating amongst my papers—papers that concern the safety of the republic! Woman, what measures are you going to take to stop this before I have your fowls all killed on the spot?"

"What can I do, Fernando?—they are hungry, I suppose. I thought you wanted to ask my advice about these prisoners—poor fellows! and here you are with your hens."

Her placid manner acted like oil on the fire of his wrath. He stormed about the room, kicking over chairs, and hurling rulers and paper-weights at the birds, apparently with the most deadly intentions, but with shockingly bad aim—shouting, shaking his fist at his wife, and even threatening to commit her for contempt of court when she laughed. At last, after a great deal of trouble, the fowls were all got out, and the servant placed to guard the door, with strict orders to decapitate the first chicken that should attempt to enter and disturb the proceedings.

Order being restored, the Juez lit a cigarette and began to smooth his ruffled feathers. "Proceed," he said to the officer, from his seat at the table.

"Sir," said the officer, "in pursuance of my duty I have taken in charge these two strangers, who are unprovided with passports or documents of any description to corroborate their statements. According to their story, the young man is an English millionaire going about the country buying up estates, while the other man is his servant. There are twenty-five reasons for disbelieving their story, but I have not sufficient time to impart them to you now. Having found the doors of the Juzgado closed, I have brought these men here with great inconvenience to myself; and I am now only waiting to have this business despatched without further delay, so that I may have a little time left to devote to my private affairs."

"Address not me in this imperative manner, sir officer!" exclaimed the Juez, his anger blazing out afresh. "Do you imagine, sir, that I have no private interests; that the state feeds and clothes my wife and children? No, sir, I am the servant of the republic, not the slave; and I beg to remind you that official business must be transacted during the proper hours and at the proper place."

"Sir Juez," said the officer, "it is my opinion that a civil magistrate ought never to have any part in matters which more properly come under the military authorities. However, since these things are differently arranged, and I am compelled to come with my reports to you in the first place, I am only here to know, without entering into any discussion concerning your position in the republic, what is to be done with these two prisoners I have brought before you."

"Done with them! Send them to the devil! cut their throats; let them go; do what you like, since you are responsible, not I. And be sure, sir officer, I shall not fail to report your insubordinate language to your superiors."

"Your threats do not alarm me," said the officer; "for one cannot be guilty of insubordination towards a person one is not bound to obey. And now, sirs," he added, turning to us, "I have been advised to release you; you are free to continue your journey."

Marcos rose with alacrity.

"Man, sit down!" yelled the irate magistrate, and poor Marcos, thoroughly crestfallen, sat down again. "Sir Lieutenant," continued the fierce old man, "you are dismissed from further attendance here. The republic you profess to serve would perhaps be just as well off without your valuable aid. Go, sir, to attend to your private affairs, and leave your men here to execute my commands."

The officer rose, and having made a profound and sarcastic bow, turned on his heel and left the room.

"Take these two prisoners to the stocks," continued the little despot. "I will examine them tomorrow."

Marcos was first marched out of the room by two of the soldiers; for it happened that an out-house on the place was provided with the usual wooden arrangement to make captives secure for the night. But when the other men took me by the arms, I recovered from the astonishment the magistrate's order had produced in me, and shook them roughly aside. "Señor Juez," I said, addressing him, "let me beg you to consider what you are doing. Surely my accent is enough to satisfy any reasonable person that I am not a native of this country. I am willing to remain in your custody, or to go wherever you like to send me; but your men shall tear me to pieces before making me suffer the indignity of the stocks. If you maltreat me in any way, I warn you that the government you serve will only censure, and perhaps ruin you, for your imprudent zeal."

Before he could reply, his fat spouse, who had apparently taken a great fancy to me, interposed on my behalf, and persuaded the little savage to spare me.

"Very well," he said, "consider yourself a guest in my house for the present; if you are telling the truth about yourself, a day's detention cannot hurt you."

I was then conducted by my kind intercessor into the kitchen, where we all sat down to partake of maté and talk ourselves into good humour.

I began to feel rather sorry for poor Marcos, for even a worthless vagabond, such as he appeared to be, becomes an object of compassion when misfortune overtakes him, and I asked permission to see him. This was readily granted. I found him confined in a large empty room built apart from the house; he had been provided with a maté-cup and a kettle of hot water, and was sipping his bitter beverage with an air of stoical indifference. His legs, confined in the stocks, were thrust straight out before him; but I suppose he was accustomed to uncomfortable positions, for he did not seem to mind it much. After sympathising with him in a general way, I asked him whether he could really sleep in that position.

"No," he replied with indifference. "But do you know I do not mind about being taken. They will send me to the comandancia, I suppose, and after a few days liberate me. I am a good workman on horseback, and there will not be wanting some estanciero in need of hands to get me out. Will you do me one small service, friend, before you go to your bed?"

"Yes, certainly, if I can," I answered.

He laughed slightly and looked at me with a strange keen glitter in his eyes; then, taking my hand, he gave it a powerful grip. "No, no, my friend, I am not going to trouble you to do anything for me," he said. "I have the devil's temper, and to-day, in a moment of rage, I insulted you. It therefore surprised me when you came here and spoke kindly to me. I desired to know whether that feeling was only on the surface; since the men one meets with are often like horned cattle. When one falls, his companions of the pasture-ground remember only his past offences, and make haste to gore him."

His manner surprised me; he did not now seem like the Marcos Marcó I had travelled with that day. Touched with his words, I sat down on the stocks facing him, and begged him to tell me what I could do for him.

"Well, friend," said he, "you see the stocks are fastened with a padlock. If you will get the key, and take me out, I will sleep well; then in the morning, before the old one-eyed lunatic is up, you can come and turn the key in the lock again. Nobody will be the wiser."

"And you are not thinking of escaping?" I said.

"I have not even the faintest wish to escape," he replied.

"You could not escape if you did," I said, "for the room would be locked, of course. But if I were disposed to do what you ask, how could I get the key?"

"That is an easy matter," said Marcos. "Ask the good señora to let you have it. Did I not notice her eyes dwelling lovingly on your face—for, doubtless, you remind her of some absent relative, a favourite nephew, perhaps. She would not deny you anything in reason; and a kindness, friend, even to the poorest man, is never thrown away."

"I will think about it," I said, and shortly after that I left him.

It was a sultry evening, and the close, smoky atmosphere of the kitchen becoming unendurable, I went out and sat down on a log of wood out of doors. Here the old Juez, in his character of amiable host, came and discoursed for half an hour on lofty matters relating to the republic. Presently his wife came out, and, declaring that the evening air would have an injurious effect on his inflamed eye, persuaded him to go indoors. Then she subsided into a place at my side, and began to talk about Fernando's dreadful temper and the many cares of her life.

"What a very serious young man you are!" she remarked, changing her tone somewhat abruptly. "Do you keep all your gay and pleasant speeches for the young and pretty señoritas?"

"Ah, señora, you are yourself young and beautiful in my eyes," I replied: "but I have no heart to be gay when my poor fellow-traveller is fastened in the stocks, where your cruel husband would also have confined me but for your timely intervention. You are so kind-hearted, cannot you have his poor tired legs taken out in order that he may also rest properly to-night?"

"Ah, little friend," she returned, "I could not attempt such a thing. Fernando is a monster of cruelty, and would immediately put out my eyes without remorse. Poor me, what I have to endure!"—and here she placed her fat hand on mine.

I drew my hand away somewhat coldly; a born diplomatist could not have managed the thing better.

"Madam," I said, "you are amusing yourself at my expense. When you have done me a great favour, will you now deny me this small thing? If your husband is so terrible a despot, surely you can do this without letting him know! Let me get my poor Marcos out of the stocks, and I give you my word of honour that the Juez will never hear of it, for I will be up early to turn the key in the lock before he is out of his bed."

"And what will my reward be?" she asked, again putting her hand on mine.

"The deep gratitude and devotion of my heart," I returned, this time without withdrawing my hand.

"Can I refuse anything to my sweet boy?" said she. "After supper I shall slip the key into your hand; I am going now to get it from his room. Before Fernando retires, ask to see your Marcos, to take him a rug, or some tobacco or something;

and do not let the servant see what you do, for he will be at the door waiting to lock it when you come out."

After supper the promised key was secretly conveyed to me, and I had not the least difficulty in liberating my friend in misfortune. Luckily the man who took me to Marcos left us alone for some time, and I related my conversation with the fat woman.

He jumped up, and, seizing my hand, wrung it till I almost screamed with pain.

"My good friend," he said, "you have a noble, generous soul, and have done me the greatest service it is possible for one man to render to another. You have, in fact, now placed me in a position to—enjoy my night's rest. Good night, and may Heaven's angels put it in my power to reward you at some future time!"

The fellow was overdoing it a little, I thought; then, when I had seen him safely locked up for the night, I walked back to the kitchen slowly and very thoughtfully.

CHAPTER XI

THE WOMAN AND THE SERPENT

I WALKED thoughtfully back because, after rendering that unimportant service to Marcos, I began to experience sundry qualms of conscience and inward questionings concerning the strict morality of the whole proceeding. Allowing that I had done something very kind, charitable, and altogether praiseworthy in getting the poor fellow's unfortunate feet out of the stocks, did all that justify the cajolery I had practised to attain my object? Or, to put it briefly in the old familiar way, Does the end sanctify the means? Assuredly it does in some cases, very easy to be imagined. Let us suppose that I have a beloved friend, an ailing person of a nervous, delicate organisation, who has taken it into his poor cracked brains that he is going to expire at the stroke of twelve on a given night. Without consulting the authorities on ethical questions I should, in such a case, flit about his room secretly manipulating his timepieces, till I had advanced them a whole hour, and then, just before the stroke of midnight, triumphantly produce my watch and inform him that death had failed to keep the appointment. Such an acted lie as that would weigh nothing on the conscience of any man. The fact of the matter is, the circumstances must always be considered and every case judged on its own particular merits. Now this affair of getting the key was not one for me to judge, since I had been a chief actor in it, but rather for some acute and learned casuist. I therefore made a mental note of it with the intention of putting it impartially before the first person of that description I should meet. Having thus disposed of a troublesome matter, I felt greatly relieved in mind and turned into the kitchen once more. I had scarcely sat down, however, before I found that one disagreeable consequence of my performance—the fat señora's claim on my undying devotion and gratitude—had yet to be faced. She greeted my entrance with an effusive smile; and the sweetest smiles of some people one meets are less endurable than their black looks. In self-defence I assumed as drowsy and vacant an expression as I could summon on the instant to a countenance by nature almost too ingenuous. I pretended not to hear or to misunderstand everything that was said to me; finally I grew so sleepy that I was several times on the point of falling off my chair, then, after each extravagant nod, I would start up and stare vacantly around me. My grim little host could scarcely conceal a quiet smile, for never had he seen a person so outrageously sleepy before. At length he mercifully remarked that I seemed fatigued and advised me to retire. Very gladly I made my exit, followed in my retreat from the kitchen by a pair of sad, reproachful eyes.

I slept soundly enough in the comfortable bed, which my obese Gulnare had provided for me, until the numerous cocks of the establishment woke me shortly after daybreak with their crowing. Remembering that I had to secure Marcos in the stocks before the irascible little magistrate should appear on the scene, I rose and hastily dressed myself. I found the greasy man of the brass buttons already in the kitchen sipping his matutinal maté-amargo, and asked him to lend me the key of the prisoner's room; for this was what I had been instructed to do by the señora. He got up and went with me to open the door himself, not caring, I suppose, to trust me with the key. When he threw the door open we stood silently gazing for some time into the empty apartment. The prisoner had vanished, and a large hole cut in the thatch of the roof showed how and where he had made his exit. I felt very much exasperated at the shabby trick the fellow had played on us, on me especially, for I was in a measure responsible for him. Fortunately the man who opened the door never suspected me of being an accomplice, but merely remarked that the stocks had evidently been left unlocked by the soldiers the evening before, so that it was not strange the prisoner had made his escape.

When the other members of the household got up the matter was discussed with little excitement or even interest, and I soon concluded that the secret of the escape would remain between the lady of the house and myself. She watched for an opportunity to speak to me alone, then, shaking her fat forefinger at me in playful anger, whispered, "Ah, deceiver, you planned it all with him last evening and only made me your instrument!"

"Señora," I protested with dignity, "I assure you, on the word of honour of an Englishman, I never suspected the man had any intention of escaping. I am very angry it has happened."

"What do you suppose I care about his escaping?" she replied laughingly. "For your sake, sweet friend, I would gladly open the doors of every prison in the Banda if I had the power."

"Ah, how you flatter! But I must now go to your husband to learn from him what he intends doing with the prisoner who has not attempted to escape."

With this excuse I got away from her.

The wretched little Juez, when I spoke to him, put me off with a number of vague, meaningless phrases about his responsible position, the peculiar nature of his functions and the unsettled state of the republic—as if it had ever known or was ever likely to know any other state! He then mounted his horse and rode away to Las Cuevas, leaving me with that dreadful woman; and I verily believe that in doing so he was only carrying out her private instructions. The only comfort he gave me was the promise he made before going that a communication respecting me would be forwarded to the Comandante of the district in the course of the day, which would probably result in my being passed on to that functionary. In the meanwhile he begged me to make free use of his house and everything in it. Of course, the misguided little wretch had no intention of throwing his fat wife at my head; still I had no doubt that it was she who inspired these complimentary phrases, telling him, perhaps, that he would lose nothing by a courteous treatment of the "English millionaire."

When he rode away he left me sitting on the gate, feeling very much disgusted, and almost wishing that, like Marcos Marcó, I had run away during the night. Never had I taken so sudden and violent a dislike to anything as I then and there did to that estancia, where I was an honoured, albeit a compulsory guest. The hot, brilliant morning sun shone down on the discoloured thatch and mud-plastered walls of the sordid-looking building, while all about wherever I cast my eyes they rested on weeds, old bones, broken bottles, and other rubbish, eloquent witnesses of the dirty, idle, thriftless character of the inmates. Meanwhile my sweet, angelic child-wife, with her violet eyes dim with tears, was waiting for me far away in Montevideo, wondering at my long absence, and even now perhaps shading her face with her lily hand and looking out on the white dusty road watching for my arrival! And here I was compelled to sit, idly swinging my legs on the gate, because that abominable fat woman had taken a fancy to keep me by her! Feeling mad with indignation, I suddenly jumped down from the gate with an exclamation not intended for ears polite, causing my hostess to jump also and utter a scream; for there she was (confound her!) standing just behind me.

"The Saints defend me!" she exclaimed, recovering herself and laughing; "what made you startle me so?"

I apologised for the strong expression I had used; then added, "Señora, I am a young man full of energy and accustomed to take a great deal of exercise every day, and I am getting very impatient sitting here basking in the sunshine, like a turtle on a bank of mud."

"Why then do you not take a walk?" she said, with kind concern.

I said I would gladly do so, and thanked her for the permission; then she immediately offered to accompany me. I protested very ungallantly that I was a fast walker, and reminded her that the sun was excessively hot, and I should also have liked to add that she was excessively fat. She replied that it did not matter; so polite a person as myself would know how to accommodate his pace to that of his companion. Unable to shake her off, I started for my walk in a somewhat unamiable mood, the stout lady resolutely trudging on at my side, perspiring abundantly. Our path led us down to a little cañada, or valley, where the ground was moist and abounding with numerous pretty flowers and feathery grasses, very refreshing to look at after leaving the parched yellow ground about the estancia house.

"You seem to be very fond of flowers," observed my companion. "Let me help you gather them. To whom will you give your nosegay when it is made?"

"Señora," I replied, vexed at her trivial chatter, "I will give it to the——" I had almost said to the devil, when a piercing scream she uttered suddenly arrested the rude speech on my lips.

Her fright had been caused by a pretty little snake, about eighteen inches long, which she had seen gliding away at her feet. And no wonder it glided away from her with all the speed it was capable of, for how gigantic and deformed a monster that fat woman must have seemed to it! The terror of a timid little child at the sight of a hippopotamus, robed in flowing bed-curtains and walking erect on its hind legs, would perhaps be comparable to the panic possessing the shallow brain of the poor speckled thing when that huge woman came striding over it.

First I laughed, and then, seeing that she was about to throw herself for protection like a mountain of flesh upon me, I turned and ran after the snake—for I had observed that it belonged to a harmless species, one of the innocuous Coronella genus—and I was anxious to annoy the woman. I captured it in a moment; then, with the poor frightened creature struggling in my hand and

winding itself about my wrist, I walked back to
her.

"Did you ever see such lovely colours?" I cried.
"Look at the delicate primrose yellow on its neck,
deepening into vivid crimson on the belly. Talk
of flowers and butterflies! And its eyes are bright
as two small diamonds—look closely at them,
señora, for they are well worth your admiration."

But she only turned and fled away screaming
at my approach, and at last finding that I would
not obey her and drop the terrible reptile, she
left me in a towering rage and went back to the
house by herself.

After that I continued my walk in peace
amongst the flowers; but my little speckled captive had served me so well that I would not release it. It occurred to me that if I kept it on my
person it might serve as a sort of talisman to protect me from the disagreeable attentions of the
señora. Finding that it was a very sly little snakey,
and, like Marcos Marcó in captivity, full of subtle deceit, I put it into my hat, which, when firmly
pressed on to my head, left no opening for the
little arrowy head to insinuate itself through.
After spending two or three hours botanising in
the cañada I returned to the house. I was in the
kitchen refreshing myself with a bitter maté, when
my hostess came in beaming with smiles, for she
had, I suppose, forgiven me by this time. I politely rose and removed my hat. Unfortunately
I had forgotten the snake, when out it dropped

on the floor; then followed screams, confusion, and scuttling out of the kitchen by madame, children, and servants. After that I was compelled to carry the snake out and give it back its liberty, which no doubt tasted very sweet to it after its close confinement. On my return to the house, one of the servants informed me that the señora was too much offended to sit in the same room with me again, so that I was obliged to have my breakfast alone; and for the remainder of the time during which I was a prisoner, I was avoided by everyone (except Brass Buttons, who appeared indifferent to everything on earth), as if I had been a leper or a dangerous lunatic. They thought, perhaps, that I still had other reptiles concealed about my person.

Of course, one always expects to find a cruel, unreasoning prejudice against snakes amongst ignorant people, but I never knew before to what ridiculous lengths it will carry them. The prejudice makes me angry, but on this occasion it had a use, for it enabled me to pass the day unmolested.

In the evening the Juez returned, and I soon heard him loud in a stormy altercation with his wife. Perhaps she wanted him to have me decapitated. How it ended I cannot say; but when I saw him his manner towards me was freezing, and he retired without giving me an opportunity of speaking to him.

Next morning I got up resolved not to be put off any longer. Something would have to be done, or I would know the reason why. On stepping out I was very much surprised to see my horse standing saddled at the gate. I went into the kitchen and asked Brass Buttons, the only person up, what it meant.

"Who knows?" he returned, giving me a maté. "Perhaps the Juez desires you to leave the house before he is up."

"What did he say?" I demanded.

"Say? Nothing—what should he say?"

"But you saddled the horse, I suppose?"

"Of course. Who else would do it?"

"Were you told to do so by the Juez?"

"Told? Why should he tell me?"

"How then am I to know that he wishes me to leave his beautiful house?" I asked, getting angry.

"The question!" he returned, shrugging his shoulders. "How do you know when it is going to rain?"

Finding there was nothing more to be got out of the fellow, I finished taking maté, lit a cigar, and left the house. It was a lovely morning, without a cloud, and the heavy dew sparkled on the grass like drops of rain. What a pleasant thing it was to be able to ride forth again free to go where I liked!

And so ends my snake-story, which is perhaps not very interesting; but it is true, and therefore has one advantage over all other snake-stories told by travellers.

CHAPTER XII

CHILDREN IN THE FOREST

BEFORE leaving the magistrate's estancia I had made up my mind to return by the shortest route, and as quickly as possible, to Montevideo; and that morning, mounted on a well-rested horse, I covered a great deal of ground. By twelve o'clock, when I stopped to rest my horse and get some refreshment at a wayside *pulpería*, I had got over about eight leagues. This was travelling at an imprudent pace, of course; but in the Banda Oriéntal it is so easy to pick up a fresh horse that one becomes somewhat reckless. My journey that morning had taken me over the eastern portion of the Durazno district, and I was everywhere charmed with the beauty of the country, though it was still very dry, the grass on the higher lands being burnt to various shades of yellow and brown. Now, however, the summer heats were over, for the time was near the end of February; the temperature, without being oppressive, was deliciously warm, so that travelling on horseback was delightful. I might fill dozens of pages with descriptions of pretty bits of country I passed that day, but must plead guilty of an unconquerable aversion to this kind of writing. After this candid confession, I hope the reader will not quarrel with me for the omission; besides, anyone who cares for these things, and knows how evanescent are the impressions left by word pictures on the mind, can sail the seas and gallop round the world to see them all for himself. It is not, however, every wanderer from England—I blush while saying it—who can make himself familiar with the home habits, the ways of thought and speech, of a distant people. Bid me discourse of lowly valley, lofty height, of barren waste, shady wood, or cooling stream where I have drunk and been refreshed; but all these places, pleasant or dreary, must be in the kingdom called the heart.

After getting some information about the country I had to traverse from the *pulpero*, who told me that I would probably reach the river Yí before evening, I resumed my journey. About four o'clock in the afternoon I came to an extensive wood of thorn trees, of which the *pulpero* had spoken, and, in accordance with his instructions, I skirted it on the eastern side. The trees were not large, but there was an engaging wildness about this forest, full of the musical chatter of birds, which tempted me to alight from my horse and rest for a hour in the shade. Taking the bit from his mouth to let him feed, I threw myself down on the dry grass under a clump of shady thorns, and for half an hour watched the sparkling sunlight falling through the foliage overhead, and listened to the feathered people that came about me, loudly chirping, apparently curious to know what object had brought me to their haunts. Then I began to think of all the people I had recently mixed with; the angry magistrate and his fat wife—horrid woman!—and Marcos Marcó, that shabby rascal, rose up before me to pass quickly away, and once more I was face to face with that lovely mystery Margarita. In imagination I put forth my hands to take hers and drew her towards me so as to look more closely into her eyes, vainly questioning them as to their pure sapphire hue. Then I imagined, or dreamt, that with trembling fingers I unbraided her hair to let it fall like a splendid golden mantle over her mean dress, and asked her how she came to possess that garment of glory. The sweet, grave, child lips smiled, but returned no answer. Then a shadowy face seemed to shape itself dimly against the green curtain of foliage, and, looking over the fair girl's shoulder, gaze sadly into my eyes. It was the face of Paquíta. Ah, sweet wife, never let the green-eyed monster trouble the peace of your heart! Know that the practical Saxon mind of your husband is puzzling itself over a purely scientific problem, that this surpassingly fair child interests me only because her fairness seems to upset all physiological laws. I was, in fact, just sinking to sleep at this moment when the shrill note of a trumpet blown close by and followed by loud shouts from several voices made me spring instantly to my feet. A storm of answering shouts came from another quarter of the

wood, then followed profound silence. Presently
the trumpet sounded again, making me feel very
much alarmed. My first impulse was to spring
on to my horse and ride away for dear life; but,
on second thoughts, I concluded that it would be
safer to remain concealed amongst the trees, as
by leaving them I should only reveal myself to
the robbers or rebels, or whatever they were. I
bridled my horse so as to be ready to run, then
drew him into a close thicket of dark-foliaged
bushes and fastened him there. The silence that
had fallen on the wood continued, and at last,
unable to bear the suspense longer, I began to
make my way cautiously, revolver in hand, towards the point the sounds had proceeded from.
Stealing softly through the bushes and trees where
they grew near together, I came at length in sight
of an open piece of ground, about two or three
hundred yards wide, and overgrown with grass.
Near its border on one side I was amazed to see
a group of about a dozen boys, their ages ranging
from about ten to fifteen, all standing perfectly
motionless. One of them held a trumpet in his
hand, and they all wore red handkerchiefs or rags
tied round their heads. Suddenly, while I
crouched amongst the leafage watching them, a
shrill note sounded from the opposite side of the
open space, and another troop of boys wearing
white on their heads burst from the trees and
advanced with loud shouts of *vivas* and *mueras*
towards the middle of the ground. Again the

red heads sounded their trumpet and went out
boldly to meet the new-comers. As the two bands
approached each other, each led by a big boy, who
turned at intervals, and with many wild gestures
addressed his followers, apparently to encourage
them, I was amazed to see them all suddenly draw
out long knives, such as the native horsemen usually wear, and rush furiously together. In a moment they were mingled together in a desperate
fight, uttering the most horrible yells, their long
weapons glittering in the sunshine as they bran-
dished them about. With such fury did they fight
that in a few moments all the combatants lay
stretched out on the grass, excepting three boys
wearing the red badges. One of these bloodthirsty young miscreants then snatched up the
trumpet and blew a victorious blast, while the
other two shrieked an accompaniment of *vivas* and
mueras. While they were thus occupied one of
the white-headed boys struggled to his feet, and,
snatching up a knife, charged the three reds with
desperate courage. Had I not been perfectly para-
lysed with amazement at what I had witnessed, I
should then have rushed out to aid this boy in
his forlorn attempt; but in an instant his three
foes were on him and dragged him down to the
ground. Two of them then held him fast by the
legs and arms, the other raised his long knife and
was just about to plunge it in the struggling captive's breast, when, uttering a loud yell, I sprang
up and rushed at them. Instantly they started

up and fled screaming towards the trees in the greatest terror; and then, most wonderful thing of all, the dead boys all came to life, and, springing to their feet, fled from me after the others. This brought me to a stand, when, seeing that one of the boys limped painfully after his companions, hopping on one leg, I made a sudden dash and captured him before he could reach the shelter of the trees.

"O señor, do not kill me!" he pleaded, bursting into tears.

"I have no wish to kill you, you unspeakable young miscreant, but I think I ought to thrash you," I answered, for, though greatly relieved at the turn things had taken, I was excessively annoyed at having experienced all those sensations of blood-curdling horror for nothing.

"We were only playing at Whites and Reds," he pleaded.

I then made him sit down and tell me all about this singular game.

None of the boys lived very near, he said; some of them came a distance of several leagues, and they had selected this locality for their sports on account of its seclusion, for they did not like to be found out. Their game was a mimic war of Whites and Reds, manœuvres, surprises, skirmishes, throat-cutting, and all.

I pitied the young patriot at the last, for he had sprained his ankle badly and could scarcely walk, and so assisted him to the spot where his horse was hidden; then having helped him to mount and given him a cigarette, for which he had the impudence to ask me, I laughingly bade him good-bye. I went back to look for my own horse after that, beginning to feel very much amused at the whole thing; but alas! my steed was gone. The young scoundrels had stolen him, to revenge themselves on me, I suppose, for disturbing them; and to relieve me from all doubt in the matter they left two bits of rag, one white and the other red, attached to the branch I had fastened the bridle to. For some time I wandered about the wood, and even shouted aloud in the wild hope that the young fiends were not going to carry things so far as to leave me without a horse in that solitary place. Nothing could I see or hear of them, however, and as it was getting late and I was becoming desperately hungry and thirsty, I resolved to go in search of some habitation.

On emerging from the forest I found the adjacent plain covered with cattle quietly grazing. Any attempt to pass through the herd would have been almost certain death, as these more than half-wild beasts will always take revenge on their master man when they catch him dismounted in the open. As they were coming up from the direction of the river, and were slowly grazing past the wood, I resolved to wait for them to pass on before leaving my concealment. I sat down and tried to be patient, but the brutes were in no hurry, and went on skirting the wood at a snail's pace. It was about six o'clock before the last stragglers had left, and then I ventured out from my hiding-place, hungry as a wolf and afraid of being overtaken by night before finding any human habitation. I had left the trees half a mile behind me and was walking hurriedly along towards the valley of the Yí, when passing over a hillock, I suddenly found myself in sight of a bull resting on the grass and quietly chewing his cud. Unfortunately the brute saw me at the same moment and immediately stood up. He was, I think, about three or four years old, and a bull of that age is even more dangerous than an older one; for he is quite as truculent as the other and far more active. There was no refuge of any kind near, and I knew very well that to attempt to escape by running would only increase my danger, so after gazing at him for a few moments I assumed an easy unconcerned manner and walked on; but he was not going to be taken in that way and began to follow me. Then for the first, and I devoutly hope for the last, time in my life I was compelled to resort to the gaucho plan, and casting myself face downwards on the earth, lay there simulating death. It is a miserable, dangerous expedient, but in the circumstances I found myself, the only one offering a chance of escape from a very terrible death. In a few moments I heard his heavy tramp, then felt him sniffing me all over. After that he tried unsuccessfully to roll me over, in order to study my face, I suppose.

It was horrible to endure the prods he gave me and lie still, but after a while he grew quieter and contented himself by simply keeping guard over me; occasionally smelling at my head, then turning round to smell at my heels. Probably his theory was, if he had one, that I had fainted with fear at the sight of him and would recover presently, but he was not quite sure at which end of me returning life would first show itself. About once in every five or six minutes he seemed to get impatient, and then he would paw me with his heavy hoof, uttering a low hoarse moaning, spattering me with froth from his mouth; but as he showed no disposition to leave, I at last resolved to try a very bold experiment, for my position was becoming unendurable. I waited till the brute's head was turned from me, then worked my hand cautiously down to my revolver; but before I had quite drawn it, he noticed the movement and wheeled swiftly round, kicking my legs as he did so. Just as he brought his head round close to mine, I discharged the weapon in his face, and the sudden explosion so terrified him that he turned tail and fled, never pausing in his lumbering gallop till he was out of sight. It was a glorious victory; and though I could scarcely stand on my legs at first, so stiff and bruised did I feel all over, I laughed with joy, and even sent another bullet whizzing after the retreating monster, accompanying the discharge with a wild yell of triumph.

After that I proceeded without further interruption on my walk, and, had I not felt so ravenously hungry and so sore where the bull had trod on me or prodded me with his horns, the walk would have been very enjoyable, for I was now approaching the Yí. The ground grew moist and green, and flowers abounded, many of them new to me and so lovely and fragrant that in my admiration for them I almost forgot my pain. The sun went down, but no house appeared in sight. Over the western heavens flamed the brilliant hues of the afterglow, and from the long grass came the sad monotonous trill of some night insect. Troops of hooded gulls flew by me on their way from their feeding grounds to the water, uttering their long hoarse laughter-like cries. How buoyant and happy they seemed, flying with their stomachs full to their rest; while I, dismounted and supperless, dragged painfully on like a gull that had been left behind with a broken wing. Presently, through the purple and saffron-hued vapours in the western sky, the evening star appeared, large and luminous, the herald of swift-coming darkness; and then, weary, bruised, hungry, baffled, and despondent, I sat down to meditate on my forlorn position.

CHAPTER XIII

BARKING DOGS AND SHOUTING REBELS

I SAT there till it was very dark, and the longer I sat the colder and stiffer I grew, yet I felt no disposition to walk further. At length a large owl, flapping down close to my head, gave utterance to a long hiss, followed by a sharp clicking sound, ending with a sudden loud, laugh-like cry. The nearness of it startled me, and looking up, I saw a twinkling yellow light gleam for a moment across the wide, black plain, then disappear. A few fireflies were flitting about the grass, but I felt sure the gleam just witnessed proceeded from a fire; and after vainly trying to catch sight of it again from my seat on the ground, I rose and walked on, keeping before me a particular star shining directly over the spot where that transient glimmer had appeared. Presently, to my great joy, I spied it again in the same place, and felt convinced that it was the gleam of firelight shining from the open door or window of some rancho or estancia house. With renewed hope and energy I hastened on, the light increasing in brightness as I progressed; and, after half an hour's brisk walking, I found myself approaching a human dwelling of some kind. I could make out a dark mass of trees and bushes, a long, low house, and, nearer to me, a corral, or cattle-pen, of tall upright posts. Now, however, when a refuge seemed so close, the fear of the terrible, savage dogs kept on most of these cattle-breeding establishments made me hesitate. Unless I wished to run the risk of being shot, it was necessary to shout loudly to make my approach known, yet by shouting I would inevitably bring a pack of huge, frantic dogs upon me; and the horns of the angry bull I had encountered were less terrible to contemplate than the fangs of these powerful truculent brutes. I sat down on the ground to consider the position, and presently heard the clatter of approaching hoofs. Immediately afterwards three men rode past me, but did not see me, for I was crouching down behind some scrubby bushes. When the horsemen approached the house the dogs rushed forth to assail them, and their loud, fierce barking, and the wild shouts of some person from the house calling them off, were enough to make a dismounted man nervous. However, now was my only chance, and, starting up, I hurried on towards the noise. As I passed the corral the brutes became aware of my approach, and instantly turned their attention on me. I wildly shouted *"Ave Maria,"* then, revolver in hand, stood awaiting the onset; but when they were near enough for me to see that the pack was composed of eight or ten huge yellow mastiff-like brutes, my courage failed, and I fled to the corral, where, with an agility surpassing that of a wild cat, so great was my terror, I climbed up a post and placed myself beyond their reach. With the dogs furiously barking under me, I renewed my shouts of *"Ave Maria"*—the proper thing to do when you approach a strange house in these pious latitudes. After some time the men approached—four of them—and asked me who I was and what I did there. I gave an account of myself, then asked whether it would be safe for me to descend. The master of the house took the hint, and drove his faithful protectors off, after which I came down from my uncomfortable perch.

He was a tall, well-made, but rather fierce-looking gaucho, with keen black eyes, and a heavy black beard. He seemed suspicious of me—a very unusual thing in a native's house, and asked me a great many searching questions; and finally, still with some reluctance in his manner, he invited me into the kitchen. There I found a big fire blazing merrily on the raised clay hearth in the centre of the large room, and seated near it an old grey-haired woman, a middle-aged, tall, dark-skinned dame in a purple dress—my host's wife; a pale, pretty young woman, about sixteen years old, and a little girl. When I sat down my host began once more questioning me; but he apologised for doing so, saying that my arrival on foot seemed a very extraordinary circumstance. I told them how I had lost my horse, saddle, and poncho in the wood, and then related my encounter with

the bull. They listened to it all with very grave
faces, but I am sure it was as good as a comedy
to them. Don Sinforiano Alday, the owner of the
place and my questioner, made me take off my
coat to exhibit the bruises the bull's hoofs had
inflicted on my arms and shoulders. He was
anxious, even after that, to know something more
about me, and so to satisfy him I gave him a brief
account of some of my adventures in the country, down to my arrest with Marcos Marcó, and
how that plausible gentleman had made his escape
from the magistrate's house. That made them all
laugh, and the three men I had seen arrive, and
who appeared to be casual visitors, became very
friendly, frequently passing me the rum bottle
with which they were provided.

After sipping maté and rum for half an hour
we settled down to discuss a plentiful supper of
roast and boiled beef and mutton, with great basins
of well-seasoned broth to wash it down. I consumed an amazing quantity of meat, as much, in
fact, as any gaucho there; and to eat as much as
one of these men at a sitting is a feat for an Englishman to boast about. Supper done, I lit a
cigar and leant back against the wall enjoying
many delightful sensations all together—-warmth,
rest, and hunger satisfied, and the subtle fragrance
of that friend and comforter, divine tobacco. On
the further side of the room my host was meanwhile talking to the other men in low tones. Occasional glances in my direction seemed to show

that they still harboured some suspicion of me, or that they had some grave matters to converse about unsuitable for a stranger to hear.

At length Alday rose and addressed me. "Señor, if you are ready to rest I will now conduct you to another room, where you can have some rugs and ponchos to make a bed with."

"If my presence here is not inconvenient," I returned, "I would rather remain and smoke by the fire."

"You see, señor," he said, "I have arranged to meet some neighbours and friends, who are coming here to discuss matters of importance with me. I am even now expecting their arrival, and the presence of a stranger would scarcely allow us to talk freely over our affairs."

"Since you wish it, I will go to any part of the house you may think proper to put me in," I returned.

I rose, not very cheerfully, I must say, from my comfortable seat before the fire, to follow him out, when the tramp of galloping horses came to our ears.

"Follow me this way—quick," exclaimed my impatient conductor; but just as I reached the door about a dozen mounted men dashed up close to us and burst forth in a perfect storm of yells. Instantly all those who were in the kitchen sprang to their feet uttering loud exclamations and looking greatly excited. Then came from the mounted men another wild outburst as they all yelled together, *"Viva el General Santa Coloma—viv—a."*

The other three men then rushed from the
kitchen, and in excited tones began to ask if anything fresh had happened. Meanwhile, I was
left standing at the door by myself. The women
appeared almost as excited as the men, except the
girl, who had glanced at me with shy compassion
in her large, dark eyes when I had been roused
from my seat by the fire. Taking advantage of
the general excitement, I now repaid that kindly
look with one of admiration. She was a quiet,
bashful girl, her pale face crowned with a pro-
fusion of black hair; and while she stood there
waiting, apparently unconcerned by the hubbub
outside, she looked strangely pretty, her home-
made cotton gown, of limp and scanty material,
clinging closely to her limbs so as to display her
slender, graceful form to the best advantage.
Presently, seeing me looking at her she came near,
and touching my arm in passing told me in a
whisper to go back to my seat by the fire. I
gladly obeyed her, for my curiosity was now thoroughly aroused, and I wished to know the meaning of this outcry which had thrown these phleg-
matic gauchos into such a frenzied state of excitement. It looked rather like a political row—but
of General Santa Coloma I had never heard, and
it seemed curious that a name so seldom mentioned
should be the rallying cry of revolutionists.

In a few minutes the men all streamed back
into the kitchen. Then the master of the house,

Alday, his face on fire with emotion, thrust himself into the midst of the crowd.

"Boys, are you mad!" he cried. "Do you not see a stranger here? What is the meaning of all this outcry if nothing new has happened?"

A roar of laughter from the new-comers greeted this outburst, after which they raised another yell of *"Viva Santa Coloma!"*

Alday became furious. "Speak, madmen!" he shouted; "tell me, in God's name, what has happened—or do you wish to ruin everything with your imprudence?"

"Listen, Alday," replied one of the men, "and know how little we need fear the presence of a stranger. Santa Coloma, the hope of Uruguay, the saviour of his country, who will shortly deliver us out of the power of Colorado assassins and pirates—Santa Coloma has come! He is here in our midst; he has seized on El Molino del Yí, and has raised the standard of revolt against the infamous government of Montevideo! *Viva Santa Coloma!*"

Alday flung his hat off and, falling on his knees, remained for some moments in silent prayer, his hands clasped before him. The others all snatched off their hats and stood silent, grouped about him. Then he stood up, and all together joined in a *viva*, which far surpassed in its deafening power their previous performances.

My host now appeared to be almost beside himself with excitement.

"What," he cried, "my General come! Do you tell me that Santa Coloma has come? O, friends, the great God has remembered our suffering country at last! He has grown weary of looking on man's injustice, the persecutions, the bloodshed, the cruelties that have almost driven us mad. I cannot realise it! Let me go to my General that these eyes that have watched for his coming may see him and rejoice. I cannot wait for daylight— this very night must I ride to El Molino, that I may see him and touch him with my hands, and know that it is not a dream."

His words were welcomed with a shout of applause, and the other men all immediately announced their intention to accompany him to El Molino, a small town on the Yí some leagues distant.

Some of the men now went out to catch fresh horses, while Alday busied himself in bringing out a store of old broadswords and carbines from their concealment in some other part of the house. The men, talking excitedly together, occupied themselves in scouring and sharpening the rusty weapons, while the women cooked a fresh supply of meat for the last comers; and in the meantime I was permitted to remain unnoticed by the fire, smoking peacefully.

CHAPTER XIV

MAIDS OF FANCY: MAIDS OF YÍ

THE girl I have mentioned, whose name was Monica, and the child, called Anita, were the only persons there besides myself who were not carried away by the warlike enthusiasm of the moment. Monica, silent, pale, almost apathetic, was occupied serving maté to the numerous guests; while the child, when the shouting and excitement was at its height, appeared greatly terrified, and clung to Alday's wife, trembling and crying piteously. No notice was taken of the poor little thing, and at length she crept away into a corner to conceal herself behind a faggot of wood. Her hiding-place was close to my seat, and after a little coaxing I induced her to leave it and come to me. She was a most forlorn little thing, with a white, thin face and large, dark, pathetic eyes. Her mean little cotton frock only reached to her knees, and her little legs and feet were bare. Her age was seven or eight; she was an orphan, and Alday's wife, having no children of her own, was bringing her up, or rather permitting her to grow up under her roof. I drew her to me, and tried to soothe her tremors and get her to talk. Little by little she gained confidence, and began to reply to my questions; then I learnt that she was a little shepherdess, although so young, and spent most of the time every day in following the flock about on her pony. Her pony and the girl Monica, who was some relation—cousin, the child called her— were the two beings she seemed to have the greatest affection for.

"And when you slip off, how do you get on again?" I asked.

"Little pony is tame, and I never fall off," she said. "Sometimes I get off, then I climb on again."

"And what do you do all day long—talk and play?"

"I talk to my doll; I take it on the pony when I go with the sheep."

"Is your doll very pretty, Anita?"

No answer.

"Will you let me see your doll, Anita? I know I shall like your doll, because I like you."

She gave me an anxious look. Evidently doll was a very precious being and had not met with proper appreciation. After a little nervous fidgeting she left me and crept out of the room; then presently she came back, apparently trying to screen something from the vulgar gaze in her scanty little dress. It was her wonderful doll— the dear companion of her rambles and rides. With fear and trembling she allowed me to take it into my hands. It was, or consisted of, the fore-foot of a sheep, cut off at the knee; on the top of the knee part a little wooden ball wrapped in a white rag represented the head, and it was dressed in a piece of red flannel—a satyr-like doll with one hairy leg and a cloven foot. I praised its pleasing countenance, its pretty gown and dainty little boots; and all I said sounded very precious to Anita, filling her with emotions of the liveliest pleasure.

"And do you never play with the dogs and cats and little lambs?" I asked.

"Not with the dogs and cats. When I see a very little lamb asleep, I get down and go softly, softly and catch it. It tries to get away; then I put my finger in its mouth, and it sucks, and sucks; then it runs away."

"And what do you like best to eat?"

"Sugar. When uncle buys sugar, aunt gives me a lump. I make doll eat some, and bite off one small piece and put it in pony's mouth."

"Which would you rather have, Anita—a great many lumps of sugar, or a beautiful string of beads, or a little girl to play with?"

This question was rather too much for her neglected little brain, which had fed itself with such simple fare; so I was obliged to put it in various ways, and at last, when she understood that only one of the three things could be chosen, she decided in favour of a little girl to play with.

Then I asked her if she liked to hear stories; this also puzzled her, and after some cross-questioning I discovered that she had never heard a story, and did not know what it meant.

"Listen, Anita, and I will tell you a story," I said. "Have you seen the white mist over the Yí in the morning—a light white mist that flies away when the sun gets hot?"

Yes, she often saw the white mist in the morning, she told me.

"Then I will tell you a story about the white mist and a little girl named Alma.

"Little Alma lived close to the river Yí, but far, far from here, beyond the trees and beyond the blue hills, for the Yí is a very long river. She lived with her grandmother and with six uncles, all big tall men with long beards; and they always talked about wars, and cattle, and horse-racing, and a great many other important things that Alma could not understand. There was no one to talk to Alma and for Alma to talk to or to play with. And when she went out of the house where all the big people were talking, she heard the cocks crowing, the dogs barking, the birds singing, the sheep bleating, and the trees rustling their leaves over her head, and she could not understand one word of all they said. At last, having no one to play with or talk to, she sat down and began to cry. Now, it happened that near the spot where she sat there was an old black woman wearing a red shawl, who was gathering sticks for the fire, and she asked Alma why she cried.

" 'Because I have no one to talk to and play with,' said Alma. Then the old black woman drew a long brass pin out of her shawl and pricked Alma's tongue with it, for she made Alma hold it out to be pricked.

" 'Now,' said the old woman, 'you can go and play and talk with the dogs, cats, birds, and trees, for you will understand all they say, and they will understand all you say.'

"Alma was very glad, and ran home as fast as she could to talk to the cat.

" 'Come, cat, let us talk and play together,' she said.

" 'Oh, no,' said the cat. 'I am very busy watching a little bird, so you must go away and play with little Niebla down by the river.'

"Then the cat ran away among the weeds and left her. The dogs also refused to play when she went to them; for they had to watch the house and bark at strangers. Then they also told her to go and play with little Niebla down by the river. Then Alma ran out and caught a little duckling, a soft little thing that looked like a ball of yellow cotton, and said—

" 'Now, little duck, let us talk and play.'

"But the duckling only struggled to get away and screamed, 'Oh, mamma, mamma, come and take me away from Alma!'

"Then the old duck came rushing up, and said—

" 'Alma, let my child alone: and if you want to play, go and play with Niebla down by the river. A nice thing to catch my duckie in your hands— what next, I wonder!'

"So she let the duckling go, and at last she said, 'Yes, I will go and play with Niebla down by the river.'

"She waited till she saw the white mist, and then ran all the way to the Yí, and stood still on the green bank close by the water with the white mist all round her. By-and-by she saw a beautiful little child come flying towards her in the white mist. The child came and stood on the green bank and looked at Alma. Very, very pretty she was; and she wore a white dress—whiter than milk, whiter than foam, and all embroidered with purple flowers; she had also white silk stockings and scarlet shoes, bright as scarlet verbenas. Her hair was long and fluffy, and shone like gold, and round her neck she had a string of big gold beads. Then Alma said, 'Oh, beautiful little girl, what is your name?' to which the little girl answered—

" 'Niebla.'

" 'Will you talk to me and play with me?' said Alma.

" 'Oh, no,' said Niebla, 'how can I play with a little girl dressed as you are and with bare feet?'

"For you know poor Alma only wore a little old frock that came down to her knees, and she had no shoes and stockings on. Then little Niebla rose up and floated away, away from the bank and down the river, and at last, when she was quite out of sight in the white mist, Alma began to cry. When it got very hot she went and sat down, still crying, under the trees; there were two very big willow trees growing near the river. By-and-by the leaves rustled in the wind and the trees began talking to each other, and Alma understood everything they said.

" 'Is it going to rain, do you think?' said one tree.

" 'Yes, I think it will—some day,' said the other.

" 'There are no clouds,' said the first tree.

" 'No, there are no clouds to-day, but there were some the day before yesterday,' said the other.

" 'Have you got any nests in your branches?' said the first tree.

" 'Yes, one,' said the other. 'It was made by a little yellow bird, and there are five speckled eggs in it.'

"Then the first tree said, 'There is little Alma sitting in our shade; do you know why she is crying, neighbour?'

"The other tree answered, 'Yes, it is because she has no one to play with. Little Niebla by the river refused to play with her because she is not beautifully dressed.'

"Then the first tree said, 'Ah, she ought to go and ask the fox for some pretty clothes to wear. The fox always keeps a great store of pretty things in her hole.'

"Alma had listened to every word of this conversation. She remembered that a fox lived on the hillside not far off; for she had often seen it sitting in the sunshine with its little ones playing round it and pulling their mother's tail in fun. So Alma got up and ran till she found the hole, and putting her head down it she cried out, 'Fox! Fox!' But the fox seemed cross and only answered without coming out, 'Go away, Alma, and talk to little Niebla. I am busy getting dinner for my children and have no time to talk to you now.'

"Then Alma cried, 'Oh, Fox, Niebla will not play with me because I have no pretty things to wear. Oh, Fox, will you give me a nice dress and shoes and stockings and a string of beads?'

"After a little while the fox came out of its hole with a big bundle done up in a red cotton handkerchief, and said, 'Here are the things, Alma, and I hope they will fit you. But you know, Alma, you really ought not to come at this time of day, for I am very busy just now cooking the dinner—an armadillo roasted and a couple of partridges stewed with rice, and a little omelette of turkeys' eggs. I mean plovers' eggs, of course; I never touch turkeys' eggs.'

"Alma said she was very sorry to give so much trouble.

"'Oh, never mind,' said the fox. 'How is your grandmother?'

"'She is very well, thank you,' said Alma, 'but she has a bad headache.'

"'I am very sorry to hear it,' said the fox. 'Tell her to stick two fresh dock leaves on her temples, and to drink a little weak tea made of knot-grass, and on no account to go out in the hot sun. I should like to go and see her, only I do not like the dogs being always about the house. Give her my best respects. And now run home, Alma, and try on the things, and when you are passing this way you can bring me back the handkerchief, as I always tie my face up in it when I have the toothache.'

"Alma thanked the fox very much and ran home as fast as she could, and when the bundle was opened she found in it a beautiful white dress, embroidered with purple flowers, a pair of scarlet shoes, silk stockings, and a string of great golden beads. They all fitted her very well; and next day when the white mist was on the Yí she dressed herself in her beautiful clothes and went down to the river. By-and-by little Niebla came flying along, and when she saw Alma she came and kissed her and took her by the hand. All the morning they played and talked together, gathering flowers and running races over the green sward; and at last Niebla bade her good-bye and flew away, for all the white mist was floating off down the river. But every day after that Alma found her little companion by the Yí, and was very happy, for now she had someone to talk to and to play with."

After I had finished the story Anita continued gazing into my face with an absorbed expression in her large wistful eyes. She seemed half scared, half delighted at what she had heard; but presently, before the little thing had said a word, Monica, who had been directing shy and wondering glances towards us for some time, came, and taking her by the hand led her away to bed.

I was getting sleepy then, and as the clatter of talk and warlike preparation showed no signs of abating, I was glad to be shown into another room, where some sheepskins, rugs, and a couple of ponchos were given to me for a bed.

During the night all the men took their departure, for in the morning, when I went into the kitchen, I only found the old woman and Alday's wife sipping bitter maté. The child, they informed me, had disappeared from the house an hour before, and Monica had gone out to look for her. Alday's wife was highly indignant at the little one's escapade, for it was high time for Anita to go out with the flock. After taking maté I went out, and looking towards the Yí veiled in a silvery mist, I spied Monica leading the culprit home by the hand, and went to meet them. Poor little Anita! her face stained with tears, her little legs and feet covered with clay and scratched by sharp reeds in fifty places, her dress soaking wet with the heavy mist, looked a most pitiful object.

"Where did you find her?" I asked the girl, beginning to fear that I had been the indirect cause of the poor child's misfortunes.

"Down by the river looking for little Niebla.

I knew she would be there when I missed her this morning."

"How did you know that?" I asked. "You did not hear the story I told her."

"I made her repeat it all to me last night," said Monica.

After that little Anita was scolded, shaken, washed and dried, then fed and finally lifted on to the back of her pony and sent to take care of the sheep. While undergoing this treatment she maintained a profound silence, her little face puckered up into an expression that boded tears. They were not for the public, however, and only after she was on the pony with the reins in her little mites of hands and her back towards us did she give way to her grief and disappointment of having failed to find the beautiful child of the mist.

I was astonished to find that she had taken the fantastic little tale invented to amuse her as truth; but the poor babe had never read books or heard stories, and the fairy tale had been too much for her starved little imagination. I remember that once on another occasion I told a pathetic story of a little child, lost in a great wilderness, to a girl about Anita's age, and just as unaccustomed to this kind of mental fare. Next morning her mother informed me that my little listener had spent half the night sobbing and begging to be allowed to go and look for that lost child I had told her about.

Hearing that Alday would not return till evening or till the following day, I asked his wife to lend or give me a horse to proceed on my journey. This, however, she could not do; then she added, very graciously, that while all the men were away my presence in the house would be a comfort to her, a man always being a great protection. The arrangement did not strike me as one very advantageous to myself, but as I could not journey very well to Montevideo on foot, I was compelled to sit still and wait for Alday's return.

It was dull work talking to those two women in the kitchen. They were both great talkers, and had evidently come to a tacit agreement to share their one listener fairly between them, for first one, then the other would speak with a maddening monotony. Alday's wife had six favourite, fine-sounding words—*elements, superior, division, prolongation, justification,* and *disproportion*. One of these she somehow managed to drag into every sentence, and sometimes she succeeded in getting in two. Whenever this happened the achievement made her so proud that she would in the most deliberate cold-blooded way repeat the sentence again, word for word. The strength of the old woman lay in dates. Not an occurrence did she mention, whether it referred to some great public event or to some trivial domestic incident in her own rancho, without giving the year, the month, and the day. The duet between these two confounded barrel-organs, one grinding out rhetoric, the other chronology, went on all the morning, and often I turned to Monica, sitting over her sewing, in hopes of a different tune from her more melodious instrument, but in vain, for never a word dropped from those silent lips. Occasionally her dark luminous eyes were raised for a moment, only to sink abashed again when they encountered mine. After breakfast I went for a walk along the river, where I spent several hours hunting for flowers and fossils, and amusing myself as best I could. There were legions of duck, coot, rosy spoonbills, and black-necked swans disporting themselves in the water, and I was very thankful that I had no gun with me, and so was not tempted to startle them with rude noises, and send any of them away to languish wounded amongst the reeds. At length, after having indulged in a good swin, I set out to walk back to the estancia.

When still about a mile from the house as I walked on, swinging my stick and singing aloud in lightness of heart, I passed a clump of willow trees, and looking up saw Monica under them watching my approach. She was standing perfectly motionless, and when I caught sight of her cast her eyes demurely down, apparently to contemplate her bare feet, which looked very white on the deep green turf. In one hand she held a cluster of stalks of the large, crimson autumnal lilies which had just begun to blossom. My singing ceased suddenly, and I stood for some moments gazing admiringly at the shy, rustic beauty.

"What a distance you have walked to gather lilies, Monica!" I said, approaching her. "Will you give me one of your stalks?"

"They were gathered for the Virgin, so I cannot give away any of these," she replied. "If you will wait here under the trees I will find one to give you."

I agreed to wait for her; then placing the cluster she had gathered on the grass she left me. Before long she returned with a stalk, round, polished, slender, like a pipe stem, and crowned with its cluster of three splendid crimson flowers.

When I had sufficiently thanked her and admired it, I said, "What boon are you going to ask from the Virgin, Monica, when you offer her these flowers—safety for your lover in the wars?"

"No, señor; I have no offering to make, and no boon to ask. They are for my aunt; I offered to gather them for her, because—I wished to meet you here."

"To meet me, Monica—what for?"

"To ask for a story, señor," she replied, colouring, and with a shy glance at my face.

"Ah, we have had stories enough," I said. "Remember poor Anita running away this morning to look for a playmate in the wet mist."

"She is a child; I am a woman."

"Then, Monica, you must have a lover who will be jealous if you listen to stories from a stranger's lips in this lonely spot."

"No person will ever know that I met you here," she returned—so bashful, yet so persistent.

"I have forgotten all my stories," I said.

"Then, señor, I will go and find you another *ramo* of lilies while you think of one to tell me."

"No," I said, "you must get no more lilies for me. Look, I will give you back these you gave me." And saying that, I fastened them in her black hair, where by contrast they looked very splendid, and gave the girl a new grace. "Ah, Monica, they make you look too pretty—let me take them out again."

But she would not have them taken. "I will leave you now to think of a story for me," she said, blushing and turning away.

Then I took her hands and made her face me. "Listen, Monica," I said. "Do you know that these lilies are full of strange magic? See how crimson they are; that is the colour of passion, for they have been steeped in passion, and turn my heart to fire. If you bring me any more of them, Monica, I shall tell you a story that will make you tremble with fear—tremble like the willow leaves and turn pale as the mists over the Yí."

She smiled at my words; it was like a ray of sunlight falling through the foliage on her face. Then, in a voice that was almost a whisper, she said, "What will the story be about, señor? Tell me, then I shall know whether to gather lilies for you or not."

"It will be about a stranger meeting a sweet,

pale girl standing under the trees, her dark eyes cast down, and red lilies in her hand; and how she asked him for a story, but he could speak to her of nothing but love, love, love."

When I finished speaking she gently withdrew her hands from mine and turned away amongst the trees, doubtless to fly from me, trembling at my words, like a frightened young fawn from the hunter.

So for a moment I thought. But no, there lay the lilies gathered for a religious purpose at my feet, and there was nothing reproachful in the shy dark eyes when they glanced back for a moment at me; for in spite of those warning words she had only gone to find more of those perilous crimson flowers to give me.

Not then, while I waited for her return with palpitating heart, but afterwards in calmer moments, and when Monica had become a pretty picture in the past, did I compose the following lines. I am not so vain as to believe that they possess any great poetical merit, and introduce them principally to let the reader know how to pronounce the pretty name of that Oriental river, which it still keeps in remembrance of a vanished race.

> Standing silent, pale her face was,
>   Pale and sweet to see:
> 'Neath the willows waiting for me,
>   Willow-like was she,

Smiling, blushing, trembling, bashful
    Maid of Yí.

Willow-like she trembled, yet she
    Never fled from me;
But her dove-like eyes were downcast,
    On the grass to see
White feet standing: white thy feet were,
    Maid of Yí.

Stalks of lilies in her hands were:
    Crimson lilies three,
Placed I in her braids of black hair—
    They were bright to see!
Lift thy dark eyes, for I love thee,
    Maid of Yí!

CHAPTER XV

WHEN THE TRUMPET CALLS TO BATTLE

In the evening Alday returned with a couple of his friends, and as soon as an opportunity offered, I took him aside and begged him to let me have a horse to continue my journey to Montevideo. He answered evasively that the horse I had lost in the neighbouring forest would probably be recovered in the course of two or three days. I replied that if he would let me have a horse, the one I had lost, together with saddle, poncho, etc., could be claimed by him whenever they turned up. He then said that he could not very well give me a horse, "with saddle and bridle also." It looked as if he wanted to keep me in his house for some purpose of his own, and this made me all the more determined to leave it immediately, in spite of the tender, reproachful glances which Monica flashed on me from under her long, drooping eyelashes. I told him that if I could not have a horse I would leave his estancia on foot. That rather put him in a corner; for in this country, where horse-stealing and cheating at cards are looked on as venial offences, to let a man leave your estancia on foot is considered a very dishonourable thing. He pondered over my declaration for some minutes, then, after conferring with his friends, he promised to provide me with all I required next day. I had heard nothing more about the revolution, but after supper Alday suddenly became very confidential, and said that the whole country would be up in arms in the course of a very few days, and that it would be highly dangerous for me to attempt travelling by myself to the capital. He expatiated on the immense prestige of General Santa Coloma, who had just taken up arms against the Colorado party then in power, and concluded by saying that my safest plan would be to join the rebels and accompany them on their march to Montevideo, which would begin almost immediately. I replied that I took no interest in the dissensions of the Banda Oriental, and did not wish to compromise myself by joining a military expedition of any kind. He shrugged his shoulders, and renewing his promise of a horse next day, retired to rest.

On rising next morning I found that the others were already up. The horses were standing saddled at the door, and Alday, pointing out a very fair-looking animal, informed me that it had been saddled for me, and then added that he and his friends would ride one or two leagues with me to put me on the right road to Montevideo. He had suddenly become almost too kind, but in the simplicity of my heart I believed that he was only making amends for the slight inhospitality of the day before.

After partaking of bitter maté I thanked my hostess, looked my last into Monica's dark, sorrowful eyes, lifted for one moment to mine, and kissed little Anita's pathetic face, by so doing filling the child with astonishment and causing considerable amusement to the other members of the family. After we had ridden about four miles, keeping nearly parallel with the river, it struck me that we were not going in the right direction—the right one for me, at any rate. I therefore checked my horse and told my companions that I would not trouble them to ride with me any farther.

"My friend," said Alday, approaching me, "you will, if you leave us now, infallibly fall into the hands of some *partida*, who, finding you without a passport, will take you to El Molino, or to some other centre. Though it would make no difference if you had a passport, for they would only tear it up and take you all the same. In these circumstances it is your safest plan to go with us to El Molino, where General Santa Coloma is collecting his forces, and you will then be able to explain your position to him."

"I refuse to go to El Molino," I said angrily, exasperated at his treachery.

"You will then compel us to take you there," he returned.

I had no wish to become a prisoner again so soon, and seeing that a bold stroke was necessary to keep my liberty, I suddenly reined up my horse and drew my revolver. "My friends," I said, "your road lies in that direction; mine in this. I wish you good morning."

I had scarcely finished speaking before a blow of a heavy whip-handle descended on my arm below the elbow, almost breaking it, and sending me off my horse, while the revolver went spinning away a dozen yards. The blow had been dealt by one of Alday's two followers who had just dropped a little to the rear, and the rascal certainly showed a marvellous quickness and dexterity in disabling me.

Wild with rage and pain, I scrambled to my feet, and drawing my knife, threatened to stab the first man who approached me; and then, in unmeasured language, I abused Alday for his cowardice and brutality. He only smiled and replied that he considered my youth, and therefore felt no resentment against me for using such intemperate words.

"And now, my friend," he continued, after picking up my revolver and remounting his horse, "let us waste no more time, but hasten on to El Molino, where you can state your case to the General."

As I did not wish to be tied on to my horse and carried in that unpleasant and ignominious manner, I had to obey. Climbing into the saddle with some difficulty, we set out towards the village of El Molino at a swinging gallop. The rough motion of the horse I rode increased the pain

in my arm till it became intolerable; then one
of the men mercifully bound it up in a sling, after
which I was able to travel more comfortably,
though still suffering a great deal.

The day was excessively warm, and we did not
reach our destination till about three o'clock in
the afternoon. Just before entering the town we
rode through a little army of gauchos encamped
on the adjacent plain. Some of them were engaged cooking meat, others were saddling horses,
while others in bodies of twenty or thirty were
going through cavalry exercises, the whole making
a scene of wonderful animation. Very nearly all
the men wore the ordinary gaucho costume, and
those who were exercising carried lances, to which
were attached little white fluttering bannerets.
Passing through the encampment, we clattered
into the town, composed of about seventy or eighty
houses of stone or mud, some thatched, others
with tiled roofs, and every house with a large
garden attached to it. At the official building
facing the plaza a guard of ten men, armed with
carbines, was stationed. We dismounted and went
into the building, only to hear that the General
had just left the town, and was not expected back
till the following day.

Alday spoke to an officer sitting at a table in the
room we were shown into, addressing him as
Major. He was a thin, elderly man, with calm
grey eyes and a colourless face, and looked like a
gentleman. After hearing a few words from

Alday, he turned to me and said courteously that he was sorry to tell me I should have to remain in El Molino till the General's return, when I could give an account of myself to him.

"We do not," he said in conclusion, "wish to compel any foreigner, or any Oriental even, to join our forces; but we are naturally suspicious of strangers, having already caught two or three spies in the neighbourhood. Unfortunately you are not provided with a passport, and it is best that the General see you."

"Sir officer," I replied, "by ill-treating and detaining an Englishman you are doing your cause no good."

He answered that he was grieved that his people had found it necessary to treat me roughly, for he put it in that mild way. Everything, he said, short of liberating me, would be done to make my sojourn in El Molino pleasant.

"If it is necessary that the General should see me himself before I can have my liberty, pray let these men take me to him at once," I said.

"He has not yet left El Molino," said an orderly standing in the room. "He is at the end of the town at the Casa Blanca, and does not leave till half-past three."

"It is nearly that now," said the officer, consulting his watch. "Take him to the General at once, Lieutenant Alday."

I thanked the officer, who had looked and spoken so unlike a revolutionary bandit, and as

soon as I had succeeded in clambering on to my
horse we were once more dashing along the main
street at a fast gallop. We drew up before a large
old-looking stone house at the end of the town,
standing some distance back from the road, and
screened from it by a double row of tall Lom-
bardy poplars. The back of the house was towards the road, and passing round to the front
after leaving our horses at the gate, we entered a
spacious *patio*, or yard. Running along the front
of the dwelling was a wide corridor, supported by
wooden pillars, painted white, while the whole of
the *patio* was shaded by an immense grape-vine.
This was evidently one of the best houses in the
place, and coming directly from the glaring sun
and the white dusty road the vine-shaded *patio*
and corridor looked delightfully cool and inviting.
A gay company of twelve or fifteen people were
gathered under the corridor, some sipping maté,
others sucking grapes; and when we came on the
scene a young lady was just finishing a song she
was singing. I at once singled out General Santa
Coloma, sitting by the young lady with the guitar
—a tall, imposing man, with somewhat irregular
features, and a bronzed, weather-beaten face. He
was booted and spurred, and over his uniform
wore a white silk poncho with purple fringe. I
judged from his countenance that he was not a
stern or truculent man, as one expects a Caudillo—
a leader of men—in the Banda Oriental to be:
and remembering that in a few minutes he would

be leaving the house, I was anxious to push forward and state my case to him. The others, however, prevented me, for the General just then happened to be engaged in a vivacious conversation with the young lady sitting by him. When I had once looked attentively at this girl I had eyes for no other face there. The type was Spanish, and I have never seen a more perfect face of the kind; a wealth of blue-black hair shading the low broad forehead, straight nose, dark luminous eyes, and crimson pouting lips. She was tall, perfect in her figure as in her face, and wore a white dress with a deep red China rose on her bosom for only ornament. Standing there unnoticed at the end of the corridor I gazed with a kind of fascination on her, listening to her light rippling laughter and lively talk, watching her graceful gestures, her sparkling eyes and damask cheeks flushed with excitement. Here is a woman, I thought with a sigh—I felt a slight twinge at that disloyal sigh—I could have worshipped. She was pressing the guitar on the General.

"You have promised to sing one song before you go, and I cannot let you off," she exclaimed.

At length he took the instrument, protesting that his voice was a very bad one; then, sweeping the strings, began that fine old Spanish song of love and war—

Cuando suena la trompa guerrera.

His voice was uncultivated and somewhat harsh, but there was a good deal of fire and expression in the performance, and it was rapturously applauded.

The moment the song was over he handed her back the guitar, and starting up hastily, bade the company adieu, and turned to go.

Coming forward, I placed myself before him and began to speak.

"I am pressed for time and cannot listen to you now," he said quickly, scarcely glancing at me. "You are a prisoner—wounded, I see; well, when I return——" Suddenly he stopped, caught hold of my wounded arm, and said, "How did you get hurt? Tell me quickly."

His sharp impatient manner, and the sight of twenty people all standing round staring at me, quite upset me, and I could only stammer out a few unintelligible words, feeling that my face was blushing scarlet to the very roots of my hair.

"Let me tell you, General," said Alday, advancing.

"No, no," said the General; "he shall speak."

The sight of Alday so eager to give his version of the affair first restored my anger to me, and with that came back the power of speech and the other faculties which I had lost for a moment.

"Sir General, all I have to say is this," I said; "I came to this man's house at night, a stranger, lost, on foot, for my horse had been stolen from me. I asked him for shelter in the belief that at least the one virtue of hospitality still survives in this country. He, assisted by these two men, treacherously disabled me with a blow on my arm and dragged me here a prisoner."

"My good friend," said the General, "I am extremely sorry that you have been hurt through an excess of zeal on the part of one of my people. But I can scarcely regret this incident, painful as it seems, since it enables me to assure you that one other virtue besides hospitality still survives in the Banda Orientál—I mean gratitude."

"I do not understand you," I said.

"We were companions in misfortune a very short time ago," he returned. "Have you forgotten the service you did me then?"

I stared at him, astonished at his words; and while I looked into his face suddenly that scene at the magistrate's estancia, when I went with the key to let my fellow-traveller out of the stocks, and he jumped up and seized my hand, flashed on me. Still I was not quite sure, and half whispered tentatively, "What, Marcos Marcó?"

"Yes," he returned, smiling, "that was my name at that moment. My friends," he continued, resting a hand on my shoulder, and speaking to the others, "I have met this young Englishman before. A few days ago, when I was on my way hither, I was arrested at Las Cuevas in his company; it was by means of his assistance that I succeeded in making my escape. He did this good deed, believing at the time that he was helping a poor peasant, and not expecting any return."

I might have reminded him that only after he had given me a solemn assurance that he did not intend attempting to make his escape, did I consent to get his legs out of the stocks. However, as he thought proper to forget that part of the affair I was not going to recall it to him.

There were many surprised exclamations from the bystanders, and glancing at that beautiful girl, who was standing near with the others, I found her dark eyes fixed on my face with an expression of tenderness and sympathy in them that sent the blood rushing to my heart.

"They have hurt you badly, I fear," said the General, addressing me again. "To continue your journey now would be imprudent. Let me beg of you to remain where you are, in this house, till your arm is better." Then, turning to the young lady, he said, "Dolores, will you and your mother take charge of my young friend till I return, and see that his injured arm is attended to?"

"My general, you will make us happy by leaving him in our care," she replied, with a bright smile.

He then introduced me as Don Ricardo simply, for he did not know my surname, to the lovely señorita—Dolores Zelaya; after which he again bade us adieu and hurried away.

When he had gone Alday advanced, hat in hand, and gave me back my revolver, which I had forgotten all about. I took it with my left hand, and put it in my pocket. He then apologised for having treated me roughly—the Major had taught him that word—but without the faintest trace of servility in his speech or manner; and after that he offered me his hand.

"Which will you have," I said, "the hand you have injured or the left hand?"

He immediately dropped his own hand to his side, then bowing, said he would wait till I had recovered the use of my right hand. Turning to go, he added with a smile that he hoped the injury would soon heal, so that I would be able to wield a sword in my friend Santa Coloma's cause.

His manner, I thought, was a little too independent. "Pray take back your horse now," I said, "as I have no further use for it, and accept my thanks for conducting me thus far on my journey."

"Do not mention it," he replied, with a dignified wave of his hand, "I am pleased to have been able to render you this small service."

CHAPTER XVI

ROMANCE OF THE WHITE FLOWER

When Alday had left us, the charming señorita, in whose care I was well pleased to find myself, led me into a cool spacious room, dimly lighted, scantily furnished, and with a floor of red tiles. It was a great relief to drop into a sofa there, for I now felt fatigued and suffered great pain from my arm. In a few moments I had the señorita, her mother, Doña Mercedes, and an old serving-woman all round me. Gently drawing off my coat, they subjected my wounded arm to a minute examination; their compassionate finger-tips—those of the lovely Dolores especially—feeling like a soft cooling rain on the swollen inflamed part, which had become quite purple.

"Ah, how barbarous of them to hurt you like that! a friend, too, of our General!" exclaimed my beautiful nurse; which made me think that I had involuntarily become associated with the right political party in the state.

They rubbed the arm with sweet oil; while the old servant brought in a bundle of rue from the garden, which being bruised in a mortar, filled the room with a fresh aromatic smell. With this fragrant herb she made a cooling cataplasm. Having dressed my arm they placed it in a sling, then in place of my coat a light Indian poncho was brought for me to wear.

"I think you are feverish," said Doña Mercedes, feeling my pulse. "We must send for the doctor —we have a doctor in our little town, a very skilful man."

"I have little faith in doctors, señora," I said, "but great faith in women and grapes. If you will give me a cluster from your vine to refresh my blood I promise to be well very soon."

Dolores laughed lightly and left the room, only to return in a few minutes with a dish full of ripe purple clusters. They were delicious and did seem to allay the fever I felt, which had probably been caused as much by angry passions as by the blow I had received.

While I reclined luxuriously, sucking my grapes, the two ladies sat on each side of me, ostensibly fanning themselves, but only, I think, trying to make the air cooler for me. Very cool and pleasant they made it, certainly, but the gentle attentions of Dolores were at the same time such as might well create a subtler kind of fever in a man's veins—a malady not to be cured by fruit, fans, or phlebotomy.

"Who would not suffer blows for such compensation as this!" I said.

"Do not say such a thing!" exclaimed the señorita, with wonderful animation. "Have you

not rendered a great service to our dear General
—to our beloved country! If we had it in our
power to give you everything your heart might
desire it would be nothing, nothing. We must
be your debtors for ever."

I smiled at her extravagant words, but they
were very sweet to hear, none the less.

"Your ardent love of your country is a beautiful
sentiment," I remarked somewhat indiscreetly,
"but is General Santa Coloma so necessary to its
welfare?"

She looked offended and did not reply. "You
are a stranger in our country, señor, and do not
quite understand these things," said the mother
gently. "Dolores must not forget that. You
know nothing of the cruel wars we have seen and
how our enemies have conquered only by bringing in the foreigner to their aid. Ah, señor, the
bloodshed, the proscriptions, the infamies which
they have brought on this land! But there is one
man they have never yet succeeded in crushing:
always from boyhood he has been foremost in the
fight, defying their bullets, and not to be corrupted
by their Brazilian gold. Is it strange that he is
so much to us, who have lost all our relations, and
have suffered many persecutions, being deprived
almost of the means of subsistence that hirelings
and traitors might be enriched with our property?
To us in this house he is even more than to others.
He was my husband's friend and companion in
arms. He has done us a thousand favours, and

if he ever succeeds in overthrowing this infamous government he will restore to us all the property we have lost. But *ai de mi*, I cannot see deliverance yet."

"Mamita, do not say such a thing!" exclaimed her daughter. "Do you begin to despair now when there is most reason to hope?"

"Child, what can he do with this handful of illarmed men?" returned the mother sadly. "He has bravely raised the standard, but the people do not flock to it. Ah, when this revolt is crushed, like so many others, we poor women will only have to lament for more friends slain and fresh persecutions." And here she covered her eyes with her handkerchief.

Dolores tossed her head back and made a sudden gesture of impatience.

"Do you then expect to see a great army formed before the ink is dry on the Geenral's proclamation? When Santa Coloma was a fugitive without a follower you hoped; now when he is with us, and actually preparing for a march on the capital, you begin to lose heart—I cannot understand it!"

Doña Mercedes rose without replying, and left the room. The lovely enthusiast dropped her head on her hand, and remained silent, taking no notice of me, a cloud of sorrow on her countenance.

"Señorita," I said, "it is not necessary for you to remain longer here. Only tell me before going that you forgive me, for it makes me very unhappy to think that I have offended you."

She turned to me with a very bright smile and gave me her hand.

"Ah, it is for you to forgive me for hastily taking offence at a light word," she said. "I must not allow anything you say in future to spoil my gratitude. Do you know I think you are one of those who like to laugh at most things, señor— no, let me call you Richard, and you shall call me Dolores, for we must remain friends always. Let us make a compact, then it will be impossible for us to quarrel. You shall be free to doubt, question, laugh at everything, except one thing only— my faith in Santa Coloma."

"Yes, I will gladly make that agreement," I replied. "It will be a new kind of paradise, and of the fruit of every tree I may eat except of this tree only."

She laughed gaily.

"I will now leave you," she said. "You are suffering pain, and are very tired. Perhaps you will be able to sleep." While speaking she brought a second cushion for my head, then left me, and before long I fell into a refreshing dose.

I spent three days of enforced idleness at the Casa Blanca, as the house was called, before Santa Coloma returned, and after the rough experience I had undergone, during which I had subsisted on a flesh diet untempered by bread or vegetables, they were indeed like days spent in paradise to me. Then the General came back. I was sitting alone in the garden when he arrived and coming out to me he greeted me warmly.

"I greatly feared from my previous experience of your impatience under restraint that you might have left us," he said kindly.

"I could not do that very well yet without a horse to ride on," I returned.

"Well, I came here just now to say I wish to present you with a horse and saddle. The horse is standing at the gate now, I believe; but if you are only waiting for a horse to leave us I shall have to regret making you this present. Do not be in a hurry; you have yet many years to live in which to accomplish all you wish to do, and let us have the pleasure of your company a few days longer. Doña Mercedes and her daughter desire nothing better than to keep you with them."

I promised him not to run away immediately, a promise which was not hard to make; then we went to inspect my horse, which proved to be a very fine bay, saddled with a dashing native *recado*.

"Come with me and try him," he said. "I am going to ride out to the Cerro Solo."

The ride proved an extremely pleasant one, as I had not mounted a horse for some days, and had been longing to spice my idle hours with a little exhilarating motion. We went at a swinging gallop over the grassy plain, the General all the time discoursing freely of his plans and of the brilliant prospects awaiting all those timely wise

individuals who should elect to link their fortunes
with his at this early stage of the campaign.

The Cerro, three leagues distant from the village of El Molino, was a high conical hill standing
quite alone and overlooking the country for a vast
distance around. A few well-mounted men were
stationed on the summit, keeping watch; and after
talking with them for a while the General led me
to a spot a hundred yards away, where there was
a large mound of sand and stone, up which we
made our horses climb with some difficulty. While
we stood here he pointed out the conspicuous objects on the surface of the surrounding country,
telling me the names of the estancias, rivers, distant hills, and other things. The whole country
about us seemed very familiar to him. He ceased
speaking at length, but continued gazing over the
wide sunlit prospect with a strange far-off look
on his face. Suddenly dropping the reins on the
neck of his horse, he stretched out his arms towards the south and began to murmur words which
I could not catch, while an expression of mingled
fury and exultation transformed his face. It
passed away as suddenly as it came. Then he dismounted, and stooping till his knee touched the
ground he kissed the rock before him, after which
he sat down and quietly invited me to do the
same. Returning to the subject he had talked
about during our ride, he began openly pressing
me to join him in his march to Montevideo, which,
he said, would begin almost immediately, and

would infallibly result in a victory, after which he would reward me for the incalculable service I had rendered him in assisting him to escape from the Juez of Las Cuevas. These tempting offers, which would have fired my brain in other circumstances—the single state, I mean—I felt compelled to decline, though I did not state my real reasons for doing so. He shrugged his shoulders in the eloquent Oriental fashion, remarking that it would not surprise him if I altered my resolution in a few days.

"Never!" I mentally ejaculated.

Then he recalled our first meeting again, spoke of Margarita, that marvellously beautiful child, asking if I had not thought it strange so fair a flower as that should have sprung from the homely stalk of a sweet potato? I answered that I had been surprised at first, but had ceased to believe that she was a child of Batata's, or of any of his kin. He then offered to tell me Margarita's history; and I was not surprised to hear that he knew it.

"I owe you this," he said, "in expiation of the somewhat offensive remarks I addressed to you that day in reference to the girl. But you must remember that I was then only Marcos Marcó, a peasant, and having some slight knowledge of acting it was only natural that my speech should be, as you find it in our common people, somewhat dry and ironical.

"Many years ago there lived in this country one

Basilio de la Barca, a person of so noble a figure and countenance that to all those who beheld him he became the type of perfect beauty, so that a 'Basilio de la Barca' came to be a proverbial expression in Montevidean society when anyone surpassingly handsome was spoken of. Though he had a gay, light-hearted disposition and loved social pleasures, he was not spoilt by the admiration his beauty excited. Simple-minded and modest he remained always; though perhaps not capable of any very strong passion, for though he won, without seeking it, the hearts of many fair women, he did not marry. He might have married some rich woman to improve his position had he been so minded, but in this, as in everything else in his life, Basilio appeared to be incapable of doing anything to advance his own fortunes. The de la Barcas had once possessed great wealth in land in the country, and, I have heard, descended from an ancient noble family of Spain. During the long, disastrous wars this country has suffered, when it was conquered in turn by England, Portugal, Spain, Brazil, and the Argentines, the family became impoverished and at last appeared to be dying out. The last of the de la Barcas was Basilio, and the evil destiny which had pursued all of that name for so many generations did not spare him. His whole life was a series of calamities. When young he entered the army, but in his first engagement he received a terrible wound which disabled him for life and compelled him to abandon the military career. After that he embarked all his little fortune in commerce and was ruined by a dishonest partner. At length when he had been reduced to great poverty, being then about forty years old, he married an old woman out of gratitude for the kindness she had shown to him; and with her he went to live on the sea-coast, several leagues east of Cabo Santa Maria. Here in a small rancho in a lonely spot called Barranca del Peregrino, and with only a few sheep and cows to subsist on, he spent the remainder of his life. His wife, though old, bore him one child, a daughter, named Transita. They taught her nothing; for in all respects they lived like peasants and had forgotten the use of books. The situation was also wild and solitary, and they very seldom saw a strange face. Transita spent her childhood in rambling over the dunes on that lonely coast, with only wild flowers, birds, and the ocean waves for playmates. One day, her age being then about eleven, she was at her usual pastimes, her golden hair blowing in the wind, her short dress and bare legs wet with the spray, chasing the waves as they retired, or flying with merry shouts from them as they hurried back towards the shore, flinging a cloud of foam over her retreating form, when a youth, a boy of fifteen, rode up and saw her there. He was hunting ostriches, when, losing sight of his companions, and finding himself near the ocean, he rode down to the shore to watch the tide coming in.

"Yes, I was that boy, Richard—you are quick in making conclusions." This he said not in reply to any remark I had made, but to my thoughts, which he frequently guessed very aptly.

"The impression this exquisite child made on me it would be impossible to convey in words. I had lived much in the capital, had been educated in our best college, and was accustomed to associate with pretty women. I had also crossed the water and had seen all that was most worthy of admiration in the Argentine cities. And remember, that with us a youth of fifteen already knows something of life. This child, playing with the waves, was like nothing I had seen before. I regarded her not as a mere human creature; she seemed more like some being from I know not what far-off celestial region who had strayed to earth, just as a bird of white and azure plumage and unknown to our woods, sometimes appears, blown hither from a distant tropical country or island, filling those who see it with wonder and delight. Imagine, if you can, Margarita with her shining hair loose to the winds, swift and graceful in her motions as the waves she plays with, her sapphire eyes sparkling like sunlight on the waters, the tender tints of the sea-shell in her ever-changing countenance, with a laughter that seems to echo the wild melody of the sandpiper's note. Margarita has inherited the form, not the spirit, of the child Transita. She is an exquisite statue endowed with life. Transita, with lines equally graceful

and colours just as perfect, had caught the spirit
of the wind and sunshine and was all freedom,
motion, fire—a being half human, half angelic.
I saw her only to love her; nor was it a common
passion she inspired in me. I worshipped her,
and longed to wear her on my bosom; but I shrank
then and for a long time after from breathing
the hot breath of love on so tender and heavenly
a blossom. I went to her parents and opened my
heart to them. My family being well known to
Basilio, I obtained his consent to visit their lonely
rancho whenever I could; and I, on my part,
promised not to speak of love to Transita till her
sixteenth year. Three years after I had found
Transita, I was ordered to a distant part of the
country, for I was already in the army then, and
fearing that it would not be possible for me to
visit them for a long time, I persuaded Basilio
to let me speak to his daughter, who was now
fourteen. She had by this time grown extremely
fond of me, and she always looked forward with
delight to my visits, when we would spend days
together rambling along the shore, or seated on
some cliff overlooking the sea, talking of the
simple things she knew, and of that wonderful,
far-away city life of which she was never tired
of hearing. When I opened my heart to her she
was at first frightened at these new strange emotions I spoke of. Soon, however, I was made
happy by seeing her fear grow less. In one day
she ceased to be a child; the rich blood mantled

her cheeks to leave her the next moment pale and tremulous; her tender lips were toying with the rim of the honeyed cup. Before I left her she had promised me her hand, and at parting even clung to me, with her beautiful eyes wet with tears.

"Three years passed before I returned to seek her. During that time I sent scores of letters to Basilio, but received no reply. Twice I was wounded in fight, once very seriously. I was also a prisoner for several months. I made my escape at last, and returning to Montevideo obtained leave of absence. Then, with heart afire with sweet anticipations, I sought that lonely sea-coast once more, only to find the weeds growing on the spot where Basilio's rancho had stood. In the neighbourhood I learnt that he had died two years before, and that after his death the widow had returned to Montevideo with Transita. After long inquiry in that city I discovered that she had not long survived her husband, and that a foreign señora had taken Transita away, no one knew whither. Her loss cast a great shadow on my life. Poignant grief cannot endure for ever, nor for very long; only the memory of grief endures. To this memory, which cannot fade, it is perhaps due that in one respect at least I am not like other men. I feel that I am incapable of passion for any woman. No, not if a new Lucrezia Borgia were to come my way, scattering the fiery seeds of adoration upon all men, could they blossom to

love in this arid heart. Since I lost Transita I
have had one thought, one love, one religion, and
it is all told in one word—*Patria*.

"Years passed. I was captain in General Oribe's
army at the siege of my own city. One day a lad
was captured in our lines, and came very near
being put to death as a spy. He had come out
from Montevideo, and was looking for me. He
had been sent, he said, by Transita de la Barca,
who was lying ill in the town, and desired to speak
to me before she died. I asked and obtained permission from our General, who had a strong personal friendship for me, to penetrate into the
town. This was, of course, dangerous, and more
so for me, perhaps, than it would have been for
many of my brother officers, for I was very well
known to the besieged. I succeeded, however, by
persuading the officers of a French sloop of war
stationed in the harbour to assist me. These foreigners at that time had friendly relations with
the officers of both armies, and three of them had
at one time visited our General to ask him to let
them hunt ostriches in the interior. He passed
them on to me, and taking them to my own estancia, I entertained them and hunted with them
for several days. For this hospitality they had
expressed themselves very grateful, inviting me
repeatedly to visit them on board, and also saying
that they would gladly do me any personal service
in the town, which they visited constantly. I love
not the French, believing them to be the most

vain and egotistical, consequently the least chivalrous, of mankind; but these officers were in my
debt, and I resolved to ask them to help me.
Under cover of night I went on board their ship;
I told them my story, and asked them to take me
on shore with them disguised as one of themselves.
With some difficulty they consented, and I was
thus enabled next day to be in Montevideo and
with my long-lost Transita. I found her lying
on her bed, emaciated and white as death, in the
last stage of some fatal pulmonary complaint. On
the bed with her was a child between two and three
years old, exceedingly beautiful like her mother,
for one glance was sufficient to tell me it was
Transita's child. Overcome with grief at finding
her in this pitiful condition, I could only kneel
at her side pouring out the last tender tears that
have fallen from these eyes. We Orientals are
not tearless men, and I have wept since then, but
only with rage and hatred. My last tears of
tenderness were shed over unhappy, dying
Transita.

"Briefly she told me her story. No letter from
me had ever reached Basilio; it was supposed that
I had fallen in battle, or that my heart had
changed. When her mother lay dying in Montevideo she was visited by a wealthy Argentine lady
named Romero, who had heard of Transita's singular beauty, and wished to see her merely out of
curiosity. She was so charmed with the girl that
she offered to take her and bring her up as her own

daughter. To this the mother, who was reduced to the greatest poverty and was dying, consented gladly. Transita was in this way taken to Buenos Ayres, where she had masters to instruct her, and lived in great splendour. The novelty of this life charmed her for a time; the pleasures of a large city, and the universal admiration her beauty excited, occupied her mind and made her happy. When she was seventeen the Señora Romero bestowed her hand on a young man of that city, named Andrada, a wealthy person. He was a fashionable man, a gambler, and a Sybarite, and having conceived a violent passion for the girl, he succeeded in winning over the señora to aid his suit. Before marrying him Transita told him frankly that she felt incapable of great affection for him; he cared nothing for that, he only wished, like the animal he was, to possess her for her beauty. Shortly after marrying her he took her to Europe, knowing very well that a man with a full purse, and whose spirit is a compound of swine and goat, finds life pleasanter in Paris than in the Plata. In Paris Transita lived a gay, but an unhappy life. Her husband's passion for her soon passed away, and was succeeded by neglect and insult. After three miserable years he abandoned her altogether to live with another woman, and then, in broken health, she returned with her child to her own country. When she had been several months in Montevideo she heard casually that I was still alive and in the besieging army;

and anxious to impart her last wishes to a friend, had sent for me.

"Could you, my friend, could any man, divine the nature of that dying request Transita wished to make?

"Pointing to her child, she said, 'Do you not see that Margarita inherits that fatal gift of beauty which won for me a life of splendour, with extreme bitterness of heart and early death? Soon, before I die, perhaps, there will not be wanting some new Señora Romero to take charge of her, who will at last sell her to some rich, cruel man, as I was sold; for how can her beauty remain long concealed? It was with very different views for her that I secretly left Paris and returned here. During all the miserable years I spent there I thought more and more of my childhood on that lonely coast, until, when I fell ill, I resolved to go back there to spend my last days on that beloved spot where I had been so happy. It was my intention to find some peasant family there who would be willing to take Margarita and bring her up as a peasant's child, with no knowledge of her father's position and of the life men live in towns. The siege and my failing health made it impossible for me to carry out that plan. I must die here, dear friend, and never see that lonely coast where we have sat together so often watching the waves. But I think only of poor little Margarita now, who will soon be motherless: will you not help me to save her? Promise me that you will take her away to some distant place, where she will be brought up as a peasant's child, and where her father will never find her. If you can promise me this, I will resign her to you now, and face death without even the sad consolation of seeing her by me to the last.'

"I promised to carry out her wishes, and also to see the child as often as circumstances would allow, and when she grew up to find her a good husband. But I would not deprive her of the child then. I told her that if she died, Margarita would be conveyed to the French ship in the harbour, and afterwards to me, and that I knew where to place her with good-hearted, simple peasants who loved me, and would obey my wishes in all things.

"She was satisfied, and I left her to make the necessary arrangements to carry out my plans. A few weeks later Transita expired, and the child was brought to me. I then sent her to Batata's house, where, ignorant of the secret of her birth, she has been brought up as her mother wished her to be. May she never, like the unhappy Transita, fall into the power of a ravening beast in man's shape."

"Amen!" I exclaimed. "But surely, if this child will be entitled to a fortune some day, it will only be right that she should have it."

"We do not worship gold in this country," he replied. "With us the poor are just as happy as the rich, their wants are so few, and easily satisfied. It would be too much to say that I love the child more than I love anyone else; I think only of Transita's wishes; that for me is the only right in the matter. Had I failed to carry them out to the letter, then I should have suffered a great remorse. Possibly I may encounter Andrada some day, and pass my sword through his body; that would give me no remorse."

After some moments of silence he looked up and said, "Richard, you admired and loved that beautiful girl when you first saw her. Listen, if you wish it you shall have her for a wife. She is simple-minded, ignorant of the world, affectionate, and where she is told to love she will love. Batata's people will obey my wishes in everything."

I shook my head, smiling somewhat sorrowfully when I thought that the events of the last few days had already half obliterated Margarita's fair image from my mind. This unexpected proposition had, moreover, forced on me, with a startling suddenness, the fact that by once performing the act of marriage a man has for ever used up the most glorious privilege of his sex—of course, I mean in countries where he is only allowed to have one wife. It was no longer in my power to say to any woman, however charming I might find her, "Be my wife." But I did not explain all this to the General.

"Ah, you are thinking of conditions," said he; "there will be none."

"No, you have guessed wrong—for once," I returned. "The girl is all you say; I have never seen a being more beautiful, and I have never heard a more romantic story than the one you have just told me about her birth. I can only echo your prayer that she may not suffer as her mother did. In name she is not a de la Barca, and perhaps destiny will spare her on that account."

He glanced keenly at me and smiled. "Perhaps you are thinking more of Dolores than of Margarita just now," he said. "Let me warn you of your danger there, my young friend. She is already promised to another."

Absurdly unreasonable as it may seem, I felt a jealous pang at that information; but then, of course, we are *not* reasonable beings, whatever the philosophers say.

I laughed, not very gaily, I must confess, and answered that there was no need to warn me, as Dolores would never be more to me than a very dear friend.

Even then I did not tell him that I was a married man; for often in the Banda Oriental I did not quite seem to know how to mix my truth and lies, and so preferred to hold my tongue. In this instance, as subsequent events proved, I held it not wisely but too well. The open man, with no secrets from the world, often enough escapes disasters which overtake your very discreet person, who acts on the old adage that speech was given to us to conceal our thoughts.

CHAPTER XVII

PASSION VERSUS PATRIOTISM

With a horse to travel on, and my arm so much better that the sling supporting it was worn rather for ornament than use, there was nothing except that promise not to run away immediately to detain me longer in the pleasant retreat of the Casa Blanca; nothing, that is, had I been a man of gutta-percha or cast-iron; being only a creature of clay—very impressionable clay as it happened—I could not persaude myself that I was quite well enough to start on that long ride over a disturbed country. Besides, my absence from Montevideo had already lasted so long that a few days more could not make much difference one way or the other; thus it came to pass that I still stayed on enjoying the society of my new friends, while every day, every hour in fact, I felt less able to endure the thought of tearing myself away from Dolores.

Much of my time was spent in the pleasant orchard adjoining the house. Here, growing in picturesque irregularity, were fifty or sixty old peach, nectarine, apricot, plum, and cherry trees, their boles double the thickness of a man's thigh; they had never been disfigured by the pruner's knife or saw, and their enormous size and rough bark overgrown with grey lichen gave them an appearance of great antiquity. All about the ground, tangled together in a pretty confusion, flourished many of those dear familiar Old World garden flowers that spring up round the white man's dwelling in all temperate regions of the earth. Here were immemorial wallflowers, stocks and marigolds, tall hollyhock, gay poppy, brilliant bachelor's button; also, half hid amongst the grass, pansy and forget-me-not. The larkspur, red, white, and blue, flaunted everywhere; and here, too, was the unforgotten sweet-william, looking bright and velvety as of yore, yet, in spite of its brightness and stiff, green collar, still wearing the old shame-faced expression, as if it felt a little ashamed of its own pretty name. These flowers were not cultivated, but grew spontaneously from the seed they shed year by year on the ground, the gardener doing nothing for them beyond keeping the weeds down and bestowing a little water in hot weather. The solstitial heats being now over, during which European garden flowers cease to bloom for a season, they were again in gayest livery to welcome the long second spring of autumn, lasting from February to May. At the further end of this wilderness of flowers and fruit trees was an aloe hedge, covering a width of twenty to third yards with its enormous, disorderly, stave-like leaves. This hedge was like a strip of wild nature placed alongside of a plot of man's im-

proved nature; and here, like snakes hunted from
the open, the weeds and wildings which were not
permitted to mix with the flowers had taken
refuge. Protected by that rude bastion of spikes,
the hemlock opened feathery clusters of dark
leaves with whitish umbels wherever it could reach
up to the sunshine. There also grew the night-
shade, with other solanaceous weeds, bearing little
clusters of green and purple berries, wild oats, fox-
tail grass, and nettles. The hedge gave them
shelter, but no moisture, so that all these weeds
and grasses had a somewhat forlorn and starved
appearance, climbing up with long stringy stems
among the powerful aloes. The hedge was also
rich in animal life. There dwelt mice, cavies, and
elusive little lizards; crickets sang all day long
under it, while in every open space the green
epeiras spread their geometric webs. Being rich
in spiders it was a favourite hunting-ground of
those insect desperadoes, the mason-wasps, that
flew about loudly buzzing in their splendid gold
and scarlet uniform. There were also many little
shy birds here, and my favourite was the wren,
for in its appearance and its scolding, jerky, ges-
ticulating ways it is precisely like our house-wren,
though it has a richer and more powerful song
than the English bird. On the other side of the
hedge was the *potrero*, or paddock, where a milch-
cow with two or three horses were kept. The man-
servant, whose name was Nepomucino, presided
over orchard and paddock, also to some extent

over the entire establishment. Nepomucino was a pure negro, a little old round-headed, bleareyed man, about five feet four in height, the short, lumpy wool on his head quite grey; slow in speech and movement, his old black or chocolate-coloured fingers all crooked, stiff-jointed, and pointing spontaneously in different directions. I have never seen anything in the human subject to equal the dignity of Nepomucino, the profound gravity of his bearing and expression forcibly reminding one of an owl. Apparently he had come to look upon himself as the sole head and master of the establishment, and the sense of responsibility had more than steadied him. The negrine propensity to frequent explosions of inconsequent laughter was not, of course, to be expected in such a sober-minded person; but he was, I think, a little too sedate for a black, for although his face would shine on warm days like polished ebony, it did not smile. Everyone in the house conspired to keep up the fiction of Nepomucino's importance; they had, in fact, conspired so long and so well, that it had very nearly ceased to be a fiction. Everybody addressed him with grave respect. Not a syllable of his long name was ever omitted—what the consequences of calling him Nepo, or Cino, or Cinito, the affectionate diminutive, would have been I am unable to say, since I never had the courage to try the experiment. It often amused me to hear Doña Mercedes calling to him from the house, and throwing the whole emphasis on the last syllable in a long, piercing crescendo—"Ne—po—mu—ci—no—o." Sometimes, when I sat in the orchard, he would come, and placing himself before me, discourse gravely about things in general, clipping his words and substituting r for l in the negro fashion, which made it hard for me to repress a smile. After winding up with a few appropriate moral reflections he would finish with the remark—"For though I am black on the surface, señor, my heart is white"; and then he would impressively lay one of his old crooked fingers on the part where the physiological curiosity was supposed to be. He did not like being told to perform menial offices, preferring to anticipate all requests of that kind and do whatever was necessary by stealth. Sometimes I would forget this peculiarity of the old black, and tell him that I wanted him to polish my boots. He would ignore the request altogether, and talk for a few minutes of political matters, or on the uncertainty of all things mundane, and by-and-by, glancing at my boots, would remark incidentally that they required polishing, offering somewhat ostentatiously to have them done for me. Nothing would make him admit that he did these things himself. Once I tried to amuse Dolores by mimicking his speech to her, but she quickly silenced me, saying that she loved Nepomucino too well to allow even her best friend to laugh at him. He had been born when blacks were slaves in the service of her family, had carried her in his arms when she was an infant, and

had seen all the male members of the house of
Zelaya swept away in the wars of Reds and
Whites; but in the days of their adversity his
faithful dog-like affection had never failed them.
It was beautiful to see her manner towards him.
If she wanted a rose for her hair or dress she would
not pluck it herself or allow me to get it for her,
but Nepomucino must be asked to get it. Then
every day she would find time to sit down in the
garden by his side to tell him all the news of the
village and of the country at large, discuss the
position of affairs with him, and ask his advice
about everything in the house.

In doors or out I generally had Dolores for a
companion, and I could certainly not have had a
more charming one. The civil war—though the
little splutter on the Yí scarcely deserved that
name yet—was her unfailing theme. She was
never weary of singing her hero Santa Coloma's
praises—his dauntless courage and patience in defeat; his strange romantic adventures; the innumerable disguises and stratagems he had re-
sorted to when going about in his own country,
where a price was set on his head; ever labouring
to infuse fresh valour into his beaten, disheartened
followers. That the governing party had any
right to be in power, or possessed any virtue of
any kind, or were, in fact, anything but an incubus
and a curse to the Banda Orientál, she would not
for one moment admit. To her mind her country
always appeared like Andromeda bound on her

rock and left weeping and desolate to be a prey to the abhorred Colorado monster; while ever to the deliverance of this lovely being came her glorious Perseus, swift as the winds of heaven, the lightnings of terrible vengeance flashing from his eyes, the might of the immortals in his strong right arm. Often she tried to persuade me to join this romantic adventurer, and it was hard, very hard, to resist her eloquent appeals, and perhaps it grew harder every day as the influence of her passionate beauty strengthened itself upon my heart. Invariably I took refuge in the argument that I was a foreigner, that I loved my country with an ardour equal to hers, and that by taking arms in the Banda Orientál I should at once divest myself of all an Englishman's rights and privileges. She scarcely had patience to listen to this argument, it seemed so trivial to her, and when she demanded other better reasons I had none to offer. I dared not quote to her the words of sulky Achilles—

The distant Trojans never injured me,

for that argument would have sounded even weaker to her than the former one. She had never read Homer in any language, of course, but she would have quickly made me tell her about Achilles, and when the end came with miserable Hector dragged thrice round the walls of besieged Troy—Montevideo was called Modern Troy, she knew—then she would have turned my argument against me and bidden me go and serve the Uruguayan President as Achilles served Hector. Seeing me silent she would turn indignantly away; only for a moment, however; the bright smile would quickly return and she would exclaim, "No, no, Richard, I shall not forget my promise, though I sometimes think you try to make me do so."

It was noon: the house was quiet, for Doña Mercedes had retired after breakfast to take her unfailing siesta, leaving us to our conversation. In that spacious, cool room where I had first reposed in the house, I was lying on the sofa smoking a cigarette. Dolores, seating herself near me with her guitar, said, "Now let me play and sing you to sleep with something very soft." But the more she played and sang the further was I from unneeded slumber.

"What, not sleeping yet, Richard!" she would say with a little laugh after each song.

"Not yet, Dolores," I would reply, pretending to get drowsy. "But my eyes are getting heavy now. One more song will send me to the region of dreams. Sing me that sweet favourite—

Desde aquel doloroso momento.

At length, finding that my sleepiness was all pretence, she refused to sing any more, and presently we drifted once more into the old subject.

"Ah yes," she replied to that argument about my nationality, which was my only shield, "I have always been taught to believe foreigners a cold, practical, calculating kind of people—so different from us. You never seemed to me like a foreigner; ah, Richard, why will you make me remember that you are not one of us! Tell me, dear friend, if a beautiful woman cried out to you to deliver her from some great misfortune or danger, would you stop to ask her nationality before going to her rescue?"

"No, Dolores; you know that if you, for instance, were in distress or danger I would fly to your side and risk my life to save you."

"I believe you, Richard. But tell me, is it less noble to help a suffering people cruelly oppressed by wicked men who have succeeded by crimes and treachery and foreign aid in climbing into power? Will you tell me that no Englishman has drawn a sword in a cause like that? Oh, friend, is not my mother-country more beautiful and worthy to be helped than any woman? Has not God given her spiritual eyes that shed tears and look for comfort; lips, sweeter than any woman's lips, that cry bitterly every day for deliverance? Can you look on the blue skies above you and walk on the green grass where the white and purple flowers smile up at you and be deaf and blind to her beauty and to her great need? Oh, no, no, it is impossible!"

"Ah, if you were a man, Dolores, what a flame you would kindle in the hearts of your countrymen!"

"Yes, if I were a man!" she exclaimed, starting to her feet; "then I should serve my country not with words only; then I would strike and bleed for her—how willingly! Being only a weak woman, I would give my heart's blood to win one arm to aid in the sacred cause."

She stood before me with flashing eyes, her face glowing with enthusiasm; then I also rose to my feet and took her hands in mine, for I was intoxicated with her loveliness and almost ready to throw all restraints to the winds.

"Dolores," I said, "are not your words extravagant? Shall I test their sincerity? Tell me, would you give even as much as one kiss with your sweet lips to win a strong arm for your country?"

She turned crimson and cast her eyes down; then, quickly recovering herself, answered—

"What do your words mean? Speak plainly, Richard."

"I cannot speak plainer, Dolores. Forgive me if I have offended once more. Your beauty and grace and eloquence have made me forget myself."

Her hands were moist and trembling in mine, still she did not withdraw them. "No, I am not offended," she returned in a strangely low tone. "Put me to the test, Richard. Do you wish me to understand clearly that for such a favour as that you would join us?"

"I cannot say," I replied, still endeavouring to be prudent, though my heart was on fire and my words when I spoke seemed to choke me. "But, Dolores, if you would shed your blood to win one strong arm, will you think it too much to bestow the favour I spoke of in the hope of winning an arm?"

She was silent. Then drawing her closer I touched her lips with mine. But who was ever satisfied with that one touch on the lips for which the heart has craved? It was like contact with a strange celestial fire that instantly kindled my love to madness. Again and yet again I kissed her; I pressed her lips till they were dry and burned like fire, then kissed cheek, forehead, hair, and casting my arms about her strained her to my breast in a long passionate embrace; then the violence of the paroxysm was over, and with a pang I released her. She trembled: her face was whiter than alabaster, and covering it with her hands she sank down on the sofa. I sat down beside her and drew her head down on my breast, but we remained silent, only our hearts were beating very fast. Presently she disengaged herself, and without bestowing one glance on me rose and left the room.

Before long I began to blame myself bitterly for this imprudent outburst. I dared not hope to continue longer on the old familiar footing. So high-spirited and sensitive a woman as Dolores would not easily be brought to forget or forgive my conduct. She had not repelled me, she had even tacitly consented to that one first kiss, and was therefore partly to blame herself; but her extreme pallor, her silence and cold manner had plainly shown me that I had wounded her. My passion had overcome me, and I felt that I had compromised myself. For that one first kiss I had all but promised to do a certain thing, and not to do it now seemed very dishonourable, much as I shrank from joining the Blanco rebels. I had proposed the thing myself; she had silently con-- sented to the stipulation. I had taken my kiss and much more, and having now had my delirious evanescent joy, I could not endure the thought of meanly skulking off without paying the price.

I went out full of trouble and paced up and down in the orchard for two or three hours, hoping that Dolores might come to me there, but I saw no more of her that day. At dinner Doña Mercedes was excessively affable, showing clearly that she was not in her daughter's confidence. She informed me, simple soul! that Dolores was suffering from a grievous headache caused by taking a glass of claret at breakfast after eating a slice of watermelon, an imprudence against which she did not omit to caution me.

Lying awake that night—for the thought that I had pained and offended Dolores made it impossible for me to sleep—I resolved to join Santa Coloma immediately. That act alone would salve my conscience, and I only hoped that it would serve to win back the friendship and esteem of the woman I had learned to love too well. I had

no sooner determined on taking this step than I
began to see so many advantages in it that it
seemed strange I had not taken it before; but we
lose half our opportunities in life through too
much caution. A few more days of adventure, all
the pleasanter for being spiced with danger, and
I would be once more in Montevideo with a host
of great and grateful friends to start me in some
career in the country. Yes, I said to myself, becoming enthusiastic, once this oppressive, scan-
dalous, and besotted Colorado party is swept with
bullet and steel out of the country, as of course it
will be, I shall go to Santa Coloma to lay down
my sword, resuming by that act my own nationality, and as sole reward of my chivalrous conduct
in aiding the rebellion, ask for his interest in
getting me placed, say, at the head of some large
estancia in the interior. There, possibly on one
of his own establishments, I shall be in my element
and happy, hunting ostriches, eating *carne con
cuero*, possessing a *tropilla* of twenty cream-coloured horses for my private use, and building up
a modest fortune out of hides, horns, tallow, and
other native products. At break of day I rose and
saddled my horse; then finding the dignified Nepomucino, who was the early bird (blackbird) of
the establishment, told him to inform his mistress
that I was going to spend the day with General
Santa Coloma. After taking a maté from the old
fellow I mounted and galloped out of the village
of Molino.

Arrived at the camp, which had been moved to a distance of four or five miles from El Molino, I found Santa Coloma just ready to mount his horse to start on an expedition to a small town eight or nine leagues distant. He at once asked me to go with him, and remarked that he was very much pleased, though not surprised, at my having changed my mind about joining him. We did not return till late in the evening, and the whole of the following day was spent in monotonous cavalry exercises. I then went to the General and requested permission to visit the Casa Blanca to bid adieu to my friends there. He informed me that he intended going to El Molino the next morning himself and would take me with him. The first thing he did on our arrival at the village was to send me to the principal storekeeper in the place, a man who had faith in the Blanco leader, and was rapidly disposing of a large stock of goods at a splendid profit, receiving in payment sundry slips of paper signed by Santa Coloma. This good fellow, who mixed politics with business, provided me with a complete and much-needed outfit, which included a broadcloth suit of clothes, soft brown hat rather broad in the brim, long riding-boots, and poncho. Going back to the official building or headquarters in the plaza I received my sword, which did not harmonise very well with the civilian costume I wore; but I was no worse off in this respect than forty-nine out of every fifty men in our little army.

In the afternoon we went together to see the ladies, and the General had a very hearty welcome from both of them, as I also had from Doña Mercedes, while Dolores received me with the utmost indifference, expressing no pleasure or surprise at seeing me wearing a sword in the cause which she had professed to have so much at heart. This was a sore disappointment, and I was also nettled at her treatment of me. After dinner, over which we sat talking some time, the General left us, telling me before doing so to join him in the plaza at five o'clock next morning. I then tried to get an opportunity of speaking to Dolores alone, but she studiously avoided me, and in the evening there were several visitors, ladies from the town with three or four officers from the camp, and dancing and singing were kept up till towards midnight. Finding that I could not speak to her, and anxious about my appointment at five in the morning, I at length retired sorrowful and baffled to my apartment. Without undressing I threw myself on my bed, and being very much fatigued with so much riding about I soon fell asleep. When I woke the brilliant light of the moon, shining in at open window and door, made me fancy it was already daylight, and I quickly sprang up. I had no means of telling the time, except by going into the large living-room, where there was an old eight-day clock. Making my way thither, I was amazed to see, on entering it, Dolores in her white dress sitting beside the open window in a dejected attitude. She started and rose up when I entered, the extreme pallor of her face heightened by contrast with her long raven-black hair hanging unbound on her shoulders.

"Dolores, do I find you here at this hour?" I exclaimed.

"Yes," she returned coldly, sitting down again. "Do you think it very strange, Richard?"

"Pardon me for disturbing you," I said; "I came here to find out the time from your clock."

"It is two o'clock. Is that all you came for? Did you imagine I could retire to sleep without first knowing what your motive was in returning to this house? Have you then forgotten everything?"

I came to her and sat down by the window before speaking. "No, Dolores," I said; "had I forgotten, you would not have seen me here enlisted in a cause which I looked on only as your cause."

"Ah, then you have honoured the Casa Blanca with this visit not to speak to me—that you considered unnecessary—but merely to exhibit yourself wearing a sword!"

I was stung by the extreme bitterness of her tone. "You are unjust to me," I said. "Since that fatal moment, when my passion overcame me I have not ceased thinking of you, grieving that I had offended you. No, I did not come to exhibit my sword, which is not worn for ornament; I came only to speak to you, Dolores, and you pur- posely avoided me."

"Not without reason," she retorted quickly. "Did I not sit quietly by you after you had acted in that way towards me, waiting for you to speak —to explain, and you were silent? Well, señor, I am here now, waiting again."

"This then is what I have to say," I replied. "After what passed I considered myself bound in honour to join your cause, Dolores. What more can I say except to implore your forgiveness? Be- lieve me, dear friend, in that moment of passion I forgot everything—forgot that I—forgot that your hand was already given to another."

"Given to another? What do you mean, Rich- ard? Who told you that?"

"General Santa Coloma."

"The General? What right has he to occupy himself with my affairs? This is a matter that concerns myself only, and it is presumption on his part to interfere in it."

"Do you speak in that tone of your hero, Dolores? Remember that he only warned me of my danger out of pure friendship. But his warn- ing was thrown away; my unhappy passion, the sight of your loveliness, your own incautious words, were too much for my heart."

She dropped her face on her hands and re- mained silent.

"I have suffered for my fault, and must suffer

more. Will you not say you forgive me, Dolores?" I said, offering my hand.

She took it, but continued silent.

"Say, dearest friend, that you forgive me, that we part friends."

"Oh, Richard, must we part then?" she murmured.

"Yes—now, Dolores; for, before you are up, I must be on horseback and on my way to join the troops. The march to Montevideo will probably commence almost immediately."

"Oh, I cannot bear it!" she suddenly exclaimed, taking my hand in both hers. "Let me open my heart to you now. Forgive me, Richard, for being so angry with you, but I did not know the General had said such a thing. Believe me, he imagines more than he knows. When you took me in your arms and held me against your breast it was a revelation to me. I cannot love or give my hand to any other man. You are everything in the world to me now, Richard; must you leave me to mingle in this cruel civil strife in which all my dearest friends and relations have perished?"

She had had her revelation; I now had mine, and it was an exceedingly bitter one. I trembled at the thought of confessing my secret to her, now when she had so unmistakably responded to the passion I had insanely revealed.

Suddenly she raised her dark, luminous eyes to mine, anger and shame struggling for mastery on her pale face.

"Speak, Richard!" she exclaimed. "Your silence at this moment is an insult to me."

"For God's sake, have mercy on me, Dolores," I said. "I am not free—I have a wife."

For some moments she sat staring fixedly at me, then flinging my hand from her, covered her face. Presently she uncovered it again, for shame was overcome and cast out by anger. She rose and stood up before me, her face very white.

"You have a wife—a wife whose existence you concealed from me till this moment!" she said. "Now you ask for mercy when your secret has been wrung from you! Married, and you have dared to take me in yours arms, to excuse yourself afterwards with the plea of passion! Passion —do you know what it means, traitor? Ah no; a breast like yours cannot know any great or generous emotion. Would you have dared show your face to me again had you been capable of shame even? And you judged my heart as shallow as your own, and after treating me in that way thought to win my forgiveness and admiration even by parading before me with a sword! Leave me, I can feel nothing but contempt for you. Go; you are a disgrace to the cause you have espoused!"

I had sat utterly crushed and humiliated, not daring even to raise my sight to her face, for I felt that my own unspeakable weakness and folly had brought this tempest upon me. But there is a limit to patience, even in the most submissive mood; and when that was overpassed, then my anger blazed out all the more hotly for the penitential meekness I had preserved during the whole interview. Her words from the first had fallen like whip-cuts, making me writhe with the pain they inflicted; but that last taunt stung me beyond endurance. I, an Englishman, to be told that I was a disgrace to the Blanco cause, which I had joined in spite of my better judgment purely out of my romantic devotion to this very woman! I too was now upon my feet, and there face to face we stood for some moments, silent and trembling. At length I found my speech.

"This," I cried, "from the woman who was ready yesterday to shed her heart's blood to win one strong arm for her country? I have renounced everything, allied myself with abhorred robbers and cut-throats, only to learn that her one desire is everything to her, her divine, beautiful country nothing. I wish that a man had spoken those words to me, Dolores, so that I might have put this sword you speak of to one good use before breaking it and flinging it from me like the vile thing it is! Would to God the earth would open and swallow up this land for ever, though I sank down into hell with it for the detestable crime of taking part in its pirate wars!"

She stood perfectly still, gazing at me with widely dilated eyes, a new expression coming into her face; then when I paused for her to speak, expecting only a fresh outburst of scorn and bitterness, a strange, sorrowful smile flitted over her lips, and coming close to me she placed her hand on my shoulder.

"Oh," she said, "what a strength of passion you are capable of! Forgive me, Richard, for I have forgiven you. Ah, we were made for each other, and it can never, never be."

She dropped her head dejectedly on my shoulder. My anger vanished at those sad words; love only remained—love mingled with profoundest compassion and remorse for the pain I had inflicted. Supporting her with my arm, I tenderly stroked her dark hair, and stooping pressed my lips against it.

"Do you love me so much, Dolores," I said, "enough even to forgive the cruel, bitter words I have just spoken? Oh, I was mad—mad to say such things to you, and shall repent it all my life long! How cruelly have I wounded you with my love and my anger! Tell me, dearest Dolores, can you forgive me?"

"Yes, Richard; everything. Is there any word you can speak, any deed you can do, and I not forgive it? Does your wife love you like that— can you love her as you love me? How cruel destiny is to us! Ah, my beloved country, I was ready to shed my blood for you—just to win one strong arm to fight for you, but I did not dream that this would be the sacrifice required of me. Look, it will soon be time for you to go—we cannot sleep now, Richard. Sit down here with me, and let us spend this last hour together with my hand in yours, for we shall never, never, never meet again."

And so sitting there hand in hand we waited for the dawn, speaking many sad and tender words to one another; and at last when we parted I held her once more unresisting to my breast, thinking, as she did, that our separation would be an eternal one.

CHAPTER XVIII

REST ON THY ROCK, ANDROMEDA!

About the stirring events of the succeeding days I have little to relate, and no reader who has suffered the malady of love in its acutest form will wonder at it. During those days I mixed with a crowd of adventurers, returned exiles, criminals, and malcontents, every one of them worth studying; the daylight hours were passed in cavalry exercises or in long expeditions about the country, while every evening beside the camp fire romantic tales enough to fill a volume were told in my hearing. But the image of Dolores was ever before my mind, so that all this crowded period, lasting nine or ten days, passed before me like a phantasmagoria, or an uneasy dream, leaving only a very confused impression on my brain. I not only grieved for the sorrow I had occasioned her, but mourned also that my own heart had so terribly betrayed me, so that for the moment the beautiful girl I had persuaded to fly from home and parents, promising her my undying affection, had ceased to be what she had been, so great was this new inconvenient passion. The General had offered me a commission in his tatterdemalion gathering, but as I had no knowledge of military matters, I had prudently declined it, only requesting, as a special favour, that I might be employed constantly on the expeditions he sent out over the surrounding country to beat up recruits, seize arms, cattle, and horses, and to depose the little local authorities in the villages, putting creatures of his own in their places. This request had been granted, so that morning, noon, and night I was generally in the saddle.

One evening I was in the camp seated beside a large fire and gloomily staring into the flames, when the other men, who were occupied playing cards or sipping maté, hastily rose to their feet, making the salute. Then I saw the General standing near gazing fixedly at me. Motioning to the men to resume their cards, he sat down by my side.

"What is the matter with you?" he said. "I have noticed that you are like a different person since you joined us. Do you regret that step?"

"No," I answered, and then was silent, not knowing what more to say.

He looked searchingly at me. Doubtless some suspicion of the truth was in his mind; for he had gone to the Casa Blanca with me, and it was scarcely likely that his keen eyes had failed to notice the cold reception Dolores gave me on that occasion. He did not, however, touch on that matter.

"Tell me," he said at length, "what can I do for you?"

I laughed. "What can you do except to take me to Montevideo?" I replied.

"Why do you say that?" he returned quickly.

"We are not merely friends now as we were before I joined you," I said. "You are my General; I am simply one of your men."

"The friendship remains just the same, Richard. Let me know frankly what you think of this campaign, since you have now suddenly turned the current of the conversation in that direction?"

There was a slight sting in the concluding words, but I had, perhaps, deserved it. "Since you bid me speak," I said, "I, for one, feel very much disappointed at the little progress we are making. It seems to me that before you are in a position to strike, the enthusiasm and courage of your people will have vanished. You cannot get anything like a decent army together, and the few men you have are badly armed and undisciplined. Is it not plain that a march to Montevideo in these circumstances is impossible, that you will be obliged to retire into the remote and difficult places to carry on a guerilla war?"

"No," he returned; "there is to be no guerilla war. The Colorados made the Orientals sick of it, when that arch-traitor and chief of cut-throats, General Rivera, desolated the Banda for ten years. We must ride on to Montevideo soon. As for the character of my force, that is a matter it would perhaps be useless to discuss, my young friend. If I could import a well-equipped and disciplined

army from Europe to do my fighting, I should do
so. The Oriental farmer, unable to send to England for a threshing-machine, is obliged to go out
and gather his wild mares from the plain to tread
out his wheat, and I, in like manner, having only a
few scattered ranchos to draw my soldiers from,
must be satisfied to do what I can with them. And
now tell me, are you anxious to see something done
at once—a fight, for instance, in which we might
possibly be the losers?"

"Yes, that would be better than standing still.
If you are strong, the best thing you can do is to
show your strength."

He laughed. "Richard, you were made for an
Oriental," he said, "only nature at your birth
dropped you down in the wrong country. You
are brave to rashness, abhor restraint, love women,
and have a light heart; the Castilian gravity you
have recently assumed is, I fancy, only a passing
mood."

"Your words are highly complimentary and fill
me with pride," I answered, "but I scarcely see
their connection with the subject of our conversation."

"There is a connection, nevertheless," he returned pleasantly. "Though you refuse a commission from me, I am so convinced that you
are in heart one of us that I will take you into my
confidence and tell you something known to only
half a dozen trusted individuals here. You rightly
say that if we have strength we must show it to

the country. That is what we are now about to do. A cavalry force has been sent against us and we shall engage it before two days are over. As far as I know, the forces will be pretty evenly balanced, though our enemies will, of course, be better armed. We shall choose our own ground; and should they attack us tired with a long march, or if there should be any disaffection amongst them, the victory will be ours, and after that every Blanco sword in the Banda will be unsheathed in our cause. I need not repeat to you that in the hour of my triumph, if it ever comes, I shall not forget my debt to you; my wish is to bind you, body and heart, to this Oriental country. It is, however, possible that I may suffer defeat, and if in two days' time we are all scattered to the winds, let me advise you what to do. Do not attempt to return immediately to Montevideo, as that might be dangerous. Make your way by Minas to the southern coast; and when you reach the department of Rocha, inquire for the little settlement of Lomas de Rocha, a village three leagues west of the lake. You will find there a storekeeper, one Florentino Blanco—a Blanco in heart as well. Tell him I sent you to him, and ask him to procure you an English passport from the capital; after which it will be safe for you to travel to Montevideo. Should you ever be identified as a follower of mine, you can invent some story to account for your presence in my force. When I remember that botanical lecture you once delivered, also some other matters, I am convinced that you are not devoid of imagination."

After giving some further kind advice, he bade me good night, leaving me with a strangely unpleasant conviction in my mind that we had changed characters for the nonce, and that I had bungled as much in my new part as I had formerly done in my old. He had been sincerity itself, while I, picking up the discarded mask, had tied it on, probably upside down, for it made me feel excessively uncomfortable during our interview. To make matters worse, I was also sure that it had quite failed to hide my countenance, and that he knew as well as I knew myself the real cause of the change he had noticed in me.

These disagreeable reflections did not trouble me long, and then I began to feel considerable excitement at the prospect of a brush with the government troops. My thoughts kept me awake most of the night; still, next morning, when the trumpet sounded its shrill reveillé close at hand, I rose quickly and in a much more cheerful mood than I had known of late. I began to feel that I was getting the better of that insane passion for Dolores which had made us both so unhappy, and when we were once more in the saddle the "Castilian gravity," to which the General had satirically alluded, had pretty well vanished.

No expeditions were sent out that day; after we had marched about twelve or thirteen miles eastward and nearer to the immense range of the

Cuchilla Grande we encamped, and after the mid-day meal spent the afternoon in cavalry exercises.

On the next day happened the great event for which we had been preparing, and I am positive that with the wretched material he commanded, no man could have done more than Santa Coloma, though, alas! all his efforts ended in disaster. Alas, I say, not because I took, even then, any very serious interest in Oriental politics, but because it would have been greatly to my advantage if things had turned out differently. Besides, a great many poor devils who had been an unconscionable time out in the cold would have come into power, and the rascally Colorados sent away in their turn to eat the "bitter bread" of proscription. The fable of the fox and the flies might here possibly occur to the reader: I, however, preferred to remember Lucero's fable of the tree called Montevideo, with the chattering colony in its branches, and to look upon myself as one in the majestic bovine army about to besiege the monkeys and punish them for their naughty behaviour.

Quite early in the morning we had breakfast, then every man was ordered to saddle his best horse; for every one of us was the owner of three or four steeds. I, of course, saddled the horse the General had given me, which had been re-served for important work. We mounted and pro-ceeded at a gentle pace through a very wild and broken country still in the direction of the Cu-chilla. About midday scouts came riding in and reported that the enemy were close upon us. After halting for half an hour, we again proceeded at the same gentle pace till about two o'clock, when we crossed the Cañada de San Paulo, a deep valley beyond which the plain rose to a height of about one hundred and fifty feet. In the cañada we stopped to water our horses, and there heard that the enemy were advancing along it at a rapid pace, evidently hoping to cut off our supposed retreat towards the Cuchilla. Crossing the little stream of San Paulo, we began slowly ascending the sloping plain on the further side till the highest point was gained; then turning we saw the enemy, numbering about seven hundred men, beneath us spread out in a line of extraordinary length. Up from the valley they came towards us at a brisk trot. We were then rapidly disposed in three columns, the centre one numbering about two hundred and fifty men, the others about two hundred men each. I was in one of the outside columns, within about four men from the front. My fellow-soldiers, who had hitherto been very light-hearted and chatty, had suddenly become grave and quiet, some of them even looking pale and scared. On one side of me was an irrepressible scamp of a boy about eighteen years old, a dark little fellow, with a monkey face and a feeble falsetto voice like a very old woman. I watched him take out a small sharp knife and without looking down draw it across the upper part of his surcingle three of four times; but this he did evidently only for practice, as he did not cut into the hide. Seeing me watching, he grinned mysteriously and made a sign with head and shoulders thrust forward in imitation of a person riding away at full speed, after which he restored his knife to its sheath.

"You intend cutting your surcingle and running away, little coward?" I said.

"And what are you going to do?" he returned.

"Fight," I said.

"It is the best thing you can do, Sir Frenchman," said he, with a grin.

"Listen," I said, "when the fight is over, I will look you up to thrash you for your impertinence in calling me a Frenchman."

"After the fight!" he exclaimed, with a funny grimace. "Do you mean next year? Before that distant time arrives some Colorado will fall in love with you, and——and——and——"

Here he explained himself without words by drawing the edge of his hand briskly across his throat, then closing his eyes and making gurgling sounds, supposed to be uttered by a person undergoing the painful operation of having his throat cut.

Our colloquy was carried on in whispers, but his pantomimic performance drew on us the attention of our neighbours, and now he looked round to inform them with a grin and a nod that his Oriental wit was getting the victory. I was determined not to be put down by him, however, and tapped my revolver with my hand to call his attention to it.

"Look at this, you young miscreant," I said. "Do you not know that I and many others in this column have received orders from the General to shoot down every man who attempts to run away?"

This speech effectually silenced him. He turned as pale as his dark skin would let him and looked round like a hunted animal in search of a hole to hide in.

On my other hand a grizzly-bearded old gaucho, in somewhat tattered garments, lit a cigarette and, oblivious of everything except the stimulating fragrance of the strongest black tobacco, expanded his lungs with long inspirations to send forth thereafter clouds of blue smoke into his neighbours' faces, scattering the soothing perfume over a third portion of the army.

Santa Coloma rose equal to the occasion; swiftly riding from column to column he addressed each in turn, and using the quaint expressive phraseology of the gauchos, which he knew so well, poured forth his denunciations of the Colorados with a fury and eloquence that brought the blood with a rush to many of his followers' pale cheeks. They were traitors, plunderers, assasisns, he cried; they had committed a million crimes, but all these things were nothing, nothing compared with that one black crime which no other political party had been guilty of. By the aid of Brazilian gold and Brazilian bayonets they had risen to power; they were the infamous pensioners of the empire of slaves. He compared them to the man who marries a beautiful wife and sells her to some rich person so as to live luxuriously on the wages of his own dishonour. The foul stain which they had brought on the honour of the Banda Orientál could only be washed away with their blood. Pointing to the advancing troops, he said that when those miserable hirelings were scattered like thistle-down before the wind, the entire country would be with him, and the Banda Orientál, after half a century of degradation, free at last and for ever from the Brazilian curse.

Waving his sword, he galloped back to the front of his column greeted by a storm of *vivas*.

Then a great silence fell upon our ranks; while up the slope, their trumpets sounding merrily, trotted the enemy, till they had covered about three hundred yards of the ascending ground, threatening to close us round in an immense circle, when suddenly the order was given to charge, and led by Santa Coloma we thundered down the incline upon them.

Soldiers reading this plain unvarnished account of an Oriental battle might feel inclined to criticise Santa Coloma's tactics; for his men were, like the Arabs, horsemen and little else; they were, moreover, armed with lance and broadsword, weapons requiring a great deal of space to be used effectively. Yet, considering all the circumstances, I am sure that he did the right thing. He knew that he was too weak to meet the enemy in the usual way, pitting man against man; also that if he failed to fight, his temporary prestige would vanish like smoke and the rebellion collapse. Having decided to hazard all, and knowing that in a stand-up fight he would infallibly be beaten, his only plan was to show a bold front, mass his feeble followers together in columns and hurl them upon the enemy, hoping by this means to introduce a panic amongst his opponents and so snatch the victory.

A discharge of carbines with which we were received did us no damage. I, at any rate, saw no saddles emptied near me, and in a few moments we were dashing through the advancing lines. A shout of triumph went up from our men, for our cowardly foes were flying before us in all directions. On we rode in triumph till we reached the bottom of the hill, then we reined up, for before us was the stream of San Paulo, and the few scattered men who had crossed it and were scuttling away like hunted ostriches scarcely seemed worth chasing. Suddenly with a great shout a large body of Colorados came thundering down the hill on our rear and flank, and dismay seized upon us. The feeble efforts made by some of our officers to bring us round to face them proved unavailing. I am utterly unable to give any clear account of what followed immediately after that, for we were all, friends and foes, mixed up for some minutes in the wildest confusion, and how I ever got out

of it all without a scratch is a mystery to me.
More than once I was in violent collision with
Colorado men, distinguished from ours by their
uniform, and several furious blows with sword
and lance were aimed at me, but somehow I escaped them all. I emptied the six chambers of my
Colt's revolver, but whether my bullets did any
execution or not I cannot pretend to say. In the
end I found myself surrounded by four of our
men who were furiously spurring their horses out
of the fight.

"Whip up, Captain, come with us this way,"
shouted one of them who knew me, and who always insisted on giving me a title to which I had
no right.

As we rode away, skirting the hill towards the
south, he assured me that all was lost, in proof of
which he pointed to scattered bodies of our men
flying from the field in all directions. Yes, we
were defeated; that was plain to see, and I needed
little encouragement from my fellow-runaways
to spur my horse to its utmost speed. Had the
falcon eye of Santa Coloma rested on me at that
moment he might have added to the list of Oriental traits he had given me the un-English faculty
of knowing when I was beaten. I was quite as
anxious, I believe, to save my skin—*throat,* we say
in the Banda Oriental—as any horseman there,
not even excepting the monkey-faced boy with the
squeaky voice.

If the curious reader, thirsting for knowledge,

will consult the Uruguayan histories, I daresay he will find a more scientific description of the battle of San Paulo than I have been able to give. My excuse must be, that it was the only battle— pitched or other—at which I have ever assisted, also that my position in the Blanco forces was a very humble one. Altogether I am not overproud of my soldiering performances; still, as I did no worse than Frederick the Great of Prussia, who ran away from his first battle, I do not consider that I need blush furiously. My companions took our defeat with the usual Oriental resignation. "You see," said one in explanation of his mental attitude, "there must always be one side defeated in every fight, for had we gained the day then the Colorados would have lost." There was in this remark a sound practical philosophy; it could not be controverted, it burdened our brains with no new thing, and it made us all very cheerful. For myself, I did not care very much, but could not help thinking a great deal of Dolores, who would now have a fresh grief to increase her pain.

For a distance of three or four miles we rode at a fast gallop, then on the slopes of the Cuchilla paused to breathe our horses, and, dismounting, stood for some time gazing back over the wide landscape spread out before us. At our backs rose the giant green and brown walls of the sierras, the range stretching away on either hand in violet and deep blue masses. At our feet lay the billowy green and yellow plain, vast as ocean, and channelled by innumerable streams, while one black patch on a slope far away showed us that our foes were camping on the very spot where they had overcome us. Not a cloud appeared in the immense heavens, only low down in the west purple and rose-coloured vapours were beginning to form, staining the clear intense whity-blue sky about the sinking sun. Over all reigned deep silence; until, suddenly, a flock of orange and flame-coloured orioles with black wings swept down on a clump of bushes hard by and poured forth a torrent of wild joyous music. A strange performance! screaming notes that seemed to scream jubilant gladness to listening heaven, and notes abrupt and guttural mingling with others more clear and soul-piercing than ever human lips drew from reed or metal. It soon ended; up sprang the vocalists like a fountain of fire and fled away to their roost among the hills, then silence reigned once more. What brilliant hues, what gay fantastic music! were they indeed birds, or the glad winged inhabitants of a mystic region, resembling earth, but sweeter than earth and never entered by death, upon whose threshold I had stumbled by chance? Then, while the last rich flood of sunshine came over the earth from that red everlasting urn resting on the far horizon, I could, had I been alone, have cast myself upon the ground to adore the great God of Nature, who had given me this precious moment of life. For here the religion that languishes in crowded cities or steals shame-faced to hide itself in dim churches flourishes greatly, filling the soul with a solemn joy. Face to face with nature on the vast hills at eventide, who does not feel himself near to the Unseen?

> Out of his heart God shall not pass:
> His image stampèd in on every grass.

My comrades, anxious to get through the Cuchilla, were already on horseback shouting to me to mount. One more lingering glance over that wide prospect—wide, yet how small a portion of the Banda's twenty thousand miles of everlasting verdure, watered by innumerable beautiful streams? Again the thought of Dolores swept like a moaning wind over my heart. For this rich prize, her beautiful country, how weakly and with what feeble hands had we striven! Where now was her hero, the glorious deliverer Perseus? Lying, perhaps, stark and stained with blood on yon darkening moor. Not yet was the Colorado monster overcome. "Rest on thy rock, Andromeda!" I sadly murmured, then leaping into the saddle galloped away after my retreating comrades, already half a mile away down in the shadowy mountain pass.

CHAPTER XIX

TALES OF THE PURPLE LAND

BEFORE it had been long dark, we had crossed the range and into the department of Minas. Nothing happened till towards midnight, when our horses began to be greatly distressed. My companions hoped to reach before morning an estancia, still many leagues distant, where they were known and would be allowed to lie in concealment for a few days till the storm blew over; for usually shortly after an outbreak has been put down an *indulto*, or proclamation of pardon, is issued, after which it is safe for all those who have taken arms against the constituted government to return to their homes. For the time we were, of course, outlaws, and liable to have our throats cut at any moment. Our poor horses at last became incapable even of a trot, and, dismounting, we walked on, leading them by the bridles.

About midnight we approached a watercourse, the upper part of the Rio Barriga Negra—Black Belly River—and on coming near it the tinkling of a bell attracted our attention. It is the usual thing for every man in the Banda Orientál to have one mare, called *madrina*, in his *tropilla*, or herd of geldings; the *madrina* always carries a bell attached to her neck, and at night her fore feet are usually hobbled to prevent her wandering far from home; for the horses are always very much attached to her and will not leave her.

After listening for a few moments, we concluded that the sound came from the bell of a *madrina*, and that her fore feet were bound, for the tinkle came in violent jerks as from an animal laboriously hopping along. Proceeding to the spot, we found a *tropilla* of eleven or twelve dun-coloured horses feeding near the river. Driving them very gently towards the bank, where a sharp bend in the stream enabled us to corner them, we set to work catching fresh horses. Fortunately they were not very shy of strangers, and after we had caught and secured the *madrina*, they gathered whinnying round her, and we were not very long in selecting the five best-looking duns in the herd.

"My friends, I call this stealing," I said, though at that very moment I was engaged in hastily transferring my saddle to the animal I had secured.

"That is very interesting information," said one of my comrades.

"A stolen horse will always carry you well," said another.

"If you cannot steal a horse without compunction, you have not been properly brought up," cried the third.

"In the Banda Oriental," said the fourth, "you are not looked upon as an honest man unless you steal."

We then crossed the river and broke into a swift gallop, which we kept up till morning, reaching our destination a little while before sunrise. There was here a fine plantation of trees not far from the house, surrounded by a deep ditch and a cactus hedge, and after we had taken maté and then breakfast at the house, where the people received us very kindly, we proceeded to conceal our horses and ourselves in the plantation. We found a comfortable little grassy hollow, partly shaded with the surrounding trees, and here we spread our rugs, and fatigued with our exertions soon dropped into a deep sleep which lasted pretty well all day. It was a pleasant day for me, for I had waking intervals during which I experienced that sensation of absolute rest of mind and body which is so exceedingly sweet after a long period of toil and anxiety. During my waking intervals I smoked cigarettes and listened to the querulous pipings of a flock of young black-headed siskins flying about from tree to tree after their parents and asking to be fed.

Occasionally the long clear sky of the venteveo, a lemon-coloured bird with black head and long beak like a kingfisher, rung through the foliage; or a flock of pecho amarillos, olive-brown birds with bright yellow vests, would visit the trees and utter their confused chorus of gay notes.

I did not think very much about Santa Coloma. Probably he had escaped, and was once more a wanderer disguised in the humble garments of a peasant; but that would be no new experience to him. The bitter bread of expatriation had apparently been his usual food, and his periodical descents upon the country had so far always ended in disaster: he had still an object to live for. But when I remembered Dolores lamenting her lost cause and vanished peace of mind, then, in spite of the bright sunshine flecking the grass, the soft, warm wind fanning my face and whispering in the foliage overhead, and the merry-throated birds that came to visit me, a pang was in my heart, and tears came to my eyes.

When evening came we were all wide awake and sat till a very late hour round the fire we had made in the hollow, sipping maté and conversing. We were all in a talkative mood that evening, and after the ordinary subjects of Banda Orientál conversation had been exhausted, we drifted into matters extraordinary—wild creatures of strange appearance and habits, apparitions, and marvellous adventures.

"The manner in which the lampalagua captures its prey is very curious," said one of the company, named Rivarola, a stout man with an immense fierce-looking black beard and moustache, but who was very mild-eyed and had a gentle, cooing voice.

We had all heard of the lampalagua, a species of boa found in these countries, with a very thick body and extremely sluggish in its motions. It preys on the larger rodents, and captures them, I believe, by following them into their burrows, where they cannot escape from its jaws by running.

"I will tell you what I once witnessed, for I have never seen a stranger thing," continued Rivarola. "Riding one day through a forest I saw some distance before me a fox sitting on the grass watching my approach. Suddenly I saw it spring high up into the air, uttering a great scream of terror, then fall back upon the earth, where it lay for some time growling, struggling, and biting as if engaged in deadly conflict with some invisible enemy. Presently it began to move away through the wood, but very slowly and still frantically struggling. It seemed to be getting exhausted, its tail dragged, the mouth foamed, and the tongue hung out, while it still moved on as if drawn by an unseen cord. I followed, going very close to it, but it took no notice of me. Sometimes it dug its claws into the ground or seized a twig or stalk with its teeth, and it would then remain resting for a few moments till the twig gave away, when it would roll over many times on the ground, loudly yelping, but still dragged onwards. Presently I saw in the direction we were going a huge serpent, thick as a man's thigh, its head lifted high above the grass, and motionless as a serpent of stone. Its cavernous, blood-red mouth was gaping wide, and its eyes were fixed on the struggling fox. When about twenty yards from the serpent, the fox began moving very rapidly over the ground, its struggles growing feebler every moment, until it seemed to fly through the air, and in an instant was in the serpent's mouth. Then the reptile dropped its head and began slowly swallowing its prey."

"And you actually witnessed this yourself?" said I.

"With these eyes," he returned, indicating the orbs in question by pointing at them with the tube of the maté-cup he held in his hand. "This was the only occasion on which I have actually seen the lampalagua take its prey, but its manner of doing it is well known to every one from hearsay. You see, it draws an animal towards it by means of its power of suction. Sometimes, when the animal attacked is very strong or very far off— say two thousand yards—the serpent becomes so inflated with the quantity of air inhaled while drawing the victim towards it——"

"That it bursts?" I suggested.

"That it is obliged to stop drawing to blow the wind out. When this happens, the animal, finding itself released from the drawing force, instantly sets off at full speed. Vain effort! The serpent has no sooner discharged the accumulated wind with a report like a cannon——"

"No, no, like a musket! I have heard it myself," interrupted Blas Aria, one of the listeners.

"Like a musket, than it once more brings its power of suction to bear; and in this manner the contest continues until the victim is finally drawn into the monster's jaws. It is well known that the lampalagua is the strongest of all God's creatures, and that if a man, stripped to the skin, engages one, and conquers it by sheer muscular strength, the serpent's power goes into him, after which he is invincible."

I laughed at this fable, and was severely rebuked for my levity.

"I will tell you the strangest thing that ever befell me," said Blas Aria. "I happened to be travelling alone—for reasons—on the northern frontier. I crossed the river Yaguaron into Brazilian territory, and for a whole day rode through a great marshy plain, where the reeds were dead and yellow, and the water shrunk into muddy pools. It was a place to make a man grow weary of life. When the sun was going down, and I began to despair of getting to the end of this desolation, I discovered a low hovel made of mud and thatched with rushes. It was about fifteen yards long, with only one small door, and seemed to be uninhabited, for no person answered me when I rode round it shouting aloud. I heard a grunting and squealing within, and by-and-by a sow, followed by a litter of young pigs, came out, looked at me, then went in again. I would have ridden on, but my horses were tired; besides, a great storm with thunder and lightning was coming up, and no other shelter appeared in sight. I therefore unsaddled, loosed my horses to feed, and took my gear into the hovel. The room I entered was so small that the sow and her young

occupied all the floor; there was, however, another room, and opening the door, which was
closed, I went into it and found that it was very
much larger than the first; also, that it contained a
dirty bed made of skins in one corner, while on
the floor was a heap of ashes and a black pot.
There was nothing else except old bones, sticks,
and other rubbish littering the floor. Afraid of
being caught unawares by the owner of this foul
den, and finding nothing to eat in it, I returned to
the first room, turned the pigs out of doors, and
sat down on my saddle to wait. It was beginning
to get dark when a woman, bringing in a bundle
of sticks, suddenly appeared at the door. Never,
sirs, have I beheld a fouler, more hideous object
than this person. Her face was hard, dark, and
rough like the bark of the ñandubuy tree, while
her hair, which covered her head and shoulders in
a tangled mass, was of a dry earthy colour. Her
body was thick and long, yet she looked like a
dwarf, for she scarcely had any legs, only enormous knees and feet; her garments were old
ragged horserugs tied round her body with thongs
of hide. She stared at me out of a pair of small
black rat eyes, then, setting down her bundle,
asked me what I wanted. I told her I was a tired
traveller, and wanted food and shelter. 'Shelter
you can have: food there is none," she said; then,
taking up her sticks, she passed to the inner room
and secured it with a bolt on the inside. She had
not inspired me with love, and there was little

danger of my attempting to intrude on her there. It was a black, stormy night, and very soon the rain began to fall in torrents. Several times the sow, with her young pigs loudly squealing, came in for shelter, and I was forced to get up and beat them out with my whip. At length, through the mud partition separating the two rooms, I heard the crackling of a fire which the vile woman was lighting; and, before long, through the chinks came the savoury smell of roast meat. That surprised me greatly, for I had searched the room and failed to find anything to eat in it. I concluded that she had brought in the meat under her garments, but where she had got it was a mystery. At length I began to doze. There were many sounds in my ear as of thunder and wind, the pigs grunting at the door, and the crackling of the fire in the hag's room. But by-and-by other sounds seemed to mingle with these—voices of several persons talking, laughing, and singing. At length I became wide awake, and found that these voices proceeded from the next room. Some person was playing a guitar and singing, then others were loudly talking and laughing. I tried to peep through the cracks in the door and partition, but could not see through them. High up in the middle of the wall there was one large crack through which I was sure the interior could be seen, so much red firelight streamed through it. I placed my saddle against the partition, and all my rugs folded small, one above the other, until I had heaped them as high as my knees. Standing on my toes on this pile, and carefully clinging to the wall with my fingernails, I managed to bring my eyes to a level with the crack, and peeped through it. The room inside was brightly lighted by a big wood fire burning at one end, while on the floor a large crimson cloak was spread, on which the people I had heard were sitting with some fruit and bottles of wine before them. There was the foul hag looking almost as tall sitting as she had appeared when standing; she was playing on a guitar and singing a ballad in Portuguese. Before her on the cloak lay a tall well-formed negro woman, wearing only a narrow white cloth round her loins, and broad silver armlets on her round black arms. She was eating a banana, and against her knees, which were drawn up, sat a beautiful girl about fifteen years old, with a dark pale face She was dressed in white, her arms were bare and round her head she wore a gold band keeping back her black hair, which fell unbound on her back. Before her, on his knees on the cloak, was an old man with a face brown and wrinkled as a walnut, and beard white as thistledown. With one of his hands he was holding the girl's arm, and with the other offering her a glass of wine. All this I saw at one glance, and then all of them together turned their eyes up at the crack as if they knew that someone was watching them. I started back in alarm, and fell with a crash to the ground. Then I heard loud screams of laughter, but I dared not

attempt to look in on them again. I took my rugs
to the further side of the room, and sat down to
wait for morning. The talking and laughter continued for about two hours, then it gradually died
away, the light faded from the chinks, and all was
dark and silent. No person came out; and at
last, overcome with drowsiness, I fell asleep. It
was day when I woke. I rose and walked round
the hovel, and finding a crack in the wall, I peered
into the hag's room. It looked just as I had seen
it the day before; there was the pot and pile of
ashes, and in the corner the brutish woman lying
asleep in her skins. After that I got on to my
horse and rode away. May I never again have
such an experience as I had that night."

Something was then said about witchcraft by
the others, all looking very solemn.

"You were very hungry and tired that night,"
I ventured to remark, "and perhaps after the
woman locked her door you went to sleep and
dreamed all that about people eating fruit and
playing on the guitar."

"Our horses were tired and we were flying for
our lives yesterday," returned Blas contemptu-
ously. "Perhaps it made us dream that we caught
five dun horses to carry us."

"When a person is incredulous, it is useless
arguing with him," said Mariano, a small dark
grey-haired man. "I will now tell you a strange
adventure I had when I was a young man; but
remember I do not put a blunderbuss to any man's

breast to compel him to believe me. For what is, is; and let him that disbelieves shake his head till he shakes it off, and it falls to the ground like a cocoanut from the tree.

"After I got married I sold my horses, and taking all my money purchased two ox-carts, intending to make my living by carrying freight. One cart I drove myself, and to drive the other I hired a boy whom I called Mula, though that was not the name his godfathers gave him, but because he was stubborn and sullen as a mule. His mother was a poor widow, living near me, and when she heard about the ox-carts she came to me with her son and said, "Neighbour Mariano, for your mother's sake, take my son and teach him to earn his bread, for he is a boy that loves not to do anything.' So I took Mula and paid the widow for his services after each journey. When there was no freight to be had I sometimes went to the lagoons to cut rushes, and loading the carts with them we would go about the country to sell the rushes to those who required them to thatch their houses. Mula loved not this work. Often when we were all day wading up to our thighs in the water, cutting the rushes down close to their roots, then carrying them in large bundles on our shoulders to land, he would cry, complaining bitterly of his hard lot. Sometimes I thrashed him, for it angered me to see a poor boy so fastidious: then he would curse me and say that some day he would have his revenge. 'When I am dead,' he often told me, 'my ghost will come to haunt and terrify you for all the blows you have given me.' This always made me laugh.

"At last, one day, while crossing a deep stream, swollen with rains, my poor Mula fell down from his perch on the shaft and was swept away by the current into deep water and drowned. Well, sirs, about a year after that event I was out in search of a couple of strayed oxen when night overtook me a long distance from home. Between me and my house there was a range of hills running down to a deep river, so close that there was only a narrow passage to get through, and for a long distance there was no other opening. When I reached the pass I fell into a narrow path with bushes and trees growing on either side; here, suddenly, the figure of a young man stepped out from the trees and stood before me. It was all in white—poncho, *chiripà*, drawers, even its boots, and wore a broad-brimmed straw hat on its head. My horse stood still trembling; nor was I less frightened, for my hair rose up on my head like bristles on a pig's back; and the sweat broke out on my face like raindrops. Not a word said the figure; only it remained standing still with arms folded on its breast, preventing me from passing. Then I cried out, 'In Heaven's name, who are you, and what do you want with Mariano Montes de Oca, that you bar his path?' At this speech it laughed; then it said, 'What, does my old master not know me? I am Mula; did I not often tell you that some day I should return to pay you out for all the thrashings you gave me? Ah, Master Mariano, you see I have kept my word!' Then it began to laugh again. 'May ten thousand curses light on your head!' I shouted. 'If you wish for my life, Mula, take it and be for ever damned; or else let me pass, and go back to Satan, your master, and tell him from me to keep a stricter watch on your movements; for why should the stench of purgatory be brought to my nostrils before my time! And now, hateful ghost, what more have you got to say to me?' At this speech the ghost shouted with laughter, slapping its thighs, and doubling itself up with mirth. At last, when it was able to speak, it said, 'Enough of this fooling, Mariano. I did not intend frightening you so much; and it is no great matter if I have laughed a little at you now, for you have often made me cry. I stopped you because I had something important to say. Go to my mother and tell her you have seen and spoken with me; tell her to pay for another mass for my soul's repose, for after that I shall be out of purgatory. If she has no money lend her a few dollars for the mass, and I will repay you, old man, in another world.'

"This it said and vanished. I lifted my whip but needed not to strike my horse, for not a bird that has wings could fly faster than he now flew with me on his back. No path was before me, nor did I know where we were going. Through rushes and through thickets, over burrows of wild animals, stones, rivers, marshes, we flew as if all the devils that are on the earth and under it were at our heels; and when the horse stopped it was at my own door. I stayed not to unsaddle him, but cutting the surcingle with my knife left him to shake the saddle off; then with the bridle I hammered on the door shouting to my wife to open. I heard her fumbling for the tinder-box. 'For the love of Heaven, woman, strike no light,' I cried. '*Santa Barbara bendita!* have you seen a ghost?' she exclaimed, opening to me. 'Yes,' I replied, rushing in and bolting the door, 'and had you struck a light you would now have been a widow.'

"For thus it is, sirs, the man who after seeing a ghost is confronted with a light immediately drops down dead."

I made no sceptical remarks, and did not even shake my head. The circumstances of the encounter were described by Mariano with such graphic power and minuteness that it was impossible not to believe his story. Yet some things in it afterwards struck me as somewhat absurd; that straw hat, for instance, and it also seemed strange that a person of Mula's disposition should have been so much improved in temper by his sojourn in a warmer place.

"Talking of ghosts," said Laralde, the other man—but proceeded no further, for I interrupted him. Laralde was a short, broad-chested man, with bow legs and bushy grey whiskers; he was called by his familiars Lechuza (owl) on account of his immense round tawny-coloured eyes, which had a tremendous staring power in them.

I thought we had had enough of the supernatural by this time.

"My friend," I said, "pardon me for interrupting you; but there will be no sleep for us to-night if we have any more stories about spirits from the other world."

"Talking of ghosts," resumed Lechuza, without noticing my remark, and this nettled me; so I cut in once more——

"I protest that we have heard quite enough about them," I said. "This conversation was only to be about rare and curious things. Now, visitors from the other world are very common. I put it to you, my friends—have you not all seen more ghosts than lampalaguas drawing foxes with their breath?"

"I have seen that once only," said Rivarola gravely. "I have often seen ghosts."

The others also confessed to having seen more than one ghost apiece.

Lechuza sat inattentive, smoking his cigarette, and when we had all done speaking began again——

"Talking of ghosts——"

Nobody interrupted him this time, though he seemed to expect it, for he made a long, deliberate pause.

"Talking of ghosts," he repeated, staring around him triumphantly, "I once had an encounter with a strange being that was *not* a ghost.

I was a young man then—young and full of the fire, strength and courage of youth—for what I am now going to relate happened over twenty years ago. I had been playing cards at a friend's house, and left it at midnight to ride to my father's house, a distance of five leagues. I had quarrelled that evening and left a loser, burning with anger against the man who had cheated and insulted me, and with whom I was not allowed to fight. Vowing vengeance on him, I rode away at a fast gallop; the night being serene, and almost as light as day, for the moon was at its full. Suddenly I saw before me a huge man sitting on a white horse, which stood perfectly motionless directly in my path. I dashed on till I came near him, then shouted aloud, 'Out of my path, friend, lest I ride over you'; for I was still raging in my heart.

"Seeing that he took no notice of my words, I dug my spurs into my horse and hurled myself against him; then at the very moment my horse struck his with a tremendous shock, I brought down my iron whip-handle with all the force that was in me upon his head. The blow rang as if I had struck upon an anvil, while at the same moment he, without swerving, clutched my cloak with both hands. I could feel that they were bony, hard hands, armed with long, crooked, sharp talons like an eagle's, which pierced through my cloak into my flesh. Dropping my whip, I seized him by the throat, which seemed scaly and hard, between my hands, and thus, locked together in a desperate struggle, we swayed this way and that, each trying to drag the other from his seat till we came down together with a crash upon the earth. In a moment we were disengaged and on our feet. Quick as lightning flashed out his long, sharp weapon, and finding I was too late to draw mine I hurled myself against him, seizing his armed hand in both mine before he could strike. For a few moments he stood still, glaring at me out of a pair of eyes that shone like burning coals; then mad with rage, he flung me off my feet and whirled me round and round like a ball in a sling, and finally cast me from him to a distance of a hundred yards, so great was his strength. I was launched with tremendous force into the middle of some thorny bushes, but had no sooner recovered from the shock than out I burst with a yell of rage and charged him again. For, you will hardly believe it, sirs, by some strange chance I had carried away his weapon, firmly grasped in my hands. It was a heavy two-edged dagger, sharp as a needle, and while I grasped the hilt I felt the strength and fury of a thousand fighting-men in me. As I advanced he retreated before me, until, seizing the topmost boughs of a great thorny bush he swung his body to one side and wrenched it out of the earth by the roots. Swinging the bush with the rapidity of a whirlwind round his head, he advanced against me and dealt a blow that would have crushed me had it descended on me; but it fell too far, for I had dodged under it to close with him and delivered a stab with such power that the long weapon was buried to its hilt in his bosom. He uttered a deafening yell, and at the same moment a torrent of blood spouted forth, scalding my face like boiling water, and drenching my clothes through to the skin. For a moment I was blinded; but when I had dashed the blood from my eyes and looked round he had vanished, horse and all.

"Then mounting my horse I rode home and told every one what had happened, showing the knife, which I still carried in my hand. Next day all the neighbours gathered at my house, and we rode in company to the spot where the fight had taken place. There we found the bush torn up by the roots, and all the earth about it ploughed up where we had fought. The ground was also dyed with blood for several yards around, and where it had fallen the grass was withered up to the roots, as if scorched with fire. We also picked up a cluster of hairs—long, wiry, crooked hairs, barbed at the ends like fish-hooks; also three or four scales like fish-scales, only rougher, and as large as doubloons. The spot where the fight took place is now called *La Cañada del Diablo*, and I have heard that since that day the devil has never appeared corporeally to fight any man in the Banda Oriental."

Lechuza's narrative gave great satisfaction. I said nothing, feeling half stupid with amazement,

for the man apparently told it in the full conviction that it was true, while the other listeners appeared to accept every word of it with the most
implicit faith. I began to feel very melancholy,
for evidently they expected something from me
now, and what to tell them I knew not. It went
against my conscience to be the only liar amongst
these exceedingly veracious Orientals, and so I
could not think of inventing anything.

"My friends," I began at length, "I am only a
young man; also a native of a country where marvellous things do not often happen, so that I can
tell you nothing to equal in interest the stories I
have heard. I can only relate a little incident
which happened to me in my own country before
I left it. It is trivial, perhaps, but will lead me to
tell you something about London—that great city
you have all heard of."

"Yes, we have heard of London; it is in England, I believe. Tell us your story about London," said Blas encouragingly.

"I was very young—only fourteen years old,"
I continued, flattering myself that my modest introduction had not been ineffective, "when one
evening I came to London from my home. It was
in January, in the middle of winter, and the
whole country was white with snow."

"Pardon me, Captain," said Blas, "but you have
got the cucumber by the wrong end. We say that
January is in summer."

"Not in my country, where the seasons are reversed," I said. "When I rose next morning it was dark as night, for a black fog had fallen upon the city."

"A black fog!" exclaimed Lechuza.

"Yes, a black fog that would last all day and make it darker than night, for though the lamps were lighted in the streets they gave no light."

"Demons!" exclaimed Rivarola; "there is no water in the bucket. I must go to the well for some or we shall have none to drink in the night."

"You might wait till I finish," I said.

"No, no, Captain," he returned. "Go on with your story; we must not be without water." And taking up the bucket he trudged off.

"Finding it was going to be dark all day," I continued, "I determined to go a little distanec away, not out of London, you will understand, but about three leagues from my hotel to a great hill, where I thought the fog would not be so dark, and where there is a palace of glass."

"A palace of glass!" repeated Lechuza, with his immense round eyes fixed sternly on me.

"Yes, a palace of glass—is there anything so wonderful in that?"

"Have you any tobacco in your pouch, Mariano?" said Blas. "Pardon, Captain, for speaking, but the things you are telling require a cigarette, and my pouch is empty."

"Very well, sirs, perhaps you will now allow me to proceed," I said, beginning to feel rather vexed at these constant interruptions. "A palace of glass large enough to hold all the people in this country."

"The Saints assist us! Your tobacco is dry as ashes, Mariano," exclaimed Blas.

"That is not strange," said the other, "for I have had it three days in my pocket. Proceed, Captain. A palace of glass large enough to hold all the people in the world. And then?"

"No, I shall not proceed," I returned, losing my temper. "It is plain to see that you do not wish to hear my story. Still, sirs, from motives of courtesy you might have disguised your want of interest in what I was about to relate; for I have heard it said that the Orientals are a polite people."

"There you are saying too much, my friend," broke in Lechuza. "Remember that we are speaking of actual experiences, not inventing tales of black fogs and glass palaces and men walking on their heads, and I know not what other marvels."

"Do you know that what I am telling you is untrue?" I indignantly asked.

"Surely, friend, you do not consider us such simple persons in the Banda Oriental as not to know the truth from fable?"

And this from the fellow who had just told us of his tragical encounter with Apollyon, a yarn which quite put Bunyan's narrative in the shade! It was useless talking; my irritation gave place to mirth, and stretching myself out on the grass I roared with laughter. The more I thought of

Lechuza's stern rebuke the louder I laughed, until I yelled with laughter, slapping my thighs and doubling myself up after the manner of Mariano's hilarious visitor from purgatory. My companions never smiled. Rivarola came back with the bucket of water and after staring at me for some time said, "If the tears, which they say always follow laughter, come in the same measure then we shall have to sleep in the wet."

This increased my mirth.

"If the whole country is to be informed of our hiding-place," said Blas the timid, "we were putting ourselves to an unnecessary trouble by running away from San Paulo."

Fresh screams of laughter greeted this protest.

"I once knew a man," said Mariano, "who had a most extraordinary laugh; you could hear it a league away, it was so loud. His name was Aniceto, but we called him El Burro on account of his laugh, which sounded like the braying of an ass. Well, sirs, he one day burst out laughing, like the Captain here, at nothing at all, and fell down dead. You see, the poor man had aneurism of the heart."

At this I fairly yelled, then, feeling quite exhausted, I looked apprehensively at Lechuza, for this important member of the quartet had not yet spoken.

With his immense unspeakably serious eyes fixed on me he remarked quietly, "And this, my friends, is the man who says it is wrong to steal horses!"

But I was past shrieking now. Even this rich specimen of topsy-turvy Banda Oriental morality only evoked a faint gurgling as I rolled about on the grass, my sides aching, as if I had received a good bruising.

CHAPTER XX

A GHASTLY GIFT

Day had just dawned when I rose to join Mariano at the fire he had already kindled to heat the water for his early maté. I did not like the idea of lying there concealed amongst the trees like some hunted animal for an indefinite time; moreover, I had been advised by Santa Coloma to proceed directly to the Lomas de Rocha, on the south coast, in the event of a defeat, and this now seemed to me the best thing to do. It had been very pleasant lying there "under the greenwood tree," while those veracious stories of hags, lampalaguas, and apparitions had proved highly entertaining; but a long spell, a whole month perhaps, of that kind of life was not to be thought of; and if I did not get to Rocha now, before the rural police were set to catch runaway rebels, it would perhaps be impossible to do so later on. I determined, therefore, to go my own way, and after drinking bitter maté, I caught and saddled the dun horse. I really had not deserved the severe censure Lechuza had passed on me the previous evening in reference to horse-stealing, for I had taken the dun with very little more compunction than one is accustomed to feel in England when "borrowing" an umbrella on a rainy day. To all people in all parts of the world, a time comes when to appropriate their neighbour's goods is held not only justifiable, but even meritorious: to Israelites in Egypt, Englishmen under a cloud in their own moist island, and to Orientals running away after a fight. By keeping the dun over thirty hours in my possession I had acquired a kind of prescriptive right to it, and now began to look on it as my very own; subsequent experience of his endurance and other good qualities enables me to endorse the Oriental saying that a "stolen horse carries you well."

Bidding farewell to my companions in defeat, who had certainly not been frightened out of their imaginations, I rode forth just when it was beginning to grow light. Roads and houses I studiously avoided, travelling on at an easy gallop, which took me about ten miles an hour, till noon; then I rested at a small rancho, where I fed and watered my horse and recruited my own energies with roast beef and bitter maté. On again till dark; by that time I had covered about forty miles and began to feel both hungry and tired. I had passed several ranchos and estancia-houses, but was shy of seeking entertainment at any of them, and so went further only to fare worse. When the brief twilight was darkening to night I came upon a broad cart-track, leading, I suppose, to Montevideo from the eastern part of the country, and seeing a long, low rancho near it, which I recognised as a *pulperia*, or store, by the flagstaff planted before it, I resolved to purchase some refreshment for myself, then to ride on a mile or two and spend the night under the stars—a safe roof if an airy one. Tying my horse to the gate, I went into the porch-like projection at the end of the rancho, which I found divided from the interior by the counter, with its usual grating of thick iron bars to protect the treasures of gin, rum, and comestibles from drunken or quarrelsome customers. As soon as I came into the porch I began to regret having alighted at the place, for there, standing at the counter, smoking and drinking, were about a dozen very rough-looking men. Unfortunately for me, they had tied their horses under the shadow of a clump of trees some distance from the gate, so that I had missed seeing them on my arrival. Once amongst them, however, my only plan was to disguise my uneasiness, be very polite, get my refreshments, then make my escape as speedily as possible. They stared rather hard at me, but returned my salutation courteously; then going to a disengaged corner of the counter I rested my left elbow on it and called for bread, a box of sardines, and a tumbler of wine.

"If you will join me, señores, the table is spread," said I; but they all declined my invitation with thanks, and I began to eat my bread and sardines.

They appeared to be all persons living in the immediate neighbourhood, for they addressed each other familiarly and were conversing about love matters. One of them, however, soon dropped out of the conversation, and edging away from the others stood a little space apart leaning against the wall on the side of the porch furthest from me. I began to notice this man very particularly, for it was plain to see that I had excited his interest in an extraordinary manner, and I did not like his scrutiny. He was, without exception, the most murderous-looking villain I have ever had the misfortune to meet: that was the deliberate opinion I came to before I formed a closer acquaintance with him. He was a broad-chested, powerful-looking man of medium height; his hands he kept concealed under the large cloth poncho he wore, and he had on a slouch hat that just allowed his eyes to be seen under the rim. They were truculent, yellowish-green eyes, that seemed to grow fiery and dim and fiery again by turns, yet never for a single instant were they averted from my face. His black hair hung to his shoulders, and he also had a bristly moustache, which did not conceal his brutal mouth, nor was there any beard to hide his broad, swarthy jowl. His jaws were the only part of him that had any motion, while he stood there, still as a bronze statue, watching me. At intervals he ground his teeth, after which he would slap his lips together two or three times, while a slimy froth, most sickening to see, gathered at the corners of his mouth.

"Gandara, you are not drinking," said one of the gauchos, turning to him. He shook his head slightly without speaking or taking his eyes off my face; whereupon the man who had spoken smiled and resumed his conversation with the others.

The long, intense, soul-trying scrutiny this brutal wretch had subjected me to came to a very sudden end. Quick as lightning a long, broad knife flashed out from its concealment under his poncho, and with one catlike bound he was before me, the point of his horrid weapon touching my poncho just over the pit of my stomach.

"Do not move, rebel," he said in a husky voice. "If you move one hair's-breadth, that moment you die."

The other men all ceased talking and looked on with some interest, but did not offer to interfere or make any remark.

For one moment I felt as if an electric shock had gone through me, and then instantly I was calm—never, in fact, have I felt more calm and collected than at that terrible moment. 'Tis a blessed instinct of self-preservation which nature has provided us with; feeble, timid men possess it in common with the strong and brave; just as weak, persecuted wild animals have it as well as those that are fierce and bloodthirsty. It is the calm which comes without call when death suddenly and unexpectedly rises up to stare us in the face; it tells us that there is one faint chance which a premature attempt to escape or even a slight agitation will destroy.

"I have no wish to move, friend," I said, "but I am curious to know why you attack me?"

"Because you are a rebel. I have seen you before, you are one of Santa Coloma's officers. Here you shall stand with this knife touching you till you are arrested, or else with this knife in you here you shall die."

"You are making a mistake," I said.

"Neighbours," said he, speaking to the others, but without taking his eyes from my face, "will you tie this man hand and foot while I stand before him to prevent him from drawing any weapon he may have concealed under his poncho?"

"We have not come here to arrest travellers," returned one of the men. "If he is a rebel it is no concern of ours. Perhaps you are mistaken, Gandara."

"No, no, I am not mistaken," he returned. "He shall not escape. I saw him at San Paulo with these eyes—when did they ever deceive me? If you refuse to assist me, then go one of you to the Alcalde's house and tell him to come without delay, while I keep guard here."

After a little discussion one of the men offered to go and inform the Alcalde. When he had left, I said, "My friend, may I finish my meal? I am hungry and had just begun to eat when you drew your knife against me."

"Yes; eat," he said; "only keep your hands well up so that I can see them. Perhaps you have a weapon at your waist."

"I have not," I said, "for I am an inoffensive person and do not require weapons."

"Tongues were made to lie," he returned, truly enough. "If I see you drop your hand lower than the counter I shall rip you up. We shall then be able to see whether you digest your food or not."

I began to eat and sip my wine, still with those brutal eyes on my face and the keen knife-point touching my poncho. There was now a ghastly look of horrible excitement on his face, while his teeth-grinding performances became more frequent and the slimy froth dropped continually from the corners of his mouth on to his bosom. I dared not look at the knife, because a terrible impulse to wrest it out of his hands kept rising in me. It was almost too strong to be overcome, yet I knew that even the slightest attempt at escape would be fatal to me; for the fellow was evidently thirsty for my blood and only wanted an excuse to run me through. But what, I thought, if he were to grow tired of waiting, and, carried away by his murderous instincts, to plunge his weapon into me? In that case I should die like a dog without having availed myself of my one chance of escape through over-caution. These thoughts were maddening, still through it all I laboured to observe an outwardly calm demeanour.

My supper was done. I began to feel strangely weak and nervous. My lips grew dry; I was intensely thirsty and longed for more wine, yet dared not take it for fear that in my excited state even a very moderate amount of alcohol might cloud my brain.

"How long will it take your friend to return with the Alcalde?" I asked at length.

Gandara made no reply. "A long time," said one of the other men. "I, for one, cannot wait till he comes," and after that he took his departure. One by one they now began to drop away till only two men besides Gandara remained in the porch. Still that murderous wretch kept before me like a tiger watching its prey, or rather like a wild boar, gnashing and foaming, and ready to rip up its adversary with horrid tusk.

At length I made an appeal to him, for I began to despair of the Alcalde coming to deliver me. "Friend," I said, "if you will allow me to speak, I can convince you that you are mistaken. I am a foreigner, and know nothing about Santa Coloma."

"No, no," he interrupted, pressing the knife-point warningly against my stomach, then suddently withdrawing it as if about to plunge it into me. "I know you are a rebel. If I thought the Alcalde were not coming I would run you through at once and cut your throat afterwards. It is a virtue to kill a Blanco traitor, and if you do not go bound hand and foot from here then here you must die. What, do you dare to say that I did not see you at San Paulo——that you are not an officer of Santa Coloma? Look, rebel, I will swear on this cross that I saw you there."

Suiting the action to the word, he raised the

hilt of the weapon to his lips to kiss the guard, which with the handle formed a cross. That pious action was the first slip he had made, and gave the first opportunity that had come to me during all that terrible interview. Before he had ceased speaking the conviction that my time had come flashed like lightning through my brain. Just as his slimy lips kissed the hilt, my right hand dropped to my side and grasped the handle of my revolver under my poncho. He saw the movement and very quickly recovered the handle of his knife. In another second of time he would have driven the blade through me; but that second was all I now required. Straight from my waist, and from under my poncho, I fired. His knife fell ringing on to the floor; he swerved, then fell back, coming to the ground with a heavy thud. Over his falling body I leaped, and almost before he had touched the ground was several yards away, then wheeling round, I found the other two men rushing out after me.

"Back!" I shouted, covering the foremost of the two with my revolver.

They instantly stood still.

"We are not following you, friend," said one, "but only wish to get out of the place."

"Back, or I fire!" I repeated, and then they retreated into the porch. They had stood by unconcerned while their cut-throat comrade Gandara was threatening my life, so that I naturally felt angry with them.

I sprang upon my horse, but instead of riding away at once stood for some minutes by the gate watching the two men. They were kneeling by Gandara, one opening his clothes to look for the wound, the other holding a flaring candle over his ashen corpse-like face.

"Is he dead?" I asked.

One of the men looked up and answered, "It appears so."

"Then," I returned, "I make you a present of his carcass."

After that, digging my spurs into my horse, I galloped away.

Some readers might imagine, after what I have related, that my sojourn in the Purple Land had quite brutalised me; I am happy to inform them that it was not so. Whatever a man's individual character may happen to be, he has always a strong inclination in him to reply to an attack in the spirit in which it is made. He does not call the person who playfully ridicules his foibles a whitened sepulchre or an unspeakable scoundrel, and the same principle holds good when it comes to actual physical fighting. If a French gentleman were to call me out, I daresay I should go to the encounter twirling my moustache, bowing down to the ground, all smiles and compliments; and that I should select my rapier with a pleasant kind of feeling, like that experienced by the satirist about to write a brilliant article while picking out a pen with a suitable nib. On the other hand, if a murderous brute with truculent eyes and gnashing teeth attempts to disembowel me with a butcher's knife, the instinct of self-preservation comes out in all its old original ferocity, inspiring the heart with such implacable fury that after spilling his blood I could spurn his loathsome carcass with my foot. I do not wonder at myself for speaking those savage words. That he was past recall seemed certain, yet not a shade of regret did I feel at his death. Joy at the terrible retribution I had been able to inflict on the murderous wretch was the only emotion I experienced when galloping away into the darkness—such joy that I could have sung and shouted aloud had it not seemed imprudent to indulge in such expressions of feeling.

CHAPTER XXI

LIBERTY AND DIRT

AFTER my terrible adventure I did not rest badly that night, albeit I slept on an empty stomach (the sardines counting as nothing), and under the vast, void sky, powdered with innumerable stars. And when I proceeded next day on my journey, *God's light,* as the pious Orientals call the first wave of glory with which the rising run floods the world, had never seemed so pleasant to my eyes, nor had earth ever looked fresher or lovelier, with the grass and bushes everywhere hung with starry lace, sparkling with countless dewy gems, which the epeiras had woven overnight. Life seemed very sweet to me on that morning, so softening my heart that when I remembered the murderous wretch who had endangered it I almost regretted that he was now probably blind and deaf to nature's sweet ministrations.

Before noon I came to a large thatched house, with clumps of shady trees growing near it, also surrounded with brushwood fences and sheep and cattle enclosures.

The blue smoke curling peacefully up from the chimney and the white gleam of the walls through the shady trees—for this rancho actually boasted a chimney and whitewashed walls—looked exceedingly inviting to my tired eyes. How pleasant a good breakfast with a long siesta in the shade after it would be, thought I; but, alas! was I not pursued by the awful phantoms of political vengeance? Uncertain whether to call or not, my horse jogged straight on towards the house, for a horse always knows when his rider is in doubt and never fails at such times to give his advice. It was lucky for me that on this occasion I condescended to take it. "I will, at all events, call for a drink of water and see what the people are like," I thought, and in a few minutes I was standing at the gate, apparently an object of great interest to half a dozen children ranging from two to thirteen years old, all staring at me with wide-open eyes. They had dirty faces, the smallest one dirty legs also, for he or she wore nothing but a small shirt. The next in size had a shirt supplemented with a trousers-like garment reaching to the knees; and so on, progressively, up to the biggest boy, who wore the cast-off parental toggery, and so instead of having too little on, was, in a sense, overdressed. I asked this youngster for a can of water to quench my thirst and a stick of fire to light my cigar. He ran into the kitchen, or living-room, and by-and-by came out again without either water or fire. "Papita wishes you to come in to drink maté," said he.

Then I dismounted, and with the careless air of

a blameless non-political person, strode into the spacious kitchen, where an immense cauldron of fat was boiling over a big fire on the hearth; while beside it, ladle in hand, sat a perspiring, greasy-looking woman of about thirty. She was engaged in skimming the fat and throwing the scum on the fire, which made it blaze with a furious joy and loudly cry out in a crackling voice for more; and from head to feet she was literally bathed in grease—certainly the most greasy individual I had ever seen. It was not easy under the circumstances to tell the colour of her skin, but she had fine large Juno eyes, and her mouth was unmistakably good-humoured, as she smiled when returning my salutation. Her husband sat on the clay floor against the wall, his bare feet stretched straight out before him, while across his lap lay an immense surcingle, twenty inches broad at least, of pure white, untanned hide; and on it he was laboriously working a design representing an ostrich hunt, with threads of black skin. He was a short, broad-shouldered man with reddish-grey hair, stiff bristly whiskers and moustache of the same hue, sharp blue eyes and a nose decidedly upturned.

He wore a red cotton handkerchief tied on his head, a blue check shirt, and a shawl wound round his body in place of the *chiripà* usually worn by native peasants. He jerked out his "Buen dia" to me in a short, quick, barking voice, and invited me to sit down.

"Cold water is bad for the constitution at this hour," he said. "We will drink maté."

There was such a rough burr-like sound in his speech that I at once concluded he was a foreigner, or hailed from some Oriental district corresponding to our Durham or Northumberland.

"Thank you," I said, "a maté is always welcome. I am an Oriental in that respect if in nothing else." For I wished everyone I met to know that I was not a native.

"Right, my friend," he exclaimed. "Maté is the best thing in this country. As for the people, they are not worth cursing."

"How can you say such a thing," I returned. "You are a foreigner, I suppose, but your wife is surely an Oriental."

The Juno of the grease-pot smiled and threw a ladleful of tallow on the fire to make it roar; possibly this was meant for applause.

He waved his hand deprecatingly, the bradawl used for his work in it.

"True, friend, she is," he replied. "Women, like horned cattle, are much the same all the world over. They have their value wherever you find them—America, Europe, Asia. We know it. I spoke of men."

"You scarcely do women justice—

La mujer es un angel del cielo,"

I returned, quoting the old Spanish song.

He barked out a short little laugh.

"That does very well to sing to a guitar," he said.

"Talking of guitars," spoke the woman, addressing me for the first time; "while we are waiting for the maté, perhaps you will sing us a ballad. The guitar is lying just behind you."

"Señora, I do not play on it," I answered. "An Englishman goes forth into the world without that desire common to people of other nations of making himself agreeable to those he may encounter on his way; this is why he does not learn to perform on musical instruments."

The little man stared at me; then deliberately disencumbering himself of surcingle, threads, and implements, he got up, advanced to me, and held out his hand.

His grave manner almost made me laugh. Taking his hand in mine, I said—

"What am I to do with this, my friend?"

"Shake it," he replied. "We are countrymen."

We then shook hands very vigorously for some time in silence, while his wife looked on with a smile and stirred the fat.

"Woman," he said, turning to her, "leave your grease till to-morrow. Breakfast must be thought of. Is there any mutton in the house?"

"Half a sheep—only," she replied.

"That will do for one meal," said he. "Here, Teofilo, run and tell Anselmo to catch two pullets —fat ones, mind. To be plucked at once. You may look for half a dozen fresh eggs for your mother to put in the stew. And, Felipe, go find Cosme and tell him to saddle the roan pony to go to the store at once. Now, wife, what is wanted —rice, sugar, vinegar, oil, raisins, pepper, saffron, salt, cloves, cummin seed, wine, brandy——"

"Stop one moment," I cried. "If you think it necessary to get provisions enough for an army to give me breakfast, I must tell you that I draw the line at brandy. I never touch it—in this country."

He shook hands with me again.

"You are right," he said. "Always stick to the native drink, wherever you are, even if it is black draught. Whisky in Scotland, in the Banda Oriental rum—that's my rule."

The place was now in a great commotion, the children saddling ponies, shouting in pursuit of fugitive chickens, and my energetic host ordering his wife about.

After the boy was despatched for the things and my horse taken care of, we sat for half an hour in the kitchen sipping maté and conversing very agreeably. Then my host took me out into his garden behind the house to be out of his wife's way while she was engaged cooking breakfast, and there he began talking in English.

"Twenty-five years I have been on this continent," said he, telling me his history, "eighteen of them in the Banda Oriental."

"Well, you have not forgotten your language," I said. "I suppose you read?"

"Read! What! I would as soon think of wearing trousers. No, no, my friend, never read. Leave politics alone. When people molest you, shoot 'em—those are my rules. Edinburgh was my home. Had enough reading when I was a boy; heard enough psalm-singing, saw enough scrubbing and scouring to last me my lifetime. My father was a bookseller in the High Street, near the Cowgate—you know! Mother, she was pious—they were all pious. Uncle, a minister, lived with us. That was all worse than purgatory to me. I was educated at the High School—intended for the ministry, ha, ha! My only pleasure was to get a book of travels in some savage country, skulk into my room, throw off my boots, light a pipe, and lie on the floor reading—locked up from everyone. Sundays just the same. They called me a sinner, said I was going to the devil— fast. It was my nature. They didn't understand —kept on ding-donging in my ears. Always scrubbing, scouring—you might have eaten your dinner off the floor; always singing psalms—praying— scolding. Couldn't bear it; ran away at fifteen, and have never heard a word from home since. What happened? I came here, worked, saved, bought land, cattle; married a wife, lived as I liked to live—am happy. There's my wife— mother of six children—you have seen her yourself, a woman for a man to be proud of. No ding-donging, black looks, scouring from Monday to Saturday—you couldn't eat your dinner off *my* kitchen floor. There are my children, six of 'em, all told, boys and girls, healthy, dirty as they like to be, happy as the day's long; and here am I, John Carrickfergus—Don Juan all the country over, my surname no native can pronounce—respected, feared, loved; a man his neighbour can rely on to do him a good turn; one who never hesitates about putting a bullet in any vulture, wild cat, or assassin that crosses his path. Now you know all."

"An extraordinary history," I said, "but I suppose you teach your children something?"

"Teach 'em nothing," he returned with emphasis. "All we think about in the old country are books, cleanliness, clothes; what's good for soul, brain, stomach, and we make 'em miserable. Liberty for everyone—that's my rule. Dirty children are healthy, happy children. If a bee stings you in England, you clap on fresh dirt to cure the pain. Here we cure all kinds of pains with dirt. If my child is ill I dig up a spadeful of fresh mould and rub it well—best remedy out. I'm not religious, but I remember *one* miracle. The Saviour spat on the ground and made mud with the spittle to anoint the eyes of the blind man. Made him see directly. What does that mean? Common remedy of the country, of course. *He* didn't need the clay, but followed the custom, same as in the other miracles. In Scotland dirt's wickedness—how'd they reconcile that with Scripture? I don't say *Nature*, mind, I say

Scripture, because the Bible's the book they swear by, though they didn't write it."

"I shall think over what you say about children, and the best way to rear them," I returned. "I needn't decide in a hurry, as I haven't any yet."

He barked his short laugh and led me back to the house, where the arrangements for breakfast were now completed. The children took their meal in the kitchen, we had ours in a large cool room adjoining it. There was a small table laid with a spotless white cloth, and real crockery plates and real knives and forks. There were also real glass tumblers, bottles of Spanish wine, and snow-white *pan creollo*. Evidently my hostess had made good use of her time. She came in immediately after we were seated, and I scarcely recognised her; for she was not only clean now, but good-looking as well, with that rich olive colour on her oval face, her black hair well arranged, and her dark eyes full of tender loving light. She was now wearing a white merino dress with a quaint maroon-coloured pattern on it, and a white silk kerchief fastened with a gold brooch at her neck. It was pleasant to look at her, and noticing my admiring glances, she blushed when she sat down, then laughed. The breakfast was excellent. Roast mutton to begin, then a dish of chickens stewed with rice, nicely flavoured and coloured with red Spanish *pimenton*. A fowl roasted or boiled, as we eat them in England, is wasted, compared with this delicious *guiso de pollo* which one gets in any

rancho in the Banda Orientál. After the meats
we sat for an hour cracking walnuts, sipping wine,
smoking cigarettes, and telling amusing stories;
and I doubt whether there were three happier
people in all Uruguay that morning than the un-
Scotched Scotchman, John Carrickfergus, his un-
ding-donging native wife, and their guest, who
had shot his man on the previous evening.

After breakfast I spread my poncho on the dry
grass under a tree to sleep the siesta. My slumbers lasted a long time, and on waking I was surprised to find my host and hostess seated on the
grass near me, he busy ornamenting his surcingle,
she with the maté-cup in her hand and a kettle of
hot water beside her. She was drying her eyes, I
fancied, when I opened mine.

"Awake at last!" cried Don Juan pleasantly.
"Come and drink maté. Wife just been crying,
you see."

She made a sign for him to hold his peace.

"Why not speak of it, Candelaria?" he said.
"Where is the harm? You see my wife thinks
you have been in the wars—a Santa Coloma man
running away to save his throat."

"How does she make that out?" I asked in some
confusion and very much surprised.

"How! Don't you know women? You said
nothing about where you had been—prudence.
That was one thing. Looked confused when we
talked of the revolution—not a word to say about
it. More evidence. Your poncho, lying there,

shows two big cuts in it. 'Torn by thorns,' said I. 'Sword cuts,' said she. We were arguing about it when you woke."

"She guessed rightly," I said, "and I am ashamed of myself for not telling you before. But why should your wife cry?"

"Woman like—woman like," he answered, waving his hand. "Always ready to cry over the beaten one—that is the only politics they know."

"Did I not say that woman is an angel from heaven," I returned; then taking her hand, I kissed it. "This is the first time I have kissed a married woman's hand, but the husband of such a wife will know better than to be jealous."

"Jealous—ha, ha!" he laughed. "It would have made me prouder if you had kissed her cheek."

"Juan—a nice thing to say!" exclaimed his wife, slapping his hand tenderly.

Then while we sipped maté I told them the history of my campaign, finding it necessary, when explaining my motives for joining the rebels, to make some slight deviations from the strictest form of truth. He agreed that my best plan was to go on to Rocha to wait there for a passport before proceeding to Montevideo. But I was not allowed to leave them that day; and while we talked over our maté, Candelaria deftly repaired the tell-tale cuts in my poncho.

I spent the afternoon making friends with the children, who proved to be very intelligent and amusing little beggars, telling them some non-sensical stories I invented, and listening to their bird's-nesting, armadillo-chasing, and other adventures. Then came a late dinner, after which the children said their prayers and retired, then we smoked and sang songs without an accompaniment, and I finished a happy day by sinking to sleep in a soft, clean bed.

I had announced my intention of leaving at daybreak next morning; and when I woke, finding it already light, I dressed hastily, and, going out, found my horse already saddled standing, with three other saddled horses, at the gate. In the kitchen I found Don Juan, his wife, and the two biggest boys having their early maté. My host told me that he had been up an hour, and was only waiting to wish me a prosperous journey before going out to gather up his cattle. He at once wished me good-bye, and with his two boys went off, leaving me to partake of poached eggs and coffee—quite an English breakfast.

I then rose and thanked the good señora for her hospitality.

"One moment," she said, when I held out my hand, and drawing a small silk bag from her bosom, she offered it to me. "My husband has given me permission to present you with this at parting. It is only a small gift, but while you are in this trouble and away from all your friends it perhaps might be of use to you."

I did not wish to take money from her after all

the kind treatment I had received, and so allowed the purse to lie on my open hand where she had placed it.

"And if I cannot accept it——" I began.

"Then you will hurt me very much," she replied. "Could you do that after the kind words you spoke yesterday?"

I could not resist, but after putting the purse away, took her hand and kissed it.

"Good-bye, Candelaria," I said, "you have made me love your country and repent every harsh word I have ever spoken against it."

Her hand remained in mine; she stood smiling, and did not seem to think the last word had been spoken yet. Then seeing her there looking so sweet and loving, and remembering the words her husband had spoken the day before, I stooped and kissed her cheek and lips.

"Adieu, my friend, and God be with you," she said.

I think there were tears in her eyes when I left her, but I could not see clearly, for mine also had suddenly grown dim.

And only the day before I had felt amused at the sight of this woman sitting hot and greasy over her work, and had called her Juno of the grease-pot! Now, after an acquaintance of about eighteen hours I had actually kissed her—a wife and the mother of six children, bidding her adieu with trembling voice and moist eyes! I know that I shall never forgot those eyes, full of sweet, pure affection and tender sympathy, looking into mine; all my life long shall I think of Candelaria, loving her like a sister. Could any woman in my own ultra-civilised and excessively proper country inspire me with a feeling like that in so short a time? I fancy not. O civilisation, with your million conventions, soul and body withering prudishnesses, vain education for the little ones, going to church in best black clothes, unnatural craving for cleanliness, feverish striving after comforts that bring no comfort to the heart, are you a mistake altogether? Candelaria and that genial runaway John Carrickfergus make me think so. Ah, yes, we are all vainly seeking after happiness in the wrong way. It was with us once and ours, but we despised it, for it was only the old common happiness which Nature gives to all her children, and we went away from it in search of another grander kind of happiness which some dreamer— Bacon or another—assured us we should find. We had only to conquer Nature, find out her secrets, make her our obedient slave, then the earth would be Eden, and every man Adam and every woman Eve. We are still marching bravely on, conquering Nature, but how weary and sad we are getting! The old joy in life and gaiety of heart have vanished, though we do sometimes pause for a few moments in our long forced march to watch the labours of some pale mechanician seeking after perpetual motion and indulge in a little, dry, cackling laugh at his expense.

CHAPTER XXII

A CROWN OF NETTLES

AFTER leaving John and Candelaria's home of
liberty and love, nothing further worth recording
happened till I had nearly reached the desired
haven of the Lomas de Rocha, a place which I
was, after all, never destined to see except from a
great distance. A day unusually brilliant even for
this bright climate was drawing to a close, it being
within about two hours of sunset, when I turned
out of my way to ascend a hill with a very long
ridge-like summit, falling away at one end, appearing like the last sierra of a range just where
it dies down into the level plain; only in this instance the range itself did not exist. The solitary hill was covered with short tussocks of yellow, wiry grass, with occasional bushes, while near
the summit large slabs of sandstone appeared just
above the surface, looking like gravestones in
some old village churchyard, with all their inscrip-
tions obliterated by time and weather. From this
elevation, which was about a hundred feet above
the plain, I wished to survey the country before
me, for I was tired and hungry, so was my horse,
and I was anxious to find a resting-place before
night. Before me the country stretched away in
vast undulations towards the ocean, which was not,

however, in sight. Not the faintest stain of vapour appeared on the immense crystalline dome of heaven, while the stillness and transparency of the atmosphere seemed almost preternatural. A blue gleam of water, south-east of where I stood and many leagues distant, I took to be the lake of Rocha; on the western horizon were faint blue cloud-like masses with pearly peaks. They were not clouds, however, but the sierras of the range weirdly named *Cuchilla de las Animas*—Ghost-haunted mountains. At length, like a person who puts his binocular into his pocket and begins to look about him, I recalled my vision from its wanderings over illimitable space to examine the objects close at hand. On the slope of the hill, sixty yards from my standpoint, were some deep green, dwarf bushes, each bush looking in that still brilliant sunshine as if it had been hewn out of a block of malachite; and on the pale purple solanaceous flowers covering them some humble-bees were feeding. It was the humming of the bees coming distinctly to my ears that first attracted my attention to the bushes; for so still was the atmosphere that at that distance apart—sixty yards—two persons might have conversed easily without raising their voices. Much further down, about two hundred yards from the bushes, a harrier hawk stood on the ground, tearing at something it had captured, feeding in that savage, suspicious manner usual with hawks, with long pauses between the bites. Over the harrier hovered a brown milvago hawk, a vulture-like bird in its habits, that lives by picking up unconsidered trifles. Envious at the other's good fortune, or fearing, perhaps, that not even the crumbs or feathers of the feast were going to be left, it was persecuting the harrier by darting down at intervals with an angry cry and aiming a blow with its wing. The harrier methodically ducked its head each time its tormentor rushed down at it, after which it would tear its prey again in its uncomfortable manner. Further away, in the depression running along at the foot of the hill, meandered a small stream so filled with aquatic grasses and plants that the water was quite concealed, its course appearing like a vivid green snake, miles long, lying there basking in the sunshine. At the point of the stream nearest to me an old man was seated on the ground, apparently washing himself, for he was stooping over a little pool of water, while behind him stood his horse with patient, drooping head, occasionally switching off the flies with its tail. A mile further on stood a dwelling, which looked to me like an old estancia-house, surrounded by large shade trees growing singly or in irregular clumps. It was the only house near, but after gazing at it for some time I concluded that it was uninhabited. For even at that distance I could see plainly that there were no human beings moving about it, no horse or other domestic animal near, and there were certainly no hedges or enclosures of any description.

Slowly I went down the hill, and to the old man sitting beside the stream. I found him engaged in the seemingly difficult operation of disentangling a luxuriant crop of very long hair, which had somehow—possibly from long neglect —got itself into great confusion. He had dipped his head into the water, and with an old comb, boasting about seven or eight teeth, was laboriously and with infinite patience drawing out the long hairs, a very few at a time. After saluting him, I lit a cigarette, and leaning on the neck of my horse, watched his efforts for some time with profound interest. He toiled away in silence for five or six minutes, then dipped his head in the water again, and while carefully wringing the wet out he remarked that my horse looked tired.

"Yes," I replied; "so is his rider. Can you tell me who lives in that estancia?"

"My master," he returned laconically.

"Is he a good-hearted man—one who will give shelter to a stranger?" I asked.

He took a very long time to answer me, then said—

"He has nothing to say about such matters."

"An invalid?" I remarked.

Another long pause; then he shook his head and tapped his forehead significantly; after which he resumed his mermaid task.

"Demented?" said I.

He elevated an eyebrow and shrugged his shoulders, but said nothing.

After a long silence, for I was anxious not to irritate him with too much questioning, I ventured to remark—

"Well, they will not set the dogs on me, will they?"

He grinned and said that it was an establishment without dogs.

I paid him for his information with a cigarette, which he took very readily, and seemed to think smoking a pleasant relief after his disentangling labours.

"An estancia without dogs, and where the master has nothing to say—that sounds strange," I remarked tentatively, but he puffed on in silence.

"What is the name of the house?" I said, after remounting my horse.

"It is a house without a name," he replied; and after this rather unsatisfactory interview I left him and slowly went on to the estancia.

On approaching the house I saw that there had formerly been a large plantation behind it, of which only a few dead stumps now remained, the ditches that had enclosed them being now nearly obliterated. The place was ruinous and overgrown with weeds. Dismounting, I led my horse along a narrow path through a perfect wilderness of wild sunflowers, horehound, red-weed, and thorn-apple, up to some poplar trees where there had once been a gate, of which only two or three broken posts remained standing in the ground. From the old gate the path ran on, still through weeds, to the door of the house, which was partly of stone and partly of red brick, with a very steep, sloping, tiled roof. Beside the ruined gate, leaning against a post, with the hot afternoon sun shining on her uncovered head, stood a woman in a rusty-black dress. She was about twenty-six or twenty-seven years old, and had an unutterably weary, desponding expression on her face, which was colourless as marble, except for the purple stains under her large dark eyes. She did not move when I approached her, but raised her sorrowful eyes to my face, apparently feeling little interest in my arrival.

I took off my hat to salute her, and said—

"Señora, my horse is tired, and I am seeking for a resting-place; can I have shelter under your roof?"

"Yes, caballero; why not?" she returned in a voice even more significant of sorrow than her countenance.

I thanked her, and waited for her to lead the way; but she still remained standing before me with eyes cast down, and a hesitating, troubled look on her face.

"Señora," I began, "if a stranger's presence in the house would be inconvenient——"

"No, no, señor, it is not that," she interrupted quickly. Then, sinking her voice almost to a whisper, she said—"Tell me, señor, have you come from the department of Florida? Have you— have you been at San Paulo?"

I hesitated a little, then answered that I had.

"On which side?" she asked quickly, with a strange eagerness in her voice.

"Ah, señora," I returned, "why do you ask me, only a poor traveller who comes for a night's shelter, such a question——"

"Why? Perhaps for your good, señor. Remember, women are not like men—implacable. A shelter you shall have, señor; but it is best that I should know."

"You are right," I returned, "forgive me for not answering you at once. I was with Santa Coloma—the rebel."

She held out her hand to me, but, before I could take it, withdrew it and, covering her face, began to cry. Presently recovering herself and turning towards the house, she asked me to follow.

Her gestures and tears had told me eloquently enough that she too belonged to the unhappy Blanco party.

"Have you then lost some relation in this fight, señora?" I asked.

"No, señor," she replied; "but if our party had triumphed perhaps deliverance would have come to me. Ah, no; I lost my relations long ago—all except my father. You shall know presently, when you see him, why our cruel enemies have refrained from shedding *his* blood."

By that time we had reached the house. There had once been a verandah to it, but this had long fallen away, leaving the walls, doors, and windows exposed to sun and rain. Lichen covered the stone walls, while in the crevices and over the tiled roof weeds and grass had flourished; but this vegetation had died with the summer heats and was now parched and yellow. She led me into a spacious room, so dimly lighted from the low door and one small window that it seemed quite dark to me coming from the bright sunlight. I stood for a few moments trying to accustom my eyes to the gloom, while she, advancing to the middle of the apartment, bent down and spoke to an aged man seated in a leather-bound easy-chair.

"Papa," she said, "I have brought in a young man—a stranger who has asked for shelter under our roof. Welcome him, papa."

Then she straightened herself, and passing behind the chair stood leaning on it, facing me.

"I wish you good day, señor," I said, advancing with a little hesitation.

There before me sat a tall, bent old man, wasted almost to a skeleton, with a grey, desolate face and long hair and beard of a silver whiteness. He was wrapped in a light-coloured poncho, and wore a black skull-cap on his head. When I spoke he leant back in his seat and began scanning my face with strangely fierce eager eyes, all the time twisting his long, thin fingers together in a nervous, excited manner.

"What, Calixto," he exclaimed at length, "is this the way you come into my presence? Ha, you thought I would not recognise you! Down—down, boy, on your knees!"

I glanced at his daughter standing behind him; she was watching my face anxiously, and made a slight inclination with her head.

Taking this as an intimation to obey the old man's commands, I went down on my knees, and touched my lips to the hand he extended.

"May God give you grace, my son," he said with tremulous voice. Then he continued: "What, did you expect to find your old father blind then? I would know you amongst a thousand, Calixto. Ah, my son, my son, why have you kept away so long? Stand, my son, and let me embrace you."

He rose up tottering from his chair and threw his arm about me; then, after gazing into my face for some moments, deliberately kissed me on both cheeks.

"Ha, Calixto," he continued, putting his trembling hands upon my shoulders and gazing into my face out of his wild, sunken eyes, "do I need ask where you have been? Where should a Peralta be but in the smoke of the battle, in the midst of carnage, fighting for the Banda Oriental? I did not complain of your absence, Calixto—Demetria will tell you that I was patient through all these years, for I knew you would come back to me at last wearing the laurel wreath of victory. And I, Calixto, what have I worn, sitting here? A crown of nettles! Yes, for a hundred years I have worn it—you are my witness, Demetria, my daughter, that I have worn this crown of stinging-nettles for a hundred years."

He sank back, apparently exhausted, in his chair, and I uttered a sigh of relief, thinking the interview was now over. But I was mistaken. His daughter placed a chair for me at his side. "Sit here, señor, and talk to my father, while I have your horse taken care of," she whispered, and then quickly glided from the room. This was rather hard on me, I thought; but while whispering those few words she touched my hand lightly and turned her wistful eyes with a grateful look on mine, and I was glad for her sake that I had not blundered.

Presently the old man roused himself again and began talking eagerly, asking me a hundred wild questions, to which I was compelled to reply, still trying to keep up the character of the long-lost son just returned victorious from the wars.

"Tell me where you have fought and overcome the enemy," he exclaimed, raising his voice almost to a scream. "Where have they flown from you like chaff before the wind?—where have you trodden them down under your horses' hoofs?—name —name the places and the battles to me, Calixto?"

I felt strongly inclined just then to jump up and rush out of the room, so trying was this mad conversation to my nerves; but I thought of his daughter Demetria's white, pathetic face, and restrained the impulse. Then in sheer desperation

I began to talk madly as himself. I thought I would make him sick of warlike subjects. Everywhere, I cried, we had defeated, slaughtered, scattered to the four winds of heaven, the infamous Colorados. From the sea to the Brazilian frontier we have been victorious. With sword, lance, and bayonet we have stormed and taken every town from Tacuarembó to Montevideo. Every river from the Yaguaron to the Uruguay had run red with Colorado blood. In forests and sierras we had hunted them, flying like wild beasts from us; we had captured them in thousands, only to cut their throats, crucify them, blow them from the guns, and tear them limb by limb to pieces with wild horses.

I was only pouring oil on the blazing fire of his insanity.

"Aha!" he shouted, his eyes sparkling while he wildly clutched my arm with his skinny, claw-like hands, "did I not know—have I not said it? Did I not fight for a hundred years, wading through blood every day, and then at last send you forth to finish the battle? And every day our enemies came and shouted in my ears, 'Victory—victory!' They told me you were dead, Calixto—that their weapons had pierced you, that they had given your flesh to be devoured of wild dogs. And I shouted with laughter to hear them. I laughed in their faces and clapped my hands and cried out, 'Prepare your throats for the sword, traitors, slaves, assassins, for a Peralta—even Calixto, de-

voured of wild dogs—is coming to execute vengeance! What, will God not leave one strong
arm to strike at the tyrant's breast—one Peralta
in all this land! Fly, miscreants! Die, wretches!
He has risen from the grave—he has come back
from hell, armed with hell-fire to burn your towns
to ashes—to extirpate you utterly from the
earth!' "

His thin, tremulous voice had risen towards the
close of this mad speech to a reedy shriek that rang
through the quiet, darkening house like the long,
shrill cry of some water-fowl heard at night in
the desolate marshes.

Then he loosened his hold on my arm and
dropped back moaning and shivering into his seat.
His eyes closed, his whole frame trembled, and
he looked like a person just recovering from an
epileptic fit; then he seemed to sink to sleep. It
was now getting quite dark, for the sun had been
down some time, and it was with the greatest relief that I saw Doña Demetria gliding like a ghost
into the room. She touched me on the arm and
whispered, "Come, señor, he is asleep now."

I followed her out into the fresh air, which
had never seemed so fresh before; then, turning
to me, she hurriedly whispered, "Remember,
señor, that what you have told me is a secret.
Say not one word of it to any other person here."

CHAPTER XXIII

THE RED FLAG OF VICTORY

She then led me to the kitchen at the end of the house. It was one of those roomy, old-fashioned kitchens still to be found in a few estancia-houses built in colonial times, in which the fireplace, raised a foot or two above the floor, extends the whole width of the room. It was large and dimly lighted, the walls and rafters black with a century's smoke and abundantly festooned with sooty cobwebs; but a large, cheerful fire blazed on the hearth, while before it stood a tall, gaunt woman engaged in cooking the supper and serving maté. This was Ramona, an old servant on the estancia. There also sat my friend of the tangled tresses, which he had evidently succeeded in combing well out, for they now hung down quite smooth on his back and as long as a woman's hair. Another person was also seated near the fire, whose age might have been anything from twenty-five to forty-five, for he had, I think, a mixture of Indian blood in his veins, and one of those smooth, dry, dark faces that change but little with age. He was an undersized, wiry-looking man with a small, intensely black moustache, but no whiskers or beard. He seemed to be a person of some consequence in the house, and when my conductress introduced him to me as "Don Hilario," he rose to his feet and received me with a profound bow. In spite of his excessive politeness I conceived a feeling of distrust towards him from the moment I saw him; and this was because his small, watchful eyes were perpetually glancing at my face in a furtive manner, only to glance swiftly away again whenever I looked at him; for he seemed quite incapable of meeting the gaze of another. We drank maté and talked a little, but were not a lively party. Doña Demetria, though she sat with us, scarcely contributed a word to the conversation; while the long-haired man—Santos by name, and the only peon on the establishment—smoked his cigarette and sipped his maté in absolute silence.

Bony old Ramona at length dished up the supper and carried it out of the kitchen; we followed to the large living-room where I had been before and gathered round a small table; for these people, though apparently poverty-stricken, ate their meals after the manner of civilised beings. At the head of the table sat the fierce, old, white-haired man staring at us out of his sunken eyes as we entered. Half rising from his seat he motioned to me to take a chair near him, then addressing Don Hilario, who sat opposite, he said, "This is my son Calixto just returned from the wars, where, as you know, he has greatly distinguished himself."

Don Hilario rose and bowed gravely. Demetria took the other end of the table, while Santos and Ramona occupied the two remaining seats.

I was greatly relieved to find that the old man's mood had changed; there were no more wild outbursts like the one I had witnessed earlier in the evening; only occasionally he would fix his strange, burning eyes on me in a way that made me exceedingly uncomfortable. We began the meal with broth, which we finished in silence; and while we ate, Don Hilario's swift glances incessantly flew from face to face; Demetria, pale and evidently ill at ease, keeping her eyes cast down all the time.

"Is there no wine this evening, Ramona?" asked the old man in querulous tones when the old woman rose to remove the broth basins.

"The *master* has not ordered me to put any on the table," she replied with asperity and strongly emphasizing the obnoxious word.

"What does this mean, Don Hilario?" said the old man, turning to his neighbour. "My son has just returned after a long absence; are we to have no wine for an occasion like this?"

Don Hilario with a faint smile on his lips drew a key from his pocket and passed it silently to Ramona. She rose, muttering, from the table and proceeded to unlock a cupboard, from which she took a bottle of wine. Then going round the table she poured out half a tumblerful for each person, excepting herself and Santos, who, to judge from his stolid countenance, did not expect any.

"No, no," said old Peralta, "give Santos wine, and pour yourself out a glass also, Ramona. You have both been good, faithful friends to me, and have nursed Calixto in his infancy. It is right that you should drink his health and rejoice with us at his return."

She obeyed with alacrity, and old Santos' wooden face almost relaxed into a grin when he received his share of the purple fluid (I can scarcely call it juice) which maketh glad the heart of man.

Presently old Peralta raised his glass and fixed his fierce, insane eyes on me. "Calixto, my son, we will drink your health," he said, "and may the curse of the Almighty fall on our enemies; may their bodies lie where they fall, till the hawks have consumed their flesh, and their bones have been trodden into dust by the cattle; and may their souls be tormented with everlasting fire."

Silently they all raised their glasses to their lips, but when they set them down again, the points of Don Hilario's black moustache were raised as if by a smile, while Santos smacked his lips in token of enjoyment.

After this ghastly toast nothing more was spoken by anyone at the table. In oppressive silence we consumed the roast and boiled meat set before us; for I dared not hazard even the most commonplace remark for fear of rousing my volcanic host into a mad eruption. When we had finished eating, Demetria rose and brought her father a cigarette. It was the signal that supper was over; and immediately afterwards she left the room, followed by the two servants. Don Hilario politely offered me a cigarette and lit one for himself. For some minutes we smoked in silence, until the old man gradually dropped to sleep in his chair, after which we rose and went back to the kitchen. Even that sombre retreat now seemed cheerful after the silence and gloom of the dining-room. Presently Don Hilario got up, and with many apologies for leaving me, explaining that he had been invited to assist at a dance at a neighbouring estancia, took himself off. Soon afterwards, though it was only about nine o'clock, I was shown to a room where a bed had been prepared for me. It was a large, musty-smelling apartment, almost empty, there being only my bed and a few tall, upright chairs bound with leather and black with age. The floor was tiled, and the ceiling was covered with a dusty canopy of cobwebs, on which flourished a numerous colony of long-legged house-spiders. I had no disposition to sleep at that early hour, and even envied Don Hilario away enjoying himself with the Rocha beauties. My door, looking out to the front, was standing wide open; the full moon had just risen and was filling the night with its mystic splendour. Putting out my candle, for the house was now all dark and silent, I softly went out for a stroll. Under a clump of trees not far off I found an old rustic bench, and sat down on it; for the place was all such a tangled wilderness of great weeds that walking was scarcely practicable and very unpleasant.

The old half-ruined house in the midst of the dusky desolation began to assume in the moonlight a singularly weird and ghost-like appearance. Near me on one side was an irregular row of poplar trees, and the long, dark lines cast from them by the moon fell across a wide, open space where the rank-growing thorn-apples predominated. In the spaces between the broad bands made by the poplar-tree shadows, the foliage appeared of a dim, hoary blue, starred over with the white blossoms of this night-flowering weed. About these flowers several big, grey moths were hovering, suddenly appearing out of the black shadows, and when looked for, noiselessly vanishing again in their mysterious ghost-like manner. Not a sound disturbed the silence except the faint melancholy trill of one small night-singing cicada from somewhere near—a faint, aerial voice that seemed to be wandering lost in infinite space, rising and floating away in its loneliness, while earth listened, hushed into preternatural stillness. Presently a large owl came noiselessly flying by, and perching on the topmost boughs of a neighbouring tree, began hooting a succession of monotonous notes, sounding like the baying of a bloodhound at a vast distance. Another owl by-and-by responded from some far-off quarter, and the dreary duet was kept up for half an hour. Whenever one bird ceased his solemn *boo-boo-boo-boo-boo*, I found myself with stilled breath straining my sense to catch the answering notes, fearing to stir lest I should lose them. A phosphorescent gleam swept by close to my face, making me start at its sudden appearance, then passed away, trailing a line of faint light over the dusky weeds. The passing firefly served to remind me that I was not smoking, and the thought then occurred to me that a cigar might possibly have the effect of relieving me from the strange, indefinable feeling of depression that had come over me. I put my hand into my pocket and drew out a cigar, and bit the end off; but when about to strike a vesta on my matchbox, I shuddered and dropped my hand.

The very thought of striking a loud exploding match was unendurable to me, so strangely nervous did I feel. Or, possibly it was a superstitious mood I had fallen into. It seemed to me at that moment that I had somehow drifted into a region of mystery, peopled only by unearthly, fantastic beings. The people I had supped with did not seem like creatures of flesh and blood. The small, dark countenance of Don Hilario with its shifty glances and Mephistophelian smile; Demetria's pale, sorrowful face, and the sunken, insane eyes of her old, white-haired father, were all about me in the moonlight and amongst the tangled greenery. I dared not move; I scarcely breathed; the very weeds with their pale, dusky leaves were like things that had a ghostly life. And while I was in this morbid condition of mind, with that irrational fear momentarily increasing on me, I saw at a distance of about thirty yards a dark object, which seemed to move, fluttering in an uncertain way towards me. I gazed intently on it, but it was motionless now, and appeared like a black, formless shadow within the shade of the trees. Presently it came again towards me, and passing into the clear moonlight, revealed a human figure. It flitted across the bright space and was lost in the shade of other trees; but it still approached, a waving, fluttering figure, advancing and receding, but always coming nearer. My blood turned cold in my veins; I could feel my hair standing up on my head, until, unable to endure the terrible suspense longer, I jumped up from my seat. A loud exclamation of terror came from the figure, and then I saw that it was Demetria. I stammered out an apology for frightening her by jumping up, and finding that I had recognised her, she advanced to me.

"Ah, you are not asleep, señor," said she quietly. "I saw you from my window come out here more than an hour ago. Finding you did not return I began to grow anxious, and thought that, tired with your journey, you had fallen asleep out here. I came to wake you and to warn you that it is very dangerous to lie sleeping with your face exposed to the full moon."

I explained that I had felt restless and disinclined to sleep, regretted that I had caused her anxiety, and thanked her for her thoughtful kindness.

Instead of leaving me then she sat quietly down on the bench. "Señor," she said, "if it is your intention to continue your journey to-morrow, let me advise you not to do so. You can safely remain here for a few days, for in this sad house we have no visitors."

I told her that acting on Santa Coloma's advice, given to me before the fight, I was going on to the Lomas de Rocha to see a person named Florentino Blanco in that place, who would probably be able to procure me a passport from Montevideo.

"How fortunate it is that you have told me this!" she replied. "Every stranger now entering the Lomas is rigorously examined, and you could not possibly escape arrest if you went there. Remain with us, señor; it is a poor house, but we are well disposed towards you. To-morrow Santos shall go with a letter from you to Don Florentino, who is always ready to serve us, and he will do what you wish without seeing you."

I thanked her warmly and accepted the offer of a refuge in her house. Somewhat to my surprise she still remained seated on the bench. Presently she said—

"It is natural, señor, that you should not be glad to remain in a house so *triste*. But there will be no repetition of all you were obliged to endure on first entering it. Whenever my father sees a young man, a stranger to him, he receives him as he received you to-day, mistaking him for his son. After the first day, however, he loses all interest in the new face, becoming indifferent, and forgetting all he has said or imagined."

This information relieved me, and I remarked that I supposed the loss of his son had been the cause of his malady.

"You are right; let me tell you how it happened," she replied. "For this estancia must seem to you a place unlike all others in the world, and it is only natural that a stranger should wish to know the reason of its sad condition. I know that I can speak without fear of these things to one who is a friend to Santa Coloma."

"And to you, I hope, señorita," I said.

"Thank you, señor. All my life has been spent here. When I was a child my brother went into the army, then my mother died, and I was left here alone, for the siege of Montevideo had begun and I could not go there. At length my father received a terrible wound in action and was brought here to die, as we thought. For months he lay on his bed, his life trembling in the balance. Our enemies triumphed at last; the siege was over, the Blanco leaders dead or driven into exile. My father had been one of the bravest officers in the Blanco forces, and could not hope to escape the general persecution. They only waited for his recovery to arrest him and convey him to the capital, where, doubtless, he would have been shot. While he lay in this precarious condition every wrong and indignity was heaped upon us. Our horses were seized by the commander of the department, our cattle slaughtered or driven off and sold, while our house was searched for arms and visited every week by an officer who came to report on my father's health. One reason for this animosity was that Calixto, my brother, had escaped and maintained a guerilla war against the government on the Brazilian frontier. At length my father recovered so far from his wounds as to be able to creep out for an hour every day leaning on someone for support; then two armed men were sent to keep guard here to prevent his escape. We were thus living in continual dread when one day an officer came and produced a written order from the Comandante. He did not read it to me, but said it was an order for every person in the Rocha department to display a red flag on his house in token of rejoicing at a victory won by the government troops. I told him that we did not wish to disobey the Comandante's orders, but had no red flag in the house to hang out. He answered that he had brought one for that purpose with him. He unrolled it and fastened it to a pole; then climbing to the roof of the house he raised and made it fast there. Not satisfied with these insults, he ordered me to wake my father, who was sleeping, so that he also might see the flag over his house. My father came out leaning on my shoulder, and when he had cast up his eyes and seen the red flag he turned and cursed the officer. 'Go back,' he cried, 'to the dog, your master, and tell him that Colonel Peralta is still a Blanco in spite of your dishonourable flag. Tell that insolent slave of Brazil that when I was disabled I passed my sword on to my son Calixto, who knows how to use it, fighting for his country's independence.' The officer, who had mounted his horse by this time, laughed, and tossing the order from the co-mandancia at our feet, bowed derisively and galloped away. My father picked up the paper and read these words: 'Let there be displayed on every house in this department a red flag, in token of joy at the happy tidings of a victory won by the government troops, in which that recreant son of the Republic, the infamous assassin and traitor, Calixto Peralta, was slain!' Alas, señor, loving his son above all things, hoping so much from him, and enfeebled by long suffering, my poor father could not resist this last blow. From that cruel moment he was deprived of reason; and to that calamity we owe it that he was not put to death and that our enemies ceased to persecute us."

Demetria shed some tears when telling me this tragical story. Poor woman, she had said little or nothing about herself, yet how great and enduring must have been her grief. I was deeply moved, and taking her hand told her how deeply her sad story had pained me. Then she rose and bade me good night with a sad smile—sad, but the first smile that had visited her grief-clouded countenance since I had seen her. I could well imagine that even the sympathy of a stranger must have seemed sweet to her in that dreary isolation.

After she left me I lit my cigar. The night had lost its ghostly character and my fantastic superstitions had vanished. I was back once more in the world of men and women, and could only think of the inhumanity of man to man, and of the infinite pain silently endured by many hearts in that Purple Land. The only mystery still unsolved in that ruinous estancia was Don Hilario, who locked up the wine and was called *master* with bitter irony by Ramona, and who had thought it necessary to apologise to me for depriving me of his precious company that evening.

CHAPTER XXIV

MYSTERY OF THE GREEN BUTTERFLY

I SPENT several days with the Peraltas at their desolate, *kineless* cattle-farm, which was known in the country around simply as *Estancia* or *Campos de Peralta*. Such wearisome days they proved to me, and so anxious was I getting about Paquíta away in Montevideo, that I was more than once on the point of giving up waiting for the passport, which Don Florentino had promised to get for me, and boldly venture forth without even that fig-leaf into the open. Demetria's prudent counsels, however, prevailed, so that my departure was put off from day to day. The only pleasure I experienced in the house arose from the belief I entertained that my visit had made an agreeable break in the sad, monotonous life of my gentle hostess. Her tragical story had stirred my heart to a very deep pity, and as I grew every day to know her better I began to appreciate and esteem her for her own pure, gentle, self-sacrificing character. Notwithstanding the dreary seclusion in which she had lived, seeing no society, and with only those old servants, so primitive in their ways, for company, there was not the slightest trace of rusticity in her manner. That, however, is not saying much for Demetria, since in most ladies—most women I might almost say— of Spanish origin there is a natural grace and dignity of manner one only expects to find in women socially well placed in our own country. When we were all together at meals, or in the kitchen sipping maté, she was invariably silent, always with that shadow of some concealed anxiety on her face; but when alone with me, or when only old Santos and Ramona were present, the cloud would be gone, her eyes would lighten up and the rare smile come more frequently to her lips. Then, at times, she would become almost animated in conversation, listening with lively interest to all I told her about the great world of which she was so ignorant, and laughing, too, at her own ignorance of things known to every town-bred child. When these pleasant conversations took place in the kitchen the two old servants would sit gazing at the face of their mistress apparently absorbed in admiration. They evidently regarded her as the most perfect being that had ever been created; and though there was a ludicrous side to their simple idolatry, I ceased to wonder at it when I began to know her better. They reminded me of two faithful dogs always watching a beloved master's face, and showing in their eyes, glad or pathetic, how they sympathise with all his moods. As for old Colonel Peralta, he did nothing to make me uneasy; after the first day he never talked to me, scarcely even noticing my presence except to salute me in a ceremonious manner when we met at table. He would spend his day between his easy-chair in the house and the rustic bench under the trees, where he would sit for hours at a time leaning forward on his stick, his preternaturally brilliant eyes watching everything seemingly with a keen, intelligent interest. But he would not speak. He was waiting for his son, thinking his fierce thoughts to himself. Like a bird blown far out over a tumultuous sea and wandering lost, his spirit was ranging over that wild and troubled past—that half a century of fierce passions and bloody warfare in which he had acted a conspicuous part. And perhaps it was sometimes even more in the future than the past—that glorious future when Calixto, lying far off in some mountain pass, or on some swampy plain with the trailing creepers covering his bones, should come back victorious from the wars.

My conversations with Demetria were not frequent, and before long they ceased altogether; for Don Hilario, who was not in harmony with us, was always there, polite, subdued, watchful, but not a man that one could take into his heart. The more I saw of him the less I liked him; and though I am not prejudiced about snakes, as the reader already knows, believing as I do that ancient tradition has made us very unjust towards these interesting children of our universal mother, I can think of no epithet except *snaky* to describe this man. Wherever I happened to be about the place he had a way of coming upon me, stealing through the weeds on his belly as it were, then suddenly appearing unawares before me; while something in his manner suggested a subtle, cold-blooded, venomous nature. Those swift glances of his, which perpetually came and went with such bewildering rapidity, reminded me not of the immovable, stony gaze of the serpent's lidless eyes, but of the flickering little forked tongue, that flickers, flickers, vanishes and flickers again, and is never for one moment at rest. Who was this man, and what did he there? Why was he, though manifestly not loved by anyone, absolute master of the estancia? He never asked me a question about myself, for it was not in his nature to ask questions, but he had evidently formed some disagreeable suspicions about me that made him look on me as a possible enemy. After I had been a few days in the house he ceased going out, and wherever I went he was always ready to accompany me, or when I met Demetria and began conversing with her, there he would be to take part in our conversation.

At length the piece of paper so long waited for came from the Lomas de Rocha, and with that sacred document, testifying that I was a subject of her Britannic Majesty, Queen Victoria, all fears and hesitations were dismissed from my mind and I prepared to depart for Montevideo.

The instant Don Hilario heard that I was about to leave the estancia his manner toward me changed; he became, in a moment, excessively friendly, pressing me to prolong my visit, also to accept a horse from him as a gift, and saying many kind things about the agreeable moments he had spent in my company. He completely reversed the old saying about welcome the coming, speed the parting guest; but I knew very well that he was anxious enough to see the last of me.

After supper on the eve of my departure he saddled his horse and rode off to attend a dance or gathering of some kind at a neighbouring estancia, for now that he had recovered from his suspicions he was very eager to resume the social pleasures my presence had interfered with.

I went out to smoke a cigar amongst the trees, it being a very lovely autumnal evening, with the light of an unclouded new moon to temper the darkness. I was walking up and down in a narrow path amongst the weeds, thinking of my approaching meeting with Paquíta, when old Santos came out to me and mysteriously informed me that Doña Demetria wished to see me. He led me through the large room where we always had our meals, then through a narrow dimly lighted passage into another room I had not entered before. Though the rest of the house was now in darkness, the old colonel having already retired to bed, it was very light here, there being about half a dozen candles placed about the room. In the centre of the floor, with her old face beaming with delighted admiration, stood Ramona gazing on another person seated on the sofa. And on this individual I also gazed silently for some time; for though I recognised Demetria in her, she was so changed that astonishment prevented me from speaking. The rusty grub had come forth as a splendid green and gold butterfly. She had on a grass-green silk dress, made in a fashion I had never seen before; extremely high in the waist, puffed out on the shoulders, and with enormous bell-shaped sleeves reaching to the elbows, the whole garment being plentifully trimmed with very fine cream-coloured lace. Her long, thick hair, which had hitherto always been worn in heavy plaits on her back, was now piled up in great coils on her head and surmounted by a tortoise-shell comb a foot high at least, and about fifteen inches broad at the top, looking like an immense crest on her head. In her ears were curious gold filigree pendants reaching to her bare shoulders; she also wore a necklet of half-doubloons linked together in a chain, and heavy gold bracelets on her arms. It was extremely quaint. Possibly this finery had belonged to her grandmother a hundred years ago; and I daresay that bright green was not the proper tint for Demetria's pallid complexion; still I must confess, at the risk of being set down as a barbarian in matters of taste, that it gave me a shock of pleasure to see her. She saw that I was very much surprised, and a blush of confusion overspread her face; then recovering her usual quiet, self-pos-

sessed manner she invited me to sit on the sofa by
her. I took her hand and complimented her on
her appearance. She laughed a little shy laugh,
then said that as I was going to leave her next day
she did not wish me to remember her only as a
woman in rusty black. I replied that I would
always remember her not for the colour and
fashion of her garments, but for her great un-
merited misfortunes, her virtuous heart, and for
the kindness she had shown to me. My words
evidently pleased her, and while we sat together
conversing pleasantly, before us were Ramona and
Santos, one standing, the other seated, both feast-
ing their eyes on their mistress in her brilliant attire. Their delight was quite open and childlike,
and gave an additional zest to the pleasure I felt.
Demetria seemed pleased to think she looked well,
and was more light-hearted than I had seen her
before. That antique finery, which would have
been laughable on another woman, somehow or
other seemed appropriate to her; possibly because
the strange simplicity and ignorance of the world
displayed in her conversation and that gentle dignity of manner natural to her would have prevented her from appearing ridiculous in any costume.

At length, after we had partaken of maté served
by Ramona, the old servants retired from the
room, not without many longing, lingering glances
at their metamorphosed mistress. Then somehow
or other our conversation began to languish, De-

metria becoming constrained in manner, while that
anxious shadow I had grown so familiar with came
again like a cloud over her face. Thinking that
it was time to leave her, I rose to go, and thanked
her for the pleasant evening I had spent, and
expressed a wish that her future would be brighter
than her past had been.

"Thank you, Richard," she returned, her eyes
cast down, and allowing her hand to rest in mine.
"But must you leave me so soon?—there is so
much I wish to say to you."

"I will gladly remain and hear it," I said, sitting down again by her side.

"My past has been very sad, as you say, Richard, but you do not know all," and here she put
her handkerchief to her eyes. There were, I
noticed, several beautiful rings on her fingers, and
the handkerchief she held to her eyes was a dainty
little embroidered thing with a lace border; for
everything in her make-up was complete and in
keeping that evening. Even the quaint little shoes
she wore were embroidered with silver thread and
had large rosettes to them. After removing the
handkerchief from her face, she continued silent
and with eyes cast down, looking very pale and
troubled.

"Demetria," I said, "tell me how I can serve
you? I cannot guess the nature of the trouble you
speak of, but if it is one I can help you out of,
speak to me without reserve."

"Perhaps you can help me, Richard. It was of

this matter I wished to speak this evening. But now—how can I speak of it?"

"Not to one who is your friend, Demetria? I wish you could think that the spirit of your lost brother Calixto was here in me, for I am as ready to help you as he would have been; and I know, Demetria, that you were very dear to him."

Her face flushed, and for a moment her eyes met mine; then, casting them down again, she replied sadly, "It is impossible! I can say no more to you now. My heart oppresses me so that my lips refuse to speak. To-morrow, perhaps."

"To-morrow morning I leave you, and there will be no opportunity of speaking," I said. "Don Hilario will be here watching you, and though he is so much in the house, I cannot believe that you trust him."

She started at the name of Don Hilario, and cried a little in silence; then suddenly she rose and gave me her hand to bid good night. "You shall know everything to-morrow, Richard," she said. "Then you will know how much I trust you and how little I trust him. I cannot speak myself, but I can trust Santos, who knows everything, and he shall tell you all."

There was a sad, wistful look in her eyes when we parted that haunted me for hours afterwards. Coming into the kitchen I disturbed Ramona and Santos deep in a whispered consultation. They started up, looking somewhat confused; then, when I had lit a cigar and turned to go out, they got up and went back to their mistress.

While I smoked I pondered over the strange evening I had passed, wondering very much what Demetria's secret trouble could be. "The mystery of the green butterfly," I called it; but it was really all too sad even for a mental joke, though a little timely laughter is often the best weapon to meet trouble with, sometimes having an effect like that of a gay sunshade suddenly opened in the face of an angry bull. Unable to solve the riddle, I retired to my room to sleep my last sleep under Peralta's dreary roof.

CHAPTER XXV

DELIVER ME FROM MINE ENEMY!

ABOUT eight o'clock next morning I bade the Peraltas good-bye, and set out on my long-delayed journey, still mounted on that dishonestly acquired steed that had served me so well, for I had declined the good Hilario's offer of a horse. Though all my toils, wanderings, and many services to the cause of liberty (or whatever people fight for in the Banda) had not earned me one copper coin, it was some comfort to think that Candelaria's never-to-be-forgotten generosity had saved me from being penniless; I was, in fact, returning to Paquíta well dressed, on a splendid horse, and with dollars enough in my pocket to take us comfortably out of the country. Santos rode out with me, ostensibly to put me on the right road to Montevideo; only I knew, of course, that he was the bearer of an important communication from Demetria. When we had ridden about half a league without any approach to the subject on his part, in spite of sundry hints I threw out, I asked him plainly if he had a message for me.

After pondering over the question for as long a time as would be necessary to work out a rather difficult mathematical problem, he answered that he had.

314

"Then," said I, "let me hear it."

He grinned. "Do you think," he said, "that it is a thing to be spoken in half a dozen words? I have not come all this distance merely to say that the moon came in dry, or that yesterday, being Friday, Doña Demetria tasted no meat. It is a long story, señor."

"How many leagues long? Do you intend it to last all the way to Montevideo? The longer it is the sooner you ought to begin it."

"There are things easy to say, and there are other things not so easy," returned Santos. "But as to saying anything on horseback, who could do that?"

"Why not?"

"The question!" said he. "Have you not observed that when liquor is drawn from a cask—wine, or bitter orange juice to make orangeade, or even rum, which is by nature white and clear—that it runs thick when the cask is shaken? It is the same with us, señor; our brain is the cask out of which we draw all the things we say."

"And the spigot——"

"That is so," he struck in, pleased with my ready intelligence; "the mouth is the spigot."

"I should have thought the nose more like the spigot," I replied.

"No," he gravely returned. "You can make a loud noise with the nose when you snore or blow it in a handkerchief; but it has no door of communication with the brain. The things that are in the brain flow out by the mouth."

"Very well," said I, getting impatient, "call the mouth spigot, bung-hole, or what you like, and the nose merely an ornament on the cask. The thing is this. Doña Demetria has entrusted you with some liquor to pass on to me; now pass it, thick or clear."

"Not thick," he answered stubbornly.

"Very well; clear then," I shouted.

"To give it to you clear I must give it off and not on my horse, sitting still and not moving."

Anxious to have it over without more beating about the bush, I reined up my horse, jumped off and sat down on the grass without another word. He followed my example, and after seating himself in a comfortable position, deliberately drew out his tobacco-pouch and began making a cigarette. I could not quarrel with him for this further delay, for without the soothing, stimulating cigarette an Oriental finds it difficult to collect his thoughts. Leaving him to carry out his instructions in his own laborious fashion, I vented my irritation on the grass, plucking it up by handfuls.

"Why do you do that?" he asked, with a grin.

"Pluck grass? What a question! When a person sits down on the grass, what is the first thing he does?"

"Makes a cigarette," he returned.

"In my country he begins plucking up the grass," I said.

"In the Banda Orientál we leave the grass for the cattle to eat," said he.

I at once gave up pulling the grass, for it evidently distracted his mind, and lighting a cigarette, began smoking as placidly as I could.

At length he began: "There is not in all the Banda Orientál a worse person to express things than myself."

"You are speaking the truth," I said.

"But what is to be done?" he continued, staring straight before him and giving as little heed to my interruption as a hunter riding at a stiff fence would pay to a remark about the weather. "When a man cannot get a knife, he breaks in two an old pair of sheep-shears and with one of the blades makes himself an implement which has to serve him for a knife. This is how it is with Doña Demetria; she has no one but her poor Santos to speak for her. If she had asked me to expose my life in her service, that I could easily have done: but to speak for her to a man who can read the almanac and knows the names of all the stars in the sky, that kills me, señor. And who knows this better than my mistress, who has been intimate with me from her infancy, when I often carried her in my arms? I can only say this, señor; when I speak, remember my poverty and that my mistress has no instrument except my poor tongue to convey her wishes. Words has she told me to say to you, but my devil of a memory has lost them all. What am I to do in this case? If

I wished to buy my neighbour's horse and went to him and said, 'Sell me your horse, neighbour, for I have fallen in love with it and my heart is sick with desire, so that I must have it at any price,' would that not be madness, señor? Yet I must be like that imprudent person. I come to you for something, and all her expressions, which were like rare flowers culled from a garden, have been lost by the way. Therefore I can only say this thing which my mistress desires, putting it in my own brute words, which are like wild flowers I have myself gathered on the plain, that have neither fragrance nor beauty to recommend them."

This quaint exordium did not advance matters much, but it had the effect of rousing my attention and convincing me that the message entrusted to Santos was one of very grave import. He had finished his first cigarette and now began slowly making himself a second one; but I waited patiently for him to speak, my irritation had quite vanished, those "wild flowers" of his were not without beauty, and his love and devotion for his unhappy mistress made them smell very sweet.

Presently he resumed: "Señor, you have told my mistress that you are a poor man; that you look upon this country life as a free and happy one; that above all things you would like to possess an estancia where you could breed cattle and race-horses and hunt ostriches. All this she has revolved in her mind, and because it is in her power to offer you the things you desire does she now ask you to aid her in her trouble. And now, señor, let me tell you this. The Peralta property extends all the way to the Rocha waters; five leagues of land, and there is none better in this department. It was formerly well stocked. There were thousands of cattle and mares; for my master's party then ruled in the country; the Colorados were shut up in Montevideo, and that cutthroat Frutos Rivera never came into this part. Of the cattle only a remnant remains, but the land is a fortune for any man, and when my old master dies Doña Demetria inherits all. Even now it is hers, since her father has lost his calabash as you have seen. Now let me tell you what happened many years ago. Don Hilario was at first a peon—a poor boy the Colonel befriended. When he grew up he was made capatas, then mayordomo. Don Calixto was killed and the Colonel lost his reason, then Don Hilario made himself all-powerful, doing what he liked with his master, and setting Doña Demetria's authority aside. Did he protect the interests of the estancia? On the contrary, he was one with our enemies, and when they came like dogs for our cattle and horses he was behind them. This he did to make friends of the reigning party, when the Blancos had lost everything. Now he wishes to marry Doña Demetria to make himself owner of the land. Don Calixto is dead, and who is there to bell the cat? Even now he acts like the only owner; he buys and sells and the money is his.

My mistress is scarcely allowed clothes to wear; she has no horse to ride on and is a prisoner in her own house. He watches her like a cat watching a bird shut in a room; if he suspected her of an intention to make her escape he would murder her. He has sworn to her that unless she marries him he will kill her. Is not this sad? Señor, she asks you to deliver her from this man. Her words I have forgotten, but imagine that you see her before you a suppliant on her knees, and that you know what the thing is she asks, and see her lips move, though you do not hear her words."

"Tell me how I can deliver her?" I said, feeling very much moved at what I had heard.

"How! By carrying her off forcibly—do you understand? Is it not in your power to return in a few days' time with two or three friends to do this thing? You must come disguised and armed. If I am in the way I will do what I can to protect her, but you will easily knock me down and stun me—do you understand? Don Hilario must not know that we are in the plot. From him fear nothing, for though he is brave enough to threaten a woman with death, before armed men he is like a dog that hears thunder. You can then take her to Montevideo and conceal her there. The rest will be easy. Don Hilario will fail to find her; Ramona and I will take care of the Colonel, and when his daughter is out of his sight perhaps he will forget her. Then, señor, there will be no trouble about the property; for who can resist a legal claim?"

"I do not understand you, Santos," said I. "If Demetria wishes me to do what you say, and there is no other way to save her from Don Hilario's persecutions, I will do it. I will do anything to serve her, and I have no fear of that dog Hilario. But when I have placed her in concealment, who in Montevideo, where she is without a friend, will take up her cause and see that she is not defrauded of her rights? I can give her liberty, but that will be all."

"The property will be the same as yours when you marry her," said he.

I had never suspected that this was coming, and was amazed to hear it.

"Will you tell me, Santos," said I, "that Demetria sent you to say this to me? Does she think that only by marrying her I can deliver her from this robber and save her property?"

"There is, of course, no other way," said he. "If it could be done by other means would she not have spoken last night and explained everything to you? Consider, señor, all this large property will be yours. If you do not like this department then she will sell everything for you to buy an estancia elsewhere, or to do whatever you wish. And I ask you this, señor, could any man marry a better woman?"

"No," said I; "but, Santos, I cannot marry your mistress."

I remembered then, sadly enough, that I had told her next to nothing about myself. Seeing me so young, wandering homeless about the country, she had naturally taken me for a single man; and, perhaps thinking that I had conceived an affection for her, had been driven in her despair to make this proposal. Poor Demetria, was there to be no deliverance for her after all!

"Friend," said Santos, dropping the ceremonious señor in his anxiety to serve his mistress, "never speak without first considering all things. There is no woman like her. If you do not love her now you will love her when you know her better; no good man could help feeling affection for her. You saw her last evening in a green silk dress, also wearing a tortoise-shell comb and gold ornaments—was she not elegant, señor? Did she not then appear to your eyes a woman suitable for a wife? You have been everywhere, and have seen many women, and perhaps in some distant place you have met one more beautiful than my mistress. But consider the life she has led! Grief has made her pale and thin, staining her face with purple under the eyes. Can laughter and song come out of a heart where fear is? Another life would change all; she would be a flower amongst women."

Poor old simple-minded Santos, he had done himself great injustice; his love for his mistress had inspired him with an eloquence that went to my heart. And poor Demetria, driven by her weary desolate life and torturing fears to make in vain this unwomanly proposal to a stranger! And after all it was not unwomanly; for in all countries where they are not abject slaves it is permissible for women in some circumstances to propose marriage. Even in England it is so, where society is like a huge Clapham Junction, with human creatures moving like trucks and carriages on cast-iron conventional rails, which they can only leave at the risk of a destructive collision. And a proposal of the kind was never more justifiable than in this case. Shut away from the sight of men in her dreary seclusion, haunted by nameless fears, her offer was to bestow her hand along with a large property on a penniless adventurer. Nor had she done this before she had learnt to love me, and to think, perhaps, that the feeling was returned. She had waited, too, till the very last moment, only making her offer when she had despaired of its coming from me. This explained the reception of the previous evening; the ancient splendid attire which she had worn to win favour in my sight; the shy, wistful expression of her eyes, the hesitation she could not overcome. When I had recovered from the first shock of surprise I could only feel the greatest respect and compassion for her, bitterly regretting that I had not told her all my past history, so that she might have been spared the shame and grief she would now be compelled to endure. These sad thoughts passed through my mind while Santos expatiated on the advantages of the proposed alliance until I stopped him.

"Say no more," I said; "for I swear to you, Santos, that were it possible I would gladly take Demetria for a wife, so greatly do I admire and esteem her. But I am married. Look at this; it is my wife's portrait"; and taking from my bosom the miniature which I always wore round my neck, I handed it to him.

He stared at me in silent astonishment for a few moments, then took the portrait into his hand; and while he gazed admiringly at it I pondered over what I had heard. I could not now think of leaving this poor woman who had offered herself with all her inheritance to me without some attempt to rescue her from her sad position. She had given me a refuge when I was in trouble and danger, and the appeal she had just made to me, accompanied by so convincing a proof of her trust and affection, would have gone to the heart of the most cold-blooded man in existence, to make him, in spite of his nature, her devoted champion.

At length Santos handed back the miniature with a sigh. "Such a face as that my eyes have never seen," he remarked. "There is nothing more to be said."

"There is a great deal more to be said," I returned. "I have thought of an easy plan to help your mistress. When you have reported this conversation, tell her to remember the offer of assistance made to her last night. I said I would be a brother to her, and I shall keep my promise. You three cannot think of any better scheme to save Demetria than this one you have told me, but it is after all a very poor scheme, full of difficulty and danger to her. My plan is a simpler and safer one. Tell her to come out to-night at midnight, after the moon has set, to meet me under the trees behind the house. I shall be there waiting with a horse for her, and will take her away to some safe place of concealment where Don Hilario will never find her. When she is once out of his power it will be time enough to think of some way to turn him out of the estancia and to arrange matters. See that she does not fail to meet me, and let her take a few clothes and some money if she has any; also her jewels, for it would not be safe to leave them in the house with Don Hilario."

Santos was delighted with my scheme, which was so much more practical though less romantic than the one hatched by those three simple-minded conspirators. With heart full of hope he was about to leave me when he suddenly exclaimed, "But, señor, how will you get a horse and side-saddle for Doña Demetria?"

"Leave it all to me," I said; then we separated, he to return to his mistress, who was no doubt anxiously waiting to know the result of our conversation, I to get through the next fifteen hours in the best way I could.

CHAPTER XXVI

LOCK AND KEY AND SINNERS THREE

AFTER leaving Santos I rode on to a belt of wood about two miles east of the road, and passing through it surveyed the country lying beyond. The only habitation near it was a shepherd's lonely rancho, standing on an open plain of yellow grass, over which a scattered flock of sheep and a few horses were grazing. I determined to remain in the wood till near noon, then proceed to the rancho to get breakfast, and commence my search for a horse and side-saddle in the neighbourhood. After unsaddling my horse and tying him to a tree, where there were some pickings of grass and herbage about the roots, I lit a cigar and made myself comfortable on my rugs in the shade. Presently I had some visitors in a flock of *urracas,* or magpies, as they are called in the vernacular, or Guira cuckoos; a graceful, loquacious bird resembling a magpie, only with a longer tail and a bold, red beak. These ill-mannered birds skulked about in the branches over me all the time I remained in the wood, scolding me so incessantly in their intolerably loud, angry, rattling notes, varied occasionally with shrill whistlings and groans, that I could scarcely even hear myself think. They soon succeeded in bringing all the other birds within hearing-distance to the spot to take part in the demonstration. It was unreasonable of the cuckoos, to say the least of it, for it was now long past their breeding season, so that parental solicitude could not be pleaded as an excuse for their churlish behaviour. The others—tanagers, finches, tyrant-birds; red, white, blue, grey, yellow, and mixed—were, I must own, less troublesome, for, after hopping about for a while, screaming, chirping, and twittering, they very sensibly flew away, no doubt thinking their friends the cuckoos were making a great deal too much fuss. My sole mammalian visitor was an armadillo, that came hurrying towards me, looking curiously like a little old bent-backed gentleman in a rusty black coat trotting briskly about on some very important business. It came to within three yards of my feet, then stopped, and seemed astonished beyond measure at my presence, staring at me with its little, bleary, blinking eyes, and looking more like the shabby old gentleman than ever. Then it trotted away through the trees, but presently returned for a second inspection; and after that it kept coming and going till I inadvertently burst out laughing, whereupon it scuttled away in great alarm, and returned no more. I was sorry I had frightened the amusing little beggar, for I felt in that exceedingly light-hearted mood when one's merriment is ready to brim over at the slightest provocation. Yet that very morning poor Demetria's appeal had deeply stirred my heart, and

I was now embarked on a most Quixotic and perhaps perilous adventure!   Possibly the very fact
of that adventure being before me had produced
an exhilarating effect on my mind, and made it impossible for me to be sad or even decently composed.

After spending a couple of hours in the pleasant
shade, the blue smoke ascending from the rancho
before me gave notice of the approaching breakfast hour; so, saddling my horse, I went to make
my morning call, the cuckoos hailing my departure
with loud, mocking shouts and whistling calls,
meant to inform all their feathered friends that
they had at last succeeded in making their haunt
too hot for me.

At the rancho I was received by a somewhat
surly-looking young man, with long, intensely
black hair and moustache, and who wore in place
of a hat a purple cotton handkerchief tied about
his head.   He did not seem to be over-pleased at
my visit, and invited me rather ungraciously to
alight if I thought proper.   I followed him into
the kitchen, where his little brown-skinned wife
was preparing breakfast, and I fancied after seeing
her that her prettiness was the cause of his inhos-
pitable manner towards a stranger.   She was singularly pretty, with a seductive soft brown skin, ripe
pouting lips of a rich purple-red, and when she
laughed, which happened very frequently, her
teeth glistened like pearls.   Her crisp black hair
hung down unbound and disordered, for she

looked like a very careless little beauty; but when she saw me enter, she blushed and tossed her tresses away from her shoulders, then carefully felt the pendants dropping from her ears to assure herself that they were safe, or possibly to attract my attention to them. The frequent glances her laughing dark eyes shot at me soon convinced me that she was one of those charming little wives—charming, that is, when they are the wives of other people—who are not satisfied with a husband's admiration.

I had timed my arrival well, for the roast lamb over the coals was just assuming a deep golden brown colour, and sending out a most delicious fragrance. During the repast which followed I amused my auditors, and myself, by telling a few innocent lies, and began by saying that I was on my return to Rocha from Montevideo.

The shepherd remarked suspiciously that I was not on the right road.

I answered that I knew it; then proceeded to say that I had met with a misfortune on the previous evening, which in the end had led me out of the right road. I had only been married a few days, I continued, and at this declaration my host looked relieved, while little gipsy suddenly seemed to lose all interest in me.

"My wife," I said, "set her heart on having a side-saddle, as she is very fond of riding; so, having business which took me to town, I there purchased one for her, and was returning with it on

a led horse—my wife's horse, unfortunately—
when I stopped last evening to get some refreshment at a *pulpería* on the road. While eating
some bread and sausage a tipsy person, who happened to be there, imprudently began to explode
some fire-crackers, which so terrified the horses
tied at the gate that several of them broke loose
and escaped. My wife's horse with the side-
saddle on him escaped with them; then mounting
my own horse I started in pursuit, but failed to
overtake the runaway. Finally it joined a herd
of mares, and these becoming terrified, fled from
me, leading me a chase of several leagues, till I
lost sight of them in the darkness."

"If your wife resembles mine in disposition,
friend," said he, with a somewhat sorrowful smile,
"you would have continued following the runaway animal with the side-saddle to the end of the
world."

"I can say this," I returned gravely, "without a
side-saddle, good or bad, I am not going to present myself before her. I intend inquiring at
every house on my way to the Lomas de Rocha
till I can hear of one for sale."

"What will you give for one?" said he, becoming interested.

"That will depend on its condition. If it is as
good as new I will give the amount it cost and two
dollars profit besides."

"I know of a side-saddle that cost ten dollars a
year ago, but it has never been used. It belongs

to a neighbour three leagues from here, and she would sell it, I believe."

"Show me the house," I said, "and I will go directly and offer twelve dollars for it."

"You speak of Doña Petrona's side-saddle, Antonio?" said the little wife. "She would sell it for what it cost—perhaps for eight dollars. Ah, pumpkin-head, why did you not think to make all that profit? Then I could have bought slippers and a thousand things."

"You are never satisfied, Cleta," he returned. "Have you not got slippers to your feet?"

She tossed up a pretty foot and displayed it cased in rather a shabby little slipper. Then with a laugh she kicked it off towards him. "There," she exclaimed, "put it in your bosom and keep it —something precious! And some day when you go to Montevideo, and wish to appear very grand before all the town, wear it on your great toe."

"Who expects reason from a woman?" said Antonio, shrugging his shoulders.

"Reason! you have no more brains than a Muscovy duck, Antonio. You might have made this profit, but you never can make money like other men, and therefore you will always be poorer than the spiders. I have said this before very often and only hope you will not forget it, for in future I intend to speak of other things."

"Where would I have got the ten dollars to pay Petrona for the saddle?" he retorted, losing his temper.

"My friend," I said, "if the saddle can be had it is only just that you should have the profit. Take ten dollars, and if you buy it for me I will pay you two more."

This proposal pleased him greatly, while Cleta, the volatile, clapped her hands with delight. While Antonio prepared to go to his neighbour's after the saddle I went out to a solitary thorn tree about fifty yards from the rancho, and spreading my poncho in the shade lay down to sleep the siesta.

Before the shepherd had been long gone I heard a great noise in the house, like banging on doors and on copper vessels, but took no notice, supposing it to proceed from Cleta engaged in some unusually noisy domestic operation. At length I heard a voice calling to me, "Señor! Señor!"

Getting up I went to the kitchen, but no person was there. Suddenly a loud knock was given on the door communicating with the second room. "Oh, my friend," cried Cleta's voice behind it, "my ruffian of a husband has locked me in—can you let me out, do you think?"

"Why has he locked you in?" I asked.

"The question! Because he is a brute, of course. He always does it when he goes out. Is it not horrible?"

"It only shows how fond he is of you," I returned.

"Are you so atrocious as to defend him? And I thought you had a heart—so handsome, too!

When I saw you I said, Ah, had I married this man what a happy life!"

"Thank you for your good opinion," I said. "I am very sorry you are locked in because it prevents me from seeing your pretty face."

"Oh, you think it pretty? Then you *must* let me out. I have put up my hair now, and look prettier than when you saw me."

"You look prettier with it down," I answered.

"Ah, down it goes again then!" she exclaimed —"Yes, you are right, it does look best that way. Is it not like silk? You shall feel it when you liberate me."

"That I cannot do, Cletita mine. Your Antonio has taken away the key."

"Oh, cruel man! He left me no water and I am perishing with thirst. What shall I do? Look, I will put my hand under the door for you to feel how hot it is; I am consumed with fever and thirst in this oven."

Presently her little brown hand came out at my feet, there being sufficient space between the floor and wood to pass it through. I stooped and took it in mine, and found it a hot, moist little hand, with a pulse beating very fast.

"Poor child!" I said, "I will pour some water in a plate and pass it to you under the door."

"Oh, you are bad to insult me!" she cried. "What, am I a cat to drink water from a plate? I could cry my eyes out"; here followed sob-like sounds. "Besides," she suddenly resumed, "it is fresh air, not water, I require. I am suffocated, I cannot breathe. Oh, dear friend, save me from fainting. Force back the door till the bolt slips out."

"No, no, Cleta, it cannot be done."

"What, with your strength! I could almost do it myself with my poor little hands. Open, open, open, before I faint."

She had evidently sunk down on the floor, sobbing, after making that practical suggestion; and casting about for burglarious implements to aid me, I found the spit and a wedge-shaped piece of hard wood. These I inserted just above and below the lock, and forcing back the door on its frame, I soon had the satisfaction of seeing the bolt slip from the catch.

Out sprang Cleta, flushed, tearful, her hair all in disorder, but laughing gleefully at having regained her liberty.

"Oh, dear friend, I thought you were going to leave me!" she cried. "How agitated I am—feel how my heart beats. Never mind, I can now pay that wretch out. Is not revenge sweet, sweet, sweet?"

"Now, Cleta," I said, "take three mouthfuls of fresh air and a drink of water, then let me lock you in again."

She laughed mockingly, and shook her hair like a wild young colt.

"Ah, you are not serious—do you not think I know?" she cried. "Your eyes tell me everything.

Besides, you could not shut me up again if you tried." Here she made a sudden dash at the door, but I caught her and held her a close prisoner.

"Let me go, monster—oh no, not monster, dear, sweet friend, beautiful as the—moon, sun, stars. I am dying for fresh air. I will come back to the oven before he returns. If he caught me out, what blows! Come, let us sit under the tree together."

"That would be disobeying your husband," I said, trying to look stern.

"Never mind, I will confess it all to the priest some day, then it will be as if it had never happened. Such a husband—poof! If you were not a married man—*are* you married? What a pity! Say again, am I pretty?"

"Say first, Cleta, have you a horse a woman can ride on, and if you have one, will you sell it to me?"

"Oh yes, the best horse in the Banda Oriental. They say it is worth six dollars—will you buy it for six dollars? No, I shall not sell it—I shall not tell you that I have a horse till you answer me. Am I pretty, sir stranger?"

"Tell me first about the horse, then ask me what you like."

"Nothing more will I tell you—not a word. Yes, everything. Listen. When Antonio comes back ask him to sell you a horse for your wife to ride. He will try to sell you one of his own, a demon full of faults like his master; false-footed, lame in the shoulder, a roarer, old as the south wind. A black piebald—remember. Offer to buy a roan with a cream nose. That is my horse. Offer him six dollars. Now say, am I pretty?"

"Oh, beautiful, Cleta; your eyes are stars, your mouth is a rosebud, sweeter than honey a thousand times."

"Now you talk like a wise man," she laughed; then holding my hand, she led me to the tree and sat down by my side on the poncho.

"And how old are you, little one?" I asked.

"Fourteen—is that very old? Ah, fool, to tell my age truly—no woman does that. Why did I not say thirteen? And I have been married six months, such a long time! I am sure I have green, blue, yellow, grey hairs coming out all over my head by this time. And what about my hair, sir, you never spoke of that? Did I not let it down for you? Is it not soft and beautiful? Tell me, sir, what about my hair?"

"In truth it is soft and beautiful, Cleta, and covers you like a dark cloud."

"Does it not! Look, I will cover my face with it. Now I am hidden like the moon in a cloud, and now, look, out comes the moon again! I have a great respect for the moon. Say, holy friar, am I like the moon?"

"Say, little sweet lips, why do you call me holy friar?"

"Say first, holy friar, am I like the moon?"

"No, Cleta, you are not like the moon, though

you are both married women; you are married to
Antonio——"

"Poor me!"

"And the moon is married to the sun."

"Happy moon, to be so far from him!"

"The moon is a quiet wife, but you chatter like
a paroquet."

"And am I not able to be quiet also, monk?
Look, I will be quiet as the moon—not a word,
not a breath." Then she threw herself back on
the poncho, feigning sleep, her arms above her
head, her hair scattered everywhere, only a tress
or two half shading her flushed face and round
heaving bosom that would not be quiet. There
was just a little mocking smile on her lips, just a
little gleam of laughing eyes under her drooping
lashes, for she could not help watching my face
for admiration. In such an attitude the tempting
little witch might have made the tepid blood of
an ascetic boil.

Two or three hours thus flew swiftly by while I
listened to her lively prattle, which, like the lark's
singing, had scarcely a pause in it, her attempt at
being still and moonlike having ended in a perfect
fiasco. At length, pouting her pretty lips and complaining of her hard lot, she said it was time to
go back to her prison; but all the time I was engaged in forcing back the bolt into its place she
chatted without ceasing. "Adieu, Sun, husband of
the moon," she said. "Adieu, sweet, sweet friend,
buyer of side-saddles! They were all lies you told

—I know, I know. You want a horse and side-saddle to carry off some girl to-night. Happy she! Now I must sit in the dark alone, alone, alone, till Antonio, the atrocious, comes to liberate me with his old iron key—ah, fool!"

Before I had been long back under my tree, Antonio appeared, bringing the side-saddle in triumph on his horse before him. After going in to release his wife he came out and invited me to take maté. I then mentioned my wish to buy a good horse; he was only too willing to sell, and in a few minutes his horses were driven up for inspection. The black piebald was first offered, a very handsome, quiet-looking animal, apparently quite sound. The cream-nose, I noticed, was a bony, long-bodied brute, with sleepy eyes and a ewe neck. Could it be that the little double-dealing witch had intended to deceive me? But in a moment I dismissed such a suspicion with the scorn it merited. Let a woman be as false as she can, and able to fool her husband to the top of her bent, she is, compared with the man who wishes to sell you a horse, openness and truth itself. I examined the piebald critically, walking and trotting him around; looked into his mouth, then at hoofs and fetlocks, beloved of windgalls; gazed with fixed attention into his eyes, and dealt him a sudden brisk blow on the shoulder.

"No weak spot will you find, señor," said Antonio the mendacious, who was certainly the greatest of the three sinners met together in that place.

"He is my best horse, only four years old, gentle as a lamb, sound as a bell. Sure-footed, señor, like no other horse; and with such an easy pace you can ride him at a gallop with a tumbler of water in your hand and not spill a drop. I will give him away to you for ten dollars, because you have been generous about the side-saddle, and I am anxious to serve you well."

"Thank you, my friend," I said. "Your piebald is fifteen years old, lame in the shoulders, broken in his wind, and has more vices than any seven horses in the Banda Oriéntal. I would not allow my wife to ride such a dangerous brute, for, as I told you, I have not been long married."

Antonio framed his face to express astonishment and virtue indignant; then with the point of his knife he scratched the figure of a cross on the ground, and was about to swear solemnly on it that I was egregiously mistaken, that his beast was a kind of equine angel, or a Pegasus, at least, when I interfered to stop him. "Tell as many lies as you like," I said, "and I will listen to them with the greatest interest; but do not swear on the figure of the cross to what is false, for then the four or five or six dollars profit you have made on the side-saddle will scarcely be sufficient to buy you absolution for such a sin."

He shrugged his shoulders and restored the sacrilegious knife to its sheath. "There are my horses," he said in an injured tone. "They are a kind of animal you seem to know a great deal

about; select one and deceive yourself. I have
endeavoured to serve you; but there are some
people who do not know a friend when they see
one."

I then minutely examined all the other horses,
and finally finished the farce by leading out the
roan cream-nose, and was pleased to notice the
crestfallen expression of my good shepherd.

"Your horses do not suit me," I said, "so I cannot buy one. I will, however, purchase this old
cow; for it is the only animal here I could trust
my wife on. You can have seven dollars for it—
not one copper more, for like the Emperor of
China, I speak once only."

He plucked off his purple headgear and
scratched his raven head, then led me back to the
kitchen to consult his wife, "For, señor," he said,
"you have, by some fatality, selected her horse."
When Cleta heard that seven dollars had been
offered for the roan, she laughed with joy. "Oh,
Antonio, he is only worth six dollars! Yes, señor,
you shall have him, and pay the seven dollars to
me. Not to my husband. Who will say now that
I cannot make money? And now, Antonio, I have
no horse to ride on, you can give me the bay with
white fore-feet."

"Do not imagine such a thing!" exclaimed her
husband.

After taking maté I left them to settle their
affairs, not doubting which would come out best
from a trial of skill. When I arrived in sight of

Peralta's trees I unsaddled and picketed my horses, then stretched myself out on my rugs. After the excitements and pleasures of that day, which had robbed me of my siesta, I quickly fell into a very sound sleep.

CHAPTER XXVII

NIGHT AND FLIGHT

When I woke I did not remember for some moments where I was. Feeling about me, my hand came in contact with the grass wet with dew. It was very dark, only low down in the sky a pale gleam of light gave promise, as I imagined, of coming day. Then recollection flashed upon me, and I sprang up alarmed to my feet, only to discover with inexpressible relief that the light I had remarked was in the west, not the east, and proceeded from the young moon just sinking beneath the horizon. Saddling my two animals expeditiously I rode to Peralta's estancia, and on arriving there carefully drew the horses into the shadow of a clump of trees growing on the borders of the ancient well-nigh obliterated foss or ditch. I then dropped on to the ground so as to listen better for approaching footsteps, and began waiting for Demetria. It was past midnight: not a sound reached me except at intervals the mournful far-away reedy note of the little nocturnal cicada that always seemed to be there lamenting the lost fortunes of the house of Peralta. For upwards of half an hour I remained lying on the ground, growing more anxious every moment and fearing that Demetria was going to fail me, when I caught a sound like a human whisper. Listening intently, I found that it pronounced my name and proceeded from a clump of tall thorn-apples some yards from me.

"Who speaks?" I replied.

The tall, gaunt form of Ramona drew itself up out of the weeds and cautiously approached me. She was shaking with nervous excitement, and had not ventured to come near without speaking for fear of being mistaken for an enemy and fired at.

"Mother of Heaven!" she exclaimed as well as her chattering teeth would allow her to speak. "I have been so agitated all the evening! Oh, señor, what are we to do now? Your plan was such a good one; when I heard it I knew an angel had flown down and whispered it in your ear. And now my mistress will not stir! All her things are ready—clothes, money, jewels; and for the last hour we have been urging her to come out, but nothing will serve. She will not see you, señor."

"Is Don Hilario in the house?"

"No, he is not—could anything have been better? But it is useless, she has lost heart and will not come. She only sits crying in her room, saying that she cannot look on your face again."

"Go and tell her that I am here with the horses waiting for her," I said.

"Señor, she knows you are here. Santos watched for you and hastened in to inform her of your arrival. Now she has sent me out only to say that she cannot meet you, that she thanks you for all you have done, and begs you to go away and leave her."

I was not greatly surprised at Demetria's reluctance to meet me at the last moment, but was determined not to leave without first seeing her and trying to change her mind. Securing the horses to a tree, I went with Ramona to the house. Stealing in on tiptoe, we found Demetria in that room where she had received me the evening before in her quaint finery, lying on the sofa, while old Santos stood by her the picture of distress. The moment she saw me enter she covered her face with her hands and turned from me. Yet a glance was sufficient to show that with or without her consent everything had been got ready for her flight. On a chair near her lay a pair of saddle-bags in which her few belongings had been stowed; a mantilla was drawn half over her head, and by her side was a large woollen shawl, evidently intended to protect her against the night air.

"Santos," I said, "go out to the horses under the trees and wait there for us: and you, Ramona, say good-bye now to your mistress, then leave us together; for by-and-by she will recover courage and go with me."

Santos, looking immensely relieved and grateful, though a little surprised at my confident tone, was hurrying out when I pointed to the saddle-bags. He nodded, grinned, and snatching them up left the room. Poor old Ramona threw herself on to her knees, sobbing and pouring out farewell blessings on her mistress, kissing her hands and hair with sorrowful devotion.

When she left us I sat down by Demetria's side, but she would not take her hands from her face or speak to me, and only wept hysterically when I addressed her. I succeeded at last in getting one of her hands in mine, and then drew her head gently down till it rested on my shoulder. When her sobs began to subside I said—

"Tell me, dear Demetria, have you lost faith in me that you fear to trust yourself with me now?"

"No, no, Richard, it is not that," she faltered. "But I can never look into your face again. If you have any compassion for me you will leave me now."

"What, leave you, Demetria, my sister, to that man—how can you imagine such a thing? Tell me, where is Don Hilario—is he coming back to-night?"

"I know nothing. He may come back at any moment. Leave me, Richard; every minute you remain here increases your danger." Then she attempted to draw away from me, but I would not release her.

"If you fear his returning to-night then it is time for you to come with me," I answered.

"No, no, no, I cannot. All is changed now. It would kill me with shame to look on your face again."

"You shall look on it again many times, De-

metria. Do you think that after coming here to
rescue you out of the coils of that serpent I am
going to leave you because you are a little timid?
Listen, Demetria, I shall save you from that devil
to-night, even if I have to carry you out in my
arms. Afterwards we can consider all there is to
be done about your father and your property.
Perhaps when the poor Colonel is taken out of
this sad atmosphere his health, his reason even,
may improve."

"Oh, Richard, are you deceiving me?" she exclaimed, suddenly dropping her hands and gazing full into my face.

"No, I am not deceiving you. And now, you
will lose all fear, Demetria, for you have looked
into my face again and have not been changed to
stone."

She turned crimson in a moment; but did not
attempt to cover her face again, for just then a
clatter of hoofs was heard approaching the house.

"Mother of Heaven, save us!" she exclaimed
in terror. "It is Don Hilario."

I quickly blew out the one candle burning dimly
in the room. "Fear nothing," I said. "When all
is quiet after he has gone to his room we will make
our escape."

She was trembling with apprehension and nes-
tled close to me; while we both listened intently
and heard Don Hilario unsaddle his horse, then
going softly, whistling to himself, to his room.

"Now he has shut himself up," I said, "and in

a few minutes will be asleep. When you think of that man whose persecutions have made your life a burden, so that you tremble when he approaches you, do you not feel glad that I have come to take you away?"

"Richard, I could go willingly with you to-night but for one thing. Do you think after what has passed that I could ever face your wife?"

"She will know nothing of what has passed, Demetria. It would be dishonourable in me and a cruel injustice to you to speak to her of it. She will welcome you as a dear sister and love you as much as I love you. All these doubts and fears troubling you are very unsubstantial and can be blown away like thistle-down. And now that you have confessed so much to me, Demetria, I wish to confess also the one thing that troubles my heart."

"What is it, Richard, tell me?" she said very gently.

"Believe me, Demetria, I never had a suspicion that you loved me. Your manner did not show it, otherwise I should have told you long ago all about my past. I only knew you regarded me as a friend and one you could trust. If I have been mistaken all along, Demetria, if you have really felt a passion in your heart, then I shall have to lament bitterly that I have been the cause of a lasting sorrow to you. Will you not open your heart more to me and tell me frankly how it is with you?"

She caressed my hand in silence for a little while and then answered, "I think you were right, Richard. Perhaps I am not capable of passion like some women. I felt—I knew that you were my friend. To be near you was like sitting in the shade of a green tree in some hot, desolate place. I thought it would be pleasant to sit there always and forget the bitter years. But, Richard, if you will always be my friend—my brother, I shall be more than content, and my life will seem different."

"Demetria, how happy you have made me! Come, the serpent is sleeping now, let us steal away and leave him to his evil dreams. God grant that I may return some day to bruise his head with my heel."

Then, wrapping the shawl about her, I led her out treading softly, and in a few moments we were with Santos, patiently keeping watch beside the horses.

I gladly let him assist Demetria to her seat on the side-saddle, for that was perhaps the last personal service he would be able to render her. The poor old fellow was crying, I believe, his utterance was so husky. Before leaving I gave him on a scrap of paper my address in Montevideo, and bade him take it to Don Florentino Blanco with a request to write me a letter in the course of the next two or three days to inform me of Don Hilario's movements. We then trotted softly away over the sward, and in about half an hour struck the road leading from Rocha to Montevideo. This we followed till daylight, scarcely pausing once from our swift gallop, and a hundred times during that dark ride over a country utterly unknown to me I blessed the little witch Cleta; for never was there a more steady, surefooted beast than the ugly roan that carried my companion, and when we drew rein in the pale morning light he seemed fresh as when we started. We then left the highway and rode across country in a north-westerly direction for a distance of eight or nine miles, for I was anxious to be far away from public roads and from the prying, prating people that use them. About eleven o'clock that morning we had breakfast at a rancho, then rode on again till we came to a forest of scattered thorn trees growing on the slopes of a range of hills. It was a wild, secluded spot, with water and good pasturage for the horses and pleasant shade for ourselves; so after unsaddling and turning loose our horses to feed we sat down to rest under a large tree with our backs against its portly trunk. From our shady retreat we commanded a splendid view of the country over which we had been riding all the morning extending for many leagues behind us, and while I smoked my cigar I talked to my companion, calling her attention to the beauty of that wide, sunlit prospect.

"Do you know, Demetria," I said, "when the long winter evenings come, and I have plenty of leisure, I intend writing a history of my wander-

ings in the Banda Orientál, and I will call my
book *The Purple Land;* for what more suitable
name can one find for a country so stained with
the blood of her children? You will never read
it, of course, for I shall write it in English and
only for the pleasure it will give to my own children—if I ever have any—at some distant date,
when their little moral and intellectual stomachs
are prepared for other food than milk. But you
will have a very important place in my narrative,
Demetria, for during these last days we have been
very much to each other. And perhaps the very
last chapter will recount this wild ride of ours together, flying from that evil genius Hilario to
some blessed refuge far away beyond the hills and
woods and the blue line of the horizon. For when
we reach the capital I believe—I think—I know,
in fact——"

I hesitated to tell her that it would probably be
necessary for me to leave the country immediately, but she did not encourage me to go on, and
glancing round I discovered that she was fast
asleep.

Poor Demetria, she had been dreadfully nervous all night and almost afraid to stop to rest
anywhere, but now her fatigue had quite overcome her. Her position against the tree was uncomfortable and insecure, so drawing her head
very gently down until it rested on my shoulder,
and shading her eyes with her mantilla, I let her
sleep on. Her face looked strangely worn and

pallid in that keen noonday light, and gazing on it
while she slumbered, and remembering all the
dark years of grief and anxiety she had endured
down to that last pain of which I had been the
innocent cause, I felt my eyes grow dim with compassion.

After sleeping for about two hours she woke
with a start and was greatly distressed to learn
that I had been supporting her all that time. But
after that refreshing slumber a change seemed to
come over her. Not only her great fatigue, but
the tormenting apprehensions had very nearly
vanished. Out of the nettle Danger she had
plucked the flower Safety, and now she could rejoice in its possession and was filled with new life
and spirits. The unaccustomed freedom and exercise with constant change of scene also had an exhilarating effect on mind and body. A new colour
came into her pale cheeks; the purple stains telling of anxious days and sleepless nights faded
away; she smiled brightly and was full of animation, so that on that long journey, whether resting in the noonday shade or swiftly cantering over
the green turf, I could not have had a more agreeable companion than Demetria. This change in
her often made me remember Santos' pathetic
words when he told of the ravages of grief, and
said that another life would make his mistress a
"flower amongst women." It was a comfort that
her affection for me had been, indeed, nothing
but affection. But what was I to do with her in

the end? for I knew that my wife was most anxious to return without further delay to her own country; and yet it seemed to me that it would be a hard thing to leave poor Demetria behind amongst strangers. Finding her so improved in spirits, I at length ventured to speak to her on the subject. At first she was depressed, but presently, recovering courage, she begged to be allowed to go with us to Buenos Ayres. The prospect of being left alone was unendurable to her, for in Montevideo she had no personal friends, while the political friends of her family were all out of the country or living in very close retirement. Across the water she would be with friends and safe for a season from her dreaded enemy. This proposal seemed a very sensible one and relieved my mind very much, although it only served to remove my difficulty for a time.

In the departmenut of Camelones, about six leagues from Montevideo, I found the house of a fellow-countryman named Barker, who had lived for many years in the country and had a wife and children. We arrived in the afternoon at his estancia, and seeing that Demetria was very much knocked up with our long journey, I asked Mr. Barker to give us shelter for the night. Our host was very kind and pleasant with us, asking no disagreeable questions, and after a few hours' acquaintance, which made us quite intimate, I took him aside and told him Demetria's history, whereupon, like the good-hearted fellow he was, he at once offered to shelter her in his house until matters could be arranged in Montevideo, an offer which was joyfully accepted.

CHAPTER XXVIII

GOOD-BYE TO THE PURPLE LAND

I was soon back in Montevideo after that. When I bade Demetria good-bye she appeared reluctant to part with me, retaining my hand in hers for an unusual time. For the first time in her life, probably, she was about to be left in the company of entire strangers, and for many days past we had been much to each other, so that it was only natural she should cling to me a little at parting. Once more I pressed her hand and exhorted her to be of good courage, reminding her that in a very few days all trouble and danger would be over; still, however, she did not release my hand. This tender reluctance to lose me was affecting and also flattering, but slightly inopportune, for I was anxious to be in the saddle and away. Presently she said, glancing down at her rusty habiliments, "Richard, if I am to remain concealed here till I go to join you on board, then I must meet your wife in these poor garments."

"Oh, *that* is what you are thinking about, Demetria!" I exclaimed.

At once I called in our kind hostess, and when this serious matter was explained to her she immediately offered to go to Montevideo to procure the necessary outfit, a thing I had thought nothing about, but which had evidently been preying on Demetria's mind.

When I at length reached the little suburban retreat of my aunt (by marriage), Paquíta and I acted for some time like two demented persons, so overjoyed were we at meeting after our long separation. I had received no letters from her, and only two or three of the score I had written had reached their destination, so that we had ten thousand questions to ask and answers to make. She could never gaze enough at me or finish admiring my bronzed skin and the respectable moustache I had grown; while she, poor darling! looked unusually pale, yet withal so beautiful that I marvelled at myself for having, after possessing her, considered any other woman even passably goodlooking. I gave her a circumstantial account of my adventures, omitting only a few matters I was in honour bound not to disclose.

Thus, when I told her the story of my sojourn at the estancia Peralta, I said nothing to betray Demetria's confidence; nor did I think it necessary to mention the episode of that wicked little sprite, Cleta; with the result that she was pleased at the chivalrous conduct I had displayed throughout the whole of that affair, and was ready to take Demetria to her heart.

I had not been back twenty-four hours in Montevideo before a letter from the Lomas de Rocha storekeeper came to justify my caution in having left Demetria at some distance from the town. The letter informed me that Don Hilario had quickly guessed that I had carried off his unhappy master's daughter, and that no doubt was left in his mind when he discovered that on the day I left the estancia a person answering to my description in every particular had purchased a horse and side-saddle and had ridden off towards the estancia in the evening. My correspondent warned me that Don Hilario would be in Montevideo even before his letter, also that he had discovered something about my connection with the late rebellion, and would be sure to place the matter in the hands of the government, so as to have me arrested, after which he would have little difficulty in compelling Demetria to return to the estancia.

For a moment this intelligence dismayed me. Luckily, Paquíta was out of the house when it came, and fearing that she might return and surprise me while I was in that troubled state, I rushed out; then, skulking through back streets and narrow lanes, peering cautiously about in fear of encountering the minions of the law, I made my escape out of the town. My only desire just then was to get away into some place of safety where I would be able to think over the position quietly, and if possible devise some plan to defeat Don Hilario, who had been a little too quick for me. Of many schemes that suggested themselves to my mind, while I sat in the shade of a cactus hedge about a mile from town, I finally determined, in accordance with my old and well-tried rule, to adopt the boldest one, which was to go straight back to Montevideo and claim the protection of my country. The only trouble was that on my way thither I might be caught, and then Paquíta would be in terrible distress about me, and perhaps Demetria's escape would be prevented. While I was occupied with these thoughts I saw a closed carriage pass by driven towards the town by a tipsy-looking coachman. Coming out of my hiding-place I managed to stop him and offered him two dollars to drive me to the British Consulate. The carriage was a private one, but the two dollars tempted the man, so after securing the fare in advance he allowed me to get in, and then I closed the windows, leant back on the cushion, and was driven rapidly and comfortably to the house of refuge. I introduced myself to the Consul, and told him a story concocted for the occasion, a judicious mixture of truth and lies, to the effect that I had been unlawfully and forcibly seized and compelled to serve in the Blanco army, and that having escaped from the rebels and made my way to Montevideo, I was amazed to hear that the government proposed arresting me. He asked me a few questions, looked at the passport which he had sent me a few days before, then laughing good-humouredly put on his hat and invited me to accompany him to the War Office close by. The secretary, Colonel Arocena, he informed me, was a personal friend of his, and if we could see him

it would be all right. Walking by his side I felt
quite safe and bold again, for I was, in a sense,
walking with my hand resting on the superb mane
of the British Lion, whose roar was not to be pro-
voked with impunity. At the War Office I was
introduced by the Consul to his friend, Colonel
Arocena, a genial old gentleman with a bald head
and a cigarette between his lips. He listened with
some interest and a smile, slightly incredulous I
thought, to the sad story of the ill-treatment I
had been subjected to at the hands of Santa
Coloma's rebellious rascals. When I had finished
he pushed over a sheet of paper on which he had
scrawled a few words to me with the remark,
"Here, my young friend, take this, and you will
be safe in Montevideo. We have heard about
your doings in Florida, also in Rocha, but we do
not propose going to war with England on your
account."

At this speech we all laughed; then when I had
pocketed the paper, which bore the sacred seal of
the War Office on the margin and requested all
persons to refrain from molesting the bearer in his
lawful outgoings and incomings, we thanked the
pleasant old Colonel and retired. I spent half an
hour strolling about with the Consul, then we separated. I had noticed two men in military uniform at some distance from us when we were together, and now returning homewards I found
that they were following me. By-and-by they
overtook me and politely intimated their inten-

tion of making me their prisoner. I smiled, and drawing forth my protection from the War Office, handed it to them. They looked surprised, and gave it back, with an apology for having molested me, then left me to pursue my way in peace.

I had, of course, been very lucky throughout all this adventure; still I did not wish to attribute my easy escape entirely to luck, for I had, I thought, contributed a good deal towards it by my promptness in acting and in inventing a plausible story on the spur of the moment.

Feeling very much elated, I strolled along the sunny streets, gaily swinging my cane, when turning a corner near Doña Isidora's house I suddenly came face to face with Don Hilario. This unexpected encounter threw us both off our guard, he recoiling two or three paces backward and turning as pale as the nature of his complexion would allow. I recovered first from the shock. So far I had been able to baffle him, and knew, moreover, many things of which he was ignorant; still, he was there in the town with me and had to be reckoned with, and I quickly resolved to meet him as a friend, affecting entire ignorance of his object in coming to Montevideo.

"Don Hilario—you here! Happy the eyes that behold you," I exclaimed, seizing and shaking his hand, pretending to be overjoyed at the meeting.

In a moment he recovered his usual self-possessed manner, and when I asked after Doña

Demetria he answered after a moment's hesitation that she was in very good health.

"Come, Don Hilario," I said, "we are close to my aunt Isidora's house where I am staying, and it will give me great pleasure to present you to my wife, who will be glad to thank you for your kindness to me at the estancia."

"Your wife, Don Ricardo! Do you tell me that you are married?" he exclaimed in amazement, thinking probably that I was already the husband of Demetria.

"What, did I not tell you before!" I said. "Ah, I remember speaking to Doña Demetria about it. Strange that she has not mentioned it to you. Yes, I was married before coming to this country—my wife is an Argentine. Come with me and you shall see a beautiful woman, if that is an inducement."

He was without doubt astonished and mystified, but he had recovered his mask, and was now polite, collected, watchful.

When we entered the house I presented him to Doña Isidora, who happened to be in the way, and left her to entertain him. I was very glad to do so, knowing that he would seize the opportunity to try and discover something from the garrulous old lady, and that he would discover nothing since she had not been let into our secrets.

I found Paquíta lying down in her room having a siesta; and while she arrayed herself at my express desire in her best dress—a black velvet which set off her matchless beauty better than anything else, I told her how I wished her to treat Don Hilario. She knew all about him, of course, and hated him with all her heart, looking on him as a kind of evil genius from whose castle I had carried off the unhappy Demetria; but I made her understand that our wisest plan was to treat him graciously. She readily consented, for Argentine women can be more charmingly gracious than any other women on the globe, and what people do well they like to be called on to do.

The subtle caution of our snaky guest did not serve to hide from my watchful eyes that he was very much surprised when he beheld her. She placed herself near him and spoke in her sweetest artless manner of the pleasure my return had given her, and of the gratitude she had felt towards him and all the people at the estancia Peralta for the hospitable treatment I had received there. He was, as I had foreseen, completely carried away by her exquisite beauty and the charm of her manner towards him. He was flattered, and exerted himself to be agreeable, but at the same time he was very much puzzled. The baffled expression was more apparent on his face every moment, while his restless glances darted here and there about the room, yet ever returned, like the doomed moth to the candle, to those lustrous violet eyes overflowing with hypocritical kindness. Paquíta's acting delighted me, and I only hoped that he would long suffer from the effect of the subtle poison she was introducing into his system. When he rose to go I was sure that Demetria's disappearance was a greater mystery to him than ever; and as a parting shot I warmly invited him to come and see us frequently while he remained in the capital, even offering him a bed in the house; while Paquíta, not to be behindhand, for she had thoroughly entered into the fun of the thing, entrusted him with a prettily worded affectionate message to Demetria, a person whom she already loved and hoped some day to meet.

Two days after this adventure I heard that Don Hilario had left Montevideo. That he had discovered nothing I was positive; it was possible, however, that he had left some person to watch the house, and as Paquíta was now anxious to get back to her own country I determined to delay our departure no longer.

Going down to the harbour, I found the captain of a small schooner trading between Montevideo and Buenos Ayres, and learning that he intended leaving for the last port in three days' time, I bargained with him to take us, and got him also to consent to receive Demetria on board at once. I then sent a message to Mr. Barker, asking him to bring his guest up to town and put her on board the schooner without coming near me. Two days later, early in the morning, I heard that she was safe on board; and having thus baffled the scoundrel Hilario, on whose ophidian skull I should have been very pleased to set my heel, and having still an idle day before me, I went once more to visit the mountain, to take from its summit my last view of the Purple Land where I had spent so many eventful days.

When I approached the crest of the great, solitary hill I did not gaze admiringly on the magnificent view that opened before me, nor did the wind, blowing fresh from the beloved Atlantic, seem to exhilarate me. My eyes were cast down and I dragged my feet like one that was weary. Yet I was not weary, but now I began to remember that on a former occasion I had on this mountain spoken many vain and foolish things concerning a people about whose character and history I was then ignorant. I also remembered with exceeding bitterness that my visit to this land had been the cause of great and perhaps lasting sorrow to one noble heart.

How often, said I to myself, have I repented of those cruel, scornful words I addressed to Dolores at our last interview, and now once more "I come to pluck the berries harsh and crude" of repentance and of expiation, to humble my insular pride in the dust and unsay all the unjust things I formerly spoke in my haste.

It is not an exclusively British characteristic to regard the people of other nationalities with a certain amount of contempt, but with us, perhaps, the feeling is stronger than with others, or else expressed with less reserve. Let me now at last rid myself of this error, which is harmless and perhaps even commendable in those who stay at home, and also very natural, since it is a part of our unreasonable nature to distrust and dislike the things that are far removed and unfamiliar. Let me at last divest myself of these old English spectacles, framed in oak and with lenses of horn, to bury them for ever in this mountain, which for half a century and upwards has looked down on the struggles of a young and feeble people against foreign aggression and domestic foes, and where a few months ago I sang the praises of British civilisation, lamenting that it had been planted here and abundantly watered with blood, only to be plucked up again and cast into the sea. After my rambles in the interior, where I carried about in me only a fading remnant of that old time-honoured superstition to prevent the most perfect sympathy between me and the natives I mixed with, I cannot say that I am of that opinion now. I cannot believe that if this country had been conquered and recolonised by England, and all that is crooked in it made straight according to our notions, my intercourse with the people would have had the wild, delightful flavour I have found in it. And if that distinctive flavour cannot be had along with the material prosperity resulting from Anglo-Saxon energy, I must breathe the wish that this land may never know such prosperity. I do not wish to be murdered; no man does; yet rather than see the ostrich and deer chased beyond the horizon, the flamingo and black-necked swan slain on the blue lakes, and the herdsman sent to twang his romantic guitar in Hades as a preliminary to security of person, I would prefer to go about prepared at any moment to defend my life against the sudden assaults of the assassin.

We do not live by bread alone, and British occupation does not give to the heart all the things for which it craves. Blessings may even become curses when the gigantic power that bestows them on us scares from our midst the shy spirits of Beauty and of Poesy. Nor is it solely because it appeals to the poetic feelings in us that this country endears itself to my heart. It is the perfect republic: the sense of emancipation experienced in it by the wanderer from the Old World is indescribably sweet and novel. Even in our ultra-civilised condition at home we do periodically escape back to nature; and, breathing the fresh mountain air and gazing over vast expanses of ocean or land, we find that she is still very much to us. It is something more than these bodily sensations we experience when first mingling with our fellow-creatures, where all men are absolutely free and equal as here. I fancy I hear some wise person exclaiming, "No, no, no! In name only is your Purple Land a republic; its constitution is a piece of waste paper, its government an oligarchy tempered by assassination and revolution." True; but the knot of ambitious rulers all striving to pluck each other down have no power to make the people miserable. The unwritten constitution,

mightier than the written one, is in the heart of
every man to make him still a republican and free
with a freedom it would be hard to match anywhere else on the globe. The Bedouin himself is
not so free, since he accords an almost superstitious reverence and implicit obedience to his
sheikh. Here the lord of many leagues of land
and of herds unnumbered sits down to talk with
the hired shepherd, a poor, bare-footed fellow in
his smoky rancho, and no class or caste difference
divides them, no consciousness of their widely different positions chills the warm current of sympathy between two human hearts. How refreshing it is to meet with this perfect freedom of intercourse, tempered only by that innate courtesy
and native grace of manner peculiar to Spanish
Americans! What a change to a person coming
from lands with higher and lower classes, each
with its innumerable hateful subdivisions—to one
who aspires not to mingle with the class above
him, yet who shudders at the slouching carriage
and abject demeanour of the class beneath him!
If this absolute equality is inconsistent with perfect political order, I for one should grieve to see
such order established. Moreover, it is by no
means true that the communities which oftenest
startle us with crimes of disorder and violence are
morally worse than others. A community in
which there are not many crimes cannot be morally
healthy. There were practically *no* crimes in
Peru under the Inca dynasty; it was a marvellous

thing for a person to commit an offence in that empire. And the reason for this most unnatural state of things was this—the Inca system of government was founded on that most iniquitous and disastrous doctrine that the individual bears the same relation to the state as a child to its parent, that its life from the cradle to the grave must be regulated for it by a power it is taught to regard as omniscient—a power practically omnipresent and almighty. In such a state there could be no individual will, no healthy play of passions, and consequently no crime. What wonder that a system so unspeakably repugnant to a being who feels that his will is a divinity working within him fell to pieces at the first touch of foreign invasion, or that it left no vestige of its pernicious existence on the continent it had ruled! For the whole state was, so to speak, putrid even before dissolution, and when it fell it mingled with the dust and was forgotten. Poland, before its conquest by Russia, a country ill-governed and disorderly as the Banda Oriental, did not mingle with the dust like that when it fell—the implacable despotism of the Czar was unable to crush its fierce spirit; its *Will* still survived to gild dreary oppression with hallowed dreams, to make it clutch with a fearful joy the dagger concealed in its bosom. But I had no need to go away from this Green Continent to illustrate the truth of what I have said. People who talk and write about the disorderly South American republics are fond of pointing to Brazil, that great, peaceful, progressive empire, as setting an example to be followed. An orderly country, yes, and the people in it steeped to their lips in every abominable vice! Compared with these emasculated children of the equator, the Orientals are nature's noblemen.

I can very well imagine some over-righteous person saying, "Alas, poor deluded soul, how little importance can we attach to your specious apologies of a people's lawlessness, when your own personal narrative shows that the moral atmosphere you have been breathing has quite corrupted you! Go back over your own record, and you will find that you have, according to *our* notions, offended in various ways and on divers occasions, and that you are even without the grace to repent of all the evil things you have thought, said, and done."

I have not read many books of philosophy, because when I tried to be a philosopher "happiness was always breaking in," as someone says; also because I have loved to study men rather than books; but in the little I have read there occurs a passage I remember well, and this I shall quote as my answer to anyone who may call me an immoral person because my passions have not always remained in a quiescent state, like hounds—to quote the simile of a South American poet—slumbering at the feet of the huntsman resting against a rock at noon. "We should regard the perturbations of the mind," says Spinoza, "not in the light of vices of human nature, but as properties just as pertinent to it as are heat, storms, thunder, and the like to the nature of the atmosphere, which phenomena, though inconvenient, are yet necessary, and have fixed causes by means of which we endeavour to understand their nature, and the mind has just as much pleasure in seeing them aright as in knowing such things as flatter the senses." Let me have the phenomena which are inconvenient as well as the things which flatter the senses, and the chances are that my life will be a healthier and happier one than that of the person who spends his time on a cloud blushing at nature's naughtiness.

It is often said that an ideal state—an Utopia where there is no folly, crime, or sorrow—has a singular fascination for the mind. Now, when I meet with a falsehood, I care not who the great persons who proclaim it may be, I do not try to like it or believe it or mimic the fashionable prattle of the world about it. I hate all dreams of perpetual peace, all wonderful cities of the sun, where people consume their joyless monotonous years in mystic contemplations, or find their delight like Buddhist monks in gazing on the ashes of dead generations of devotees. The state is one unnatural, unspeakably repugnant: the dreamless sleep of the grave is more tolerable to the active, healthy mind than such an existence. If Signor Gaudentio di Lucca, still keeping himself alive by means of his marvellous knowledge of the secrets

of nature, were to appear before me now on this
mountain to inform me that the sacred community
he resided with in Central Africa was no mere
dream, and should offer to conduct me to it, I
should decline to go with him. I should prefer
to remain in the Banda Oriental, even though by
so doing I should grow at last to be as bad as any
person in it, and ready to "wade through slaugh-
ter" to the Presidential Chair. For even in my
own country of England, which is not so perfect
as old Peru or the Pophar's country in Central
Africa, I have been long divided from nature, and
now in this Oriental country, whose political mis-
deeds are a scandal alike to pure England and im-
pure Brazil, I have been reunited to her. For this
reason I love her with all her faults. Here, like
Santa Coloma, I will kneel down and kiss this
stone as an infant might kiss the breast that feeds
it; here, fearless of dirt like John Carrickfergus,
I will thrust my hands into the loose brown soil
to clasp the hands, as it were, of dear mother Nature after our long separation.

Farewell, beautiful land of sunshine and storm,
of virtue and of crime; may the invaders of the
future fare on your soil like those of the past and
leave you in the end to your own devices; may the
chivalrous instinct of Santa Coloma, the passion
of Dolores, the loving-kindness of Candelaria
still live in your children to brighten their lives
with romance and beauty; may the blight of our
superior civilisation never fall on your wild

flowers, or the yoke of our progress be laid on your herdsman—careless, graceful, music-loving as the birds—to make him like the sullen abject peasant of the Old World!

CHAPTER XXIX

BACK TO BUENOS AYRES

The meeting of my fellow-travellers took place next day on board the ship, where we three were the only cabin passengers. On going down into the little saloon I found Demetria waiting for us, considerably improved in appearance by her new dress, but looking pale and anxious, for she probably found this meeting a trying one. The two women looked earnestly at each other, but Demetria, to hide her nervousness, I suppose, had framed her face in the old, impassive, almost cold expression it had worn when I first knew her, and Paquíta was repelled by it; so after a somewhat lukewarm greeting they sat down and made commonplace remarks. Two women more unlike each other in appearance, character, education, and disposition it would have been difficult to find; still I had hoped they might be friends, and felt keenly disappointed at the result of their first meeting. After an uncomfortable interval we all rose. I was about to proceed to the deck, they to their respective cabins, when Paquíta, without any warning of what was coming, suddenly burst into tears and threw her arms about Demetria's neck.

372

"Oh, dear Demetria, what a sad life yours has been!" she exclaimed.

That was like her, so impulsive and with such a true instinct to make her do the right thing always! The other gladly responded to the embrace, and I hastily retreated, leaving them kissing and mingling their tears.

When I got out on deck I found that we were already on our way, sails up, and a fresh wind sending us swiftly through the dull green water. There were five steerage passengers, disreputable-looking fellows in ponchos and slouch hats, lounging about the deck smoking; but when we got outside the harbour and the ship began to toss a little, they very soon dropped their cigars and began ignominiously creeping away out of sight of the grinning sailors. Only one remained, a grizzly-bearded, rough-looking old gaucho, who firmly kept his seat at the stern, as if determined to see the last of "The Mount," as the pretty city near the foot of Magellan's Hill is called by the English people in this region.

To satisfy myself that none of these fellows were sent in pursuit of Demetria, I asked our Italian captain who they were and how long they had been on board, and was much relieved to hear that they were fugitives—rebels probably—and had all been concealed for the past three or four days in the ship, waiting to get away from Montevideo.

Towards evening it came on very rough, the

wind veering round to the south and blowing half a gale, a very favourable wind, as it happened, to take us across this unlovely "Silver Sea," as the poets of the Plata insist on calling it, with its villainous, brick-red, chopping waves, so disagreeable to bad sailors. Paquíta and Demetria suffered agonies, so that I was obliged to keep with them a good deal. I very imprudently told them not to be alarmed, that it was nothing—*only sea-sickness*—and I verily believe they both hated me with all their hearts for a little while in consequence. Fortunately I had anticipated these harrowing scenes, and had provided a bottle of champagne for the occasion; and after I had consumed two or three glassfuls to encourage them, showing how easy this kind of medicine is to take, I prevailed on them to drink the remainder. At length, about ten o'clock in the evening, they began to suspect that their malady was not going to prove fatal, and seeing them so much better, I went up to get some fresh air. There at the stern still sat the stoical old gaucho looking extremely miserable.

"Good evening, old comrade," said I, "will you smoke a cigar?"

"Young master, you seem to have a good heart," he returned, shaking his head at the proffered cigar, "do, for God's sake, get me a little rum. I am dying for something to warm my inside and stop my head from going round like a top, but nothing can I get from these jabbering foreign brutes on board."

"Yes, why not, my old friend," said I, and going to the master of the boat, I succeeded in getting a pint of rum in a bottle.

The old fellow clutched it with eager delight and took a long draught. "Ah!" he said, patting first the bottle, then his stomach, "this puts new life into a man! Will this voyage never end, master? When I am on horseback I can forget that I am old, but these cursed waves remind me that I have lived many years."

I lit my cigar and sat down to have a talk with him.

"Ah, with you foreigners it is just the same—land or water," he continued. "You can even smoke—what a calm head and quiet stomach you must have! But what puzzles me is this, señor: how you, a foreigner, come to be traveling with native women. Now there is that beautiful young señora with the violet eyes, who can she be?"

"She is my wife, old man," said I, laughing, a little amused at his curiosity.

"Ah, you are married then—so young? She is beautiful, graceful, well educated, the daughter of wealthy parents, no doubt, but frail—frail, señor; and some day, not a very distant day—but why should I predict sorrow to a gay heart? Only her face, señor, is strange to me; it does not recall the features of any Oriental family I know."

"That is easily explained," I said, surprised at his shrewdness, "she is an Argentine, not an Oriental."

"Ah, that explains it," he said, taking another long pull at the bottle. "As for the other señora with you, I need not ask you who *she* is."

"Why, who is she?" I returned.

"A Peralta, if there ever was one," he returned confidently.

His reply disturbed me not a little, for after all my precautions this old man had perhaps been sent to follow Demetria.

"Yes," he continued, with an evident pride in his knowledge of families and faces which tended to allay my suspicions; "a Peralta and not a Madariaga, nor a Sanchez, nor a Zelaya, nor an Ibarra. Do I not know a Peralta when I see one?" And here he laughed scornfully at the absurdity of such an idea.

"Tell me," I said, "how do you know a Peralta?"

"The question!" he exclaimed. "You are a Frenchman or a German from over the sea, and do not understand these things. Have I borne arms forty years in my country's service not to know a Peralta! On earth they are with me; if I go to heaven I meet them there, and in hell I see them; for when have I charged into the hottest of the fight and have not found a Peralta there before me? But I am speaking of the past, señor; for now I am also like one that has been left on the field forgotten—left for the vultures and foxes. You will no longer find them walking on the earth; only where men have rushed together sword in hand you will find their bones. Ah, friend!" And here, overcome with sad memories, the ancient warrior took another drink from his bottle.

"They cannot all be dead," said I, "if, as you imagine, the señora travelling with me is a Peralta."

"As I imagine!" he repeated scornfully. "Do I not know what I am talking about, young sir? They are dead, I tell you—dead as the past, dead as Oriental independence and honour. Did I not ride into the fight at Gil de los Medanos with the last of the Peraltas, Calixto, when he received his baptism of blood? Fifteen years old, señor, only fifteen, when he galloped into the fight, for he had the light heart, the brave spirit, and the hand swift to strike of a Peralta. And after the fight our colonel, Santa Coloma, who was killed the other day at San Paulo, embraced the boy before all the troops. He is dead, señor, and with Calixto died the house of Peralta."

"You knew Santa Coloma, then?" I said. "But you are mistaken, he was not killed at San Paulo, he made his escape."

"So they say—the ignorant ones," he returned. "But he is dead, for he loved his country, and all who are of that mind are slain. How should he escape?"

"I tell you he is not dead," I repeated, vexed at his stubborn persistence. "I also knew him, old man, and was with him at San Paulo."

He looked at me for a long time, and then took another swig from his bottle.

"Señor, this is not a thing I love joking about," said he. "Let us talk of other things. What I want to know is, what is Calixto's sister doing here? Why has she left her country?"

Receiving no reply to this question he went on: "Has she not got property? Yes, a large estancia, impoverished, ruined, if you like, but still a very large tract of land. When your enemies do not fear you then they cease to persecute. A broken old man, bereft of reason—surely they would not trouble him! No, no, she is leaving her country for other reasons. Yes, there is some private plot against her; some design, perhaps, to carry her off, or even to destroy her and get possession of her property. Naturally in such a case she would fly for protection to Buenos Ayres, where there is one with some of her blood in his veins able to protect her person and her property."

I was astonished to hear him, but his last words were a mystery to me.

"There is no one in Buenos Ayres to protect her," I said; "I only will be there as I am here to shield her, and if, as you think, she has an enemy, he must reckon with me—one who, like that Calixto you speak of, has a hand quick to strike."

"There spoke the heart of a Blanco!" he exclaimed, clutching my arm, and then, the boat giving a lurch at that moment, almost dragging me down in his efforts to steady himself. After another sip of rum he went on: "But who are you, young sir, if that is not an impertinent question? Do you possess money, influence, powerful friends, that you take upon yourself the care of this woman? Is it in your power to baffle and crush her enemy or enemies, to protect not only her person, but her property, which, in her absence, will become the prey of robbers?"

"And who are you, old man?" I returned, unable to give a satisfactory answer to one of his searching questions, "and why do you ask me these things? And who is this powerful person you speak of in Buenos Ayres with some of her blood in his veins, but of whose existence she is ignorant?"

He shook his head silently, then deliberately proceeded to take out and light a cigarette. He smoked with a placid enjoyment which made me think that his refusal of my cigar and his bitter complaints about the effects of the ship's tossing on him had merely been to get the bottle of rum out of me. He was evidently a veteran in more senses than one, and now finding that I would tell him no more secrets he refused to answer any questions. Fearing that I had imprudently told him too much already, I finally left him and retired to my bunk.

Next morning we arrived at Buenos Ayres, and cast anchor about two miles from shore, for that was as near the land as we could get. Presently we were boarded by a Custom House officer, and for some time longer I was engaged in getting out our luggage and in bargaining with the captain to put us on shore. When I had completed these arrangements I was very much surprised to see the cunning old soldier I had talked with the evening before sitting in the Custom House boat which was just putting off from the side. Demetria had been looking on when the old fellow had left the ship, and she now came to me looking very excited.

"Richard," she said, "did you notice that man who was a passenger with us and who has just gone off in the boat? It is Santa Coloma."

"Oh, absurd!" I exclaimed. "I talked with that old man last night for an hour—an old grey-bearded gaucho, and no more like Santa Coloma than that sailor."

"I know I am right," she returned. "The General has visited my father at the estancia and I know him well. He is disguised now and has made himself look like a peasant, but when he went over the side into the boat he looked full into my face; I knew him and started, then he smiled, for he saw that I had recognised him."

The very fact that this common-looking old man had gone on shore in the Custom House boat proved that he was a person of consequence in disguise, and I could not doubt that Demetria was right. I felt excessively annoyed at myself for having failed to penetrate his disguise; for some-

thing of the old Marcos Marcó style of speaking
might very well have revealed his identity if I
had only had my wits about me. I was also very
much concerned on Demetria's account, for it
seemed that I had missed finding out something
for her which would have been to her advantage
to know. I was ashamed to tell her of that conversation about a relation in Buenos Ayres, but
secretly determined to try and find Santa Coloma
to get him to tell me what he knew.

After landing we put our small luggage into a
fly and were driven to an hotel in Calle Lima, an
out-of-the-way place kept by a German; but I
knew the house to be a quiet, respectable one and
very moderate in its charges.

About five o'clock in the afternoon we were together in the sitting-room on the first floor looking
down on the street from the window, when a well-
appointed carriage with a gentleman and two
young ladies in it drew up before the door.

"Oh, Richard," exclaimed Paquíta in the greatest excitement, "it is Don Pantaleon Villaverde
with his daughters, and they are getting out!"

"Who is Villaverde?" I asked.

"What, do you not know? He is a Judge of
First Instance and his daughters are my dearest
friends. Is it not strange to meet them like this?
Oh, I must see them to ask for papa and mamita!"
and here she began to cry.

The waiter came up with a card from the Señor

Villaverde requesting an interview with the Señorita Peralta.

Demetria, who had been trying to soothe Paquíta's intense excitement and infuse a little courage into her, was too much amazed to speak; and in another moment our visitors were in the room. Paquíta started up tearful and trembling; then her two young friends, after staring at her for a few moments, delivered a screech of astonishment and rushed into her arms, and all three were locked together for some time in a triangular embrace.

When the excitement of this tempestuous meeting had spent itself, Señor Villaverde, who stood looking on with grave, impassive face, spoke to Demetria, telling her that his old friend, General Santa Coloma, had just informed him of her arrival in Buenos Ayres and of the hotel where she was staying. Probably she did not even know who he was, he said; he was her relation; his mother was a Peralta, a first cousin of her unhappy father, Colonel Peralta. He had come to see her with his daughters to invite her to make his house her home during her stay in Buenos Ayres. He also wished to help her with her affairs, which, his friend the General had informed him, were in some confusion. He had, he concluded, many influential friends in the sister city, who would be ready to assist him in arranging matters for her.

Demetria, recovering from the nervousness she had experienced on finding that Paquíta's great friends were her visitors, thanked him warmly and accepted his offer of a home and assistance; then, with a quiet dignity and self-possession one would hardly expect from a girl coming amongst fashionable people for the first time in her life, she greeted her new-found relations and thanked them for their visit.

As they insisted on taking Demetria away with them at once she left us to make her preparations, while Paquíta remained conversing with her friends, having many questions to ask them. She was consumed with anxiety to know how her family, and especially her father, who made the domestic laws, now, after so many months, regarded her elopement and marriage with me. Her friends, however, either knew nothing or would not tell her what they knew.

Poor Demetria! she had, with no time given her for reflection, taken the wise course of at once accepting the offer of her influential and extremely dignified kinsman; but it was hard for her to leave her friends at such short notice, and when she came back prepared for her departure the separation tried her severely. With tears in her eyes she bade Paquíta farewell, but when she took my hand in hers, for some time her trembling lips refused to speak. Overcoming her emotions by a great effort, she at length said, addressing her visitors, "For my escape from a sad and perilous position and for the pleasure of finding myself here amongst relations, I am indebted to this young friend who has been a brother to me."

Señor Villaverde listened and bowed towards me, but with no softening in his stern, calm face, while his cold grey eyes seemed to look straight through me at something beyond. His manner towards me made me feel a kind of despair, for how strong must have been his disapproval of my conduct in running off with his friend's daughter —how great his indignation against me, when it prevented him from bestowing one smile or one kind word on me to thank me for all I had done for his kinswoman! Yet this was only the reflected indignation of my father-in-law.

We went down to the carriage to see them off, and then finding myself for a moment by the side of one of the young ladies I tried to find out something for myself. "Pray tell me, señorita," I said, "what you know about my father-in-law. If it is very bad, I promise you my wife shall not hear a word of it; but it is best that I should know the truth before meeting him."

A cloud came over her bright, expressive face while she glanced anxiously at Paquíta; then bending towards me she whispered, "Ah, my friend, he is implacable! I am so sorry for Paquíta's sake." And then with a smile of irrepressible coquetry she added, "And for yours."

The carriage drove away, and Demetria's eyes looking back at me were filled with tears, but in Señor Villaverde's eyes, also glancing back, there was an expression that boded ill for my future. His feeling was natural, perhaps, for he was the father of two very pretty girls.

Implacable, and I was now divided from him by no silver or brick-coloured sea! By returning I had made myself amenable to the laws I had broken by marrying a girl under age without her father's consent. The person in England who runs away with a ward in Chancery is not a greater offender against the law than I was. It was now in his power to have me punished, to cast me into prison for an indefinite time, and if not to crush my spirit, he would at least be able to break the heart of his unhappy daughter. Those wild, troubled days in the Purple Land now seemed to my mind peaceful, happy days, and the bitter days with no pleasure in them were only now about to begin. Implacable!

Suddenly looking up, I found Paquíta's violet eyes full of sad questioning fixed on my face.

"Tell me truly, Richard, what have you heard?" she asked.

I forced a smile, and taking her hand assured her that I had heard nothing to cause her any uneasiness. "Come," I said, "let us go in and prepare to leave town to-morrow. We will go back to the point we started from—your father's estancia, for the sooner this meeting you are thinking about so anxiously is over the better will it be for all of us."

APPENDIX

THE country, called in this work the Purple Land, was discovered by Magellan in the year 1500, and he called the hill, or mountain, which gives its name to the capital, Monte Vidi. He described it as a hat-shaped mountain; and it is probable that, four centuries ago, the tall conical hat, which is worn to this day by women in South Wales, was a common form in Spain and Portugal.

In due time settlements were made; but the colonists of those days loved gold and adventure above everything, and finding neither in the Banda, they little esteemed it. For two centuries it was neglected by its white possessors, while the cattle they had imported continued to multiply, and returning to a feral life, overran the country in amazing numbers.

The heroic period in South American history then passed away. El Dorado, the Spaniard's New Jerusalem, has changed into a bank of malarious mist and a cloud of mosquitoes. Amazons, giants, pigmies,

"The Anthropophagi, and men whose heads
Do grow beneath their shoulders,"

when closely looked for, turned out to be Red Indians of a type which varied but little throughout the entire vast continent. Wanderers from the Old World grew weary of seeking the tropics only to sink into flowery graves. They turned away sick at heart from the great desolation where the splendid empire of the Children of the Sun had so lately flourished. The accumulated treasures had been squandered. The cruel crusades of the Paulists against the Jesuit missions had ceased, for the inhuman slave-hunters had utterly destroyed the smiling gardens in the wilderness. A remnant of the escaped converts had gone back to a wild life in the woods, and the Fathers, who had done their Master's work so well, drifted away to mingle in other scenes or die of broken hearts. Then, in the sober eighteenth century, when the disillusion was complete, Spain woke up to the fact that in the temperate part of the continent, shared by her with Portugal, she possessed a new bright little Spain worth cultivating. About the same time Portugal discovered that the acquisition of this pretty country, with its lovely Lusitanian climate, would nicely round off her vast possessions on the south side. Forthwith these two great colonising powers fell to fighting over the Banda, where there were no temples of beaten gold, or mythical races of men, or fountains of everlasting youth. The quarrel might have continued to the end of time, so languidly was it conducted by both par-

ties, had not great events come to swallow up the
little ones.

At the beginning of the nineteenth century the
English invasion burst like a sudden terrible
thunderstorm on the country. Montevideo on the
east and Buenos Ayres on the west side of the sea-
like river were captured and lost again. The storm
was soon over, but it had the effect of precipitating
the revolution of 1810, which presently ended in
the loss to Spain of all her American possessions.
These changes brought only fresh wars and calamities to the long-suffering Banda. The ancient
feud between Spain and Portugal descended to
the new Brazilian Empire and the new Argentine
Confederation, and these claimants contended for
the country until 1828, when they finally agreed
to let it govern itself in its own fashion. After
thus acquiring its independence the little Belgium
of the New World cast off its pretty, but hated
appellation of Cisplatina and resumed its old joyous name of Banda Oriental. With light hearts
the people then proceeded to divide themselves
into two political parties—Whites and Reds. End-
less struggles for mastery ensued, in which the
Argentines and Brazilians, forgetting their solemn
compact, were for ever taking sides. But of these
wars of crows and pies it would be idle to say
more, since after going on for three-quarters of a
century they are not wholly ended yet. The rambles and adventures described in the book take us
back to the late sixties or early seventies of the

last century, when the country was still in the condition in which it had remained since the colonial
days, when the ten years' siege of Montevideo
was not yet a remote event, and many of the people one met had had a part in it.

THE END